First Light

Book One of the Torus Saga

Michael Berg

ISBN: 978-0-6486874-0-5

Cover design by: Channelee

First printing (paperback): Amazon Publishing 2019

First published as an Amazon Kindle ebook Copyright © 2013

For all permissions contact: torussaga@gmail.com

Michael Berg is a professional writer residing in Australia. He dedicates this work The Torus Saga, to those with an open mind connected to the heart who seek the many mysteries and progressions of life.

Also in the Torus Saga by Michael Berg:

Book Two: Volition

Book Three: The Last Year

FIRST LIGHT

Chapter 1

Raynie O'Day sat alone in the library of the old nineteenth century house, reading a book she had just found after a long search.

'This is simply beautiful,' she thought when she paused for a moment to look out through the window where the moon was a glow just above the horizon to the east. As she sat pondering her place and picturing her lone small section of the universe there in the library within the isolated house miles from any neighbours, she could feel a sense mystery in life as her companion.

A short while later when she was reading chapter three about atomic fields, the rustle of leaves on the large Oak trees in the garden out beyond the window caught her attention. She loved the sound of the wind in the trees and the release it gave her as she would spend time just listening.

"A storm must be coming," she said aloud to herself. "I wonder if...?" she trailed off as a light outside caught her eye when for a moment she was unsure of what it could be. Logic had defied her for a few seconds as she had been so absorbed by the reading and dream like thinking. Then she realized the light was a vehicle driving up the valley toward the old house, and it would arrive within a minute.

Raynie had not seen Jake Sinclair for almost six months as their investigations had taken them on individual trails of discovery. Now their meeting was about to take place and she had actually been looking forward to this moment for over a month. She rushed out of the library and down the hallway to the kitchen where she put some more water on to boil. As she hung the pot over the wood fire stove, the broadcast playing featured an on the hour news bulletin.

"This is news for the hour. A widespread early winter storm is bearing down on the southeast. This storm is forecast to be severe with near gale force winds about higher parts and some low-level snow. The Weather Bureau is saying this could be the biggest storm since the great storms of the twenties."

As Raynie went to look out the kitchen window after hearing the news, she saw the headlights shine brightly for a moment before disappearing as the car parked at the other end of the house. Raynie left the kitchen to greet him at the front door, where Jake was already out of his vehicle and gathering a few belongings from the back seat. She ran from the door to greet him, taking his luggage bag as he struggled to collect some books into one stack to carry inside.

"Well hello," he said. "So nice to see you again."

"Hi yourself," she replied swinging the bag into his leg and he pretended to almost spill the books piled on his arm. "Let's go in."

Jake followed her quickly up the path chased by a collection of swirling leaves caught up in the increasing winds.

"Good to see you looking so happy," he said as they stood face to face at the door.

"Good to feel happy too. Some coffee is on. Come to the kitchen."

"It will do nicely," Jake replied pushing the door closed behind him.

"There is a storm coming."

"Yes I know. I had the broadcast on as I drove."

The pot was boiling when they entered so Raynie set about making the coffee. "We'll go through to the library if you like," she suggested after preparing a tray with coffee and cups.

"I have a lot of information to show you."

Raynie led Jake down the long wood paneled hallway until they reached the lighted doorway of the library.

"Here we are," she said as they entered.

Jake looked around the room, taking a moment to contemplate where he was to spend the next few hours talking. He liked Raynie, and like her he was fond of such night vigils immersing himself into the spirit of both surroundings and the quest at hand.

"What elevation are we at here?" he asked a moment later as Raynie set the coffee down on the desk. "Around twelve hundred meters isn't it?"

"Yes. We are at just over twelve hundred. We could see a bit of snow out of this storm as they have said snow to low levels."

"Yes I thought so. I do love the snow."

"Me too."

Raynie poured two coffees and then glanced out the nearby window noticing a few spots of rain on the glass.

"The rain has started. Hey. I will be back in just a minute," she said as she rushed out of the library and headed back down the hall.

Jake looked out the window Raynie had glanced through and noticed the rain was increasing with large some spots being blown hard onto the glass. As he watched, he felt a sense of knowing. Somehow this night would prove crucial to their journey and quest ahead. It was as if they were being guided together to this meeting almost by some other force or sense.

"I just stoked the kitchen fire some more. If it gets cold here, I want the kitchen to stay warm. We will need it. Sit down. Let's talk."

They both drew their chairs closer to the desk from either side, enthusiastically embracing the hot coffee mugs and eager to embrace the details of their research.

"This is what I have been reading tonight." She presented the book open at the Atomic Fields - Quantum Phasing chapter to Jake. "It details the constant shift of sub-atomic resonance at the quantum level. Various details are provided on the resonance fields generated and their interaction with each other. There is also mention of how quantum particles themselves seem to resonate out of some field beyond description."

"Interesting," Jake replied. He read for a few minutes whilst Raynie sipped her coffee watching him.

"It gets a bit technical but also there is something else. Whilst scientific in nature, it leads to some method to observe atoms at the quantum level," Raynie continued after seeing Jake pause his reading.

"I see here there is some imagery," Jake said looking up from the book. "Is this part of the explanation?"

"Not sure, but lovely colors, and if you stare at them for some time they seem to take on much more depth. It is almost as if there are images within the image."

"Perhaps it is a type of code for some connection?"

"Could be."

"They might give us some information on what the text may lead to." Jake said as he drained the last of his coffee and reached for the pot. "The storm seems stronger."

"It has come up quickly. We should go and get more firewood."

"Okay."

Raynie opened the large doors leading from the library to the courtyard outside, but the wind immediately challenged her hold on the door.

"Let's go via the kitchen."

She led Jake back down the hallway to a cupboard by the door leading outside.

Raynie gave Jake a coat as she took one for herself.

"Come on," she said beckoning him to follow.

He nodded and followed her out along the path across the yard to a gate leading to the woodshed. The cold rain beat upon them both as they ran with Raynie shining a torch on the way ahead. A few snowflakes were already drifting amongst the downpour strangely defying the course of the wind as they were blown about caught in miniature eddies and currents.

"I'll just get the light," Raynie said as she shone a torch along the wall after they entered the wood shed.

A single light revealed a large stack of wood and a hand cart just beside the door. They both started filling the cart with logs working fast as lightning flashes were beginning to show through the open door behind them casting shadows and adding eeriness to the scene. The storm was soon directly overhead in a fury much faster than they had expected hastening them as they stacked the last logs onto the cart and covered them with a tarpaulin.

Raynie killed the light and they left the shed casting themselves into the elements outside for the return trip through the yard to the house.

When they arrived back at the kitchen, the broadcast was still on featuring a reporter talking to a meteorologist about the current storm.

"I'll stoke the fire and then let's go back to the library," Jake offered.

"Sure. How about some more coffee to warm us up after the cold outside?"

Raynie made another coffee pot as Jake tended the fire.

"The wind sure is furious out there," he said as the kitchen door shuddered in its frame.

"Certainly a night to be indoors. I'm glad you arrived before the storm hit."

"Yeah, me too. How's the coffee coming? I think the fire should be good for an hour or so."

"Coffee is ready now in fact. Let's get back to the library."

"I have information about some relics and locations to help us," Jake said after they had once again sat at the desk in the library. "There are relics found in sites I think are keys or a means to understand some other details. It is about the best I can come up with."

"Relics? Sites? What are these places like?"

"I am not sure entirely. I suppose they look like ceremonial sites but I don't have a definitive description. Other information I have seen indicates someone has to be aware of these things to be able to see them."

"Aware..." Raynie trailed off thinking for a moment. "For some people to be able to see them they need more than just eyesight?"

"I thought similar but it is still a bit beyond me. What is being aware to be able to see?"

"Perhaps our language cannot quite describe it well enough."

"Maybe you are right. I think we need to work more on the details. Maybe these relics could be analysed against the text and imagery I have found and maybe then we will find some more clues. The relic sites I have looked into are not what you would expect."

They had both been looking through the information for almost half an hour and it was the first time they had been silent since meeting.

"The sites are more like what you could describe as a midden. A place where indigenous peoples would leave food scraps like shells and bones. It may depend on the location I guess."

"There is one of those on the hills at the back of this property."

"These midden sites are arranged in specific patterns, not like the random dump of scraps you see in most of them. In the past, most archeological diggings at these places have come in at the sides but if you take a top down view you then notice the pattern."

"Interesting. I want to show you the one on this property tomorrow, but the snow might be a struggle. Hey, let's go back to the kitchen and check the fire."

"Sounds good."

"Are there any snow skis here?" Jake asked as Raynie added more wood to the fire in the stove.

"Why yes. There are some in the store room. We can ski to the midden site if we need to."

"Boots?"

"Adjustable boots."

"Great. Skiing in the morning then. I certainly didn't think it would happen."

After a few more hot drinks and another hour of in depth discussion, they fell tired and decided it was time to retire for the night.

Raynie was stoking the fire in the kitchen sending sparks flying from dying embers as Jake appeared through the kitchen door the next morning.

"Good morning to you Raynie. It looks cold outside. There must be two feet of snow."

"Yes, and good morning to you Jake. There is a lot of snow so it could be difficult to find what we are looking for today."

Twenty minutes later they had finished breakfast and were donning ski gear in preparation for the potential discovery to be had in the field. Despite the heavy snow and some earlier doubts, they both felt as if enthusiastic as if something was awaiting their arrival.

Snow was falling in a steady stream as they made their way outside, and within moments they were both coated white as they skied slowly out through the yard towards the gate they had taken the night before.

"Keep high on this slope so we can make good progress up the hill," Raynie said pointing in the direction they were to take.

After fifteen minutes of steady skating they reached the crest of the hill where they stopped again to survey the scene. Raynie indicated the way ahead without speaking, pointing in the general direction of their destination with a ski stock.

A stand of pine trees could be made out after they had skied for another twenty minutes.

"There is where we need to get to," Raynie said as they paused for a moment to rest. "The midden is just on the down side of the hill from those pines."

"This looks similar to the sites I have been studying," Jake said.

"I thought there might be something here. See how the trees appear to be planted in some semi-circular pattern and they open to face the direction of the midden as if they are some type of ceremonial place," Raynie said as they arrived on scene and she took the snow shovel from her backpack. The wind had returned and continued to build in intensity causing the snow to swirl around them.

"Here, hold on to this whilst I survey precisely where we should look," she said handing Jake the shovel. Raynie carefully studied the surroundings looking back towards the stand of pines and then made imaginary lines back towards them as she lined up the position to dig.

"Right here could be a good place," she said indicating just a few yards to their left.

Jake moved across to where she was pointing and began to dig through the snow.

"Look!" Jake exclaimed after he had dug deep enough through the snow and had penetrated into the soil. "Can you notice the layers here? They appear to be organized as opposed to some random discarding of rubbish. How did you first notice this place?"

"I was walking out here just two days ago when I noticed the trees and then I literally stumbled across this midden when my foot caught a stone sticking out of the grass. I scratched around and saw some bones and thought this must be a place of significance or of some history in the least. I will dig for a bit whilst you take a look at the arrangement and see if it is what you have been researching."

She took the shovel from Jake and started to carefully excavate just to the side of the hole he had made.

"I'll try to trace a circle in the snow so we can then get to more of the soil if it makes sense."

"Good idea," Jake replied. "These sites seem to always be made out in circles, so dig around there."

Raynie continued to trace out a curve making her way slowly away from Jake as he scrambled about in the loosened soil looking for answers. After about fifteen minutes she had dug a curve in the snow some ten feet long.

"Here, I'll take the shovel now," Jake said. "I think we are definitely onto something but it looks like we need to dig more towards the center of this circle as opposed to around."

"There was a stone…" Raynie trailed off as she walked through the snow to what she thought was the center of the midden. Jake followed and started digging next to the place where she had stopped. After breaking through the snow to the soil, they found nothing.

"Well, maybe a little over here," she said as they stood wondering where to go next. She kicked at the powder snow sending billowing clouds into the wind. On the third kick she struck something hard. "This is it!"

Jake dug around her foot with renewed enthusiasm, sending more snow into the air until he had uncovered a slab approximately two feet square. He dug around the edge and rubbed away the remaining soil to reveal the entire stone. What appeared to be an abstract picture of an eye was carved very shallow into one corner.

"This is great. Those other sites I have seen have the same symbol."

Raynie helped Jake lift the stone slab eager to see what lay beneath. The snow and wind was blowing hard partially filling in the hole as they struggled with the stone. Their enthusiasm for answers kept Raynie and Jake going undeterred in anticipation of a discovery despite the arduous conditions of the setting, and after a short struggle they pushed the stone to the side of the opening to reveal a smaller slab roughly half the size of the first with the same eye decal.

"Try the shovel," Raynie said as they stood up after being unable to move the smaller slab with their hands.

Jake grabbed the shovel and after a few attempts he managed to move the slab revealing a small carved stone underneath. He saw some small inscriptions on the stone he immediately recognized.

"I think we have what we came for," he said as he picked up the stone. "Let's put these slabs back and return to the house."

The howling gale fought against them as they skied off keeping their trail high on the hillside in a traverse. Skiing was difficult as they stayed close together so as not to lose each other in the white out conditions. When they arrived back at the house, snow was piled high against the kitchen door forcing them to dig feverously so they could get back inside and out of the elements.

The small glow in the fire was a welcome greeting and Raynie quickly moved to stash her ski gear and then put more wood on. Jake stashed his gear, filled the pot with some water, and then helped her make a hot drink and prepare some food for a meal before they went to the library to talk.

"You know. This could be a significant find. I have seen these markings before." Jake said as he turned to face Raynie who was sitting relaxed in one of the old leather wing backed chairs used for reading. "Let's take a closer look." He took the stone from his pocket and sat next to Raynie in the accompanying chair. "See here? This line with what appears as segments running along each side in a twisted pattern resembles DNA."

She leaned in closer to examine the markings Jake was referring to. Before she spoke, she felt a sense of companionship being so close to Jake physically, "Yes, I see what you mean. They remind me of what I was reading about last night just before you arrived."

"Reading? I recall the quantum phase…"

"Yes. I'll get the book. I have marked the pages of most interest to me and thought may be of use to us."

She opened the book to the marked page referring to DNA sequencing and re-organisation during quantum molecular phase shifting.

"DNA sequencing undergoes a state of flux when excited through sub atomic reverberations phasing in synchronicity with harmonic vibrations in certain wavelengths." she read out loud.

"Sounds like resonance to me."

"Well, I thought there is some underlying pattern emitting from some type of universal blue print or coding giving rise to matter…and fluctuating matter."

"Fluctuating matter? Sounds like atoms going in and out of existence. Well, existence as we know it. Let's look for some hint as to coding or information to explain how it happens. This stone may be a key to the DNA aspect going by how it appears to hold pieces of the sequencing within each image. And see here? This appears to be a cross section of the brain but quite abstract, and there is a link going from this area of the brain continuing on to the main DNA sequence feature."

Raynie and Jake continued to discuss their find for an hour comparing information and theories about the carved stone with the text she had supplied. "Time we had a break," Raynie said putting the book down. "I think some tea is in order. I've had enough coffee for now."

She made off to the kitchen leaving Jake behind lost in thought. As she entered the kitchen, she turned the broadcast on for company.

"This is a breaking news update for May six twenty eighty eight. The authorities have just advised of another small nuclear detonation off the California coast in the past hour. This follows on from the two detonations just three days ago. Authorities advise this detonation took place on an abandoned oilrig decommissioned thirty-three years ago not yet removed from the site. All maintenance robotics on location have been destroyed. It is believed a number of personnel were recently visiting the site to commence removal procedures but there is no word of any human casualties. Authorities have placed an increased state of alert for all aligned authorities including Australia. Further information will be provided when it comes to hand. In other news…"

"Jake, come quickly!" Raynie shouted down the hall.

He was awakened from his stream of thought and came running. "What is it?" he said as he entered the kitchen.

"There has been another nuclear detonation. This time off California."

"What is going on over there?"

"A heightened state of alert is in place, even for Australia."

"Any details or why?"

"No further information besides the actual explosion and where it took place on an abandoned oilrig. Robotics have been destroyed. No advice on human casualties."

"When is the next update?"

"Anytime. They said there would be more information when it comes to hand. There has to be a connection with those other explosions."

"Well. Those other explosions were near to some sensitive sites used for developing new energy. It is said they are on the verge of a breakthrough in renewable and virtual infinite sources. Something to do with quantum molecular fusion.

"And here we are looking at quantum mechanics and atomic fields. Perhaps a co-incidence in a way."

"Is there really such a thing as co-incidence as many may see it though? Or is it somehow timely?

Chapter 2

Dawn was grey and white - brilliant, yet without direct sunlight. As he awoke, his vision was of mostly just a grey surface appearing as two dimensional without depth. It seemed the closest to nothing he had ever seen. A moment later he decided the emptiness was an illusion as there was as much on offer with this dawn as with any other. It was new, had never occurred previously, and like any other, presented opportunity.

His way of living lately had been somewhat different to the years previous. His decisions and the events took him to places he remembered dreaming of many years ago and in recent times. Now he was on course to see them become reality. The series of events leading to this place and why were a result of people he had met, information he had researched, and the response of others to his enquiries. His life would never be the same. What he was doing now was changing him for good, and he could never return to his ways of old – thankfully.

Now with another dawn greeting him holding promise he held dear, his spirit lightened a little. Never one to dwell, he told himself the grey abyss in front of him was actually the wall of his sleeping quarters. As he awoke further he was now aware of where he was and felt comfortable. He was in a space station in low Earth orbit. This was the eleventh dawn he had seen today and none of them bored him. He was in space.

His life was an adventure in both his own mind and the way he treated his friends and associates. Everyone could count on spirited company when he was around with barely a dull moment. Full of life, people at times almost would draw upon him for inspiration themselves. He knew this but did not mind as he was a giving person and he freely gave his energy where he deemed it to be required.

"Ninety minutes to Earth descent," came over the announcer.

'Good,' he thought, 'time for one more sunrise.'

He had made his way from quarters and was sitting in the mess section of the space station eating breakfast, though this could be dinner or lunch considering the speed at which he was orbiting the Earth. As he sipped a cup of tea, he stared out the porthole window beside his table admiring the expanse of bright blue ocean some two hundred and twenty miles beneath him. The sun shone brightly glittering off the surface here and there and this sight filled him with awe even though this was his third trip into space. He could never tire of this situation since he had finally realized the dream of venturing into the cosmos - one he had held since childhood. There was nothing more he wanted more at this moment than to be where he was.

An island appeared in his field of view so he hit the zoom button located next to him just below the porthole. The window was actually a lens. He zoomed in on the island of Hawaii showing the great volcanoes of Kilauea and Mauna Loa where lava flows and eruptions come from a number of volcanic cones.

Without warning his view was suddenly obscured by what appeared to be a window. Momentarily baffled by what he saw he then realized a space craft had passed into close up view.

He ordered some more tea as he watched the craft edge closer. Thrusters erupted from a number of places on the ship it edged closer for docking with the station. A few moments later a slight jolt then indicated the shuttle had docked.

"All passengers for transfer to Earth are requested to check in to the departure lounge. Descent will be in sixty minutes," came the announcer.

A few minutes later he left his seat to join other passengers for descent to Earth. After check in and allocation of his seat, he moved to the suit-up area in preparation for boarding of the ship in full space wear. It was here he began to talk to the others who were to accompany him on the trip back to Earth.

"Have you heard?" a woman who was amongst the group asked him. "Two days ago two small proximity radiation bombs and now a third explosion off California."

"Yes I heard about those."

Descent would take thirty minutes and their destination was in the New Mexico desert at the huge space port.

Shortly after, everyone was directed to fit their space suits and prepare for boarding the descent vehicle. The woman who had spoken to him earlier gained his attention as she requested to be seated beside him.

"We'll travel together into this," she said grabbing his hand.

"Descent will commence in fifteen minutes," came over the announcer.

"Well here we go," he said as they both moved to the airlock when directed. Minutes later they were both seated with safety belts locking them to their seats.

"Five minutes to descent. All passengers prepare for launch position."

Their seats were adjusted to an incline so as to minimize the effects of forces during their descent. She grabbed his hand and a minute later the vehicle broke away from the docking port as they began their journey to Earth.

"Ladies and Gentlemen. Our trip will take us on a single Earth orbit as we descend on a trajectory to enter the atmosphere over the Pacific Ocean. Our descent speed will initially be seventeen thousand miles per hour slowing to eleven thousand miles per hour during atmospheric buffering. Once inside Earth's atmosphere we will then gradually slow to four hundred miles per hour on a thirty seven degree angle for landing at New Mexico Space Port. Estimated time to landing is forty seven minutes. We hope you enjoy your trip with us and thank you for traveling with Space Ventures – the leader in Earth orbit transits."

Plasma fueled engines then fired as the vehicle increased speed away from the space station.

As they passed over the continent of Australia, plasma rockets fired again and soon after the turbulence of the atmosphere began to shake the vehicle. Within a few minutes they were traveling under a blue sky streaming towards the west coast of North America at breakneck speed. They crossed the coast near San Francisco, on a turning trajectory to line up with spaceport runway eleven in New Mexico.

"Passengers, we will be arriving at New Mexico Space Port in eleven minutes. Please remain in your seats until the vehicle has reached a full stop. Connecting flights from spaceport are on standby for international and internal passengers. Once again, thank you for flying with Space Ventures."

"Where are you flying to?" the woman asked him letting go of his hand.

"I'm off to Australia to see some friends I have there. And you?"

"Home to San Francisco. I work at Berkley University researching propulsion systems. I was in space testing a few of the new systems. By the way, my name is Jenna Atkinson." She had noticed Lyle a few times during her stay at the station. His manner and general energy interested her but she remained guarded in appraoch to him depsite conveying an open friendliness.

"Hello Jenna. I am Lyle. Lyle Shrewsbury. I work as a consultant archeologist doing research and I advise on the impacts of resource planning covering culturally significant material. I have just been mapping and studying geographical data for this purpose at the station."

"Passengers, please prepare for landing in four minutes," the announcer said. A slight bump indicated to them the vehicle had touched down on runway eleven where it then taxied to the docking area for passengers to disembark. After a short while they were de-suited and given the standard anti-sickness gravity medications dispensed for all personnel returning to Earth.

"Would you like to have some coffee?" Jenna asked. "My flight is on standby but I can wait for the next one in an hour."

"It would be nice," Lyle replied. "I can connect in two hours for the trip south."

"Ladies and Gentlemen. This is New Mexico Space Port administration. Due to recent events involving detonations, some flights are required to take alternative routes to destinations in the east and to international destinations. We apologize for the delays and request you enquire as to your amended flight details when checking in."

"It won't affect us," Lyle said as they walked the passageway towards the main lounge of the spaceport terminal. He noticed several flights taking off and marveled at the expanse of this facility out beyond the window - the lights of each ship twinkling like stars. There were seventeen runways in all at the spaceport. Twelve were designated for Earth bound flights and five were for transfer to and from space. The sheer size of the place was astounding appearing to stretch all the way to the sunset behind the distant mountains.

"Well, let's go and board then," Jenna said rising from her seat and extending her hand to Lyle. They had finished coffee where they talked about the recent events and a little about themselves. Lyle had decided to put off his trip to Australia and to accompany Jenna for a few days. He felt at ease with her as she did with him. Their rapport was instant since the very first meeting prior to descent from orbit and he felt comfortable and excited about the prospect of a few days in the Bay City. They made their way through the throng of passengers and visitors populating the main lounge, to internal departures for the thirty-minute transit to San Francisco. As they were about to reach the departure area, Lyle noticed a group of military police checking all outgoing passengers situated at the access gates.

"I suppose there will be police everywhere after those detonations," Jenna said.

They reached the cordon of officers and were then directed to large scanning units for full body scans.

"Alert level is red," an officer said to them as he indicated where they should go. "All persons are required to take mandatory scans."

"No problem," both Lyle and Jenna said in unison as they took up individual scanning units beside each other. The magnetic resonance imaging devices hummed into action and they could feel a gentle wave sweep their bodies.

"You are clear,' the same officer told them indicating the way to proceed with his hand. They proceeded to check in where Jenna had her ticket processed and Lyle purchased one for his trip with her.

"Just going to San Francisco for a few days," he replied to the check-in officers' query on his change of destination. "I will be traveling onto Australia from there."

Lyle confirmed his seat was beside Jenna prior to proceeding to the boarding gates. They passed through the gates and then boarded the HyperJet along with the twenty-three other passengers.

Ten minutes later the engines fired up and they began to taxi towards the runway.

"Ladies and Gentlemen. This is your pilot speaking. We will be taking off from runway four tonight for our thirty-minute ride to San Francisco. Our cruising speed will be mach five at an elevation of fifty thousand feet. Ascent will take seven minutes and descent into San Francisco will take five minutes. We hope your enjoy your flight."

The HyperJet slowly lined up at the end of the runway, paused a moment, and then the pilot fired up the four rocket engines. The lights of the spaceport then became a blur as the jet sped along the runway and into the night sky.

"Ladies and gentlemen. This is your captain speaking. We have now reached cruising altitude and our current speed is three thousand eight hundred and fifty miles per hour. We expect to arrive at San Francisco in approximately fifteen minutes. Descent will commence in seven minutes."

"I suppose you worked on these jets," Lyle said.

"Well. No. I work only on fusion propulsion," Jenna replied smiling as she recalled recent advances her research had made. "I just completed work looking into advances with plasma drive engines and how protein strings can be used for propulsion systems. We leave the Earth bound stuff to a separate division."

"Interesting. I am off to the Moon for a while after my stint in Australia. It will be my fourth trip to space."

"But I thought you examined culturally significant sites."

"Yes, but this time I am assigned to examine the long-term contamination repercussions for a mining base."

"It certainly sounds a bit different." She said smiling at him as they held each other's gaze for a moment. "I can't wait to ride into space again."

"Riding aboard HyperJet Space is quite an experience."

"I did work on the engines for it after the incident a few months back where there was a problem and a ship plummeted until they could restore power."

"I remember. It didn't stop me from wanting to go though."

"Ladies and gentlemen. Descent is in one minute," the HyperJet captain said.

Lights atop the Bay Bridge came into view as they lined up to land at San Francisco airport. The city looked amazing just after dusk as vehicles both ground based and airborne traveled busily around lighted transit ways and in the sky above.

"I know a great place down in old China Town," Jenna said feeling glad to see her home city again. "We'll take a JetCab from the airport."

The HyperJet landed and taxied to the terminal where they disembarked and then made their way to the JetCab stand. With a sudden thrust, the cab ascended to five hundred feet and traveled the eight miles to the city in two minutes. After landing at the central cab hub, they made their way on foot guided by Jenna. People were everywhere in the city of five million people. The streets were a throng of pedestrians with vendors hawking them at almost every step as others made them promises. Although San Francisco had undergone a large modernization, there still remained those bound to the streets fighting to make a living or to simply survive.

"Here is the place," Jenna remarked as they stopped outside Fong's Restaurant and Bar. Set in a traditional sense decorated with lanterns and ornate dragon figures, the bar appeared to defy the times as if it had been there for more than a hundred years.

"I know it looks a little old, but the food here is terrific."

"Well. Those don't look old," Lyle said pointing to the multiple holographic projectors all showing the latest news concerning the recent events and providing advice about the heightened state of security. As they were about to enter, two men suddenly pushed past them both very eager to be inside. "Hey…."

"Don't worry," Jenna said noticing Lyle's disdain. "You'll get used to it." Once inside they were shown to a booth table behind some curtains in the far corner.

"This is nice and private for us. Thank you," Jenna said to the waiter who had ushered them to the table.

They sat down immediately in front of a unique statue set into an alcove in the wall. "Demon statue with protection," Jenna said seeing Lyle look the figure up and down. "See there?" She pointed to a small urn placed in front of the statue figure filled with food, trinkets, and some other items. "Those are offerings made to keep the demon spirits at bay."

"Yes I know," Lyle replied. "I have seen similar figures in my work, but none quite like this. I cannot make out or be sure what the headdress on the demon is for. It almost seems out of step with the rest of it. To be frank, more like a space helmet for want of a more accurate description. And see the inscription here? Translated it reads, Demon Lunar. What is it? Moon demon?"

"Szechwan beef, pork dumplings, egg rolls…and green tea madam and sir," the waiter said placing their meal on the table in front of them fifteen minutes later. As they ate, they continued to discuss the merits of the statue behind them, intrigued by its' appearance and keen to speculate on the truth of its' meaning.

Suddenly a man of Chinese appearance was at their booth as they sat sipping green tea at the end of their meal. "Please let me stay, sit with you a while."

"What? Why?" Lyle asked him as the man did not wait for an answer but just sat down next to him.

"You must let me stay. People are after me," the man said. "Much trouble."

"What trouble?"

"Friend already taken, others look for me."

"Why?' Jenna asked.

"Better you not know details but to say I have important information they want. Just make out I am friend you see." He pulled the plate of left over beef to himself and began eating as if he was sharing a meal with them.

"Hey. We don't want trouble," Lyle said trying to force the plate away from him.

"No, no. You not get trouble. Just friend you see." He took the plate back and leaned low over it scooping food up with chopsticks. Two men then paused outside the thin curtains separating the booth from others in the restaurant a moment later. All three of them pretended to be busily eating and drinking at the table doing their best to ignore the potential intrusion. After the men had gone, they took up where the conversation had left off.

"Why are you in trouble?" Lyle asked.

"Information I have, they want."

"What information?"

"To do with ancient memories. Dangerous information, and powerful."

"Powerful. What do you mean?"

"Cannot explain here. Trust me, I am not bad, good you see. Look." He pointed to the demon statue behind them. "Demon. Strange, yet a coincidence I meet you here. I think we are meant to meet."

"What about the demon?" Jenna enquired leaning closer in towards the man.

"This demon connected to power. Much power."

"Yes. But it is myth. Stories," Lyle added.

"There is truth in demon. Can you help me? I must escape."

"We can help you. Fong can get us out of here." Jenna said as she rose from her seat and pushed past the curtains heading for the kitchen. She returned a minute later. "Fong will help. This place has a tunnel to take us under the building next door and out into an alley behind it. We must leave now. I think I saw those two men again."

"Then you can tell us more," Lyle said getting up out of the seat. "Though, I am unsure why I am so willing to talk with you suddenly."

"Sometimes life brings us the things we need without so much thinking. I will tell you more but we need better place where nobody can listen."

"We'll go to my place," Jenna said. "I live near California Avenue just off Hyde Street."

"Good," the Chinese man said. "Get away from inner city." The three of them made off to the kitchen after Lyle first checked to see of the way was clear. It wasn't.

"Walk beside us," Jenna said pushing the man to the right. They slowly walked the few yards to the kitchen door but were seen.

"Hey you," one of the men shouted. "Stop!"

Jenna, Lyle, and the Chinese man broke into a run as they burst through the swing doors to the kitchen. Fong was waiting inside and directed them to what looked like a tall cupboard.

"In here," he said, as he gave the Chinese man a wink. They hurried inside to find a false back to the cupboard leading to stairs going down into a tunnel. As

Fong closed the door behind them, the two assailants came into the kitchen looking around.

"Gentlemen, how can I help you?"

Chapter 3

A commander's voice sounded, "This is HAARP station Alaska. Come in HAARP Norway."

"This is HAARP station Norway. We register your call. Standing by for instructions."

"Okay Norway. We have you on-line. Please stand by for a resonance settings update."

"Standing by."

"We are engaging resonance generator now and increasing to eleven point zero Schumann." Tobias Engelmann said as he flicked an array of switches bringing the entire array on-line. The massive antenna array covering an area of seven acres deep within the Alaskan wilderness hummed into action, emitting a faint glow as it came online.

"Norway. Set your array to eleven point zero Schumann in the one eight zero gigahertz bandwidth. We are requested to heighten status."

"Okay Alaska. We copy. Band width set, array engaged." The antenna located in the northern region of the Scandinavian country hummed into action, sending a similar faint glow into the Arctic night sky.

"Norway. Maintain this frequency until further advice," Tobias added.

"Confirmed Alaska. Heightened status engaged and holding until further advice."

Tobias looked out the station window across the valley illuminated by the glow of the HAARP array. A blanket of stars with a half moon shone above with the Pole Star looking almost close enough to touch. As he watched, the star seemed to be getting closer, confounding him for a moment. When the Pole Star then appeared from behind the light, he realized it was not actually the star itself, but a HyperJet on its' way to the station. Runway lights then flicked on automatically sending bright beams heavenward and a few moments later the jet made landing. Tobias quickly checked all instruments then put on some outdoor gear to go and meet the visitors. With a heightened alert status, such visits were not unexpected, but somehow he felt unsure of this sudden visit to the station.

Two electric snow mobiles were located just outside the main doors to the station but he did not to take one, instead deciding to walk the hundred yards to the hanger at the end of the runway.

Three officers each armed with laser pulse rifles emerged from the hanger - their large figures could be seen in the glow coming from the array.

"This is a turn up," Tobias said aloud to himself, pausing for a moment. He could not think of why these officers needed to be armed.

With still about fifty yards between him and the three officers, he suddenly heard them yell. "Stay there! Remain where you are! You are under arrest."

Tobias immediately stopped where he was for a moment wondering why they would demand he not move and also be placed under arrest. Then he ran. He knew something was very wrong and he had seen keys were in the snow mobile ignition of whichever one of the two he decided to take.

Responding to his actions, the officers opened fire as he ran towards the snow mobiles amongst a volley of their laser pulses. One struck the ground right beside him sending him scrambling onto the seat of the first snow vehicle. He turned the key bringing it instantly to life and he accelerated away taking the only road out of the station.

One of the officers took a snow mobile in chase whilst the other two entered the station command center throwing all vicinity lights on. Two rows of high intensity bulbs alongside the road illuminated Tobias and his pursuer as their machines threw snow high into the air behind them.

"They'll alert anyone and everyone. How am I going to get out of here?"

He turned left into a forest of aspen trees he knew well. There were numerous paths he could take through the terrain to try and lose his pursuer, so he rode on powering between tree trunks under low hanging branches and over half frozen creeks. The officer fired a few shots from his pulse rifle now and then but was mostly concerned with negotiating the track through the forest.

Tobias was racing, his heartbeat almost in his mouth and with the officer now some one hundred yards to the rear. He took a sharp right turn dropping into a small gully, killed the headlight and continued on chancing his way in the silvery moonlight.

He decided his only option for a way out of here quickly and secretly would be John Matheson. Tobias knew of John who was an ex-serviceman now resigned to a life as a bush pilot by a river four valleys away from the station. There was no other option for Tobias. All his belongings were back at the base and he would risk certain arrest should he decide to go back and retrieve them.

After ten more minutes of riding by starlight and having passed around the end of a low ridge in the wide valley, he switched the headlight back on and increased speed. Almost at the same instant, a brown bear appeared directly in front of him in the light. In this racing state Tobias was fast with reflexes in going around the bear. "What the hell are you doing here?" he yelled. "Everything's going bloody weird tonight."

After a while travelling as fast as he dared, he could see the river shining in the moonlight like a silvery ribbon cutting its way through the valley. When he neared the cabin, Tobias could see Matheson's plane parked on a gravel bar jutting out in a bend of the river, and a minute later he arrived and jumped off the snow mobile almost before he had reached a full stop.

"John. John, you there?" he shouted. John Matheson appeared on the verandah of the small hut silhouette against the light beaming out into the night from inside.

"Yeah. Is it you Tobias?"

"Sure is mate. Can I come in?"

"Of course. What's the problem?"

"I was chased out of HAARP station."

"What for? You work for them."

"I don't know. They fired at me with laser pulse rifles."

"Come in. Let's have a drink. I reckon you need one." He led Tobias into the hut and poured two glasses of whiskey. "Sit here by the fire and tell me about this."

"I just don't know. It was working fine, and we went to heightened weapons status. I was monitoring the situation and then a HyperJet landed. They told me to stay where I was and under arrest with rifles poised and all. I made a runner, jumped on the snow mobile and took some short cuts through the forest to get here." He finished off his whiskey and felt a little more relaxed.

"Why would they want you?"

"Cannot figure out why. Was just doing my job."

"Maybe you know too much about the array. It is a pretty sensitive thing there. Perhaps they want to keep it quiet and with this situation developing…who knows."

"They could be looking to upscale the military and bring in a new team to combat or perform some operations. But why take me out?"

"You know them. One minute you are all in sync with the authorities, next moment you are virtually a criminal, all because you have too much information in your head."

"You mean silence me? Why would I talk?"

"It's why I left the service a few years back. I was getting to know too much for their liking. If you ask me, they had another agenda going. Better to be safe than risk any information getting out."

"They will be after me forever. John, I have to get out of here."

"I bet I know what you are going to ask next. Can you fly…?"

"Can you? Look, I know you don't fly at night, but just think. They'll be combing these valleys anytime soon. They cannot risk me getting away. Perhaps they'll take you for good measure…well, on their part. The file on you must be extensive."

"Yeah, you're right there. It would be very extensive. I will help you mate. I just installed a long-range fuel cell system in the old DeHavilland Beaver and it is ready to go. I was going to go on a flight in the morning before dawn but I guess we'll just have to bring it forward a few hours."

"Thanks John. I'm sorry to put this on you suddenly."

"You know me. Always willing to help a just cause."

"What time is it?"

"Just after eleven. Grab the gear out on the verandah and I'll meet you at the plane in a minute."

"Are you really sure John? Look mate, I have brought you into this."

"Tobias. We are friends. Doing this is okay. If I can't help you, then what am I good for?"

The engine was revving hard with the Beaver swaying under the power whilst being held it back by the brake. A moment later, John gunned the accelerator to full and then let the brake off sending the plane immediately rushing over the gravel bar in the river. With a heave on the control stick they became airborne barely fifty yards later, sending them soaring into the night sky. He kept the throttle at maximum to gain altitude before leveling off a bit once they had reached sufficient speed to stay in the air.

"I'll stay low in the valleys for a while on an easterly trajectory and keep us under any radar. Once we are over the main highway, I'll get us to ten thousand and it will be straight flying from there."

"Where will we head to?" Tobias asked.

"I can fly us at least three thousand miles in this thing. We can be near Vancouver before lunch time tomorrow." He flicked the switch on an instrument used to navigate the way through tight terrain. "I normally only use this thing for rainy and foggy days. Never tried it at night before."

"Isn't it a bit risky?"

"We are going to have to take the risk. We don't have a choice. It would be way too hazardous flying at night without it."

They flew on for a short while longer in silence until John spoke. "Okay, let's go to ten thousand feet," he said turning off the instrument as they crossed the main highway.

The Beaver's engine then went to full throttle as he pulled back on the controls taking the plane up a thirty-degree pitch. As he did, the on-board radar confirmed his unspoken fears as three blips showed clearly on an intercept course coming fast. Tobias saw this and immediately knew what was happening.

"No problem," John said. "I have a handy little gadget I made for this plane to help us." He flicked a couple of switches located on a small box at the bottom of the flight control panel. "They won't see us now unless they catch us visually by sight. This little baby has some pretty high tech photonic microchips inside. They will see this plane continuing on the same heading. Same thing will happen too if they try satellite tracking. We are now emitting a distortion field to fool them. Ha, you could almost call it a cloaking device." He altered their course to turn southwest, whilst the homemade radar scrambler sent out a signal to the HyperJets showing them continuing southeast.

The pilots aboard each of the HyperJets continued their pursuit maintaining the same direction, and soon John and Tobias reached altitude high above the cold ocean on a heading directly for Vancouver Island.

Chapter 4

Jenna, Lyle, and their new companion had made their way on foot taking an alternating path from China Town through the Tenderloin district and then along Hyde Street in an attempt to conceal their precise destination. No sign of the two men could be seen as they approached the front path of Jenna's typical wooden San Franciscan house. She unlocked the front door and hurried them inside. Lyle and the Chinese man who still looked nervous, sat down in the lounge room whilst Jenna went to the kitchen to make some coffee.

"Now. First of all, tell us your name," Lyle asked.

"Chan Lee."

"Okay Chan Lee. I am Lyle and this is Jenna's house. What is this about power? Dangerous power?"

"I will tell you only if you promise to not tell anyone else," Chan replied.

"We'll keep a secret, won't we Jenna."

"I'm good with secrets. But this meeting. How come you seem willing to feel safe with us and potentially give us some secretive information?"

"It is because I can sense you are good. I am a man who is aware of the energies people have and both of you have good energy. And…I am also very much aware of coincidence in life taking us to places we are meant to be. This is what I have felt since I first met you. What I say is very special. Hardly known to anyone. It starts with why these explosions take place."

"Nuclear ex…?" Lyle began.

"Yes, they are for a special reason. They seek to limit the freedom of people."

"You mean the authorities?"

"Yes authorities. They have an idea but are not sure on all details. You know those bombs went off near the experimental research place for new energy."

"I have heard of it," Jenna chimed in. "What about…?"

"Yes, me too," Lyle added. "What about it Chan?"

"They have almost unlocked secrets of potential universe energy using torus vortexes. Many die to prevent this information coming to light. And there are others who also want this knowledge and are not the authorities. They are making these explosions now to scare people so they can bring in this new technology as a way to say they are protecting them."

"What information are you speaking about?" Lyle began to get a little impatient.

"Linked to ancient memories and the secret of awakening energy potential. They do not know how to understand, but some of us, very few, have knowledge. Not all information but key. Key to put with other information and work out this puzzle."

"Are they stones? Tablets? Carvings? Crystals? And what is it about torus vortexes – what are they?'

"The vortexes can draw energies in and create a means to harness or use these energies. And no. Not crystals or the like. Some information is written and others are figures with coding as pictograms."

"This sounds a bit last century to me," Jenna said. "A bit like mythology."

"No, not myth," Chan replied. "This is true. Knowledge is only held by some."

"Why haven't we heard of this before?" Lyle enquired.

"They say nothing. Why would they? Such things make them rich, powerful."

The coffee pot sounded and Jenna left to go fetch it from the kitchen.

"Is there any cultural significance to this?" Lyle asked. "Something in legend?"

"No. Not really," Chan replied. "Some of this is from old China long before their development at the start of this century. Other is found in different countries. Spread across the globe."

"Do they have teams working on this?"

"Yes teams. Some are already experimenting with technology to try to make it work. But they fail so far. They only know so much. And the others are trying similar – they are a dark group."

Jenna returned with the coffee pouring them each a cup. "I heard you from the kitchen talking about technology experiments. I have worked on some complex ideas in the past few years. What are you talking about?"

"I cannot say precisely,' Chan answered. "I know only a piece of the puzzle."

"Where are these pieces?" Lyle asked intrigued from his career-based perspective.

"I do not know all of them, only some. Some are secrets in China, others are here, and some in other places. It is all I know."

"Where in China?" Lyle asked.

"Near Dunhuang at the edge of the Gobi desert."

"I have not been there. I must look it up."

"Yes do. I know I can trust you. I could sense so when you rescued me and I am sure you are the ones I am meant to meet. My insights are good enough to rely on what appears as chance to be the way forward. There are ancient caves on the old Silk Road near Dunhuang. Go there. You might find something."

"Really, why do you trust us?" Jenna asked.

"I was told I would meet two people here in San Francisco today who could help."

"How would anyone know it would be us?"

"No person is certain on such things. My inner being senses told me it was you when we met. You were sitting by the demon and in the statue is a small clue, and since I saw you talking about it, I figured it must be you. Sometimes life events just lead you to wherever you are meant to be…without question as if it is too good to be true, but it is true because life is always the path…or the way whatever. I have experience with this and now I am experiencing it again with you."

"A bit sketchy," Lyle added.

"So be it," Chan replied. "But I take a chance you see."

"Maybe it was a good chance to take. I study culturally significant sites and Jenna here is a propulsion scientist."

"See how I am right. What chances are there of meeting the very type of people who can help. Go to Dunhuang and look about the old town."

"How will we know who to ask?" Jenna enquired. "The entire thing sounds vague. Why would we even embark on such a journey?"

"This choice is yours, but I can sense you are already giving it great consideration. If you travel to Dunhuang, find a man in the old town. Then look for tattoo on left side of face. Dragon head tattoo. He will help you."

"Why should we do this? It is all very sudden and seems a bit unreal?"

"Alaska. Experiment station built right on top of clue to this puzzle. The authorities know this site is special. And please, do not see this as 'unreal' as you say. It is very real and I am confident you can help."

"So what details do you know?" asked Lyle.

"I can tell you just this." He handed him a piece of paper with some Chinese style lettering. "First you translate. But only some know translation. This not traditional Chinese. Believe this is right. This is not about computers or machines we have today or have ever had. It is information so when all details come to light, then those with information can find this energy. And the Song peoples in China had a spirit in life relevant to this understanding. This too is relevant. Perhaps research the Song to discover more in principle to determine your feelings for this venture."

"More coffee?" Jenna offered.

"No thanks," Chan replied. "I must go and tell others of this meeting and what happened to my friend."

"Is it dangerous? What others?"

"Yes, a lot of danger, but it must be done. Otherwise this effort is all in vain. These other people are working to help prevent this information coming to light for the authorities everywhere."

"Do you have a copy of this code?" Lyle waved the piece of paper toward Chan.

"Yes some information, but not here. It comes to light for those who are aware of understanding. You go to Dunhuang, seek dragon head tattoo on left side of face. He will tell if you can help. We have people watching. We must be sure to keep it secret. There are dark others too who are not the authorities."

"Don't worry we are not authorities, or the others," Lyle said smiling at Chan.

"I go now."

"Where will you go?" she asked him.

"Down Hyde Street to the bay. Someone will come get me."

Chan left keeping to the shadows as he made his way downhill towards the water's edge. An historic cable car passed him by with bells chiming as it then made a stop just past him. Two men appeared who then looked up and down the street making Chan feel very nervous. He hid himself deep in the shadows of an apartment block main entrance for a few minutes until the men had moved on, and then quietly and quickly traveled the remaining half-mile down to the bay. Here he made contact with an associate and was quickly taken inside an old warehouse nearby Fisherman's Wharf where he then boarded a high speed boat without lights taking him out over the water past Alcatraz to be lost in the darkness.

****

Jake stared at the carved stone he held in his hand, his thoughts lost to theories and information he and Raynie had been going over for the past couple of hours. His eyes rested on some very small inscriptions appearing to be Chinese lettering.

'These I just cannot figure,' he thought to himself.

Raynie was taking a shower, so he was alone in the kitchen.

'A stone located here in Australia with Chinese lettering?' He thought of the research he had undertaken in the past six months recalling how some information was about coding of some type and how it was sourced at various special sites.

'Why was this site potentially one of those?' he asked himself. It seemed co-incidental where the very place they had chosen to meet could be one of these sites.

'Why this place?' he asked himself again. Thoughts and ideas were tumbling around in his mind and he was not sure if it was beginning to actually confuse himself. Then he recalled their talk last night and the idea someone must be 'aware' in order to decipher any of this stuff. 'Aware of what?' he wondered.

"You look deep in thought," Raynie said entering the kitchen.

"Well yes. But at least now we have something tangible to work with," he replied. "It is a start, but what to do next?"

"You know, Lyle might be able to help us. He's due in Australia anytime now."

"Yeah, he might shed some light with all his work on cultural sites, but I have a hint this might even be somewhat beyond him. Well...at least to some extent."

"You know we were to meet him in Sydney, but with all this snow I think we might be stuck here for a few days longer. I think we should bring him in on all this stuff now. He can help us I'm sure."

"Hmm...the thought had crossed my mind. To bring him in on it I mean."

"Maybe we should call him. See what he is up to or where he is?"

A few moments later Lyle's holographic phone sounded, "Hi. Lyle here."

"Hello Lyle. It's Raynie, how are you?" A three dimensional image of her appeared resonating over the device.

"Raynie. So good to see you. I am great. How are you?"

"Same here. Always good where I come from. Where are you? On your way to Sydney?" HyperJets were equipped to take calls at any time.

"Um...no. I am in San Francisco."

"San Francisco. Whatever for?"

"Well, I met this person during descent from space...the space station. We struck up a bit of a friendship and sort of hooked up. I am at her place now."

"Ah...her place?"

"Yes. Her name is Jenna. Jenna Atkinson."

"Is she nice?"

"Very nice. And...we have just had a very interesting time together."

"I don't really want the details..."

"We have been talking about some very interesting stuff and met a strange man. A Chinese guy called Chan Lee. He gave us some odd information."

"Odd?"

"Yes odd. Information about some coding tied in with energy forces."

"It barely makes sense."

"I know. It barely makes sense to us, but there is something in it worth a further look. This guy Chan was adamant we were meant to find him based on something like an intuition."

"Say again, codes and forces?" Raynie stopped and thought for a moment to consider what she was just told.

"I reckon you and Jake might like it considering the research you guys have been doing."

"We are stuck in snow here. Biggest storm in years so we cannot get to Sydney. It will be at least two or three days. Most arterial transit lines near here are blocked."

"I'm going to stay here with Jenna a couple more days. We'll think about this stuff we have just been given and decide what to do with it. Hang on a minute."

Lyle asked Jenna about her thoughts when she replied, "I'm not due back for a while. We have a top priority project on but I asked for some leave just to have a chance to get my head clear."

"Hey Raynie. Jenna just told me she has some time off work, so yeah, I'll stay here a few more days yet."

"We can meet up in a week say. Jake and I have something to work on."

"Okay."

"Right, we'll call you in three days and make some solid plans."

"Sounds good. Looking forward to seeing you guys. Bye for now."

"Bye sweetie." Raynie ended the call and switched to the online video news to get an update.

The device changed mode to show a newsreader giving updates on both situations - the explosions and the storm. After a minute or two of viewing, she decided there was nothing new on either front and switched off.

"Any news?" Jake asked her looking up from where he had just stoked the fire with more wood.

"Strange. Lyle is San Francisco and has met someone called Jenna Atkinson. They were given some information he thinks we might be interested in. He is staying there a few more days and I told him we would meet in a week."

"In Sydney?"

"Yes."

"What info?"

"Something very much like what we are looking at here."

"We need all the help we can get. I have been going over this stuff in my head again and again and not getting far. What I can't figure is the reason why this stone would be here. Nothing explains it. See the inscriptions here just under this pictogram? It looks Chinese."

"Perhaps Lyle can shed some light. He said he and Jenna met this Chinese guy Chan Lee who gave them the information they have."

"You're right. We should leave it until then."

"Good idea and you know another idea? We could go for a ski again. The sky has cleared a lot and there are only flurries of snow now. Let's go out and have some fun." They put their ski gear back on and headed back outside from the kitchen, making way to the gate at the back of the house to the open fields beyond.

Chapter 5

John and Tobias were flying high over the sea just south of Prince of Wales Island and were making good time with their flight. The sky was crystal clear with stars and a half moon making for an almost metallic gleam off the ocean waters thousands of feet below. Green light illuminated the scene from above as the Aurora Borealis made a light show in the sky and both men were now used to the smell of the old Beaver's engine.

"I love those lights," John said as they both gazed at the spectacle above them.

"Strange they show this far south."

"You have a point there, but I have seen some unusual activity coming out of solar weather readings online. Maybe they are a result of a large solar flare."

"What about interference from the solar flare?" Tobias asked.

"Hey, where is your head? The place you've just been working at provides shielding for this type of thing nowadays."

"Oh yeah. Slipped my mind for a bit. All this action has left me a little dumbfounded."

"I'll put the Beaver down at Port Hardy then we'll make it to Vancouver by road from there. I estimate we have about four hours flying time left so we should arrive around six in the morning. A friend of mine can hide the plane for us just in case anyone comes looking."

"I've been trying to figure why those guys wanted to arrest me so badly. Still have no answers. It is not like I was privy to any sensitive information up there. I just was a station operations guy. You know, flick switches on and off, monitor the array, and make a few commands."

"Don't beat yourself up over it mate. I reckon like we said earlier - they just want you to cover their own backsides. Anyone with any details on the place is never let go lightly, and with these detonations happening I guess you had to make some adjustments to the array."

"Yeah. I had to tell Norway to upscale their frequency to. Up to eleven Schumann."

"Eleven. Man it is high. I reckon something else is going on. Eleven could almost interfere with anything. Was there a terrestrial reflection, some wide spectrum spread?"

"No. It was a straight beam up, with no cover for land based systems. I suppose a frequency along those lines might have damaged their systems as well. And what about this nuclear thing off California? I wonder what it is all about."

"No idea, but it has to have something to do with those other bombs. Sounds like there is some heavy stuff going down."

"You're telling me. And now we are both in on it. Sorry mate."

"No problem."

"So what you going to do?"

"I'm coming with you. There is nothing back there for me now. The authorities will put a trace on me so I should hide this plane. Poor old Beaver, has served me well, but someone else will find a use for her." A signal on the flight control dashboard told them they had reached international air space. "I'll leave this thing on," John said tapping his radar scrambler. "It is likely the authorities are going to be all over air control to track us."

"Will they be able to?"

"Not if I can help it." He turned the plane to the left. "I'll take us down to three thousand feet over the Hecate Strait and hug the east coast of the Queen Charlotte Islands."

High above them at over fifty thousand feet, a squadron of military HyperJets headed northward towards Palmer in Alaska with their lights making a diamond shape as they flew in formation.

Three hours later John and Tobias could see the northern tip of Vancouver Island as dawn's first light caressed the snow capped peaks of the coastal mountains on the mainland of Canada.

"We should be at Port Hardy within the hour," John said taking the plane even lower to an altitude just under two thousand feet. "I'll radio ahead to my friend there and tell him we are coming." He engaged the plane's radio for the first time during the entire flight. "This is Old Beaver, come in Sound Man."

"Sound man?" Tobias was curious.

"Yep. We use call signs up here. Saves giving away our registration number or name." He went back to the radio, "Come in Sound Man."

Almost a minute passed. "This is Sound Man. You're up early Old Beaver. What can I do for you? And...what you doing in these parts?"

"Um...we have had to leave somewhat in a hurry. Can you help us?"

"Sure Old Beaver. Fly on in. When are you arriving?"

"About forty minutes Sound Man. I'll bring her down just up the valley from your position."

"Okay. Copy Beaver. See you then."

"All good," John said turning to Tobias. "We call him Sound Man because he spends so much time out in the sounds fishing. I guess you know about the Beaver."

"Yeah. Figured so."

The plane came down with a hard bump and then John strained the controls to bring it to a halt in time before they hit the rock face looming up in front of them. He cut the engine and made a turn with the last of the plane's momentum as they rolled along the gravel bar.

"Nice landing," Tobias said, glad they had made it safely.

"Pretty run of the mill," laughed John knowing what Tobias was going through. "I'll just grab my little gadget and we'll be off."

After a brief search, they located Soundman.

"There he is over there," John said as he pointed over to the left in the direction of a small clump of trees.

"Hi you guys," he said as they greeted him. "Hi. I'm Sound Man." He shook Tobias' hand. "Hey Beaver," he said turning to John and also shaking his hand. "Good to see you guys."

"This is Tobias. We've been on a fun flight together."

"Yeah, I bet. You guys are sought after I reckon. I have been hacking into authority transmissions since you radioed through. Boy are they in a frenzy looking for you. We'd better get going."

"The plane?" John asked.

"No problem, I have someone on it already. They'll be here in fifteen minutes to take it away for you. I trust they didn't get your registration?"

"No chance. They won't even know it's a Beaver."

"Good. I have a vehicle just up the hill."

They followed Sound Man to a small truck like utility often found in these parts parked on a dirt track just a hundred yards away.

"Get in. We have no time to lose." He engaged the almost silent engine and then hit the accelerator sending clouds of dust in a vortex behind them as they quickly gained speed.

"You'll get used to his driving pretty soon," John said noticing the discomfort on Tobias' face as they sped away at eighty miles per hour.

"I'm sure I will."

"We'll stop off at my place for just a minute. Should be there in about two," Sound Man added. They reached his house perched high on a ridge overlooking the sea stretching beyond the horizon to the north.

"Here, take these." He handed them two bags. "Full of stuff you'll need." They continued on after Sound Man's house reaching hair-raising speeds along the winding road bounded by a steep hillside both up and down.

"We'll hit the transit way in ten minutes for clear driving from there on to Victoria."

"Hey, thanks for this," John said slapping him on the shoulder.

"No problem for the Old Beaver. Any day you can call on Sound Man. You too Tobias. I reckon on Beaver's judgment and if he thinks you're alright, then it's okay with me."

"Thanks mate," Tobias replied glad to be in the company of people he could trust, particularly at such high speed.

"So what you been up to?" Sound Man asked.

"Tobias here is in a bit of trouble through no fault of his own. He was stationed up at HAARP."

"You military?" Sound Man asked.

"Was. Not now I guess. They wanted me for some reason."

"You know how it is," John said. "Once you know too much they take you out."

"Ah yes. Well have no fear. Where you guys going?"

"We thought…well, after Vancouver, we might head down to Seattle then take it from there."

"You're going to need to get across the border. Don't worry, I thought ahead, figured you would want some special assistance. Most of what you will need is in those bags. And I know someone in Vancouver who can get you some identification."

A few minutes later they came to the only transit way on the island taking them through to Victoria.

"This is not like those transits on the mainland, but we should get there in good time."

A high whirring sound could be heard as the engine increased their velocity to one hundred and fifty miles per hour as sunshine began to break through the trees to their east side, making for a flickering stroboscopic light effect due to their speed.

"We should be there shortly yeah?" Tobias asked.

"Yep. We'll make for Goldstream on the west side of the city, where my contact is," Sound Man replied.

Chapter 6

Lyle woke, not sure where he was at first, then it all came to him like a flood as he remembered the events of the previous day. He walked over to the large bay windows of the lounge room and could see the sun shining on the communications tower on the hill south of the city. It made for a dream like scene as the lights of buildings and skyward traffic shone brightly in the early morning. JetCabs formed a steady line going from the airport to the central hub downtown, even at this early hour as people went to work.

After gazing outward for a few minutes, his vision shifted noticing Jenna's library of books on shelves set into one wall of the room. Titles ranged from Propulsion Physics, Cooking, Classics, Natural History, to Mythology, and Meditation.

'A pretty rounded person,' he thought to himself. He settled on the Mythology section and grabbed what appeared to be an antique volume titled Ancient Lore of the Forest. Such things always interested him and he made himself comfortable sitting in a large chair set near the window.

After about ten minutes of reading, Jenna had awoken and greeted him with a good morning, herself taking in the view through the bay window as she did most mornings.

"Good morning," he replied. "How did you sleep?"

"Like a babe. I always sleep better back on Earth. I think yesterday was quite exhausting. How about some breakfast." She left and went to the kitchen to make a meal, leaving him alone to continue his reading.

Through the open door leading to the kitchen he could hear her softly singing to herself with such harmony it seemed to add to his reading as if her voice was some enchantment coming from some mystical forest. Returning to the book, he came across a chapter titled 'Pictograms and their Meaning in Forest Lore.' Almost instantly he was struck by surprise as he viewed a page showing pictures of symbols used in past times. It was unmistakable, one picture held uncanny resemblance to the lettering he had seen on the piece of paper given to him by Chan Lee. At this, he diverged for a moment wondering about the fate of Chan after their meeting the day before. He had been adamant of dangers present concerning the information he possessed and wondered too what dangers may present to both himself and to Jenna if they were to take on board Chan's request and pursue these matters.

He read the text explaining the pictogram. 'Lettering symbols were often used in forest ceremonies to conjure up what believers saw as way to access and harness powers to give them eternal awareness of their surroundings and provide deeper understanding of forest lore. Scribes would spend many months and sometimes years researching the method by which to create the symbols and then how to use them in ceremonial practice. Outsiders to these events would often discard these letters as meaningless and were deemed to be unaware by scholars who practiced forest rights.'

"Very interesting," he said aloud to himself.

"What is?" Jenna enquired, returning with a tray of breakfast.

"Oh this book," he said showing her the title. "Where did you get it?"

"I came across it during a holiday when I was going through an interest in mythology stage. I found it at an antique market in a small town. So what is interesting?"

"This," he said showing her the page he was on. "See this lettering here? It is very similar to things Chan showed us." He placed the piece of paper on the book so she could see the similarity.

"Well yes it is. I see how close they are to each other. I haven't read this book in years, perhaps six or seven. And I love the piece of paper. I rarely see such things – simple messages written on paper."

"I think we should follow this up," he said taking the paper back off the book. "It seems a little too co-incidental we met each other at this time, met Chan, and now you have this book."

"I'm not really a believer in co-incidence in the normal sense. If you break down the word, co as in company or cooperate, and incident, you could get cooperative incident."

"I couldn't agree more. I was just using the word…well, as something to say."

"Yeah, I know. Have some breakfast."

An hour later they boarded an historic Hyde Street cable car for the trip downhill to the bay side. The sun was sparkling off the water on this beautiful spring day with boats already busily ferrying passengers. As they stood at the wharf gazing westward, a flotilla of large authority ships could be seen stationed directly in front of the Golden Gate Bridge. Lyle flicked on his holographic phone to see if there was any news on why they were stationed there, appearing to be blocking any traffic from heading out to sea. After a few minutes of switching channels he was unable to find any information about the vessels either on a national news or local news front, and so turned it off. Jenna was gazing out across the blue waters the entire time embracing the scene, feeling her love for living in this city and soaking up the sea smells carried on a gentle breeze.

"I suppose those ships are out there because of the bomb on the oilrig," Lyle said to her breaking the relative silence.

"The ships? Oh sorry, I was somewhere else then thinking about Chan Lee and his request. Yes, you could be right. I would expect a clamp down on ocean traffic considering the blast was only three hundred miles from here. I came across some information about two months back. Apparently they found lanthanides for use in fuel cells where the rig is located."

"The rare earth elements market is pretty tight at this time, even with off Earth mining. Three years ago I was looking at extraction in parts of northwest Australia and we had to do an assessment for the local first peoples. It reminds me, my trip to the Moon is supposed to involve similar materials but of much higher density which means a much higher yield."

"Hmm… the Moon. You must be excited."

"To be honest, yes. I have always wanted to go there. They want my expertise on assessing extraction methods. I don't see any cultural significance involved this time though."

"Hey, would you like to take a walk out to Golden Gate Park?"

****

Tobias and John left the house of Sound Man's contact and made their way to the old English style harbor in Victoria. After some cosmetic changes to their appearances and being given passports with new identities, they were on their way to a meeting with a person who could take them to the border. They boarded the ferry for Vancouver and now stood at the bow, gazing towards the islands in the distance.

"I know the cafe district in the city. I have been to a few cafes and bars there over the years. You know the ones," John said.

"Yeah. I've tried those myself. You get all types. Locals, tourists, and the hard up crowd trying to score something, or do you out of some cash."

"Speaking of cash. Hold on tight to the satchel Sound Man gave you. We are going to have to be careful on foot through the city and we'll need every cent of it to get us where we are going."

As the ferry rounded the final headland, the city came into full view with the mountains behind to the east. After docking, they disembarked and made their way straight for their next contact at Oakridge in the inner city. Vancouver was ultra modern with several towers stretching to over one hundred stories and many connected by pedestrian tunnels elevated high above the streets below. Now and then they passed entrances to the catacombs of the city existing below street level.

"I can never tire of this place," Tobias said looking around him all the time as they walked. "It is as if it has become the center of the modern world. Since all the work was done in the sixties to upgrade the buildings and the infrastructure, you could almost say it was a frontier city for a new world."

"I agree there," John replied. "I sort of miss the place when I am away, but even still with all its glory, it is hard to beat the wilds up north for some real outdoor experience."

Two lines of JetCabs streamed overhead between the tallest buildings on their way to and from the main hub with HyperJet passengers. Despite just having flown Beaver Air with John, these things made Tobias a little nervous as they appeared they flew too close to each other for his liking.

Ten minutes later they arrived at the house of Sound Man's contact and he greeted them at the door.

"Howdy guys, come in. I'm known in these parts as The Fixture," he said as he shook hands with both of them. They followed him inside, each taking up a seat in the lounge room. "You two have a bit of a mess on your hands, and in them."

"What do you mean in them?" John asked.

"I guess you all forgot about one important thing. Well, by now the authorities will have tracked you to this vicinity, so we have no time to lose."

"Oh bloody hell!" John said loudly realizing both he and Tobias had overlooked one important detail.

"I've just figured," Tobias said looking a little forlorn.

"Let's get to work then," The Fixture said moving to a cabinet at the side of the room and removing a device similar to an arm brace. "Time to remove those service personnel identification chips then. Who is first?"

Tobias held out his arm and The Fixture put the brace on extending from the base of his hand up to his elbow. He then flicked a couple of switches and Tobias felt a steel rod put pressure on his skin on the inside of his forearm.

"Ready?"

"Yeah, I'm ready."

"You'll feel a sharp pain for about two seconds no more. Here we go."

He flicked a third switch and the rod against Tobias' skin thrust into his arm, grabbed the microchip located in the tissue and pulled it out.

"Now you John."

He did the same for John and within a minute the entire procedure was over. Then he took both the chips, each about two millimeters long and placed them in a high-pressure heating kiln located on top of the cabinet. "We cannot smash them as they are too strong. This baby will render them inoperative."

As he did this, signals on the scanners held by five separate military officers in downtown Vancouver went blank. "Damn it, lost the signal," said the lead officer. "All officers remain in position. We have a cordon. I'll call for back up. We'll proceed with visual pursuit."

"I bloody well forgot all about those chips," John said rubbing his forearm. "In fact, even though my service chip was still there, I had been overlooking it past few years. Maybe I was in a bit of a dream by the river and you are here to wake me up."

"Now let's get you on your way. I reckon on having bought you about an hour before even this place will be swarming with those looking for you."

The twenty-mile journey was fast, as the guidance systems steered them along at one hundred and fifty miles per hour along the main transit way to the border. Vehicles of all sizes formed a long line of traffic in both directions, all of them kept at equal distance apart by the position tracking systems. When they were nearing the border, the transit way became an elevated tunnel twenty metres above the old highway routes. The Fixture slotted the vehicle into the transit track inside the clear tunnel after disengaging manual driving. As they came to the border post, The Fixture took manual control and parked the vehicle in the bay reserved for those not actually making the crossing.

"It's up to you guys now. If I were you, I would go through each as a single to minimize the chance of being seen together."

"I'll go first," said Tobias. "I hope these cosmetic changes are enough to throw them off visually." He left the vehicle and proceeded on foot via the elevated walkway to the gates ahead of them. The other two watched a little nervously as he approached an officer who was checking credentials.

The officer scanned his electronic passport with the system returning a green light to indicate all was in order. "Are you chipped? Consumer number please."

"Um…no consumer chip. I haven't done the uptake yet."

"Okay. I'll do a full body scan then." He directed Tobias into a full body scanner device and the resonance imaging hummed into action. It returned an all-clear signal. "You know. You should get a consumer chip to save these scans and make life a lot simpler for yourself. All your details are stored in those little things and you won't have need for cash. Just swipe your arm over the scanner and you're done."

"Thanks," said Tobias, a little disgusted at the entire idea of the technology.

"Where is your destination?"

"I'm going on to San Francisco. Have some friends there I haven't seen in ages. Um…which way to the public transit vehicles?"

"Take the corridor on the left there and it will take you all the way to where you want to go."

"Thanks and have a nice day."

"Same to you sir."

After seeing Tobias pass through the post successfully, John took his turn a little buoyed by what he had seen. "Well thanks Fixture. I'm sure we owe you one."

"No problem. Seeing you guys get through is all the reward I need. Each little victory against the system gives me a warm feeling inside."

John approached the post then presented himself for assessment. He went through an identical process to Tobias and was given the green light to proceed. As he walked towards the corridor on the left leading to the public transit vehicle hub, the officer called out to him. "Excuse me sir. Wait a moment."

A shot of nerves went through John. He had made it and felt sure he was free to go on. What could be happening now? He turned to face the officer who was indicating he should return to the scanning area. As he made his way back, he gained a little calm over his nerves.

"We have a residue reading showing on the scanner here. It has just come up. Have you ever been involved with military service sir?"

"No officer. I once consulted with the service."

"In what capacity was it sir?"

"I was asked to assist in developing some photonic micro chip development for shielding systems at an installation up north," John replied, careful not to be too precise on the location at which he had done the work.

"Please present your bags for visual inspection."

"Okay, but I only have some personal items."

"We will see sir."

John presented his bags and the officer proceeded in emptying their contents on the stainless steel table between them. After a few seconds searching, the officer held up the small stealth device John had brought with him from the plane.

"What device is this?" he was asked looking over its' exterior.

"Just a little project I have been working on. I am on my way to Seattle to show it some electronics gurus I know down there."

"What does it do?"

"Oh…it is a high speed processor. I am going to get their opinion on its viability for use in surveillance systems."

"Do you have authority to possess this device?"

"Well, no. As I said, it is a little personal project I have been working on."

An announcer system advised the next southbound public transit was leaving in three minutes and all passengers should now board.

"Look. I really need to go now," John said worried he was going to miss joining Tobias.

"Okay sir. I will let you proceed, but you will need authority for this device. I am going to log it into our system here and you will receive orders to proceed to authority offices in Seattle and have it approved." He handed it back to John. "Have a nice day sir."

"Thank you officer. You too."

John hastily made his way down the corridor and was the last passenger to join the vehicle.

As they pulled away from the terminal, the officer at the border post scanning area received a message to look for any individual possibly in possession of a stealth like device as he was a fugitive sought by authorities. Immediately he recalled John's passage just a few minutes before and raised the alarm back to authority control.

"We are going to have to get off this thing straight away," John said. "I just had the third degree on my stealth device."

The transport driver announced their journey ahead. "Ladies and Gentlemen, you are aboard public transit bound for Los Angeles. Our estimated time to arrival is ten hours. We will be traveling at one hundred and fifty miles per hour. First stop is Bellingham, Seattle, Portland, Sacramento…"

"Bellingham is our destination now," John said. "We'll have to make our way from there."

Fifteen minutes later the vehicle stopped at Bellingham. John and Tobias both hurriedly disembarked and then made their way out of the transit terminal. They ran through the town before seeing a secluded bar where a few local drinkers were inside despite the early hour. They each bought a drink and then sat in the dim light of one of the vacant booths in the corner behind a pool table. As they sat trying to be inconspicuous, they discussed how to move on and make their way south to San Francisco.

"They'll be looking for both of us I guess," Tobias said. "After Alaska, I can see them seeing us as travelling together."

"Maybe we should spilt and make our way separately. I can make contact with someone I know in Tacoma who has a seaplane. It can get to places out of reach of the authorities at airports. Also, there is a motor cycle dealer I know in Seattle who can help you. He'll give you a bike pretty cheap. You have the cash?"

"Yep. Safe and secure."

"Cool. Give me some and you take the rest. We'll have to make it on foot from here. Once we get to Seattle, I'll fix you up and then I'll go on to Tacoma on foot again. We're going to have to divert and not go direct to the bay area. I suggest we meet in Boise, Idaho, and then we can take more transit passage from there through Reno and go in from the northeast. They have the idea we are heading in roughly the same direction with the destinations we foolishly gave at the border post. Remind me never to do it again."

"Yeah, your idea sounds good John. I'll probably beat you to Boise with a head start riding while you're walking and then flying."

"No problem. Just lay low and I'll call you when I am close."

They decided it was the right time to leave, so they stopped at a local store and picked up a few food items then departed Bellingham. For the next five hours they tracked near the main transit way, keeping to the forest and bush lands just out of sight of any vehicles. When they stopped to eat just outside the town of Everett, they had covered just over half the distance to Seattle.

"When we get there, we'll go and buy the motorbike straight away and then you can head off," John said. "Head east on the main transit taking you over the Blue Mountains. It will be late by the time you start so most of your trip will be at night. I should be in Boise by tomorrow evening."

They continued on after eating, still keeping out of sight from anyone who would be inclined to stop them, until they could see the early evening lights of the Seattle outskirts in the distance. After a short rest, John took them to his contact on the northern edge of the city.

The motorcycle dealership was closed when they arrived - only the lights were on in the house at the rear. Within half an hour they had purchased a bike and Tobias was ready to set off at a time when the sun was just past setting and the eastern sky had begun to take on a nighttime shade.

"I'm going to stay here tonight and make my way to Tacoma at dawn," John said as he helped Tobias with the riding gear. "Take it easy, you don't want to attract any attention. Find an old motel at Le Grande up in the mountains and stay there. You'll need a break and they'll be sure to accommodate any latecomers. I reckon you should be in Boise by lunch time tomorrow."

"It'll be slow going. This thing is not built for transit ways," Tobias said as he mounted the bike. "How far will its' fuel cell take me?"

"You should get all the way. So take it easy and I will be seeing you."

Tobias rode off under the lights of the almost deserted streets with the flickering of amber lights shining his way ahead creating a mesmerizing mix as he sped the bike along. Now alone, he began to go over everything happening so far, wondering still why the authorities wanted him so badly. Although he had some answers, further questions arose as he thought about what they would do after they arrived in San Francisco. He knew a couple of people in the city but he was originally from Los Angeles so his knowledge of the place was sketchy.

After joining the military to continue his interest in electronics and for the promised travel to unique places, his first post at HAARP had taken up the past three years of his life. Prior to his posting, he had been on the east coast a number of times and had marveled at the sheer scope of the great cities there, each surpassing anything he had seen in technological development and scale. There were buildings almost reaching the sky interconnected by transit ways with lines of airborne traffic weaving in and out. Millions of people traveled the suspended walkways above the streets amidst a general buzz of energy and organized efficiency.

The wired world of the mid twenty first century was on the way out for the most developed nations. Where super poles one hundred and fifty feet high for conducting electricity and data once lined the streets in a matrix immersing the lower buildings and the people, the new cities were now becoming a suspended environment. In the densest population centers, city dwellers rarely touched the earth, instead living a life played out above ground. The enormous grid lines and wire sets were becoming a relic of the past where some fringe inhabitants and society outcasts still dwelled among the remnants of the old suburban areas.

Tobias was a child of the sixties, a time of great upheaval and changes to the world mostly unimagined in the previous decades since the suppressive years in the second quarter of the twenty-first century. During those years, people suffered largely at the hands of magnates and corporations who had taken a stranglehold and controlled the lives of most people in the western world though resources and energy. As this happened, more and more influence had eroded traditional values for the sake of economic development and market dominance with nearly entire populaces moved to and near high-rise buildings to save the open land for food and resource use.

In the decades through the late thirties, forties, and fifties, it was decided preservation of cultures was what determined the diverse character of humanity. Now the Earth was in an apparently more balanced state with dreams seemingly waiting to be fulfilled, and yet power was still maintained through a consolidated business model, largely un-noticed by the masses. The Earth's population of eight billion lived under the guise of renewed freedom, but was still being manipulated as those in elite positions grew stronger. They were the providers of new developments in technology seductive in appeal and touted as beneficial for people. And as they offered this tantalizing view of the future, they bore down controlling the people, building dependence, and constructing product as part of the human condition.

The road ahead stretched into the darkness lit only by his motorcycle headlight and now and then by other traffic. Tobias felt more and more comfortable as he left Seattle far behind and the chances of attracting attention seemed less. After crossing the Columbia River, his passage soon steered him to the foothills of the Blue Mountains, as John had said. He took on the challenge of riding up the twisting road to ascend their heights, for a while thinking of nothing else besides him and the road. Then, as he arrived at La Grande and found a motel, he rested until dawn.

Chapter 7

Jenna took Lyle by the arm as they walked the remaining city block along the boulevard at Fisherman's Wharf. The scene was one of glittering lights, people laughing as they walked, others eating and drinking al fresco, and of street musicians adding melody to the salt laden air. She kept her hold on him as they walked along through the late night crowd who were out in San Francisco - a twenty-four hour city, hardly ever sleeping, and never closing. As they walked, they could see the lights of the guarding vessels still blocking seaward passage out beyond the Golden Gate Bridge. No further news had been released about the bombing at the abandoned oilrig off the coast and they had given up on their quest to find out more.

"Hey, let's stop here," Jenna said as they came across a bar situated at the water's edge.

They sat down at a table closest to the edge, catching each others' eyes for a moment before a waiter came to take their order.

"Scotch and soda for me," Lyle said, being the first to break their gaze.

"I'll have the same please," Jenna added, still looking at Lyle.

The waiter left them to gaze out at the reflection of the night-lights on the water, before returning with their drinks a minute later.

"You know, I've been thinking about Chan Lee's information most of the day," Lyle said after taking a sip. "I feel some inclination to investigate further. I don't know if it is me, my profession, or both."

"I agree with you there. Anyway, how can you separate yourself as such? It seems as though Chan was right in a sense. With us meeting prior to descent from space, going to Fong's, his advice of how he was going to meet people who could help him, and your inclination to look at this further. Well…it seems right somehow. I am not sure where I can exactly fit in, but I do have an interest in this type of stuff, and with my line of work researching, I might be able to help."

"It is amazing how life can coast along setting you up for a series of events you cannot predict, and yeah, the separation is something I see now, thanks. I am sure you could help with whatever it is we might do. I was meant to go to Sydney in the next few days, but with the entire current goings on, I wonder if it might be better if my friends come here instead. Then we can all put our heads together and see what happens from there, and…," he pondered for a moment. "Take on this sense of adventure."

"Are they able to travel here at such short notice?"

"I'm sure they can. Jake travels a lot and Raynie is never one to shy away from something mysterious. With the snow there in Australia and with what Chan told us, it makes sense we gather here."

They remained silent for a few moments sipping their drinks and considering what events may lay ahead in the immediate future.

"Guess what," Jenna said breaking their silence. I can easily take more time off work. I am way ahead with my current project and I am sure they will not miss me anytime soon. I'll just have to give them some details and advice on the next stage of testing I was to undertake and they can go ahead without me."

"I have an extended break until my Moon trip scheduled for six weeks time. I have some briefings to go over and then report for pre-flight training, but until then…let's do it then?"

"Yes Lyle. I feel excited. This is shaping up as some sort of investigation or adventure or both."

"Why don't I call Raynie now? I wonder what time it is in Sydney?" He checked the world time on his holographic phone. "Okay, it is mid afternoon there. I'll call now." He retrieved Raynie's number and set his phone down so as to capture her holographic image.

"Hello Lyle. How are you…and Jenna?" Raynie said appearing as a miniature figure in the air over the device.

"We are both fine. And you?"

"Good. The snow has eased. How is San Francisco?"

"Great. We are down at the wharf just having a drink."

"Sounds nice."

"How is the snow?"

"There has been over two feet in all. They expect the main transit way to Sydney will be open tomorrow. We need to get the local roads clear first though. It should be by the next day."

"So two days then?"

"Yes, by then it should be okay. When are you arriving?"

"I'm not coming now."

"Why sweetie? Anything wrong?"

"No. Quite the opposite actually. All good on this front."

"Then why aren't you…?"

"A good reason. I wonder if you and Jake can come over here."

"I can't see any reason why we can't come. Do you have something for us?"

"Sure have and I think it would be great if you two could come over to San Francisco. We can discuss some details when you get here."

"Well, we are kind of stuck here. We found something we have both been looking for which is…um, something we just cannot work out why. Why it was here I mean. So yes, we are kind of stuck and frankly were wondering where it might lead to next."

"How about you get yourselves over here and we can put all this together. I think we may have your next heading."

"Oh great! Jake will be pleased. He is just out getting some wood for our fire at the moment. I'll tell him as soon as he gets back in."

"Good. So you'll arrange a HyperJet flight from Sydney then?"

"Yeah, but in two or three days. I will make a booking after we get off the phone."

"Okay. Do so and call me as soon as you arrive."

"Alright, will do. Hey this sounds exciting!"

"I think it is."

"Okay sweetie, take care and we will see you in a few days. Bye"

"Cool, see you then Raynie. Bye." He ended the call and Raynie's holographic image disappeared.

Jenna attracted the waiter's attention after Lyle had concluded the call. "This is making me hungry," she said. "How about you?"

"Yeah, I could eat." The waiter came over and took their order for food and another round of drinks. When he returned with the drinks, they both downed them quickly and ordered another two rounds. Ten minutes later their food arrived and they tucked in, feeling ravenous now by both their energy levels and the few alcoholic drinks they had consumed.

Before long they had ordered three more rounds of drinks and both of them felt the persuasion of the alcohol. Swept up in the moment, they left the table and walked along the boulevard. They stopped by a Cuban musician with salsa tunes beckoning them to join others who were already moving to his rhythms, and so they danced a while in an embrace alluding to the growing feelings they had for each other.

****

Tobias awoke startled at first, until he realized where he was a moment or two later. He immediately then rose out of bed, washed his face, and dressed. Ten minutes later a knock came at the door and a breakfast tray was left. After eating, he paid his bill and set off again on the motorbike. The sun was early in the eastern sky, casting a golden glow over the mountains surrounding him. Before long, he was making way downhill as he approached the Snake River shining like a golden serpent in the early light. There was only an hour and a half of riding left until he reached Boise and so he decided to stop a while by the river to admire the sun's caress of the valley floor.

To the west, John's bike dealer friend had offered to drive him all the way, much to his delight. When a roadblock came into view, John knew the authorities had covered every route out of the city.

"Pull over," John said readying himself to get out of the vehicle as soon as they had stopped. His friend brought the vehicle to a halt and John immediately left with grateful thanks, heading straight into a small forest by the roadside. Sirens sounded and lights flashed as the authorities had seen them pull up short of the roadblock. The chase was on and this time he had no vehicle or plane to use for escape.

He ran on through the forest, hearing the military follow him in. Panic overtook him a little as he was unfamiliar with this territory and was a little blind on direction. He kept on running, his breathing loud as he exerted himself to the fullest. He kept going smashing through branches and jumping holes. Still they were behind him and seemed to be getting closer.

'It must be only five miles or so to get there,' he thought.

He was running as hard as he could, and his pursuers would not give up. He could hear dogs barking - they had trackers with them. Sweat ran down his face, inside his clothes. They were gaining, the dogs becoming more excited as they closed in on him. He crossed a road and took to the bushes on the other side. This was easier now than the forest. Still they came closer. He tripped and fell becoming covered in dirt and mud. He was almost instantly back up on his feet and kept running, thankful for the time he had spent maintaining fitness going up and down the mountains in Alaska. They were too close now for comfort but they had lost sight of him. The dogs ran with their noses to the ground, sniffing out his trail. He kept on, but fell again. His chest was heaving, his legs aching.

He pulled out his holographic phone as he ran. "Shane, you there?" he said into the microphone without engaging holographic mode.

"Yeah, who is this?"

"It's John. John Matheson. Can you help me?"

"John. Yeah. What's wrong, you sound like you're running."

"I am." He caught his breath for a moment. "Can you fly me?"

"Fly you? Yeah sure. I am at the plane now. Just finished some maintenance. Where are you?"

"About three miles away."

"I'll get her started. See you soon."

John kept running through the bushes, his pursuers still closing in. His conversation had slowed him a little. He fell again and thought for a moment, this is it - they will catch me. Then a large truck vehicle came into view and so he crossed the road when it was almost upon him. A little stroke of luck as this thing could put some space between them. He continued on, his legs almost giving out. He stumbled again and for a few minutes made his way by crawling. His upper body was heaving, as this effort was taking it out of him. He crashed through bushes, barely ten inches from the ground. He could hear the dogs barking. They were still at least one hundred yards behind.

He kept half crawling half running and came upon a house. Two people, a couple had just arrived and he stayed low so they would not see him. They would be sure to tell the authorities who were still coming. Then he was back on his feet when he was well past the house. His arms felt like lead, his legs a little less after the crawl. He ran. He kept running. The dogs with their officers were still behind.

'Only about a mile and a half to go now,' he thought.

He could see water in the distance. Surely Shane's place was not too far now. The effort was almost making him sick feeling sure he could vomit. Then he saw a way through a forest, and he was within the last half mile. He ran in and his pursuers followed less than a minute later. He had gained more ground as they had set the dogs to regain his trail. He ran on through the trees - a stand of young pines each positioned well apart from the other. There were no branches but he ducked around tree trunks and over some fallen logs. He could see a row of houses and so he ran as fast as possible towards them. He reached the houses but found them to be joined together with no way through. He thought frantically. He ran along behind them, at last finding access by way of a community park separating two blocks of town houses. He ran through and there were people everywhere.

"What the hell?" he said aloud.

He looked to his left and saw a man running from another row of houses. The man ran into the crowd and fired a shot, instantly killing an innocent person. "Bloody hell!"

He kept running and to his left he saw a road overpass. The killer ran the opposite way. John ran through the overpass and could see the water clearly and then he found his bearings. Shane's place was only a few hundred yards further on. He looked across the water as he ran and could see a mass of people gathering further along near where the shooting had taken place, for a few moments consuming his pursuers. Suddenly there was a dog at his side. He slowed a little and called "come on boy." It followed him for a moment, and then ran off.

A minute later he could hear the sound of a plane engine revving and so he again broke into a run, almost sprinting this time. He was close. He rounded a corner on the road and there was Shane standing on one of the plane's landing floats. He ran up to him and they both boarded without a word. They took off and finally John could rest and catch his breath as Shane took the plane up in a steep incline.

Tobias arrived at the outskirts of Boise and pulled up on his bike at a rest area. He meandered about for a few minutes and then his holographic phone rang. "Hi, is it you John?"

"Yep. Sure is. I'm flying there now. Bloody chased half the way to the plane, but I am alright. We're going to land this thing on the river near Nampa. I'll make my way from there. Go to the Boise HyperJet terminal now and get us tickets. There is a change of plans. We need to get south, fast. I'll meet you there."

"See you there."

Tobias rode onto into the city and straight to the terminal securing them tickets on a jet leaving in three hours. He decided to try and get a sale on the bike within the waiting time and so rode out to where he had seen a dealership when he entered the city. After a little haggling, he secured a reasonable amount of cash not much less than they had paid. He then had two hours remaining until the flight so he took a bit of time to walk around the inner city.

John greeted him in the departure lounge fifteen minutes before takeoff was scheduled. They exchanged stories on what had happened to them both since they last had contact as they made their way to board the jet. A stewardess directed them to their seats and within minutes the jet was airborne.

An hour later after successfully exiting the San Francisco domestic HyperJet terminal, they were both on their way in a JetCab to the city center. Tobias felt uneasy during this flight as the cab joined others in a line heading towards the city.

"Don't worry too much Tobias, these things have specialized guidance systems. They cannot crash into each other."

"Where will we go? I only know a couple of people here and they probably would not want us turning up on their door at random."

"I have a great friend here. We did some propulsion systems work a few years back. She'll let us stay a while."

They landed shortly after and went to a bar for a settling drink in celebration after all they had gone through and to catch their breath. The latest news was playing on all of the large holographic projectors in the bar. "Authorities advise due to recent explosions in the mid west and off the coast of California, all sea traffic is on hold. The current state of alert is high red so passengers for all HyperJets leaving and entering the United States can expect rigorous scanning. Further information as to the origins of the explosions reveals authorities are following several leads concerning a group of activists. As to the reason for the explosions, authorities will not comment."

"Well, there you have it. No real news. I bet Jenna would be interested."

"Jenna?" Tobias asked.

"Yes, Jenna. She is my friend I told you about. We should go to her place now. I could do with a decent rest away from the public."

****

Jenna rose from the reading chair to answer a knock at the front door. She opened it to find Chan Lee standing there. "Come in, come in."

"Thank you. I will come in."

"What brings you back?" she asked him as they made their way to the lounge room to join Lyle who was already there.

"Have much news. Must tell you now and leave quickly."

Lyle greeted Chan as he entered the room and was unable to also ask why he had returned before Chan let his reasons known.

"I have been checking your backgrounds and I am convinced our chance meeting is the right solution no matter how remote it may seem. We must move on the information I gave you quickly if you are going to help. Bad people are trying what they can. They are already in Duanhang. We must travel quickly."

"We can't do it yet," Lyle replied. "People are coming to meet us from Australia in two days, maybe three."

"Bad people are getting close, they know about man with dragoon head tattoo. They are looking for him."

"Do they have the same information you gave us?"

"No. They have something else. I did not know they would be so advanced in their search. Thought there would be few weeks for us to move. Now, they are a present danger."

"Can we stop them?"

"No. They have weapons and backup people helping them. We best go now."

"How much time? I mean, can we wait until our friends arrive?"

"Two days at most. Much better if we go today. I will not come with you as they might get to know I have help here in America. I will leave today, but you must follow. We need your help or I am afraid they will obtain too many details to be stopped in time."

"Okay," Jenna chimed in. "This is still a bit sudden Chan. You say you checked our backgrounds. I can only assume you have contacts. For us though, we have no backgrounds check on you Chan."

"Can you consider Jenna, when you are at work, do you rely heavily on your instinct from knowledge to guide where you look next?"

"Well, yes I do. It is different though. I work according to specific outcomes for the research."

"Perhaps you can consider this as the same. There is a specific outcome, though not obvious. This will come over time. I am only asking you to trust yourself. There is nothing for me choosing to deceive you. What could I gain from sending you to China if I was deceitful?"

Jenna and Lyle thought this over for a moment. They could see nothing they could have or do for Chan to make him want to deceive them. Lyle then looked into Jenna's eyes asking her if she wanted to go. He had embraced the idea with more enthusiasm than the degree of caution she held.

"We will come in two days," she said finally providing both Chan and Lyle a sense of relief.

"They do not know I have seen you or I am here. Just be prepared. Be careful and do not ask about anything. Just go to Dunhuang like I said. I must go, am leaving today for China on jet."

"Alright Chan, we will see you in Dunhuang?"

"Perhaps. Just go to Mogao Caves. I know in my heart you are the people to help us. I will be in communication again soon, and be alert to coincidences."

Chan left leaving Jenna and Lyle to hastily begin planning for the trip to China, whilst considering what he meant by being alert to coincidences. They had begun packing and organizing a few things when another knock came at the door.

"Chan must have come back," Jenna said as she went to answer.

To her surprise, John and Tobias were there to greet her. "John, come in," she said grabbing his arm.

"Hi Jenna, this is Tobias, a friend of mine."

"Welcome Tobias, come in."

They went inside and did a round of introductions with Lyle.

"I'll fix us some drinks. Gee, it is all happening today."

For a while they all sat in the lounge room exchanging news and stories. John explained how he and Tobias were on the run from authorities for no real reason, and by now they would be classified as fugitives. He asked if they could lie low there for a while, but soon learned of the impending trip to China for Jenna and Lyle.

"Hmm... well, I was hoping to be out of the action for a while and try to plan our next moves," he said rubbing his temple. "I suppose we could just move on. Why a trip to China?"

Jenna and Lyle explained all the details to them, including the chance meeting with Chan Lee. They explained the thoughts they had put together themselves based on the information he had given, and the fact he had just re-visited them not long ago. Lyle also added details of Raynie's and Jake's pending arrival in San Francisco, and how he and Jenna intended to discuss all this with them, proposing they join them in going to China.

"Sounds like some pretty hairy stuff from Chan Lee. I wonder..." John trailed off considering his situation being at a loose end with Tobias.

Tobias asked if there was anything they could do to help. Lyle was not sure on what it could be, but he was turning an idea over in his mind.

"What if you come with us?" Jenna voiced his thoughts.

"I am not sure. Are we going to get out of here easily?" John was curious yet a little hesitant. "Perhaps we could make it if we left soon enough. I know someone here who could give us new passports. But yes, we would have to leave within a couple of days at most."

"It is our plan," Lyle added.

"Alright. But first I need some rest for a few hours. How about you Tobias?"

"I might go for a bit of a tour down to the wharves," he replied. "Time to get my head all around this."

"It's settled then," Jenna said. "I'll make bookings for six on a HyperJet to Beijing." She immediately did so and returned to advise a jet booking had been made departing in sixty hours.

Lyle decided to research their destination some more to give them details on the path to where they were going, and about the Mogao Caves. He switched his holographic phone on and placed it on the coffee table before entering the research details. Immediately the phone showed a hologram of the earth with his present location. He decided to magnify the image expanding the projection to five feet in diameter. With a wave of his hand from left to right, the sphere slowly rotated showing the expanse of the Pacific Ocean, with the Asian coast coming into view. Once China showed clearly on the three dimensional image, he stopped its' rotation. By pointing his finger through the details representing the Chinese capital Beijing, the image then changed to reveal a three dimensional image two miles above the city.

Buildings of immense size loomed out toward him, their dimensions truly astounding. After substantial development, this city had taken on almost alien proportion. Ranked in the top three cities on Earth, Beijing contained a population exceeding thirty million people with the infrastructure to match. He then switched from static view to real time. The image changed to fill in gaps between the super structures, revealing hordes of people and busy airborne traffic lanes.

Lyle navigated to information about the city's transit system via a control panel holographic image appearing to the right of the main image. He entered in their trip details for information on how to get to Dunhuang. A locally accented voice in English then announced HyperJets were available from Beijing to Lanzhou with a flight time of thirty minutes. Transit ways were available then to Yumen with conventional driving available onwards to Dunhuang at this time due to flight travel restrictions in place.

He then traced the route in static global mode to find they would be traveling through some of the most ancient parts of China, crossing the Great Wall and then traversing it for some distance before arriving at Yumen. This interested him greatly as he had only been near to that part of the world on a fairly rushed trip just over eight years prior when conducting work on researching the cultural impacts of an advanced deep space tracking system to be built.

For as much of his thirty-two years of life as he could remember, he had dreamed of visiting the Gobi Desert, only to eventually be frustrated on coming so close previously. This time by going to the very beginnings of the ancient Silk Road trade route, he would be closer than ever in realizing his dreams. He then entered Mogao Caves into the control panel.

The projection view switched to reveal a vast array of grottos or caves chiseled into a cliff face alongside a seasonal river. Almost eight hundred caves in total were located there with over half of them featuring murals. These images rendered over centuries spanning a millennia or more, were a mixture of interpretations travelers had made of deities in the past. The Chinese referred to them as 'peerless caves' decorated with expansive interpretations forming a kaleidoscope of images including many carvings and statues. Each period featured its' own artistic style, but a common thread permeated them all.

'Very interesting,' Lyle was thinking and he began to ask himself, if his lifelong fascination with the Gobi Desert might, in some way, be linked to this place.

Satisfied with the details, he switched off the holographic phone and calculated the travel time to gain estimation on the precise time of arrival for the party of travelers in Dunhuang. Taken from their departure scheduled in sixty hours, he came up with an approximate three days before they would be there.

A moment later, Jenna joined him asking what he was doing. Lyle explained to her the details of their trip, the marvel of the caves at their destination, and gave her the estimated time of arrival.

"You had better call Raynie and Jake now Lyle, to see if they can make it."

"Good idea."

He called Raynie who answered in her usual cheerful way.

"Hi Lyle. Jake and I are excited about meeting you and Jenna."

"When are you leaving? We need to hurry up here."

"We're in luck. They say the road linking to the main transit way to Sydney will be clear all the way in twelve hours or so. With the HyperJet flight, I would say we allow about twenty four hours."

"Okay then. We'll see you in a day more or less. Also, what do you think about a sudden trip to China?"

"China! Why?"

"I'll tell you when you get here. We will have about a day here before we go. There are two others coming with us as well. You will find out why when you arrive."

"Thirty hours, then to China. I think Jake will like it as some of his research seems to have links with China, as does our recent discovery here. We will see you then."

Chapter 8

Raynie and Jake sped along the road bordered by walls of snow as they were heading to the main transit way for the drive to Sydney. Driving was mostly a fully automated experience when traveling the transits, as high-powered computer guidance systems did the work. Traditional type driving was also still available where people required transit away from the elevated tunnels. Sleek in design with high-powered electric engines running on tiny fuel cells – a small single power cell coupled to the operating systems and motors driving the wheels. Each cell held a dynamic anti-matter threshold containment module requiring only initiation to work. Energy sourced from the perpetual state of the proximity threshold between matter and anti matter, drew upon the transition of particles expelled during intense electromagnetic discharge. Equipped with automatic sensors and advanced safety systems, they were virtually impossible to crash, even during those times of actual manual operations.

Vehicles were almost silent when running, with most noise coming from the flexible carbon nano tube tires on the surface of the road. These tires always remained flat on a road surface and the axles horizontal. With suspension located at the apex of each axle where the passenger compartment was connected, the vehicles cambered according to the forces at play, enabling such high speeds to be reached and maintained. Advanced hydraulics operated by high-speed early photonic chip technology, brought instant response providing passengers and cargo with a smooth, almost un-noticeable ride.

When used in the advanced transit ways closer to the main cities found in nearly all major cities of the world, vehicles drove within an elevated tube as if on a rail system where all modes of operation were automated. Passengers were provided with holographic projectors rendering information in high definition three-dimensional imaging so they could often be content to sit back and relax being entertained during the longer trips. Speed was limited to two hundred miles per hour for fast movement along the tubes.

"Doesn't the countryside look beautiful," Raynie said gazing out the side window at the fields of white under a pale blue sky.

"Sure does," Jake replied as he drove at high speed through the twisting bends. "I expect we will get a nice view when on the transit from twenty meters up. They reported snow was on the ground all the way to the outskirts of the city."

The onboard navigation hologram hanging in mid air just to the side of his forward vision indicated ten minutes at current speed until they reached the main transit way for the journey to Australia's largest city.

"After last night and going through the book again, I think I am beginning to get a picture on some of this stuff," Jake said as they entered the main transit way and the car went into full automation mode. The scenery in the foreground then began to blur a little as they increased speed to two hundred miles per hour.

Two hours later, they entered Sydney, once a sprawling metropolis, now a city focused on high-rise at the center. A lot of the remnants of old suburbia had been removed from the land now converted to vast fields for growing food to feed the population. Buildings rose towards the clouds in this geologically and tectonically stable region, enabling architects to design towers reaching two hundred floors. Through advances in construction and stabilization methods, many cities defied their surroundings, some reaching unfathomable heights in seismically active zones compared to the cities of old, and in others not burdened with such activity, reaching almost twice their height.

Their vehicle changed transit lanes and took them at high speed towards the HyperJet Airport. As they neared the terminal, a museum of early flight came into view. Old jet airliners and planes seemingly ancient were parked at the entrance as exhibitions in a time-line of flying history.

"Would you fly in one of those?" Raynie asked pointing a large double decked passenger jet from the early twenty first century.

"I suppose so. They were heralded for their capacity and standard of luxury at the time, but nothing like a HyperJet though."

They boarded their flight as scheduled and once again marveled at the city as it receded below them as their jet approached the altitude where hypersonic drive was engaged. After just over four hours of flight time at speeds exceeding three thousand five hundred miles per hour, the HyperJet captain announced they were now on approach to San Francisco International Airport.

Amongst the glittering lights of San Francisco in the distance, the city's towers could just be made out amidst the general light haze streaming into the night sky. Twenty minutes later they eagerly walked the passenger departure hall of the jet terminal, ready to immerse themselves into the buzz of the city's goings on. A line of JetCabs awaited as they left the main building where they boarded for the short ride to the city center.

As they left the central cab hub, a lot of people were staring at the many holographic projectors located throughout. Looking up to the pedestrian transit ways above, they noticed similar groups had gathered around projectors like the people did on the streets. It appeared as though some news story had grabbed their attention, so they walked over to the closest projector available to see what the fuss was about.

"The authorities have approved the implementation of mandatory human micro chips. With recent events concerning nuclear detonations, it has now become necessary for all civilians to have identification chips in view of security maintenance and control. The bill states all citizens are to have the chips by the end of the year twenty ninety..."

The address went on to explain how this bill is in the best interests of the public at large and how it is a main weapon in the struggle against insurgency threatening many great nations.

After it concluded, advertising in support of the scheme, immediately appeared on all projections.

"Ladies and gentlemen, be the first to have your mandatory chip. For all those taking up this scheme immediately, we offer significant discounts on many of the things you need in life for happiness. With this offer, we will reduce costs for food and personal items by up to twenty percent for a limited time. Be safe now. Don't wait to be caught out. Join the beginning of the electronic payment revolution. With your new chip, we can meet all your needs from payment through to medical records and anything you currently manage in your own personal database. Go online now for early benefits and know your family is safe. As an additional special offer, those who obtain their chips in the first forty eight hours of this scheme, will be entitled to their choice of consumer number or name for their chip, so don't wait, you can customize your own personal account now."

They were taken aback with this news. Whilst the population at large would accept this information given by authorities as a benefit to them all, they both held grave reservation on what it would actually mean for the people. After deciding to move on, they took to a leisurely walk. Half an hour later they arrived at Jenna's place where she welcomed them lovingly at the front door.

"Lyle has told me a lot about you two. I think we have something special. Come in, come in." They entered the house and were introduced to the other three waiting in the lounge room. Raynie greeted Lyle with a hug – now both in their early thirties, they had been friends a decade now since their early twenties.

"Did you see the latest news?" Lyle asked.

"Yes we did. A big worry," Jake replied.

"We just had our military tags taken out," Tobias added.

"And, I for one am not going to get another one inserted, even if it is the civilian version," John said with a determined thoughtful look on his face. As an electronics specialist, he had already begun to think of ways around being 'chipped' again.

Both Raynie and Jake as historical archivists by profession, began to talk about it being an unprecedented move since the early twenties where corporations had collaborated with governments at the time in an attempt to bring in similar technology for a cash-less world. This had been mostly rejected as systems at the time were incapable of processing all facets of the global market, so the authorities had decided the technology was not yet ready.

"Well, we made it in time," Raynie said changing the course of the conversation. "We still have a day left before we depart. What shall we do tomorrow?"

"I think we should put all our information together to give a focus point on what we look at ahead," Lyle said.

"Yeah, I want to talk about it," Jake added. "So how do you and Tobias come into the picture?" he asked John.

"I'm an old friend of Jenna here," he replied. "Both Tobias and I are on the run from the authorities you could say. But…we are innocent of any real wrong doings. We have made it here from Alaska over the past two days and I brought us here to Jenna's to plan our next move. Jenna and Lyle explained their recent events and meetings, and without any real heading or plan, Tobias and I decided we could be of use in their endeavors. I guess you could say we are part of a team somewhat."

"Us too," Raynie said.

"We need more gear to take with us," Lyle added. "Some relatively low tech stuff, all legal. It might help us to decipher what we are going to look at."

"And I'll take Raynie and get us some new clothes," Jenna added. "Sort of a girl thing."

"Good idea. This stuff I have on has seen better days, especially after the chase yesterday," John said as he looked himself over.

As the early sun shone brightly over the bay, Jenna and Raynie made their way to the central shopping district in search of new clothes for the entire traveling party. The central district never closed and so they had decided on dining out for breakfast before going shopping, leaving the others to fend for themselves at Jenna's place. The two women walked the streets in an excited frame of mind, glad to just have each other's company as new friends.

Jenna took Raynie by the arm and led her down a street to where she knew they could get a nice meal. As they entered the street level café, news, and advertising for the microchip scheme was playing on all of the projectors.

"This is big news," Jenna said. "I am with John on not getting one, but hey, let's not talk about it now."

"I agree," Raynie replied. "Though just to add, there is no chance for me either."

They sat at a welcoming booth table by the front window of the café where the light of the day was streaming in. After placing their orders, they discussed their mission ahead for the day as Jenna suggested various places to go shopping. When their meals arrived, they began eating but were then interrupted by someone who had burst into the café through the front doors. He was a man in his later years appearing a bit rough and unkempt. After looking around to see who was inside, he began to speak loudly telling everyone not to get these new microchips and they were the work of the authorities who wanted to control all lives on the planet. A few other customers jeered at him, with some replying to his rant telling him he was a crazy old man and to go home. Others just listened, knowing the apparently crazy man spoke words of truth.

A little later, Jenna and Raynie decided it was time to go shopping and walked to Union Square in the city center for an elevator to take them to the world above. As they rode up to the pedestrian transit forty stories above street level, they were again bombarded with advertising on the elevators' four holographic projectors. Everything from lifestyle products, clothing, appliances and the new microchip scheme came across with endless catch phrases and reasons why one seller was better than another.

An advert for automated air freshener caught Raynie's attention. "I thought they banned those things years ago after it was found a lot of the scents actually contained carbonates effectively diminishing brain function."

"Yeah they did. But they are making a comeback. See the banner text now appearing?"

Text began to scroll across the bottom of the projection guaranteeing the product to be carbonate free and how it could actually enhance brain function.

"I doubt it," Jenna said. "But, by the looks of it today, I reckon a lot of people around here could do with a little brain enhancement."

"Don't they get it with nano implants?"

"Yes some do. I have worked with a few scientists who have the inserts and they claim to be able to process calculations at a much faster rate than previous because of the enhanced DNA maintenance function they carry out."

The elevator doors opened and they stepped out onto the tube walkway stretching between the buildings. Jenna took them to the left where she knew she could find a store selling the latest in clothing wear.

"You'll find some nice clothes here," she said as they reached the end of the walkway opening out onto a large indoor esplanade fronted by shops.

They struggled between the masses of people crowding the area as she led Raynie to a store she knew well on the far right side of the esplanade.

Upon reaching the store, a service person greeted them, "What would you like today ladies? City wear, casual, or outdoor wear?"

"We'll take outdoor wear," Jenna replied. "But first, we will get the men sorted out and then we can shop at our leisure. Please show us the male section."

"With our current technology, you know one size fits all, except for height."

"Four men all between six foot and six foot six inches."

"Well then, now we can get down to business." The service attendant took four different styled outdoor suits off the rack. "Now. These Geiga suits can all accommodate the height range as you advised. Do you like the styles?"

"They look fine to me. What do you think Raynie?"

"Yes. Great suits."

Clothing had taken on an entire new dimension in recent years for those living in the more advanced societies. Gone were the old style shirts and pants prone to wear and tear. Nanotechnology now played a big part in clothing design and styles. Clothes for those fortunate to be able to afford them were now one-piece suits incorporating technology developed through discoveries in plant-based materials preventing them from becoming soiled or wet. They could still be prone to wear, mostly in adverse environments, but were much longer lasting and retained their original new look for almost their entire life cycle. The technology was woven into the fabric of each to provide a bacteria free thermally regulated environment for the wearer.

With the advances made in medicine with nanotechnology, nearly all consumers now had access to the atomic world. Programmed to optimize the human body, anyone who needed it was capable of taking them on board personally to re-shape their body and retain condition for most of their average one hundred and twenty year lives. On one level were the corporations responsible for the development of this technology - their thinking was people with healthy long lives could provide a longer and more productive life of consumption in-turn adding to the profit of the large corporations. Unbeknown to the population at large was the fact most corporations were owned or being acquired by the authorities.

Through constant upkeep and repairs of the Telomeres found at the ends of chromosomes, the cell based nanotechnology retained cell reproduction at high quality thus sustaining the integrity of DNA condition. Under the guise of the freedom to live happy and healthy lives, people took to this technology without hesitation. Some elected not to have the implants of nanotechnology - mostly those fortunate enough physically to only require specific treatments as they aged. Jenna and Raynie were of this later group, and so had both decided they did not require any of the nano medicines.

"Now for us," Jenna said when the attendant had finished packing the men's' clothes. "Take us to the ladies section please."

"You will love our brand new stock," the attendant told them as he led them away. "A new line of women's Geiga Suits. The styles are just out of this world and the price is right too."

He took two body suits off the rack and instantly both women fell in love with the clothing.

"Aren't they just great."

Indeed the suits were very appealing to the eye in a style appearing quite futuristic. They had lavish lines to accentuate the female form. Flowing designs and decals offered sensuality with organic impressions immersed the entire body into the suit. When they returned from the fitting rooms to examine themselves in the mirror, the women were taken aback. The clothes made them look sheer and effervescent as if illuminating something from deep within them.

"It's like my soul is showing on the outside," Raynie said as she ran her hands down her sides.

"Yes and how sexy we look," Jenna added laughing at herself. "You have a sale. No need to pack these, we will wear them now."

"Okay ladies. And see the label here. Vandervals force enabled. You know what it is don't you."

"Sure do," Jenna said. "It means we can literally move up walls with these things."

"Yes. There are pads built into the suit mostly for a bit of adult fun you know."

"Vanderva...?" Raynie began to ask.

"Yes. Vandervals. It is a force of millions of tiny hair-lets enabling grip onto to any surface. They developed it from studies into how some wild life can walk up walls where it looks as if there is nothing to grip onto. The mass of hairs does all the work providing a large area contacting the surface. When we walk, beneath our feet is mostly air. Well, these are much different, but the hair-lets are synthetic though."

"You are right," the attendant added. "And you voice command it to work. The discreet gripping pads are here on the forearms and on the knees."

"Are the men's suits the same?"

"Yes they are."

They left the clothing store and continued on for another hour browsing the shops before deciding it was time to leave. As they descended the elevator back to street level, they were again bombarded with adverts on the microchip scheme by the three-dimensional holographic projections.

"Gee, they are really going hard on the sell," Raynie commented.

"It's not going to convince me though. But...I wonder how we are going to avoid having one?"

"I think John might be thinking the same Jenna."

"Let's go through China Town and visit Fongs. I'm hungry and I want to check out the demon statue again."

Jenna took Raynie to the venue and showed her the table where she and Lyle had met Chan Lee. Whilst they ate, conversation was about the statue behind them.

"See the writing underneath? It means Moon Demon or something. There, see those inscriptions, they are a bit like some of the stuff Chan gave to Lyle."

Raynie leaned in and saw what Jenna was referring to - small inscriptions ran along the left side of the statue in a vertical array.

"I have seen this one on the stone Jake and I found," she said putting her finger on one of the symbols. Immediately she thought it had glowed a little and felt warmer to the touch. "What was it?" she said drawing her hand away. "It felt like a tingle."

"Yes I saw it too as if it went slightly blurry for half a second. We'll tell the others about it when we get home."

"Here you go ladies. Your meals as ordered. Please allow me to serve you again should you wish for anything else."

They were both surprised at their appetite as they spent the next hour eating and ordering again from the waiter.

"You can feel the pressure here Jenna. Jake and I were at an old farmhouse and this is so different."

"I get the pressure thing. I see it when I go to work at Berkley. So many people appear to be in a trance or something. Lucky my job is about new ideas and research all the time. It saves the boring factor creeping in."

"It is fortunate we can do what our passion is. Such things seem so lost these days with so much in life being provided...or a product. I wonder if some have lost sight of their organic self. You know...the one free from all the organizing and management of life living in the moment."

"We get a mix of both. Work can make me busy and for others with families, they have a lot to manage. I guess it has always been this way, it's just what we focus on and how mindful we are about where we spend our time and how we think about it."

"Or not think about it."

They arrived at Jenna's home and presented themselves to the others who were deep in discussion about the journey ahead and of the findings so far. On seeing the two women, the men were immediately drawn out of their conversation, giving them both praise and accolades for their appearances.

"We bought suits for you guys too," Raynie said as she removed them from the bag. "Nano, thermo, breathing, Geiga grip suits to keep you guys cool."

"We just had an experience...a little extraordinary, didn't we Raynie."

"Yes. Lyle, you will be interested I guess. One of the images on the statue..the one at Fong's. Jenna and I stopped for lunch there. Well, it had some sort of fuzzy resonance to it when I put my finger over the image. The inscription was similar to the one on the stone we found Jake."

"Maybe you had a few drinks at Fong's too?"

"Don't be silly. I'm serious."

"I saw it too Jake."

"Well, I wonder how many other people might have done the same. Did they get a fuzzy feeling?"

"How can I tell? It just seemed real. We had no drinks other than water."

"I have an idea," Lyle interjected. "In my work I have read of similar relics changing when touched by an individual who is free from mind and can therefore connect somehow. Their stories speak of the resonance as Raynie put it. It is said to bring on a sense of essence within the item...or image. Some are relics carved like the stone you found. But it is more like a tale, or a myth if you will. It has never been documented scientifically. Perhaps there is some residual energy somewhere...maybe the statue holds an electrical charge. Some people can be more sensitive to such things than most others."

"I think I will go to Fong's now and see it for myself,' Jake said. "I want to see if it has the same response for me."

"I'll come too. I have seen this statue before and...here, let me touch the inscription on your stone just in case."

Lyle reached across and took the stone from Jake and then ran his fingers over the lines of each of the inscriptions. "Okay. Let's go. We'll take three dimensional images using a holographic phone so we have some more to work with."

Jake and Lyle left the house and proceeded to Fong's and were able to get access to the statue immediately as there were only a few patrons about. They located the small inscription Raynie had touched and they both tried their own hand in turn. Upon contact with the statue, they both experienced the same sensation as Raynie whilst noticing the faint glow coming from the within the inscription.

"Interesting," Jake said. "I'll take some images now and then we might as well go back to Jenna's place." He took over a dozen three dimensional photos of the statue as Lyle removed it from its alcove so he could also photograph its' rear side.

A short while later, they arrived back at Jenna's to find she had prepared some fresh coffee and food. Lyle noticed how luscious she looked in the suit, as did Jake upon seeing Raynie sitting back at an angle in a lounge chair with one arm draped along the chair's headrest.

"Anything interesting happen?" Raynie asked.

"Yes," replied Jake. "Same as you described for both of us. We took some photos as well."

He placed his holographic phone on the table bringing the three-dimensional images into life.

"Magnify one hundred times," he said. Instantly the image became one hundred times larger, immersing all who were gathered about to examine his find. Jake placed his hand onto the part of the image showing the inscription. "Magnify one hundred times. Again the image changed now focusing only on the selected area, with the remainder disappearing into a haze and then into thin air at the image edges.

"What is this?" he exclaimed.

They were now able to see the inscription in much more detail than could be seen in the dim lighting at Fong's. It revealed a network of patterns resembling DNA. Each strand was connected to another with exquisite detail as if yet more could be hidden within.

"Magnify two hundred times."

Again the image flickered then changed into precisely what Jake was imagining. Each of the DNA strands were interlaced with yet more strands slightly different in appearance. He captured an image at this resolution and then returned to the previous resolution where he also captured an image.

"I'm going to take a look at these over time. Raynie, do you have the book there?"

"Sure," she rose up from the chair and went to the room she had shared with Jake, bringing it back a moment later. "Here you go."

Jake opened the book to the section he and Raynie had been studying over the past few days.

"Here, Atomic Fields - Quantum Phasing. I am thinking these seemingly endless strands have something to do with such phasing. Where it appears to be DNA or similar, you can fix on a point and establish a pattern, but…with magnification, you see further strands at a much lower level, yet with equal detail. So where you think you have a fixed point to determine a pattern, you then find no such fixed point exists as the rest of this sequencing is still going through some form of osmosis or separation to become more condensed or intricate. Essentially, what appears to be happening is something like matter in a constant state of flux. Perhaps we need to look deeper and find if there is any energy at play in the spaces appearing, well…at this level, as rifts between each strand in flux."

"Did I hear someone mention flux?" John appeared, followed by Tobias.

They had been in Jenna's small lab working on some technology idea John had for getting around the mandatory microchip implants.

"We have just been working on the very thing. Flux I mean. Tobias has some experience from HAARP where they generate frequencies designed to flux and confuse anyone they don't like."

"Yeah, and I…um, we think we might have come up with something," Tobias added.

"Do tell us," Jenna pleaded. "I would hate to have one of those chips."

"Well. We have some time to work on it…about eighteen months so there is no great hurry, but I think we can come up with something. See this device I built?" John held out the stealth device he had taken from the Beaver. "Well, in effect, it is a stealth device or cloaking device. It mimics the transmitted patterns a radar receives in order to pin point a target. We used it to get away from

Alaska. So…what I am thinking, sorry, what we are thinking, is if we modify and somehow shrink its' component size down a little, then we can do the same for the scanners they will use to read those microchips. In effect, stick one of these behind your ear and for the authorities' sake, you appear as though you are fully integrated into their database. We can program it as we need so their file appears legitimate and up to date."

"What about their coding and encryption?" Jenna asked.

"We need to work on it, and likely is the hardest part. I imagine they will have random generators putting out coding for authentication security. You would be a little naïve to think they wouldn't be thinking of such things. We will need to hack into their systems without them knowing so this device can generate the same authentication signatures.

"It will take us some time," Tobias added. "Those systems will have the highest security specs of anything running civilian operations. But…I think with my experience with coding along with John's expertise, we should be able to come up with something reasonably quickly."

"Then we will need to subtly test it out over a period before we actually begin to use it. And, knowing their paranoid state of minds and how they will be changing code in an on-going sense, we are going to have to maintain this in parallel and keep one step ahead in development ourselves."

"Sounds like a lot of work," Jake added, looking up from the book where he had been only partly listening to the conversation.

"Exactly. And it is why I propose Tobias and I do not come to China with you. Instead, we stay here and continue work with this technology. If it is okay with you Jenna…please?"

"Um…yes, it's fine John. You are always welcome here. Will it be a security concern though?"

"We thought about it and both of us feel that if we can manage to lay low here and continue using these new identifications we have, then we should be okay."

"There was a risk they might be looking for you at any HyperJet terminal," Lyle added.

"Yes we thought of the risk. Tobias and I think it best we stay behind and work on this baby. Like we said, it could be months yet before we bring it on-line and even though there is still time until the mandatory cutoff date, it is best we get started straight away."

"Well…it is settled then, you present a good case. I'll change our flight booking now."

When it came for Raynie, Jake, Jenna, and Lyle to depart, John and Tobias asked them to stay out of trouble and remain in regular contact.

"Of course John. Tobias, please make sure John takes good care of my house."

"I will Jenna."

During the JetCab to the airport, the city once again sparkled in the late evening sky, but this time an additional haze was being ejected from an aircraft situated over the city center.

"Do you have any idea Jenna? Have you seen it before?" Lyle asked.

"I cannot say I have seen it but I might have an idea on what it could be. There was some work, though quite covert, on the development of a targeted nano spray where the technology was dispersed over cities and programmed to affects systems…anything they wanted to basically. The nano bits are attracted to resonant frequencies emitted by their technology like an antenna in reverse. There was no word though on it being operational as yet."

Chapter 9

Traveling at hypersonic speed and flying at seventy thousand feet near the edge of space, they could see the line of sunset stretching along the curvature of the Earth. As they breached the line of the suns' rays, light filled the passenger section of the jet in an aurora of ethereal beams. Jenna was gazing out the window next to her and the sunlight made her appearance so striking, Lyle filled with emotion as he was drawn towards her. Since their first meeting on the space station, he felt attracted to her in a way he had never experienced as if there was some deeper connection in a sense beyond what words could ever say. She was a beautiful woman, intelligent, willing to seek answers, intuitive, authentic in her presence, and not afraid to be forthwith. They were of similar age - both in their late thirties. His admiration of her strengths grew with each time he cast eyes upon her, and as she sat there with her head turned a little to the side bathed in the colored light, his passion to be with her grew even more.

With the events of recent days and now this trip to China full of anticipation and discovery, he felt enthusiasm and a general sense of well-being. His work had showed him many visions of wonder and beauty across the globe, in space, and soon it would take him to the Moon, yet he began to feel she was the most wonderful thing he had ever encountered. Seeing the sun shining off her Geiga suit was beauty in apparition. Similar to what Raynie had first said about the suit bringing her soul to the surface, he too was almost seeing the same in Jenna. She was caressed by light appearing in a dream like state.

He leaned over a little closer to her and she turned to face him. They looked at each other for a moment in silence and he was sure her feelings were being projected towards him. Within a short time, they had developed a relationship where they were both perfectly comfortable with each other and silence between them was not an issue. She smiled, as she knew where he was in his mind and heart, and she felt confidence with her intuition in sharing those feelings.

"It's beautiful," she said whispering to him and turning her eyes back out the window. "Seeing the gold ocean beneath us with the arc of space almost close enough to touch is enchanting. And see the clouds? It is like we are floating in the heavens."

"I see them. We are floating in the heavens."

They both continued their gaze out the window for a few more minutes in silence. The only sound was a faint swish coming from the four rocket engines on the wings of the aircraft. It seemed like all the passengers inside the HyperJet were taken with this view upon and over the world they knew, as a general hush was evident throughout the passenger cabin.

Jake and Raynie were sitting opposite to them, both also gazing out the window.

"Hey Lyle, come and see this," Jake said breaking the silence. Lyle left his seat and went to see what Jake was talking about. As he did, Raynie went to join Jenna.

Both men peered upward out the jet window to see the space station way above them lit up for all to see. It was an immense mass of modules joined together to form a structure one mile in length and half a mile wide. The lights located all over the station made it the brightest object in the sky, even visible on some days around sunrise and sunset. As they stared at it, they noticed some smaller lights moving about next to the station.

"Some traffic up there today," Lyle said.

The captain of the jet interrupted him, "Ladies and gentlemen. If you take a look out the left side windows, you will see the Conglomerate Internationale space station. We are currently about two hundred and seven miles below the station, but its lights can clearly be seen."

They continued to watch the station seeing it gradually fade from view as the jet moved more and more into stronger sunlight beyond the line of sunset.

Jenna and Raynie had joined them, leaning over to catch a view of the station, but had since returned to their seats. Now they sat talking quietly, careful not to be too loud so as to avoid the men catching a hint of their conversation. Jake and Lyle turned back to look at them after the station had faded from view, and when they noticed their attention, the two women gave them a smile.

"You can only guess what they are talking about," Jake said quietly.

"What did you say?" Raynie asked.

"Oh, he just said we can only guess what you two are discussing," Lyle added.

"Guess all you like," Jenna said looking directly at Lyle. "Women's talk."

The two men left the women to their conversation, turning their attention to matters before them during their trip to China. They went over the logistics of traveling on land to Dunhuang, and of the traits and customs they might find from locals along the way.

"Mostly locals are helpful and willing to communicate," Lyle said.

"My only trip to China previously took me to the old parts of Shanghai and I was unfortunate to come across a gang of thieves who were intent on stealing some of my tech hardware. There is a thriving market in the old city streets for parts."

"As always there are criminals like all places. So many people struggling to live, you can reckon on why they would be looking out for any targets to make some cash. Wait until you see the central city in Beijing. It is a city to behold with all the development there, particularly with such a high population. The network of sky towers is amazing and covers an area the size of Manhattan Island."

Not long after, the nation of Korea was receding into the distance below them as the HyperJet began its descent stage into Beijing. Still traveling at just over mach three, it was not long before they had crossed the Yellow Sea and the coastline of China appeared below.

"Ladies and Gentlemen. Our flight is on approach to Beijing. We will be going sub sonic in eleven minutes. Please remain in your seats," the captain announced.

As they crossed the low coast to the east of the great city, they could see the city itself rising in the haze ahead. Two sonic booms indicated they had slowed to sub sonic speed as the jet took a steep pitch descending to line up with the main runway at Beijing. Details of the city became clearer as they came into land, its' towers truly astounding in height and complexity.

There was a huge central sector located mostly above the ground with the sprawling elements of the old city all around. Many of the old buildings were gone having surrendered to both age and to the rapid expansion and development of the city since the early twenty first century. Now Beijing was mostly a mixture of traditional Chinese styles decorating the enormous buildings and ultra modern architecture.

After passing through customs, the four passengers went to the lounge area to wait for their connecting flight to Lanzhou, due to depart in ninety minutes. "Perhaps we could take a quick JetCab flight around the city," Raynie suggested. "It looked so magical when we were flying in. I suppose if we just take a half hour flight or so, then we will have sufficient time to get back and make our connecting flight."

"Great idea," Lyle responded. "It would be good to see this place in the flesh as opposed to just a holographic view." They checked their luggage in for the connecting flight and ten minutes later were boarding a JetCab.

Massive towers loomed around them as they flew at five hundred feet above the streets. Even in the broad daylight, there was a glittering effect to the city caressing the eye and inspiring thoughts of wonder and mystery. Traditional Chinese lanterns, some over forty feet in diameter, were hanging from the translucent pedestrian walkways linking each building at the fifty-story level. Large projectors cast three-dimensional images of culture, news, and advertising into the air, immersing the buildings and the people as if they were transported to a total holographic world. Ancient music mixed with electronic beats and rhythms filled the atmosphere in compliment of the projected scenes. Colours filled in other spaces as the immense glass structures caught sunlight and passed it on as if they were all prisms designed to project the entire spectrum. It seemed as if the city was energized with life from the street below up to the tops of the buildings above.

The largest of the buildings towered to one hundred and eighty stories and were gathered in the most central part of the city giving it a crystalline appearance. Far below, millions walked the streets, among them musicians, hawkers, shop keepers, restaurateurs, and pedestrians.

Jenna exclaimed pointing to a sight just above the cab where a floating restaurant could be seen. "Look. I have never seen anything like it!"

The moving building was traveling slowly along the same route as they were, but some two hundred feet higher. It was a floating palace decorated in the most traditional Chinese way and reminiscent of the ancient life in the city centuries before. Diners were treated to the spectacle of this city as they slowly made their way through what appeared as an enormous crystal filled with effervescent colour and sound. Evening would soon come to this great city of the east bringing it to life in ways begging to be witnessed. In the lengthening sun, it was a mere hint of its' nighttime beauty, yet still astounding to any new visitor and also to many who lived here.

As their JetCab rounded the farthest corner of the city center, they were met with the sight of the whole city block appearing like a giant crystal peaking at the center. It was nearly indescribable and a most rewarding sight to any who were able to see it from the air. "Much better than the holographic image," Lyle said. 'Much much better."

The JetCab then took a swift arcing left turn and headed straight back towards the airport. When they arrived in the internal departures area, the first call for boarding their flight to Lanzhou was being made.

"Let's get on board then," Jake said as they stood in a group for a moment deciding what to do. "These flights are not pre-booked seats, and I want a good one next to the window."

"I'm with you," Raynie said as she looped her arm in his.

Jenna decided this was the best way to go and followed Raynie's lead herself, taking up Lyle's arm as they followed immediately behind.

Thirty minutes later, they took one last look at Beijing as they flew to three thousand feet at six hundred miles per hour, before the HyperJet quickly accelerated from sub sonic speed to over mach three in three minutes.

China's Great Wall stretched into the distance snaking its way over mountains and along ridge tops as they flew at fifty thousand feet during the short flight to Lanzhou. Its' wonder was equal from the air as it was at ground level with most of the wall now restored to its original glory as a centerpiece of the nations' attraction for visitors. The flight path took a parallel line to its traverse over the mountains for half an hour before the wall swung away to their right as they began approach to their destination.

After touchdown, the four took to the main center of the city where they decided to discuss the next leg of their trip from Lanzhou to Dunhuang, over some authentic Chinese cuisine. Glimpses of the perilous mountains circling the city could be seen framed by the city's avenues as they walked amongst the central towers. Suddenly through these glass canyons, they caught sight of one unique mountain featuring a large white pagoda building at the summit.

"Baita, White Pagoda Mountain," Lyle said as they all stood for a moment. "I checked it out on the holographic phone as we came in on descent."

"Perhaps we should take a look," Jake said.

"Yes, let's go and see," Raynie added, always intrigued by the mystery of mountain top monuments and monasteries of the east.

"First let's eat though. This place looks okay," Jenna said pointing to a restaurant diagonally opposite across the street.

"Waiter," Lyle asked. "How is the best way to travel to Dunhuang? We are touring and wonder if the road is good for driving?" He knew the way after having researched the route, but he thought any insight from a local person could be valuable.

"Ah, City of Sands. You can fly there. Much easier. Road is good to main highway turnoff, but can be dangerous after. Bandits sometimes attack road you see. No rocket jets to Dunhuang though. You travel by jet plane, but it gets you there safe. You best fly."

"I think we will drive as we will really need our own transport," Lyle said after the waiter left.

"But he said it would be dangerous," Jenna said looking a little worried. Raynie too felt the same.

"We can handle it if we are prepared and travel wisely. What do you say Jake?"

"I think driving is best. The road is good he said. We still have some time up our sleeve. A few more hours should not make any difference. Plus, it will give us a chance to look around and we will have our own transport when we arrive there as you said. Also, consider how we project our thoughts and expectations into this journey. It has been working for us so far when you think about the information we have found and our time together, plus with John and Tobias back at your house Jenna. And think of Chan."

"Something is happening…" Jenna trailed off then looked to Raynie.

"We can drive. But Jenna and I are going to keep our eyes open."

"Well, let's finish up here and go and get a vehicle. Our first trip is up the pagoda mountain," Jake said.

Half an hour later, they had finished their meal and hired a utility type vehicle featuring room for four people and extra compartments at the rear.

Raynie brought up city sights on her own holographic phone. "Five Springs. We can go there after we get back from the mountain. It is supposed to be a beautiful place."

"Okay," Jake relied. "Then we set out for Dunhuang."

As they wound up the steep mountainside towards the summit, the white pagoda stood in clear view, gleaming in the late light of the afternoon. When they arrived, the intricate carvings of the pagoda caught the light in a way where the dragons featured at each tier of the tower appeared to have glaring eyes.

"A bit eerie," Jenna said as they stopped the base of the building towering over one hundred feet above.

Just inside the building at the bottom of the stairs leading to its' top levels, an old Chinese man was sitting in contemplation. He was aroused from his meditative state by their entrance, his eyes following them as they began their ascent. This late in the day there were no other visitors at the site, so they had the entire pagoda to themselves aside from the solitary old man, and this gave them a sense of place not possible when it was full of tourists. The view from the top was astounding showing them the entire city of Lanzhou circled by mountains with some early evening lights adding a twinkle effect to the scene. More dragon figures adorned the top of the pagoda with their presence exaggerated by the low light.

They each looked upon the figure heads of dragons contemplating their seemingly coincidental run of encounters with such forms. The four of them stood there for a while taking in the view and after breaking the silence of contemplation over the dragons, began talking softly about the prominence of this tower over the city below. They could also smell a sweet scent to the air as thermal breezes carried the many blossoms amongst the city streets up to meet their position on the mountain.

After a while of soft talk and simply smelling the air, they descended back down, their footsteps echoing on the old stone stairs. Upon reaching the bottom, they found the old man still there standing silhouette in the doorway. "You must see Five Springs," he said. "You like the dragons of Baita? I know you like, otherwise you would not be here at this time. Go to the springs, you will find more you like." With this, he left them taking an old walking path down the mountain away from the road.

"Strange," Jake said as they stood there watching him disappear into some bushes as the track took a turn.

"Well, I said we should see the Five Springs, but it is getting late. Maybe they are open to night time visitors," Raynie said.

"Let's get there then," said Lyle as he turned and started for their vehicle.

Sunset gave Lanzhou a mystical glow as they descended down the mountain, with the Yellow River a golden ribbon meandering through the valley floor and taking on the reflection of the evening city lights. Jake engaged the heads up map display in the vehicle to show the route for them to take to the Five Springs.

"We head north west of Gaolin Mountain to get to the springs."

Ten minutes later they arrived to a wondrous spectacle of gardens illuminated by thousands of tiny lights creating a scene instantly intriguing. It was a popular place as they encountered dozens of others who had chosen to experience the site at this particular time. Walking through the crowds was in contrast to the serenity recently experienced at the pagoda, but the sheer delight in the spectacle was enchanting in itself. Children could be heard softly laughing, and couples were in embrace swept up in the romance of the evening light.

"Juyue Spring," Lyle said as they stood gazing at the near full moon in its silky waters. "Ju is to hold in your hands and yue is moon."

Suddenly they became aware of company at the spring and turned to see the old man they had encountered at the pagoda. "How did you get here...?" Jake began to ask.

"The mind travels and so the body follows," was his reply. "This spring is to hold the moon. Watch and you shall see deep into the light of reflection and beyond. Again, the mind travels and so the body follows."

They all turned back to the reflection to see it was now quite still in the water. Instead of its silvery appearance as it was just a moment before, the moon seemed to have more of a golden glow and Jenna was sure she could see movement within the image despite the calmness of the waters' surface.

"The mind travels," she said softly.

For a few moments they all stood transfixed in their gaze captivated by the change in appearance of the reflection. When they had finished gazing at the water, they found themselves alone again at the spring - the old man had slipped silently away.

"This is becoming a bit familiar. The moon demon statue, the advice from Chan to seek a dragon head tattoo, this old man turning up, the dragons on the pagoda, and now this strange moon reflection." Lyle voiced what the others were thinking as they pondered the strange connection of events.

Chapter 10

They stopped to obtain some supplies on their way out of the city before the trip along National Highway three one two leading to the town of Wuwei. Lyle bought four laser pulse pistols from a licensed weapons dealer just in case they ran into any trouble or encountered bandits as they had been told before.

After driving two hours they arrived at the Qilian Shan Mountains where they met with the Great Wall at ground level for the first time. Under the clear night sky, the wall was alight with modern versions of ancient lanterns following its course into the distant mountainsides. To compliment this sight, the moon provided enough glow to light up the distant snow-covered peaks of the mountains bordering the desert, making for a spectacular dream like scene.

For the next few hours, they continued their drive under the clear night sky, flanked by the mountains to the left and the wall to their right. Very few other vehicles were using the highway and it felt to them as if they were venturing towards a frontier. When finally they left the wall as it headed away to the mountains and eventually to its end in the north, they felt a sense of loss as it had been their companion in the nearly deserted landscape.

"The highway is not kept very well in this area," Lyle said reading from the holographic map projected from the dashboard. "It is so people are not encouraged to live in the remote places deemed too inefficient to maintain. Dunhuang is still a vibrant city, but the population is on the decline, so in the future only those who need to be there will be there."

Immediately the road deteriorated showing signs of a route far less traveled and reminiscent of the highways of old. Their vehicle now on manual control, continued to provide a smooth ride, but Jake as driver had to remain alert. The scenery around them was quickly turning to desert with great silvery dunes beginning to appear on either side of the road under the moonlit sky.

When vehicle headlights appeared to be coming at them from a distance to their left, the felt some concern as Lyle told them the map showed no roads branching off the one they were traveling. For a short time the lights disappeared behind a sand dune, only to re-appear again this time much closer.

"I think they are driving over the dunes. We should be careful," Jenna said as Jake drove on.

Again the lights disappeared behind a dune and this time they did not re-appear for a minute or two. Then as they rounded a bend, threading their way between two towering dunes, the vehicle could be seen directly ahead and stationary in the middle of the road. It was evidently not a ground-based vehicle as it was hovering about ten feet off the ground. Jake brought them to a stop about one hundred feet from the craft in front of them.

"What the hell is it?" he said as they peered out the front window. "I don't like the look of this."

"I have a hint on what it might be," Jenna answered. "You know I work in propulsion systems. Well, it looks like a working version of a craft I thought was still experimental."

A moment later, three armed officers exited the craft via a ramp protruding from its' side.

"Now I really don't like this," Lyle said as he gave them each one of the laser pulse pistols he had bought. "Don't show these. We need to keep the peace here. I'll be our talker. I've been negotiating with various types of locals in many situations for some years now."

He began to get out of the vehicle when an announcer voice sounded first in Chinese and then in English, "Do not get out of your vehicle. Remain where you are. This is the first and final notice. Any further movement will be met with force."

The three officers were now only fifty feet away with their weapons at the ready.

"The guy in Lanzhou said it would be dangerous, but these three don't look like bandits to me," Jake said just as Raynie took his left hand squeezing it a little.

The four of them then waited in silence as the officers covered the remaining ground to their vehicle. When they reached them, they could see all three of the officers were Chinese dressed in national military uniforms. Two of them stood just a slight distance away whilst the third came up to the driver side window.

"Show me your passports," he demanded. They all handed their passports to Jake who presented them to the officer. "What is the purpose of your trip?"

Lyle answered, "We are touring on our way to Dunhuang."

"Why?"

"We are two couples seeking the origins of the Silk Road."

"Why?"

"We are interested in historical places."

"I see. Why are you traveling now?"

"We left Lanzhou when it was evening and decided to keep traveling through the night."

"It is dangerous on this road at night. Did you not know this?"

One of the officers who was looking at a scanner readout, indicated something to the questioning officer.

"Our scanner tells me you have weapons."

"Ah…yes. We thought in case there was trouble."

"Wait." He left the window and went over to the officer who was reading the scanner. After checking their passports and reading some details, he returned to the vehicle window. "Your passports are valid. Again, why are you here?"

"Like I said, we are touring."

"Are you sure?"

"Yes."

"Where did you get this vehicle?"

"We hired it in Lanzhou."

"Yes, it checks out. You can go. But you must continue to Dunhuang. Do not stop, otherwise you will be arrested on suspicion."

"Suspicion?"

"Yes. This location is within the patrol radius of the national space launch facility. Any traffic warned not heeding the warning within three hundred miles, will be detained."

"I see officer. I was aware of the launch area, but I did not think we would be near enough…"

"Did not think. Taking the time to do so would be in your best interests. Now leave and do not stop."

He handed back the documents then indicated to the other officers to return to their craft. They all watched them go back in via the ramp and then silently move away from the road allowing them to pass. Jake hit the accelerator and they sped away.

"Perhaps there is a launch tonight," Jenna said breaking their silence. "With all the action going on, I can imagine everyone is at a high state of alert, and feeling a bit sensitive."

They drove on for about another hour, winding their way between the towering dunes when headlights appeared in front of them and heading their way.

"Another patrol?' Raynie said.

"Cannot be sure, we are over four hundred miles from the launch facility now, but you never know," Lyle replied as he checked their position on the holographic display.

As the oncoming vehicle approached, they felt sure it was ground based and therefore unlikely to be another patrol. Then it stopped at about a distance of five hundred feet.

Jake kept going thinking of the warning not to stop given by the officer as he slowed down a little.

"Just to be sure," Lyle said as he handed out three laser pistols. "Don't get trigger happy. I'll hold yours for you Jake while you drive. It's here if you need it."

The other vehicle had started moving again and was now two hundred feet ahead. Jake slowed to twenty miles per hour. When they were within eighty feet of the oncoming vehicle, it stopped and turned sideways to block the road.

With dunes reaching high on either side, Jake realized there was no means to avoid the other vehicle, so he brought them to a halt.

"We need to be real smooth here," Lyle said.

"It's what us two women are all about," Jenna said as an expression of reassurance.

"Don't anyone get out. I have been in a similar situation to this before," Jake said. "Best stay in the vehicle, it will give us cover."

Two men disembarked the other vehicle and started towards them, both brandishing laser pulse rifles. Jake was busy keeping one eye on them, and the other assessing any possible means of escape. The only way was to either back track from where they had come, or to give the vehicle full revs and traverse the sand dune on the right side of the vehicle parked ahead.

As the two assailants entered the headlights of their vehicle, they raised their rifles aiming directly through their front windscreen shouting 'come out Chan Lee!'

The second they did this, Jake switched the headlights to high beam, monetarily blinding the two men. Immediately after, he gunned the accelerator to full and swerved quickly to pass around the other vehicle. They hit the dune fast pitching almost sideways as Jake fought to keep control on the shifting sand. The two assailants began firing at them after coming out of their temporary daze, their laser pulses striking but bouncing off their vehicle harmlessly. As they passed around the other vehicle, the two men were running back to get in, still firing their rifles as they ran. When they were in, their driver then stepped hard on acceleration in pursuit.

"Don't fire," Jake said busily steering the vehicle at high speed. "They want Chan, so they'll want us."

He drove on fighting hard to keep control. High-speed warning lights and sounds began to scream at him as he drove as fast as possible barely avoiding the dunes and rocks beside the road. Then he failed to adjust in time and the vehicle struck a large rock with the impact knocking Jake unconscious. Automated systems on board then brought them to a halt, allowing their pursuers to close in on them rapidly.

Lyle took hold of Jake's arm and pulled him out of the driver seat, with the two women then shuffling him into the back seat. Lyle trod on the accelerator and they were off again amidst a volley of laser pulses.

"How's he going?" he asked noticing Jake was becoming conscious.

"He'll be alright," Raynie replied as she applied pressure the open cut on his forehead.

"Yeah, I'll have full brain ops back soon," Jake smiled as he stroked his temple. "You just keep driving, and fast."

Jenna scrambled through to the front seat as Lyle kept going hard at the wheel. Distance was now beginning to grow between them and their pursuers who had ceased firing at them. Soon enough, the other vehicle was lost to sight behind but in no way did Lyle let up on the intensity in his driving.

Another hour of fast driving saw them finally reach the sandy city, its' lights a welcome sight in the pre-dawn morning after their eventful journey and confrontation.

"We are at a good time. Let's find somewhere to stay and park this vehicle out of sight." Lyle said as took a sweeping left turn.

They found lodgings complete with indoor parking used to keep vehicles out of the regular sand storms affecting the city. Soon after, they were finally able to relax and take stock of their journey.

Chapter 11

Tobias and John had been working hard all day on a design to counteract the signals emitted by the personal microchips. John had spent the first half of the day sourcing one of the chips from numerous contacts he had throughout California. He was finally able to find one, so he had taken a JetCab over to Oakland and returned with some additional programming language information. The early evening light had caught his eye on his return trip as the cab traveled across the bay. Whilst observing the lights of the city, he had noticed several incoming authority HyperJets. As he watched them quickly land at the civilian airport, he was struck.

"Why are they landing there?" he said aloud to himself.

"What was it mate?"

"Oh I just wondered why the military was landing here in the city," he said to the cab pilot.

"Not sure mate, maybe to do with the latest news today. Don't tell me you don't know."

"Know what?"

"They announced we are on high level alert. Practically in a state of war, but don't ask me who with."

"What do you mean?"

"I mean we are almost at war. Those detonations and some other stuff have the big office all edgy. They are clamping down on everything. I reckon on those jets being part of proceedings."

"Proceedings?"

"Yeah. I'll bet there are some surprises in store for us yet."

He brought the JetCab in on approach to the central city terminal. John's last clear sky vision was of yet another group of authority jets on approach to the airport, before the cab became immersed amongst the towers and skyscrapers. The terminal forty floors above street level was very busy with people hurrying everywhere and numerous cabs landing and taking off.

Now back at Jenna's house he had decided to take a break as he had been working with Tobias on algorithms and programming the chip for the past four hours.

"I'll grab a beer hey. I trust you bought some this afternoon?"

"You bet. Tobias never forgets his beer."

"Where are we at time wise?" John asked returning with two beers.

"Eleven past eleven to be precise," Tobias replied. They sat for a moment in silence, each savoring the fresh cold ale.

"Plenty of action in the sky tonight. I forgot to tell you when I arrived back."

"Yeah?"

"Authorities. I think we are going to see something happen. Two sets of their planes landed at the airport instead of at their base."

"What? Surely they are not after us."

"I reckon there is some big end stuff going on somewhere. The cab pilot said were are almost at war."

"Who with?"

"Well there is the question. Nothing is clear. Those bombs, the action up at HAARP. Who knows?"

"Now, this programming thing. My contact in Oakland gave some advice on the floating point signaling they are using to authenticate these little bastards. The stuff we have worked on today mostly concerns the actual identification algorithms used to spot each device in the system. I think we need to begin on the authentication as no doubt, this is going to tie in real time with their systems. It isn't going to be easy to crack because they are going to appoint the best, actually, they probably already have, to develop a feasible regenerating algorithm for people as they transit, purchase, or check in to anywhere in the system."

"While you were gone I figured there would be some nanotechnology involved aside from the obvious chip components. With those medical systems being wide spread, they are likely to be using some type of link to establish a number of gateways for authentication…and security I suppose."

"Yep, sounds right to me. We are going to have to stay one step ahead of them, which is why I have asked the guy in Oakland to keep us in the loop. He has a contact with access to the central ops where they develop the chips. They are certainly going to be working overtime trying to make this entire system foolproof so it cannot be compromised. What is on our side to an extent is the fact these systems are relatively new. The previous attempt some years back failed due to the incompatibility of many systems to integrate the sets of algorithms required to generate the nano signals. As we now know from my trip to Oakland today, those signals are extremely complex in nature as they re-build themselves in real time. Some can be almost in a constant state of flux, but there has to be a key there."

"Something to keep a core linkage or authentication?"

"Precisely. Whilst they can float about all the time or whenever they so choose, one point remains in the capacity to link in to central processing and feed data through…well authenticate data. I suggest we have another beer though before we start."

Tobias laughed in agreement at John's suggestion. "I'll fetch them this time."

"You know?" John said half an hour later feeling a bit tired of the work. "I think we need to go out for a bit of fun. I have been up in Alaska for a while, and so have you and we had the bloody hectic time being chased all the way past

Seattle. What do you say to a bit of an excursion to China Town or to the wharves? It is never too late to go out in this town."

"Alright then. I think you make a good point there. Maybe it will help us relax and perhaps think of some new ideas on our issues here."

"Let's go then."

They left Jenna's house and walked generally in a direction where they could still choose either the wharves or China Town. As they strode along the pavement, they noticed there was a general hum in the air coming from people conversing around them, and from holographic projections encountered along the way. A hyped sense could indeed be felt as if the city was on alert, or an event was about to occur.

"I wonder how the others are faring."

"Yeah, me too," John replied looking skyward. "Chan Lee was sure of impending danger, but not too clear on what it was. I think the girls can look after themselves though, same with Jake and Lyle."

"Just the dangerous ones whoever they may be are the ones to keep a look out for."

"I do think we are onto something though. It seems a little too co-incidental this contact was suddenly made and we were all brought together on all this. Otherwise we would have been living out our individual lives watching this other stuff develop. Now we are all cast together and working on things we could have barely considered just a few days back."

"Well, all good I say. I am glad you helped me out of the situation at HAARP considering where I could have ended up through no fault of my own. I am beginning to understand why you left few years back."

"You could say I saw something coming. There was just too much secrecy and similar crap for it to be anything other than trouble. One step out of line or too much knowledge, and suddenly you disappear."

"Yeah. I am a pretty quiet person, happy to go about my business, then before I know it, I am branded a fugitive."

"Well, we are both in the same club now. The chase was a stuff up. I thought they would get me with those bloody tracker dogs."

"Well. Which way do we turn?" Tobias said as they stopped on a street corner waiting for an historic cable car to amble past. "Left to the wharves, or right to China Town?"

"Let's go the wharves. I want to get some fresh air tonight."

"Right. Wharves it is." They continued on downhill, past Coit Tower clearly visible to their right with three dimensional laser projection beams streaking skyward from the top.

John cast a glance westwards towards the Golden Gate Bridge and was astounded to see a large flotilla of craft under the bridge. "Hey, check it out."

"Gee, looks serious. What is going on?"

"I figured there was going to be something serious after seeing those jets earlier. Now seeing this, I am convinced."

They continued downhill towards the wharf precinct noticing large numbers of people seemed to be doing the same. As they arrived, there was a crowd much larger than the usual late night partygoers. Most were in groups talking amongst themselves whilst looking seaward to the gathering under the bridge. The two men decided on a small bar less crowded than the rest. They bought a beer each then found a table outside where they too discussed the spectacle before them. It was clear to anyone some type of event was unfolding due to the sheer numbers of water craft gathered in the one place.

"I'm not much one for the news," John said reaching into his pocket. "But maybe I'll check out online services and see if there is any information on this."

"Didn't the cab pilot mention something?"

"Yeah he did. But I expect any news on this stuff will be brief. The authorities are not known for their transparency on these types of affairs."

"Similar to the big corporation thing. Sure we get advice on how markets and nations are being shaped and controlled through so called innovations in economics. But, there is seldom anything tangible seen as a true proviso of what the actual intent is."

"I have to agree there. They tell us corporations are being kept in check and governmental control is for the best interests of the people, and most buy the line. But you cannot tell me mandatory microchip insertion for every citizen is a 'best interest' thing."

"It might do a lot of them some good though."

"Ha. You are right there." John switched his holographic phone to online news and the three-dimensional holographic newsreader appeared on the table.

"…so authorities advise. Latest information suggests all citizens should be prepared for nationally significant events to arise over the coming days and to expect some restrictions to come into place. The recent detonations and some information the government will not specify has rendered all international travel subject to authority, with exceptions only for personnel assigned to special duties or pre-designated missions. These missions include scientific persons, police, military associates, executive corporate, essential infrastructure, and services. All other persons are advised international travel other than for these purposes, requires application for approval through city central authority offices."

"Nationally significant events?" John shut the phone service down. "Sounds typical and evasive."

"Hey let's leave it then for a while. We are here to socialize and take some time to forget this stuff."

"Yeah, you're right. I have been too wrapped up in it for the past few days."

Whilst they sat enjoying their beers, two women took a table nearby John and Tobias. One of them caught Tobias' eye as she sat down giving him a faint smile. They both looked to be in their early thirties. Tobias took the initiative telling John they should go and join them, so they both approached the other table.

"Good evening," Tobias said politely. "My buddy and I have been hard at work over the past few days and would certainly enjoy some delightful company for a conversation."

"Um…well, why not," one of the women replied. "You're not dangerous are you?"

"Dangerous? Well only when we need to be I suppose."

Tobias and John took up a chair each joining the women.

"Hi. I'm Tobias and this is a mate of mine John."

"Hello Tobias. I am Asper and this is my best friend Lorraine."

"Hello Asper and Lorraine," Tobias said shaking each of their offered hands.

"Hi Asper. Hi Lorraine," John repeated the same.

The four of them sat talking for a while until Tobias went off to get the next round of drinks.

"So what have you two been working on?" Asper asked John.

"Oh a few things. Some electronics work mostly about developing new technology."

"What is it for?"

"Systems integration mostly. But hey, it is probably too high end for us to be talking about now."

"Um…not so," Lorraine said. "Both Asper and I work on data management which sort of ties in with systems integration."

"I see. Then perhaps you can get your head around what we do."

"Sure. So what do you think of this stuff going on? In the news I mean, and those craft out near the bridge?"

"A bit weird isn't it," John replied. "Typical though, we don't get any real details for a decent view into what is happening. I suspect they want to hold their hand pretty close to their chest and save any real information ending up in the wrong hands."

"You would think so. Where we work, there are strict secure lines for all to follow," Asper chimed in. "Sometimes it is like we feel as if they see us as a threat."

Tobias returned with the next round of drinks, handed them out and then sat down. "So what you all talking about?"

"Mostly work stuff Tobias," Lorraine said.

"Ah. John and I came out tonight to get away from work. What do you do?"

"Data systems management." At this, Tobias cast a quick sideways glance to John who immediately recognized his intent.

"Where do you live?"

"We share a place not too far from Haight Street. Do you know the area?"

"Yes, and its' history," Tobias said with a wry smile. "It's where the hippy movement started around one hundred and twenty years ago. I wonder if there are any of those old hippies left." They all laughed and the conversation then took a more casual turn.

Over the next hour they discussed various topics, each in turn, taking on a slant as the four of them consumed more alcohol. By the time they reached an impasse, the time had gone past two in the morning.

"Well...what, um what do we do now?" John said with a bit of a slur.

"Let's go somewhere else, I like a variety," Asper answered.

They left the bar and wandered for a few seconds trying to make a decision.

"Let's grab the car up Hyde Street then," Lorraine said taking John by the arm. The others followed and they staggered a little for the next quarter mile until they had reached the bottom of the infamous hill. A minute later, the historic car took them as they all hung off the standing platform to the rear.

"You guys sure are nice," Asper said as they disembarked the car at the top of the hill. "Why don't we just go back to our place for a while? We have more drinks there."

"Come with us. Asper and I would love you to come."

"Okay."

"Cool with me," Tobias added.

****

Captain Steve McCray was now in command of the US military facility HAARP in Alaska. Events over the past few days had seen this normally quiet station transform into a hub. He could feel the pressure rising given the situation and so ordered his personnel about expecting strict compliance and immediate action. Five HyperJets were at the ready for scramble at any time, each capable of mach eight.

McCray was a man of action demanding the best of all resources at his disposal as part of his dedication in fulfilling the expectations of his senior officers. As he stared out the station window at the jets standing at the ready, he went through all the procedures he had been trained to execute in circumstances like these. Such a heightened alert level without any clear evidence of who the enemy was frustrated him. Being one for detail, this ambiguity left him a little nervous, and so he had been taking this out on his personnel, giving stern and short commands. He turned around after hearing footsteps behind him, to see a communications officer waiting to report. "What is it officer?"

"Sir. We have advice from central command we are to receive a special weapons cache at zero six hundred hours today."

"I had a feeling we might. What are the details of this cache?"

"I cannot advise sir. Command has placed top-level restrictions on this information due to the sensitive nature of proceedings. We are advised to take delivery and hold awaiting further orders sir."

"Great…" he trailed off in thought. 'Just what I bloody need, more uncertainty.' "Are any special ops assigned to accompany this material?"

"Yes sir. There will be a team of seven arriving with the cache. Four weapons operators, two science officers, and one unit command officer sir."

"Why us. Why not Palmer?"

"Command advises two such caches and accompanying teams are being sent to the Palmer base sir. We are advised of this in order to coordinate any offensive action required sir."

"Alright officer, return to station. We have three and a half hours."

McCray hit the communications device on his tunic. "Attention all officers on duty for zero six hundred. We are to receive further hardware at this time. I expect all designated personnel to be on full standby to receive further instructions at zero five hundred hours."

****

Asper, Lorraine, John, and Tobias all laughed together, each of them becoming increasingly swept away with the effects of alcohol. Lorraine gave John a hug after taking her shot at a game of pool. He responded tightly, feeling her warmth and feminine shape pressed against him. She looked into his eyes and suddenly kissed him, prolonging their embrace a little further.

"Hey you two," Asper laughed as she took her shot in the game of doubles.

"Hey you yourself," Lorraine replied.

A couple of hours went by as they played pool, drank some more, and spent time in conversation before John decided it was time to take leave. "I think Tobias and I should get going. The sun is coming up."

"Leave now?" Asper grabbed Tobias. "I won't let him go."

"Yeah stay some more," Lorraine added giving John another hug.

Tobias looked at John, his face saying he would like to stay. John took this message and figured they could leave it sometime before they needed to go. "Open another bottle then."

Asper giggled as Lorraine went to the bar for a new bottle of wine. "How's this, you like red?"

"I do," Tobias said. "Open it up. I'm sure John will indulge some more."

They were nearly finished with the bottle when their impulses took over. Lorraine and John retired to her room, leaving Asper and Tobias alone in the lounge. Swept away with alcohol-induced urges, they embraced each other passionately. When the kiss ended, Asper grabbed another bottle and took it with her as she led Tobias to her room.

Chapter 12

Raynie was fascinated with the market place in the city of Dunhuang as she hurried about looking for items to spark her interest. They had spent the afternoon going through the city center doing the things typical tourists would do in such a place. Careful to appear as ordinary as possible, they had also changed prior to leaving their motel in order to fit in and not attract attention by wearing the Geiga suits.

As the colors of sunset began in the western sky, Jake decided it was time to eat and talk. All the wanderings had made him hungry and upon this suggestion, he was greeted with unanimous agreement as the others suddenly realized their own hunger. Casting a glance along the city's main street, he saw a restaurant on the next block and so indicated they should all follow him there.

The atmosphere inside was cool and dark with ornaments adorning nearly every available space. Lanterns cast a low light sufficient only to illuminate each table and booth, adding a sense of history to the scene. Jake led them to a booth table and as they sat, a waiter greeted them. They placed their order and were then left to themselves.

"This is quite a place. Nice choice Jake," Raynie said breaking the momentary silence.

"Something caught my eye as soon as I saw it. Did you notice the doorway as we came in? The figurines on the posts on each side reminded me a little of the dragons we saw at the pagoda yesterday."

"Yeah, I saw those," Lyle responded. "Perhaps though, such figures are common place."

"The land of dragons."

"Show us what you bought," Jenna said to Raynie.

"I just bought a few things as I didn't want to be weighed down with a horde of goodies. I bought some small trinkets and charms, and a few other ornamental items. Here take a look."

Raynie reached into her bag and emptied the contents on the table for them all to see. Amongst the items, was a small bracelet featuring a string of Chinese lettering appearing as if it could be a message or perhaps a proverb, so common in this culture.

"See this," she said holding it up. "I bought it from an old man at a stall half hidden away in the corner of the market place. He said it was for the acceptance of wisdom or something. Not so much a charm, rather an item of destiny. As soon as he said so I just had to have it."

"An item of destiny. I have come across a number of such things in my work," Lyle added. "It does look genuine, not like some tourist souvenir." He held it up to his face and by chance it framed his left eye.

"Look, his destiny is foretold through his eye apparent," Jenna laughed.

"Perhaps it is," Raynie added. "The forces of destiny are to behold. Tell us oh wise one, what do you see?"

"I see four people wandering the desert sands. Two couples make four and together they shall be as ordained in the comic cycle of deliverance." With this he turned to his right and gave Jenna a quick kiss. They all laughed, with Raynie and Jake's eyes meeting for more than a quick glance.

"Ah, destiny may indeed be foretold through the eye of the bracelet. I saw you two," Jenna said winking at Raynie.

The waiter then returned to the table with their order and they immediately began to eat in earnest. He noticed the bracelet as Lyle put it on the table next to Raynie.

"Ah. Order of the Dragon. Seek knowledge I see. You will meet great teacher soon."

"Can you read the letters?" Raynie asked.

"Yes. Dragon of great wisdom will bequeath upon you tasks and discovery in your life. See here, this is dragon of great wisdom and these tell of what you will encounter for higher knowledge."

"Thanks. I think I will wear it now." Raynie interrupted her meal to put on the bracelet – a perfect fit.

"See. It fits you as if it is meant to be." The waiter then left them to their meal.

When they had finished eating, they all felt relaxed and content just to sit a while, have a few drinks, and talk about the journey behind them and ahead of them.

"I suppose we just need to search the city in the right places to find the man with the dragon head tattoo Chan told us about," Lyle was considering their options. "But he did say old town and then the caves."

They sat for a while longer as the sun gradually slipped below the horizon and the city took on an enchanted feeling. By the time they left it was after seven in the evening and so they decided to wander the old town and look for anything interesting. The market place had come into its' night time life where shoppers had mostly given way to people out in the old town to experience the festive traits of this ancient Chinese city. Tourists and locals occupied the streets, each looking for the moment to make the night memorable amongst food vendors, musicians, and dancers.

As they walked amongst the crowd, a group of three men were searching for a particular person. These men had intent to find their target and quietly take him out of the scene as their captive. As they pushed past the group of four among the crowd on the street, something told them they had all met before but such was their uncertainty, after a moment they decided the four of them were mere travelers amongst the many on the city streets.

After the earlier encounter they had discussed the men briefly, with all agreeing they must be the men they had encountered in the desert. Moving on, the four of them continued to scout the market place area looking for any sign of the person they sought. An hour had passed as they made their way around searching the many faces illuminated by the dazzle of the night-lights, and those half hidden in the mysterious shadows cast at conflicting angles.

"Well. Our search seems to be going nowhere. Perhaps we should split into two groups and meet back here again later," Lyle suggested.

"Good idea. I'll take Raynie and check the street over there," Jenna agreed, pointing to her right. "It looks like there are a few old establishments. Perhaps they could be hiding some secrets."

"Okay. We'll meet here again in two hours. It will be ten thirty by then."

"See you then," Jenna said as she took Raynie's arm leading her into the street she had indicated.

Jake and Lyle took a street in the opposite direction, it too leading to an even older part of the city.

"I know we need patience, as this search could last for days, even weeks. But I feel urgency here like Chan was on about. I hope we find something tonight. There has been a hint of synchronicity about our travels so far and I hope it continues and keeps up the momentum," Jake said as he and Lyle headed into a more dimly lit street than those closest to the market place.

"I know what you mean, or should I say what you feel. I am thinking along the same lines about the momentum we have. It seems weird yet I get a feeling what Chan is pointing us to is about the synchronicity of events. When you think about most events in life, or ventures you take, there are those events leading to it…sometimes you don't realize as you go along. It seems to be happening for you."

"Can it be everything seems a little too right, too connected? Perhaps there are forces or persons playing this out, away from our conscious recognition?"

"It too is on my mind, but then it gets counteracted with a gut feeling to go along with it and see where it takes us. The encounter in the desert sure made it look like something is on our side."

They continued on in silence checking one street after another for any signs of life or a feeling to look further. It was when they had entered a darker, even more dimly lit area, when something caught their attention. As they entered the narrow lane they noticed a cafe - the only business open for trading among all the lanes and streets they had seen.

"We'll check in there," Lyle said. "Ask some questions."

Just then a light rain began to fall – something they thought a little unusual considering they were in a city bordering on the fringes of a vast sandy desert. As they approached the eatery, the sole yellow street lamp outside glistened off the musty wet cobblestones deepening the sense of history they felt. Upon reaching the front door they found the place empty except for a man who appeared to be cooking in the kitchen behind the counter. When they entered, he did not break from his chores and they wondered if he had even noticed there were two people inside.

A soft light only partially filled the cafe. All other light was a mix of the street lamp shining in, and reflections of the many ornaments and decorations along the walls and hanging from the ceiling. They took a seat at the counter bar quietly, for some reason not wanting to disturb the man at work in the kitchen. As they sat there for a moment in silence, they looked around at the various ornaments and decorations pondering the meaning of each.

"See it?" Jake said pointing to a small-framed pictogram located behind the bar. Lyle turned to see what Jake meant, immediately seeing the pictogram. As if by some coincidence, the man then stopped what he was doing and came to the bar.

"Torus of Eternity," he said answering their unasked questions. "It shows life and its' creative force."

"I see. Um…what exactly does it mean?" Lyle asked.

"It is for the forces at play beyond our understanding, yet retained deep in our memories."

"The part looks like DNA sequencing."

"You are correct. It is DNA we need to unlock. An understanding, hard to put in your western terms. Now how can I help you gentlemen?"

"How about a couple of coffees just for now. We have already eaten tonight."

"Okay. Two coffees coming up."

He turned to make the coffees leaving them to continue contemplating the pictogram.

"You know what. Those sequences remind me of the ones we saw on the figurine of the moon demon in San Francisco."

"I thought similar just as you spoke," Jake replied. "Maybe we are onto something."

"Yeah maybe, but remember, we only just arrived Dunhuang and we did speculate on this being a little too easy."

The man then returned with their coffees, "Enjoy gentlemen, but please excuse me if I go back to preparing in my kitchen. My most regular customer is due to arrive in an hour and I always ensure I have his meal ready to his taste when he arrives."

"Certainly. Just one more question. Um…where did you get the pictogram?"

"Why, from my most regular customer. He told me it would heighten my awareness beyond the pressures of life to calmly be a positive influence for my business."

"Do you think we might be able to speak with him when he arrives?"

"I can ask him. He is a solitary man, so he may not be so forthcoming when you ask him questions."

"Thanks. We'll keep it brief. Both of us are very interested in antiquities and old pictograms. We just want to get a little more understanding ourselves."

Jake checked his watch seeing it was just after nine, "After this coffee, we could go for a walk for half an hour or so, see if there is anything else we can find."

"Good idea," Lyle replied.

Raynie and Jenna had been wandering for half an hour looking into whatever establishment they thought may lead to some information. Upon realizing they were making their way further into a warehouse area and without any success so far, they decided to try the direction Lyle and Jake had taken. Ten minutes later they were crossing the central market place, once again momentarily immersed in the festivities. As lights danced and flickered around them, they noticed the three men who had earlier crossed their paths, but this time with a sense of foreboding.

"I don't like it," Jenna said grabbing Raynie's arm. "Let's keep low. Those guys look very intent, and angry."

A line of dancers suddenly invaded their space and they elected to be swept along with them as a means of cover. As the line took a turn back towards the center of festivities, Jenna lead Raynie away from the group, taking the same street the two men headed down around an hour earlier. Feeling somewhat more at ease, the women walked into the dimmer light glad to be free of the melee and the prospective gaze of those who appeared more and more to be their enemy.

"Well. What do we have here," Lyle said grabbing Jenna's arm from behind. Instantly she felt a surge of panic in the split second before she recognized his voice.

"Don't do it, we just had a scare."

"What? A scare…."

"Yeah those men are still circling and they look angrier than before."

"We are glad to see you two," Raynie added taking Jake's arm.

"And so are we. We wanted to come find you but thought we would not have the time. Lyle and I have a tentative meeting lined up in about half an hour. So it's great we caught up with you. Now we can all go."

"What have you found?" Jenna asked.

"Not so much what, but whom. We stopped at this cafe and noticed a pictogram reminding us of the demon figurine in San Francisco. When we asked about it, the owner told us its meaning and where it came from. It so happens the person who gave it to him is his most regular customer, and is due for dinner anytime soon. He told us we might get a little more information, but was hesitant to say any more. It is our best lead yet."

"We ought to go back now anyway," Lyle said. "Perhaps he might show up early and we don't want to miss him."

Ten minutes later they were standing outside the restaurant under cover to avoid the rain - now a steady drizzle bringing out more of the musty smell of the old city stones.

They entered and discreetly as possible, all glanced towards the only occupant aside from the owner who was in the kitchen. Immediately they all saw it was a woman sitting alone eating.

Jake led them to a table, "It is a man whom we need to see."

As they sat, the owner turned, coming over to them. "Ah, you are back I see. Good time too, I have some fresh soup just made. Would you like some? And your friends?"

"Sure," came a unanimous reply.

"My regular customer will be here soon. Perhaps he will talk to you about the Torus."

"There it is, see," Jake said indicating to the pictogram behind the bar.

"Yes, I see it does look a little familiar," Raynie replied. They huddled together for the next few moments discussing the torus and the possibility of success in meeting someone who might give them a lead. The owner then returned with four bowls of soup, bringing them to a hush. It was a welcome meal even though they had eaten earlier. Somehow, their eagerness had given them an appetite and the soup was also some comfort in the damp cool night.

When they had finished, Jake walked over to the bar and ordered them each a coffee. As he sat down again upon return to their table, the bells over the front door chimed, announcing the unmistakable most regular customer.

Dressed in a dark hooded coat against the elements, his face was barely visible as he made his way to his usual table in a corner near the far end of the bar. Before sitting, he removed his coat, placing it on a chair opposite to where he would sit. Lyle glanced his way as if to be momentarily distracted by the man's actions, and suddenly felt a rush of excitement. In a fleeting second, he felt sure he recognized the man. Discreetly he turned to Jenna, disguising his words with actions as if they were lovers. He whispered softly to her, very close to her ear as the others watched them fascinated.

"What is it?" Raynie asked leaning toward Jenna after Lyle broke their embrace.

"Lyle is sure he recognizes the man who just came in, the most regular customer. He is sure he is the same man we saw at the Baita pagoda."

The owner came out to serve the man his meal he had prepared before his arrival whereupon he greeted his customer with an exalted handshake and affirmation his favorite dishes were as tasty as ever. Upon his return to the bar, he prepared their coffee then came over to serve them.

"I will speak to him after he finishes his main courses. Perhaps then, he might invite you to share tea after his meal. He likes a meaningful conversation, but is always hesitant to whom he speaks."

"Those sequences we saw on the demon statue and again here on the torus, remind me of something I was looking at in Australia," Raynie said, breaking a momentary silence in the group. "I think we should take another look at the stone we found."

"Agreed. The inscriptions on the stone seem to resemble both the torus and the statue in ways. I have been thinking a combination of the inscriptions and pictograms might reveal more," Lyle replied.

"Sounds similar to the reading on quantum phasing I did. I showed some of the information to Jake, but before he arrived, I read a bit deeper into the work. It appears as though quantum phasing comes through some type of opening up or tuning into its' existence. To get there, coding of some manner had to be sequenced...um, you could say released."

"Sounds like a propulsion system," Jenna chimed in.

"You could say so," Raynie replied. "In a manner of speaking, the whole thing could be about propulsion, but in an awareness and vibration sense."

"We were working on a system using phasing ions with high localized magnetic field fusion resonance generators. By applying these fields to the ions, there is artificial plasma generated which in-turn gives off strong repulsing reactions resulting in a kinetic transference of the matter. This then applies a force strong enough to drive ships. Well...supposedly. The research is still new, unproven but...with what we saw in San Francisco, I would not be surprised at all, if ..."

"Sounds advanced Jenna," Lyle said thinking of his mission to the moon, for a moment.

Raynie caught his eyes drift away, "Tell us your thoughts."

"The Moon actually. My mission is in a month or so, and all the tech talk made me think of the trip."

"It ties in maybe," Jake suggested. "We mentioned the moon demon earlier. I've been thinking perhaps the image of the demon is not a warning of things to come, but a warning to those unfit at the time to properly interpret information."

"My time there is to study impact of development on lunar integrity. We are past just entering new places and junking them now."

"Yeah, but there are no traces of anything remotely resembling artifacts found on the moon. They've covered just about all of it at ground level haven't they?" Raynie asked certain there was no evidence of any moon relics.

"You're right. There is no record of any find. I don't think there is any moon connection. More symbols or code is what we could look for now and see if there is a common thread."

"It could relate. There is other meaning to look for beyond what seems obvious. If we are getting the nature of this information at all and how synchronicity plays such a part, then we could be open to circumstances relating in any way, to being opportunities," Jake said certain there was more to his thoughts.

"I get your meaning. We need to pay attention to any details during these times or missions, as we are actually immersing ourselves into events as part of what we are looking for," Raynie said excitedly. "Playing this as a game you could say, instead of just watching and collecting information."

"So…after all, I guess I should keep my eyes wide open when I go to the moon?"

Raynie laughed thinking how their conversation had just taken one turn after another, leading to some insight as to why they were actually on this journey of discovery at all. The others all picked up on her sensing the break in the moment as they each considered similar ideas in their own ways. Their sudden commotion in an otherwise quiet setting raised an inquiry from a man at the corner table - his eyes briefly turning towards them.

Chapter 13

Tobias walked into the room just a moment before John began testing a new algorithm to reprogram the personal identification microchip signals.

"You might like to watch this," John said accepting a beer. "I think this one is going to be close. We need to mimic the original pathways through an upgrade in programming. These things can take a lot of information and I'm just cracking them wide open with this. Well I hope to."

He pushed his finger through the holographic button to his right, setting a sequence in motion appearing above him in three dimensions. The view was spectacular. An algorithm pictured in complex detail displayed a complex nano image, and then transformed it showing billions of indistinguishable tiny pathways seen as a carpet of motion. John had programmed change to the original nanotechnology algorithm from a dodecahedron image representing the twelve dimensional layers of data processing, to something resembling an object in a state of flux. The image appeared to radiate before suddenly disappearing to travel just above light speed as both men witnessed a residue of light then remain for a fraction of a second.

"I'm getting two distinct transmission signals, one back to my receiver and also the original signal. If I use this signal by sending it out through this transmitter, then we can fool any system check and make it appear as though we actually have a chip. I'll have to keep working on it as they are bound to have placed random algorithms in all sorts of layers to keep security levels up."

"How will you do it? We could be on the move."

"Now I have the fix on this, I can now download it to the transmitter. The calculations can be real time and update the child devices anywhere at light speed. The only real gap you might ever get is if you are off the Earth. Two to seven seconds at the most."

"Sounds alright to me. But…what about systems authentication? Is there any way they can possibly detect it as a dummy signal?"

"I'm trying to get around it at each stage of development. The floating-point calculations should do the trick. I am getting it to work in a similar way to the device I used in the Beaver for throwing those dummy signals."

****

Steve McCray had just about had enough. It was a lot of work getting this urgent response to a call up at HAARP and keeping the team together. Now there were seven officers as a weapons deployment team operating at the site out of his command. He liked absolute clarity and control over situations where he was placed in charge, so having this additional crew working right under his nose and telling him nothing, made him furious. Aside from this though, he did observe them with an inkling of interest.

The equipment they were now unpacking and setting up in a section of the aircraft hanger, appeared entirely new to him. The main unit looked familiar enough being a Radome – a dome made of hexagonal pieces in use for over one hundred years now, but its composition appeared to be of some new material he was not certain he had ever seen before.

'Perhaps it is a new carbon nano-composite', he thought.

Carbon nano-composites were an extension of the carbon nano tubes developed earlier in the century, but were actually programmed compounds, for alteration then using software. He stared at it for a few moments wondering if he might detect any slight shift or flux in its' appearance. He saw none. The team was still installing various devices within the dome and to external couplings, so it was yet to be engaged.

Steve was then distracted away from his momentary stare by his second in command officer who was seated behind him at a monitor station.

"You getting any readings from the thing yet?" he asked.

"No sir. I have conducted a number of structural scans to attempt any detection of potential signal interference to the antenna array. Nothing as yet."

"Well, keep going, and make sure you maintain a low spectrum profile. We don't want them knowing we are trying to take a look at their equipment. This is purely my order out of my own interests."

"Acknowledged sir. If they detect anything, it should look like one of the resonance profiles the array emits in its' relay back to this station."

"Good." His gaze returned to the window looking out towards the hangar.

****

"Exquisite! Look at it. I think I have it," John said as he and Tobias watched the holographic image before them. The projection had increased in brightness, producing a more dazzling image of the complex carpet of nanotechnology.

"Now check this." He brought up a corresponding image of the technology sourced earlier from his trip across the bay.

"See it? The authentication signatures are the same on each. I am pretty sure I have nailed it. Those bastards won't be able to tell my signal from theirs."

"Well cheers," Tobias offered his beer as a celebration and they toasted the success of their endeavor.

"I'll begin working on developing a control panel enabling full integration into their systems," Tobias said after taking a mouthful of beer. "The recent changes they made at HAARP are linked into a central database with access to the entire network."

"We have it now and with this baby up and working, all we have to do is work out those control algorithms, and we are in. They are never going to know."

"Yeah, but what if they do some type of upgrade or modifications? I suspect they will keep changing their systems and not just sit on anything for the sake of keeping it secure and untraceable."

"This thing I have here should track any types of modifications. With this matching signal baseline, it should download as if it is just part of their operations."

"We're having a good day, aren't we?"

"You bet. It is all running pretty smooth for the last few days. We'll keep this simulation running to prove it and see if there are any potential breaks creeping in. I suggest you make a start on putting together all your knowledge on the systems operations at HAARP and then we can go from there."

****

"What is it now?" McCray stormed into the office where he had earlier been observing the team setting up in the hangar. "This bloody weapon. Now we are getting power fluctuations."

"They are connecting the Radome to the power grid here at the station sir."

"Why didn't they tell me? What's the use of being in command when they come here and steal your bloody power? Is the array affected?"

"No sir. The array is still maintaining resonance as set earlier. These fluctuations are part of the general power grid here at the station. The isolators for the array are still holding."

"Well, keep me informed. Do you have any other readings?"

"Yes sir. As the weapon is now powered sir, there are readings all over our operations systems. It appears as though it has linked in to the central control operations. They must have some element of control or capacity to link in and issue virtual commands."

"What the bloody hell is it for? This weapon is beyond anything else. Even those bloody new mother ships for the HyperJets don't have near the capacity."

"Affirmative sir. Shall I maintain this station?"

"Yes. Keep going. I am going to get some inside information on this deployment. I want to know about everything happening at this base." Steve began to wonder. Previously he had never called his service into question relying on his stout manner and capacity to work things how the military liked. Now he was having doubts and for the first time in his career he felt something he wouldn't like was coming.

Chapter 14

"Excuse me please sir. I was wondering if my friends and I could talk to you for just a moment please." Lyle asked after wandering over to the regular customer. The man was slowly sipping a cup of green tea. For a few seconds he did nothing else before raising his head a little and turning only his eyes in Lyle's direction. Immediately Lyle recognized the man as the one they had encountered at the White Pagoda.

"You are most welcome. Ask your friends over."

Lyle turned and indicated for the others to come over to the table. They promptly arose - Jake grabbing a chair for himself.

"I have been expecting you since our meeting much further back down the road," he said as the others sat down. His face was welcoming, with a hint of a smile at the corners of his mouth. Upon recognizing the man, the others felt a little eased and were immediately comfortable in his presence.

"Juyue Spring, you found it yes?"

"We did. It was a beautiful place and the light…" Raynie replied.

"Set you upon a journey within the spring," the old man interrupted her as if to speak what she was thinking.

"Indeed. There was something there I cannot really explain."

"None of us could," Jenna added.

"But you could feel it yes?"

"Sure, there was a certain magic," Raynie continued. It was like something stirring you deeply inside. I imagine all people who see the spring would take similar feelings away."

"One should always take notice of such times. They are important to you and to others and different for all. It is what we do with this whether we respond or simply leave it to memories. Too often people are just glimpsing at things. They do not take enough time to feel them."

"Umm, how is it you are here? It seems funny as we travel, you are showing up where we go," Jake asked him as the man took another couple of sips of tea. It was the question on all their minds.

"I am a guide. I go where I am needed. No one tells me to go or asks me. Where I feel I am needed, I go."

"Are you guiding us then?"

"I cannot say whole heartedly. You tell me."

"Let's put a few things together then. We came to China because we were shown some information from a person, Chan, who we met in San Francisco."

"Ah yes, Chan. Go on."

"Do you know Chan?"

"Many Chans in China. Tell me more."

"Chan Lee told us of some important information potentially dangerous."

"Dangerous, yes, many people in China are dangerous as in other places."

"Well he said the information related to energy and to look for someone with a dragonhead tattoo."

"Ah, many dragonhead tattoo in China."

"He also said there was something relating to some type of consciousness needed to activate or decode the energy. We met him in a Chinese restaurant …and had this statue, um…figure of a Moon Demon."

"Moon Demon. I have heard of this. You know even if it named as a demon, it is not necessarily a bad omen. Demons are used to frighten off some, like those who cannot understand the meaning behind them."

"We figured it as well. Pictograms on the statue caught our attention. It was if they might be part of this code."

"Yes. Tell me more."

"Then we came to China to see if we could meet this person with the dragon head tattoo, and we saw you at the White Pagoda."

"I recall."

"Then you told us to go to Juyue Spring, the moon spring where we felt something. First the Moon Demon, the Moon Spring, and um…here we are at Dunhuang."

"Have you met this dragon person?"

"No," Jake continued. "But, Lyle and I came to this café earlier and we saw the torus picture up there behind the bar."

Everyone's head turned toward the picture as Jake pointed it out, except the old man.

"In the picture there are symbols almost matching the ones we saw on the statue back in San Francisco. Then we were told you gave the picture to the owner here and you would be in later. We thought we would like to ask you about the picture."

"Eternity, never ending. See the torus, it continues like infinity. Hmm… perhaps I am here to guide you."

He took a few moments to pour some more tea from the small pot and take a few sips. The others sat in silence as he did this, considering what he had just said to them.

"I am not sure why you say to guide us," Lyle said finally breaking the silence. "We are not even sure about what we are doing. It is just all of us are so interested in this type of thing so we thought it worth looking at. A bit of mystery makes life interesting and so here we are. Although, I think I speak for all of us in regards to the danger element here, and say the danger is not so interesting."

"Yes, I see," the old man replied. "But is it not inherent for danger to almost always be a part of following or seeking mystery? Be it a physical danger as Chan indicated, or a challenge as an upheaval to your usual way of thinking. This may not present itself as dangerous, but it is a challenge and a step away from what you might say as a typically comfortable way to see the world and life."

Jake interjected, "And we have this stone piece Raynie and I found in Australia. It too has symbols similar to the demon statue and again here in the torus."

"Show me the piece."

"Here it is," Jake said as he reached into his pocket and placed the piece on the center of the table. "See the markings here?"

"Indeed. Interesting you found this in Australia. Not so many relics or the like often appear in such a place. It must have been put there deliberately, in association."

"What do you mean in association?"

"Such a piece was found in a place linked to the indigenous peoples of the nation, yes?"

"Umm…it was in a midden where people would discard their unwanted food waste."

"Well then, this piece is fortunate to have found you. No doubt it had rested in the place you found it for many years. It is likely it has been there at least for a long time, if not longer."

"Why would it be there? It seems a long way from anywhere else?"

"Safety. Such things are very precious, not in a material way, but as part of this code as you say."

"But how? If it came from elsewhere, who took it to Australia?"

"It remains uncertain. Without the remnants of buildings and writings, Australia is a mystery. The indigenous people have their dreaming worthy of deep respect, and it is upon them we must rely to find out the mysteries."

"Is it important?" Jenna asked.

"How do you mean?"

"Australia, is it important for…um, finding this code or whatever it is?"

"One cannot be sure beyond this discovery of the stone piece. But, it is as I said a land more mysterious than has been previously thought and like any other, it is important for realizing the true human condition."

"Is the condition a part of this code or whatever it is we are looking at?"

"Indeed. One must be in synchronicity for human potential to even begin to unlock your code. I would not call it a code, but it will do for now."

"Chan did mention…" Raynie began

"Yes he did," Jake interrupted. "Sorry Raynie."

"Is there a place near this city we can get further information?" Lyle asked keen to piece some more of their prospective journey ahead together.

"Did Chan not mention the caves?"

"He told us of the Buddhist Mogao Caves."

"Then go there. But first I will give you this."

The old man handed a copy of the Torus of Eternity picture to Lyle.

"Take this and study it. I only give copies to those I know who are potentially able to gather feeling of this and so I am of the feeling I can guide your intentions as you seek information be it for your own or for a wider good. There is much to tell, but not enough time. As Chan has told you, movement must be fast on this. We have known of others who seek the same but they seem not right for what is ahead. It is about your intentions. Let me add to this by saying the Song peoples were great achievers in the fields of printing, knowledge, and technology. You will also learn the Song eventually fought off the great hordes from the Mongol, Genghis Kahn, due to their strength. Not in arms, but in spirit."

"Interesting. Chan did mention the Song in San Francisco. I will research this as we travel," Lyle added.

"Yes do so. You are small in this knowledge yet you possess ability to understand great things. For now, I have nothing else to say. You need to understand this is a path of self-discovery as much as one of unearthing great things. To speak anymore would give you too much reliance on my words. You must develop this understanding from within."

He left them to themselves turning back to his tea and appearing to drift away to other thoughts. They left his table and turned to go outside the café. Returning to the musty lane now damp and slippery with a strange light mist in the air, they took to the walk back to their accomodation grateful for what seemed an insight into both mind and self.

****

Mark Broden as captain of the ship Enceladus, pondered the reason for his executive passenger aboard ship, as his vessel headed northward on the Bering Sea towards Anchorage Alaska.

A call from his first officer brought him out of this moment. "Sir. We are within five hundred miles of destination. Navigation is indicating increasing inclement conditions when we pass the Elution Islands. There is no threat to the vessel."

"Thank you."

Mark steered the ship with precision as he thought about of the type of mission he was on. All his work aboard the Enceladus had been purely scientific study, with the ship equipped to analyze the composition of materials to a depth of nearly ten miles below the ocean bed. It was at the leading edge of any technology of similar type. Bow to stern it was three hundred feet and encased in a carbon composite shell, and like a Chameleon, it could blend with its surroundings so as provide no visible sign of its presence using a sensitive new stealth design technology for blending with surroundings in a manner of stealth, be it ship, craft, or infrastructure.

****

McCray stared at the scene before him. Most of the central HAARP complex was awash with lights. None of this was his doing and so these experiments or whatever the team of specialists was conducting, annoyed him as more operations at his base went beyond his control.

"What were they doing now?" he almost voiced his thoughts with an angry punch, displaying enough to make those around him tense.

"Sir. The specialists are…"

"Yes. I know. Conducting more tests."

"Um…no sir. They have powered up their device and advise all calibrations have been set. They are standing by at readiness."

"At readiness are they. For what? Something else I have no command over?"

"It may appear as such sir. Though I am sure you still have overall command of this base should any situation call upon your expertise to conduct operations sir."

"Yes. Yes. Thank you. I am sure I have the support of all my officers. It just annoys me all this secrecy. Normally I get first or second look in on these matters, but this time, virtually nothing. What do they have anyway?

"I don't know sir. There is also more to report."

"More?"

"Yes. A scientific ship is making heading to Anchorage for the dispatch of personnel and equipment to this base."

"How do you know?"

"The specialists told me sir."

Just then, the intense light around the base softened to a peculiar colour resonating somewhere between purple and pink, and it had some type of inner glow. From a distance, the valley cast a soft purple and pink glow upon the snowbound open plains fringed by forests.

A flare then erupted within the glow of the base simultaneously taking all command systems offline.

"What the…" McCray stammered. He barely had time to complain before the flare receded and all systems came back to normal status. "Check it out!" he barked.

"Right on it sir."

Two minutes later the officer returned. "They advise it was a system purge."

"System purge. What?"

"To keep the system at stable levels. Stop any build up of energy sir."

"Right. Well how often are they going to do this?"

"They said it should not happen again because it only takes place on the first purge since installation. It should then remain stable."

"Well let's hope it does."

****

All four fell tired as they entered the motel room. It had been a long and strenuous series of events and now it had all caught up to them after the leaving the café to walk through the rain. Within minutes of arriving they were in bed talking briefly of the day as they fell asleep one by one. Outside the weather had more vigor now, soaking the city, where the twinkle of light seen earlier, had now become a dour mish mash of colour, tempered by the greyness of the gathering water in the streets and plazas.

In a lane in the old section of the city, a sole dim light inside a cafe, revealed two men in conversation. Their discussion focused on the meeting earlier with the group of four travelers. In soft tones they spoke in detail of why this group was on their journey and how events along the way would shape outcomes in the future.

They discussed the activation of the torus and how to then best manage the results. Unleashing its potential in all immediacy would invite attention - something they were keen to avoid on any account. When the rain became heavier distracting them for a moment, their discussion shifted to how unusual it was for such heavy rain in the city on the desert fringe.

Chapter 15

John and Tobias were silently walking along a passageway inside the local technology security station for servicing the area around Jenna's house. They had been able to access the building using an encryption code from personal identification devices positioned behind their ear. John had set up a fake authorization code enabling them immediate un-questioned access. Their objective was to hack into main central systems from the access point and obtain vital encryption data.

Continuing on, there was surprisingly little in the way of resistance as they made their way along a narrow corridor. John suspected the authorities were confident their systems were intruder and fool proof, and so they had relaxed security in the physical sense. Now as they were both only moments away from obtaining the last key ingredient to his binary recipe, John felt some comfort in his ability to have overcome the reasonable odds he considered would have prevented him from making progress to this point.

Tobias bumped into him when he suddenly stopped. "What is it?" he asked, his view ahead blocked by Johns shoulders.

"Just the central hub door. I think it has encrypted locking. I will have to take a few moments to break the code."

He took a small device out of his jacket pocket and placed it on the door adjacent to the locking mechanism. After entering a few commands via the device interface, a slight whirring could be heard as the locking mechanism released - they were in.

The central hub of this operations centre was a small room about ten feet square with a hardware panel on one wall. John went straight to the panel and immediately set about decrypting the lock. It took less than a minute before he was able to open the door and reveal the single processing unit hardware inside.

"As I thought," he said. "Mainly photonic circuitry coupled with interfacing to transmission hardware. See the line up there?" He pointed to a thin white line on the white wall.

"Yeah?"

"Well, it leads to the transmitter...carries a lot of data through the thin line. Old fibre optics systems would have run at less than one percent of the capacity this thing has."

"What do we do next?"

"I'll break into the box and tap into the main data stream. It has photonic nodes for linking to the main data distribution pathways. Afterwards I can obtain the floating encryption coding used for updating the identification chips."

He set to work on these tasks whilst Tobias kept a careful watch.

"See this?" he indicated a very small cube attached to the centre of the panel he had revealed. "It is the quantum unit. Main processor. All of the photonic hardware comes from this cube."

"So the encryption data is inside?" Tobias asked.

"Basically. This unit takes the encryption updates as they arrive from central systems, and then forwards it out across the network. It needs to be fast. Updates come through at least one thousand times per second. I need to tap into it via a photonic inlet."

He set about this task using various small devices and input peripherals as Tobias returned to keeping watch. Within a minute John had gained access and was copying the encryption generation data from the quantum cube. He knew his way around this type of thing well after years of studying, working, and inventing. Such a task was a snack to him and he paused for a moment considering this may well be why they were intent on chasing him from Alaska.

"There," he said. "I have it. I'll disconnect and we are out of here."

They quietly closed the door behind them as they exited the building emerging into bright sunlight. After casually walking towards the street to mix amongst other pedestrians, they quickened their pace, wasting no time in leaving the vicinity.

"How is the progress so far," Tobias asked after John had been working for a while since their arrival back at Jenna's house.

"Good. Any time now and I think I will have broken into the coding and we are set. Central systems will virtually have to be re-built for this to fail. They depend on the algorithms I picked up on. Sort of cumbersome really when you consider the capacity of the technology available."

"So you think we can ride with this for a while then?"

"Yeah I would say. Not sure though on what could happen or develop in the future, but for now and during this identification chip roll-out, I reckon we are a safe bet."

"I'm going to take a walk and escape this whole thing for a while," Tobias said. "I have some thoughts to go through."

"I think I will stick with this a little longer. After, it is just programming these fake identification devices I have put together. I'll see you when you get back."

It was a nice walk downhill from the house down to the bay side as Tobias walked along a street of historical and wonderfully decorated wooden houses. Each one he found fascinating as he surveyed the many vistas held by gates and windows, gardens and trees. His spirits lifted the further he walked, glad the owners of the houses had gone to such effort to make their residences offer such visual treats.

Ahead of him, the bay caught the sunlight and was a splendid alluring view of gold and blue forming a backdrop to the street. The scenes reminded him of the simplicity still to be found everywhere, so often overlooked by many people as they hurried about in life.

Asper watched him certain he was unaware of her following about fifty yards behind. It was her job to keep an eye on Tobias, and aside from their intoxicated initial rendezvous, she had noticed a level of tension in him was evident in almost every breath. This walk seemed to be doing him some good and she knew her job would soon take on a new direction as she came closer to finding out what he and John were up to.

Tobias sensed there was something else not part of his increasingly buoyant mood. There was no sense of unease, yet he felt something was happening. He turned suddenly with a gut feeling telling him he was being watched. As he turned, he noticed a person disappear behind a nearby bush, and for some reason he felt a sense of familiarity.

She was unsure whether or not he had recognised her. He was still visible through a gap in the branches of the bush she was standing behind. She stood there for a minute more, watching as he went out of sight down the hill. She gave it a moment more before re-starting the chase and enacting a plan to accidentally come across him sometime as he walked towards the wharves down by the bay.

Suddenly he was right beside her, startling her almost out of her wits. "I am surprised," he said. "When I sensed someone was following me, I certainly did not expect you Asper."

She motioned to speak.

"Don't speak," he interrupted. "Walk with me will you? I am curious to know why. You don't intend to harm me do you?"

"Oh no..."

"Good. Let's walk then. It is a great day and this is a fine place."

"Okay."

"See how the sunlight catches the water out by the island? Sort of takes you away. It sparkles and catches your eyes," Tobias said with a glance at Asper.

"I do love the bay."

"The light can be deceptive. It appears as though you are immersed in some type of paradise almost in a trance, but you are only yards away from the crowds at the wharves."

"Yes it has a magic. I guess it is what draws so many people here. I have lived in this city for long enough to have memories of it as a girl. It seemed even more enchanted then through a child's eyes, yet... it is as if it renews itself in a self perpetuating way."

"Interesting way to describe it. I would have to agree."

"I did enjoy our evening."

"Me too," Tobias said this honestly as he felt a degree of conflict pondering the reason Asper was following him.

"I felt a connection. But in these times, you need to be hesitant on taking those things further."

"I agree. It seems through all we have with this technology and lifestyles, we sometimes forget how to simply meet each other."

"They are utterly swept up in supporting and consuming technology."

"A cycle of work, pay, play. It all started years ago and now with the high end manufacturing becoming automated."

"You seem to have a view on this."

"I always have. Sure. I do some technology, but mostly it is a selective thing, not a dependence thing."

"I'm similar. Just the one portable device for me."

"Even it can be bad with tracking and..." Asper said trailing off.

They then fell silent and they continued without talking as they walked the final few hundred yards to the wharf area. When they arrived, they both hesitated a moment to survey the scene, and then turned to face each other. Asper felt she could just leave.

Tobias sensed this in her eyes, "Leave if you like. I am not going to force you to stay. I am interested in you...and why you were following me. It seems a little strange. We do connect, yet you have this other... um, agenda. Well at least I know to look out now and for whom."

"No need. I'll stay. I like you. Perhaps we have more in common than we think."

"Maybe we do. We could find somewhere to sit and chat?"

Chapter 16

Driving the short distance to the Mogao Caves was relatively uneventful except for encountering what some people referred to as ancients. They were people who lived life as many had done for years with barely any influence from the modern world and appeared as though they belonged to times more than a century ago. As they approached their destination, the light was glowing upon the cliff edges seeming to mystify the atmosphere as it cast an elevated glow and sense to the small valley containing the caves. After arriving, the first thing they noticed was the smell of musty sand and rain in the desert location.

"I think we should find somewhere to sit and get a feel for this place," Jake suggested.

"I agree," Lyle added. "We have almost no leads here so there is no need for us to rush in and continue this quest...whatever it is."

"My thoughts precisely. I think we need to take stock a little and approach this place with some reservation. Blending in as some of the many tourists should do the trick. Also, I suggest we dress in the new gear. Those Geiga suits will keep us comfortable and I have already noticed some very well dressed people about."

"There are bound to be some scientific teams here too, so perhaps a blend in with such a group or to be seen as a science group may be better cover than tourism?"

"What are you two talking about?" Jenna interrupted. "Did I hear we are going in as a science team cover? Well we all are scientists in a way actually."

"Yes. So we wear the suits. They should assist our cover."

"I have been looking forward to dressing up in those sexy suits," Jenna said looking at Lyle a moment before turning to Raynie.

"Um, yeah," Raynie chimed in with a giggle.

Lyle kept the vehicle on course towards the small settlement at the caves keeping a look out for somewhere they could stop. After rounding a corner they suddenly came across a group of forty or so people gathered near one of the largest buildings in the area.

"A lot of scientists," he said before anyone else could speak. "Perhaps we will fit in quite well. The crowd of scientists all appear to wearing the latest suits."

"Good. A peak group will get preferential treatment. We need to attach ourselves," Jake added.

"How will we do it?" Raynie asked.

"I think it should be okay. Take a look at them. They appear to be a number of smaller groups gathered for the one event. If we can attach to the crowd in a non-descript way, I think we can blend in."

"Oh look!" Jenna exclaimed.

She pointed towards a stall where the latest in scientific wear was available for all entrants. A sign posted on a wall advised it was compulsory for all entering the caves to wear a suit as they controlled body temperature and emissions sufficiently to avoid any damage to the ancient art works in the caves.

"Well, all solved then. Park over there and we will take the teahouse at the edge of the garden," Jake said. A moment later the vehicle was parked and they changed into their Geiga wear.

"Right. All set. Let's go," Lyle said as he led the way through the garden towards the teahouse they had chosen.

Lyle was the first to speak once they were inside, "I think we had better make some type of plan and get going. See the group? It appears as though they might be getting ready to move."

The others turned to see the small groups appearing to be getting ready for something.

"I think we just take a look around and see if we find anything of interest. We don't really know what we are here for aside from those few things Chan told us. The information we were given back in the city should help us some, but as usual we are unclear on exactly what to do."

"So we go on as we have before. A little blind yet with eyes wide open," Raynie added.

They began to merge with the other groups gathered outside the entrance to caves.

"Something must be about to happen," Jenna said as the others looked around at the groups on approach to the gate. "Perhaps a new discovery?"

A few of the other scientists who were filing in through the gate, looked at the new group of four who had joined them for a moment. One man was sure he had not seen them in the preliminary lectures prior to the trip to the caves and began to discuss them with a colleague. In response, his colleague was dismissive thinking more of what lay ahead and not in the least concerned with strangers. There was no strategic significance to the caves, so he felt satisfied the group of four were likely enthusiasts.

His companion remained a little suspicious however, not so easily dismissing the group as his colleague had done.

Jake had been secretly analysing the groups around them as they entered the gate, looking for any signs of suspicion. He had noticed the brief moment between the other two men and whispered to Lyle, "We need to watch ourselves very carefully."

"Yes. I saw it too. I have many questions running through my head. This appears to be a significant event of some artefact type and I wonder what exactly is going on. I cannot see any official teams here though. These groups look like they have just come together."

"Why is there no security I wonder?" Jake asked.

"It is playing on my mind. No security also means there is no official line for this site or event. I think we are on the verge of something here never before seen, or at least been notified to the authorities yet."

Raynie and Jenna were just ahead of the two men as they entered the caves complex through the gate. The entire crowd of scientists were moving in the same direction obviously towards a specified location.

As they passed cave ninety-six, they were stunned by the sheer height of the cave. It was the tallest of all and housed the tallest Buddha statue at over one hundred and ten feet. Continuing on, they passed cave two four nine known to feature figures swirling around a demon and dating back to the sixth century.

The group had now amassed outside of what was a small and rather drab entrance to a cave listed on the holographic guide as having been closed to the public since the caves were recognised and protected as significant.

When they entered the cave after waiting their turn amongst the groups filing in, they noticed a few very old and much faded murals featuring Buddha at what looked like the centre of a world. After passing through the initial chamber with the murals, some steep stairs then lead underground. They all filed slowly down the stairs until they reached the chamber of interest. Its' expanse was surprising as it could easily be amongst the biggest of the entire Mogao caves complex with this main chamber stretching to almost one hundred by one hundred feet.

Once the entire group had entered and gathered in the far end from the entry point, a muffled sound of low conversations filled the chamber. The escort for the entire group then brought them all to silence with an "attention please."

The guide described the characteristics of the chamber they were in, including an image of Buddha sitting in the centre of a torus - itself adorned with many small images showing human life in different situations. Another feature appeared to be a carving faintly resembling the torus of the image. Parts of the carving appeared to be missing or more accurately, deliberately left out. There was no other feature equal to these two in size – the only other being a small statuette sitting in an alcove in the wall. It appeared to be some type of demon. Lyle immediately saw its similarity to the figure they had seen in San Francisco and his heart jumped.

The guide interrupted his thoughts, "You will notice the statuette appears to be indicating towards something. When we examined this closely, we came to no conclusion until we took a more lateral view. See the carving over there? Well the demon is not indicating towards the carving as it appears. It is actually a distraction from the lateral meanings behind the Buddha gestures or Mudras where we began to understand more. The demon statue is merely the balance here in this equation for it is very similar to an equation yet different in its own sense. To cut it short so we can move on, when we deciphered the gestures we then looked at the symbols from within the torus and in the carving. This answer showed us a sequence for touching the symbols, which themselves released an unlocking mechanism for access to the third chamber in this cave. Watch now as I initiate the sequence."

The guide moved closer to the Buddha feature and touched three symbols at different places surrounding the figure. He then moved across to the carving and the wall midpoint between the two features, gently slid to one side. A gap of approximately fifteen inches wide was visible with no light coming from within.

"Now despite the apparent size of this cave, this doorway leads to yet another staircase leading to a chamber about forty feet below this room. Please follow me in an orderly manner. I will switch on the lights as we enter the doorway." He moved through the door by turning sideways and then hit a switch just inside. The light illuminated the stairs just sufficiently to see, leaving most of the walls and ceiling in shadow.

"You will find we need to travel down eighty eight stairs to reach the third chamber," he said as the group made their way in. "The room down there is quite big enough for all of us. We have measured it at eighty eight feet square, so we should all be comfortable."

Chapter 17

Steve McCray was in one of his usual moods. He stood once again at the main windows gazing out over the compound toward the specialized team who had just been advised of the Enceladus having arrived at Anchorage for immediate transfer to HAARP.

"Sir?"

"Yes. What is it?"

"The personnel from the Enceladus have left Anchorage and have communicated ahead to the specialized team we have stationed here sir."

"What! No contact made to me as the Commander prior to this? I am going over to talk to them now!"

He stormed out of the office and strode over to the building housing the team, with a look of complete determination to get some answers. His first officer watched him knowing trouble lay ahead.

"When Steve gets mad, everyone pays," he whispered just low enough to be out of earshot for others in the room.

"What the hell is this?" Steve demanded from the leader of the team. "No clearing communications through me at this state ...um, level of alert. How the hell can I command this place with... Oh forget it! Just tell me what I want to know for now. No run around you see. Who are these personnel arriving and what is their purpose? And...do they have more of this type of equipment you lot seem to be so fascinated with?"

"We appreciate your position Steve, but we are under orders to only provide information upon discretion. But, I think it is time you did get some more to know a little more. I see you are running a tight command here, so at this stage we can release some information to you."

"Well. Finally a little light on the subject," Steve replied calming down some.

"Basically we are going to amplify this HAARP facility to a level beyond how it has operated. We will do this with technology from the Enceladus. Largely experimental technology - this is the real first time deployment."

"But why? I thought the output here went up straight after the California incident."

"It did, but this new level of technology will make it look miniscule."

"So what will it do?"

"It remains a secret other than to say it will affect the systems of many operations and facilities in a lot of places."

"I see...and people? We all know these transmissions have affects on delta and theta brain waves. How will they cope?"

"No affect in this instance..."

"What?"

"Well. No affect other than what is commonly known."

"How do you mean?"

"Far more subtle where brain waves are unaffected, but the brain can be influenced…"

"I get it. This has to do with the nanotechnology consumption in recent years. I knew you lot had an agenda somewhere."

"No Steve it is not as such. We are not going to suddenly take over people's brain patterns. We will have to leave it there. You will receive more advice closer to operations commencing in full. You will need it. Otherwise, I cannot say any more."

"Just report to me on some regular basis, and include me in any frontline operational decisions. I need to run this place properly."

"Okay. Sorry Steve."

He left the building and returned to the main office to await arrival of the group from Anchorage.

****

Lorraine viewed John as he went about working on a small piece of hardware, and she felt satisfied at how well the secret holographic camera had been deployed. Her instructions were to continue building a relationship and watch John without being found out about why she was doing it. She had taken a liking to him after their first meeting and considered him a candidate for a genuine friend, except for this reconnaissance. This had overwhelmed her at times, as finding and keeping friends had become increasingly difficult for her, and now she felt a little torn between her duties and her feelings.

He reminded her of people she had once known before they had become high-rise dwellers. They retained some old world type values, yet could easily embrace and use technology to their advantage. Her friends had gone too far though and were amongst those too eager to adopt the trans-human state growing in popularity. They were now amongst the growing numbers of humans integrating with technology as part of a systematic lifestyle of work and consumption in the growing super towers located in most of the world's significant cities.

Outside of these places, there were those who aspired to life in the high rise, and who led their lives trying to raise their status. Lorraine was neither of these types, although she held some interest in technology herself. When her friends took their first implants, she knew then her association with them was over. It was strange to her, as they had presented initially as being opposed to the idea, but then quickly succumbed to offerings of improved health and life through technology.

She leaned in closer to see what John was doing in more detail. She saw he appeared to be working on an algorithm for a small photonic device linked to a processor unit on the desk. It took her a moment to realize what she was looking at as she worked on analyzing the situation. On the side of the receiving device was a small port she had only seen in virtual space as a holographic image, and she felt sure she knew what it was. He was teleporting data.

"How did he get...?" she asked out loud to herself.

Data teleport was unknown to the general populace - only a few technical people knew of its schematics and operations. The capacity to transmit all data simultaneously was almost infinitely faster than streaming it through any previous method.

For a brief moment she felt a sense of arousal brought on from the relief to know John was probably working on her side. She looked away lost for a moment to thoughts of the future, and to images in her mind of John. Questions came to her causing her to return back to his image. As she stared at him working, she took mental note of all she thought to ask him given the chance, whilst maintaining her cover until confirming John's intentions.

A few minutes later, he stopped what he was doing and left the room, so Lorraine decided it was time to meet him in person again. She checked her appearance, grabbed a bag and light jacket, and then headed out towards the heritage wooden house. To hasten her journey, she decided to travel via Aero Tram - a novel addition to the antique vintage trams still operating from the city center down Hyde Street. Aero Trams ran along lines suspended twenty meters above street level. Surrounded in window space except for a thin hardware strip in the middle of the floor, passengers were treated to unparalleled views of the city and the bay area, with trips extending from the city center across the famous Golden Gate Bridge and the Bay Bridge, then further to the outer areas.

As she rode the tram staring out to the sky beyond, she noticed a configuration of aircraft in the far distance. She treated the sight casually at first considering so many aircraft filled the skies in these times, but her thoughts took a turn when she noticed the size of the configuration.

"There must be at least one hundred aircraft," she said quietly to herself.

A slight sense of alarm arose within. She had control over her responses and felt only a little phased for a moment before considering the recent events off the coast and the increased activity by the authorities, the appearance of such a large number could only mean some type of event was about to unfold or was already unfolding.

****

Raynie was the first of the four to enter the final chamber in the cave. As she took the last step down onto the floor, she immediately felt an elevated sense as if the chamber was resonating energy of some type. Looking around, she noticed how others were dealing with this sensation. Some seemed to stagger at times as they tried to stand still, others stood calmly with a sense of peace about them. Lyle, Jake, and Jenna joined her seconds later - they too visibly changing as they stepped onto the floor of the chamber.

"I guess it is like a feeling of nostalgia mixed with anticipation, mixed with feeling good," she whispered as they huddled together.

"Sums it up well," Jake replied. "There is some good type of feeling, mixed with an elevated sense of knowing it is right there."

"Ladies and Gentlemen," the guide brought all in the chamber to be quiet. "As you can no doubt tell, or feel, this chamber has a unique character. Since the discovery of this chamber two months ago, only eight people have been here prior to your group today. Please, may I draw your attention to the center of this chamber and to the figure resting on the round pedestal?"

The entire group stood surrounding the center figure, all eyes gazing over it for a minute before the guide spoke again.

"Take note of the details at the base of the figure. They are reminiscent of those found in the chambers above us."

Again there was silence as all stood studying the figure.

Jake whispered to Raynie, "See the similarity?"

"Yes, I know," she replied.

"At this time," the guide announced. "We have only a fragment of the information surrounding these chambers. We do believe there is more information to add to these details, but our team has come up with no answers. It is why we have invited you here today, to help us decipher this mystery. Please take time to study the information and draw some conclusions, if you can. Our team would be grateful for any advice based on your expertise."

The group of scientists once again fragmented into the same smaller groups.

After ten minutes of study, one group called for the others to allow them to shine an ultra violet light on the figure, explaining it could reveal more details. All agreed and so the requesting group quickly set up their lighting rig and then switched it on.

A glow came from otherwise unlit or shadowed sections of the chamber, astounding those present for a few seconds. Images similar to those on the figure lit up the darker corners forming a band around the entire chamber. For a moment, all stood aghast at the site, before they hurriedly entered into conversation speculating on the nature of the decals.

Jenna was silently looking around her as Raynie, Jake, and Lyle discussed the glowing imagery. Her eyes rested on one man who seemed to be attached to a group, yet not really participating in their conversation. To Jenna, it appeared as if he was almost looking at their group, his head leaning slightly to one side. For a brief moment, his face seemed to light up as if the glow of the chamber was his as well.

During this she noticed there was form to the light coming from the man's face. In an instant she recognized the form as a dragon head only visible under such light conditions.

"We need to talk to him," she said interrupting the others.

With a slight push, she ushered Lyle into position to see whom she was referring to. He saw the image on the man's face at once and with a hint of excitement, nodded to confirm Jenna's recommendation.

Over the following ten minutes, they all discussed the chamber and its' link to the man with the dragon head tattoo. They kept a watch on him without giving themselves away, noticing he continued to look occasionally in their direction. The man then vacated the chamber, ascending the stairs to the chamber above. Lyle and Jenna decided they should stay behind whilst Raynie and Jake followed the stranger.

"It looks best for some of us to stay and not appear as obviously following the man. A split group will not seem suspicious. I have seen a few others split as well. Perhaps they need a rest from the sensations inside this chamber?" Lyle said.

When they reached the chamber above, the man was nowhere to be seen and both Jake and Raynie felt their energy levels drop.

"Let's go outside, perhaps…" Jake was saying when Raynie interrupted him pulling his arm and gesturing towards the exterior.

"I know he is out there."

Brilliant sunlight temporarily blinded them as they went outside. A few seconds later, their focus had returned and they saw the man sitting on a seat under a nearby tree writing something on paper. The tree itself was almost perfect in form, abounding with life and appearing strong. They walked over to him, his tattoo no longer visible in the plain light of day. As they came close, he raised his eyes to greet them and gestured they sit beside him.

"Amazing chamber yes?" he both stated and asked them.

"Yes," they replied in unison.

"You now know why you were sent here. There are details at this location to be understood and acted upon if those who threaten this knowledge are to be kept at bay."

Raynie and Jake only nodded their understanding.

"The chamber is so very interesting, it is difficult to know what to think isn't it?" he said in a louder voice. "We are being watched," he added under his breath.

"It certainly is," Jake replied. "What about the images only visible with ultra violet light?"

"Remarkable how those gestures were key," Raynie added.

"They are visible in such light for only a few to see. It is not until this time since they were created, where using ultra violet light has been considered. For you, think of this as a reflection of your higher intuitions. You must take this," he said to Jake slipping him the paper he had written on. "Do not read it here. Keep it secret…always."

"I think I saw our watcher," Raynie said. "He was looking our way prior to us entering the cave."

"Yes, he is part of the people we should be concerned with. I have trailed him for some time now through China."

"Is there any danger?" Jake asked.

"Of course. I told you so in San Francisco."

"Chan?" Raynie and Jake whispered together.

"Yes. I have different appearances. This work is important and it would be foolish to look the same wherever I go. It is here you must talk to me and now you have. What I am giving you needs to be done in this place, as the information comes to you and also the feelings within the lower chamber. There would be nothing gained to have simply told you about the deepest chamber in this cave. As you can tell, it has a special feeling associated with it for the activation of memories. Now return below ground and take pictures of all you see. You will need this information as well to assist you."

"In what?" Jake asked.

"Again, I am so very impressed with the cave," Chan said aloud as a diversion.

"It is magnificent," Raynie added.

"I will leave now. Remember to read all written on the paper and study what you know."

He left them and returned to the cave. As Raynie and Jake did the same a minute or two later, they passed Chan at the entrance where he was reading some inscriptions there. The person who had been watching them was nowhere to be seen, his work apparently done.

"Who was the man watching us I wonder?" Raynie said as they began the stairs back down to the deepest chamber.

"No doubt someone we should also keep a look out for, and likely to be part of the team who chased us in the desert, but for now, let's get back to the others, get those images, and then make for a place where we can go through this information Chan has given us."

When they greeted Jenna and Lyle, the lights had now been turned off and the luminescent images had disappeared. Jake stood holding his holographic camera with a look of disappointment on his face.

Reading his thoughts, Jenna smiled and said to him, "Fear not, we already took some images before the lights went out."

"Someone was watching us," Raynie said when they had exited the caves and had some space to themselves.

"I figured as much," Lyle said. "We saw a man return before you did. He gave Jenna and I a look...somewhat discerning."

"Yes, he made us a little edgy."

"We need to be more vigilant now."

"Chan..." Jake started.

"Chan! Did you see him? Where?"

Raynie leant in close and spoke in a lower voice than the others, "He had the dragon head tattoo. It was Chan all along."

This brought silence for a minute as Lyle and Jenna contemplated the turn of events.

"He said we needed to be here to feel this chamber as he gave us more information. Intrinsically they are linked. He gave us a sheet of paper we need to keep secret. So I think we need to depart Mogao and go back to our rooms at Dunhuang to look it ov..."

"I think only part of it is a good idea, the going back to our rooms part. Once there, we should leave and find another place to stay," Lyle interrupted.

As they turned to leave, they noticed other groups emerging from the caves. "Well at least our departure may be less suspicious with these others leaving as well."

Three hours later, they were gathered in the same cafe in the older part of the city where they had first discussed the torus. The owner recognized them immediately and came over to serve them. A few other people were in the establishment, a couple, and middle-aged man, and two women sitting together.

"How may I serve you today?"

"Um...some green tea. I can smell it from here," Raynie said ordering for them all. The others all said yes in agreement, and the owner left them to make the tea.

"Perhaps he could tell us where else we could stay," Jake proposed. "No harm in asking him I guess."

"I agree. He might know of a place away from the tourist hordes and any other visitors to the city at the moment," Jenna replied. "He seems to be on our side."

"Side?" Lyle challenged laughing. "Taking sides? Whose side? What side? Inside?

"All of the above and more." This brought them all to silence as they contemplated the 'more' part of Jenna's statement. There would certainly be more than the sides they had become accustomed to. Already, the experience at the caves had changed them as they began to grasp the activation meaning behind their journey to discover more about what Chan was alluding to, particularly the torus.

When the owner returned with a pot of tea and four cups, he seemed even more enthusiastic toward them. "Have you thought about the torus and your meeting here the other night? How was your trip to the caves?"

"How did you...?" Jake began to ask.

"I know. My customer tells me what he considers worth knowing, both good and bad. I must say my most regular customer is quite impressed with your integrity. He can sense from all of you, the thirst for knowledge and synchronicity...um, and decency of character. He says you are an unlikely group to help us and you must have fortitude to go on this journey you are on with very little knowledge as to why."

"Perhaps you can help us some more," Lyle asked. "We are very grateful for the hospitality you have given us and we feel we are amongst friends here. But, we think there are others who we may not consider as friends and they make us nervous."

"Hmm. I expected this."

"Well, we were wondering if you could recommend another place to stay here in Dunhuang? Somewhere a little away from the popular places."

"You can stay at my own home. I have plenty of room for all four of you. It is best what you say and keep out of sight. They will likely have determined where you are staying and the vehicle in which you travel. My home has a workshop attached to it for my hobbies. Your vehicle will fit in there. Where is it now?"

"We thought it was better to walk most of the way here than to drive. It is at our motel," Jake replied.

"Well. You must have your tea, return to your motel, and then drive to my home. I will give you the route to take. Anyone who may follow you will be easy to see and if they are tracking you electronically, I have a little surprise for them."

"Surprise?"

"Yes, one of my hobbies. I will return shortly with the bill. On there I will write the details you need."

"More paper with writing. These old fashioned ways to communicate are so interesting," Jenna said when the owner had returned with the bill. "It keeps those electronic tracking devices at bay. Any communications sent through the system would be intercepted for sure."

"Let's go back but casually and in a round-a-bout way," Lyle added. They had all changed from their Geiga wear after returning from the caves prior to going to the cafe - appearing now as two couples holding hands like the many tourists about Dunhuang in the evening.

****

Tobias, Asper, John, and Lorraine sat in the lounge room of the wooden house - the night sky visible through the large bay windows. Amongst the stars, a myriad of orbital and other craft also lit up the sky. These sights often made people stop a moment just to gaze at the beauty of the light show and ponder the role of the many spacecraft. Some would say they are just commercial satellites servicing the needs of society, and others would speculate about conspiracy and they were constantly watching us.

Their conversation focused on the plight John had taken to decipher an algorithm for the personal identity chips. After setting up a chance meeting with John, Lorraine had contacted Asper to come along for dinner at the house where John and Tobias were staying. It was then everything had been brought out into the open.

Lorraine had advised both Asper and her were members of a group who stood for values outside those of the consumer corporations and central systems. Their group also investigated people who could be considered as members or networked associates. They operated on a basis like John and Tobias, plus the other four in China, where they accepted technology for what it could do for them, but refused to take on the trans-humanism values espoused to by those in control.

"I think we need some more information," John said. "There is an extra data security requirement where the chip authenticates for the latest updates to prevent data hacking. I knew there was one, but there is also a second. It was hidden in the first algorithm...very clever."

"But these things will update so fast, how will we intercept?" Tobias asked.

"Ah. See this?" John held out what appeared to be no more than a very tiny lens. "Data teleport sender and receiver. This enables all data to be received simultaneously, no streaming involved. I am pretty sure they are also working hard on this technology, so we are going to need this if we are to have a definite chance of beating these chips."

"How does it work?" Asper enquired.

"Glad you asked me. It has a tachyon emitter. This sends out a signal just above light speed to the receiving device setting the space for the data to occupy. All of this takes nano seconds with the tachyon sort of…punching a hole in normal time and space. So without going into the physics of faster than light, basically it arrives virtually the instant it was sent."

"Oh, almost a juxtaposition yet virtually?"

"Hmm…maybe. It is difficult to conceive I know. Try working with it. But if you just consider a moment like an epiphany where a lot of information or sense comes to you at once and whilst you consider it coming to you, it actually begins inside you."

Lorraine was listening intently as John spoke to Asper.

"I remember there was a time when faster than light speed was deemed impossible," Lorraine said with a laugh.

"Yeah I recall," Tobias added.

"Now we are at the brink of going beyond," John said. "It was just back in those days when the corporations were the only ones driving science, there was little to no resources put into the research and so instruments for even beginning to detect tachyon emissions were unheard of."

"But…" Tobias was deep in thought at this moment. "How does the receiver even begin to work if tachyons travel faster than light, the very speed at which the receiver exists?"

"Again, good question. I'll just sum it up as the physics are far too complex to explain. The lens you see is in a constant state of flux. It is one of the newest instruments made to facilitate data teleport. Whilst it appears as solid, it actually must contain a percentage of tachyons to create the flux and receive faster than light transmissions. With their slowest speed being just above light speed by the tiniest amount, the tachyons are held in this state awaiting engagement. The work science has done in recent years developing flux is astounding when you think these machines are barely solid."

"I wonder how far central systems have developed this." Lorraine asked. "I suspect they are a fair way along the path."

"Indeed," John replied. "This technology I have was borrowed in part from them. I could see where they were going when I left the service, so I took a little with me, well…rather copied it. Since then I have made some changes and added some other modifications obtained from various contacts I have."

"Reminds me of the chip we used on the Beaver," Tobias said his facial expression lost a little to the recollection of the event.

"Pretty similar, just a lot more data power. If I am right, in the near future this technology may take on teleport of physical objects, but I think it will be more of a blend of data teleport and replication. It has to do with organizing matter atomically so organic matter is an entirely different subject, beyond our reach."

"So what are we going to do?" Tobias asked. "I am thinking…"

"We are going to need to contact someone in the high rise to get the information we need. The authorities will have agents looking for the very thing we are creating here and no doubt they will be using the latest encryption methods to remain undetectable. This is on top of what I have already mentioned. I know someone who might be able to help us get inside information."

"Top level?"

"Near enough."

Chapter 18

San Francisco Bay glittered in the early morning sunlight as they rode the elevator car towards the top of the eastern tower in the city center. One of eight interlinked towers covering eight city blocks, it housed over sixty thousand people. Each of the eight towers included parklands with water features, facilities for outdoor amusements, and market gardens to give residents a sense of a complete life forty stories above street level.

The four passengers all knew otherwise, seeing life in the high rise as an illusion where such features were designed to placate the minds of those who lived here. When a person becomes almost permanently removed from the Earth beneath them and living in manufactured environments, their hearts became indifferent to the essence of this organic interaction – an elemental interaction for humans since their beginning.

John broke the silence as the car began to slow for their destination over one hundred floors above the streets.

"Welcome to floor one hundred and twenty seven. You will not be required to check in, as this is a non-restricted zone."

"Non-restricted? I thought these were purely residential and commercial allotments," Asper said as they disembarked.

"They are," John replied. "It is a new condition. I suspect it could be associated with this alert level the city is under."

"You can bet there is a lot they are not telling anyone," Tobias said as they walked towards the reception area.

Each floor had a reception lounge where a holographic concierge service was available for residents and visitors, along with a space designated as a general social meeting place. The concierge automatically detected their arrival and appeared before them, floating in the air.

Before it could say anything, John said 'no service' and it disappeared.

"We don't need it," he said to the others. "I know where to go."

He led them along a transparent walkway offering views to the internal structure of the building where people could be seen taking morning walks in the parklands. A waterfall led into a lake where the early morning colors were reflected as if it was a natural feature.

"How do they do it?" Lorraine asked as they stopped to gaze at the scene for a moment.

"Mirrors," John replied. "All part of the manufactured nature going on here." Despite their objections to this way of life, they all agreed it was an awe-inspiring sight as it appeared so convincing where if one was to be in amongst the trees, one could easily forget they were suspended so high above the city below.

"Okay, here we are. We will need to use one of these transports, as the walk could take too long and we need to get this over with quickly."

John firmly believed in operating fast and precise so as to avoid any unnecessary time wasting. Since leaving the service, he had made it an imperative based on his knowledge of the authority's inner workings, and what could happen if he was caught trying to obtain technology. Citizens were encouraged to use technology as much as possible, but to go any further and understand its' workings, was strictly forbidden. He thought again of this in its' paradoxical sense where the authorities espoused to a heightened life experience through technology, yet underneath, retained the utmost in control to ensure compliance and general ignorance. They boarded the transport and stood together on a platform as it automatically drove along taking them to the destination John had stated.

Behind them someone was watching. He noticed the group of four as they stood gazing at the interior of the building. It was his nature and his job to be suspicious and when his suspicions were aroused, and he was almost always proven correct. The two women and two men dressed in the latest Geiga wear like many others were not like the many others. It was the way they talked together and the looks in their eyes. The tallest man, whom he had heard to be called John, was of the most suspicion. And no doubt those two women were very keen to be a part of whatever it was he was doing. The other man, Tobias, looked a little lost and not as fiercely determined as John. He had been warned about such dreamers too. Given the chance, they could very likely decide to involve themselves in extreme actions.

He maintained a distance from them as he followed their transport along the internal passageway, careful to retain a posture and air about him to avoid looking suspicious. His assignment was to track two fugitive ex-service people who had taken to leaving Alaska in a hurry and had avoided any successful apprehension as they made their way to San Francisco. It was only through a stroke of luck he had even been given this assignment. Behaving like an inebriated person at a bar, covertly he was seeking to uncover information when by chance he was able to just catch a sentence from Tobias who fortunately for him, was actually inebriated.

This was the clue leading him to follow their conversation about using high intensity listening technology. He heard Tobias mention the trip from Alaska, and thought such a journey was uncommon enough to warrant further investigation. By covertly using his holographic phone as opposed to his official issue technology, he was able to access information on the wanted fugitives.

The authorities did not want to detain Tobias and John at this point, rather allow them to further carry out whatever it was they were doing in the hope of the two men leading them to others who might oppose them. There was no room for dissent from any citizen. Tolerance was out of the question for anyone breaching the rules of conduct and psychological behavior. New systems would come online in two weeks, so the authorities were now dispatching agents across cities and across the virtual systems to combat any movement or data considered in opposition to their motives.

Citizens around the world would suddenly be thrust into a life even more convenient for them, more technologically reliant, and unconsciously, even more controlled. He thought for a moment as he followed them, of how successfully the authorities had everyone believing the hard times of the past where corporations and governments deliberately manipulated lives on mass scales, were long gone. Consumed as they were with their daily work and their struggles to maintain and elevate their individual status, they were mostly unaware of the change already occurring.

Where once multinational corporations had almost taken over the thoughts and actions of most citizens with their convenience through technology advertising the comfort and health benefits, such control was now in the hands of just a few. Enormous revenues were gained through centrally owned and driven corporations legislated to replace the previous concepts of privately owned multinationals at the mercy of the stock market. It too was gone.

He laughed a little to himself as his thought of how absurd those who had tried control through stocks and poor fiscal and economic policy, now seemed. He was a man for the system and its' capacity impressed him. Nothing in those erroneous ways of the past could even approach the level of manipulation now controlled by those who held high office. He drew a sense of power from this, drawing a deep breath and doubling his efforts to track the group ahead.

He saw them come to a stop outside one of the many residential doors along the passageway. Pretending not to notice, he continued to approach them and then passed by, appearing as if he was intent on his own destination.

John and the others had been silently riding the transport until they stopped, and did not notice the man until he was almost upon them. Casting only a sideways glance at the man as he brushed by, John took careful note of the face he saw - something he had often done since leaving the services. He was very good at remembering faces and where he had seen them. At this time with his objective in mind, he took particular notice for a brief half second, vigilant in noticing every small detail.

"Come in," came a voice from the door itself, which then opened automatically.

"Welcome. Hello John and friends."

"Hi Raman. So I am still on your face recognition list."

"Yes. Of course good man. You are someone I can always trust. You can access my door at any time. Well, almost any time…you know."

"Thanks," John replied shaking Raman's hand. "This is Asper, Lorraine, and Tobias. All very good friends of mine."

"Hello to you and welcome to my home."

"Thanks," the others said together.

"Let us go through to the lounge and have refreshments. I know you are here for something and not just a social visit," Raman said to John.

"You know me," John replied as they all walked into the lounge and sat down. "Always there is something new and I am onto something now."

"Yes. I know. With all this trouble off shore, there is bound to be something very new…and big about to happen. Such events are normally the precursor for some other measure."

"I see your distrust of the authorities is as strong as ever."

"Indeed. Even stronger. You cannot work on the inside without having suspicions when you return to the outside."

"So you are working alone now Raman?"

"Yes, very much so. My links to the systems are as good as ever, but my main focus is on trying to stay at least one step ahead of any developments they might come up with."

"Does it pay for this place?"

"No not really. Money is no longer an issue. I made one patented device just a year or so back. All of this I own…well as much as you can own. I am a free agent you could say."

"But not an official agent."

"Correct. Now would you like coffee?"

"Sure," the other three replied together again. They had sat silently as Raman and John talked.

"Yeah, me too," John added getting up to walk with Raman as he went to the kitchen to make the coffee.

By the time everyone had finished their drink, John had outlined his story thus far to Raman, and indicated on the type of technology he would require to overcome the security and secretive encryption the authorities would deploy.

"You can bet on there being agents in these buildings now," Raman said as the group discussed this issue widely.

"I think it is almost a given. We need to remain aware of any incursion they might make into groups like ours. Asper and Lorraine are part of a larger organization looking into issues they deem fit for attention."

"Yeah, it is how we met these two," Lorraine added.

"Well," Raman said with an air of confidence, "So long as you have me on your side you can feel pretty confident of staying in the game, as long as you don't make any stupid moves."

"One thing concerns me," Tobias interjected. "John said these identification algorithms would update at light speed and the security at faster than light. Aside from beyond light speed, the personal chip updates will have gaps like he said if for instance you are located any distance from the Earth where the update could take two seconds or more. The networks he described to me are very fast but still linger in contrast to the light speed threshold. Why would they do this? Why not make it all faster than light?"

"Simple," Raman replied, "They don't have the technology developed sufficiently to deploy at such a large scale. Most of this is being hurried in using existing technology with a few add on pieces. Until they can deploy on a global scale, they have to keep it to the security."

"Okay then, but they will be continuing to work on it..."

"Certainly and with extra effort. Once they get a taste of things to come, they will want more and more. It is their way."

"Are you safe here? From agents or investigation I mean," Asper asked Raman.

"Yes..."

"You can count on it," John interrupted. "None safer. Now this tech I need."

****

They had found their way to the restaurant owners' residence the night before without incident, and had spent the night talking about their trip to the caves and speculating what might lie ahead.

"Those mudras...the gestures, were very similar to the markings Raynie and I found in Australia," Jake said as the four of them talked over lunch.

"Yes Jake," Raynie replied jabbing him in the ribs, "You have told us quite a few times now."

"I just can't get over the disparity or whatever here. The stone we found in the snow and the gestures being connected. It just seems such a remote possibility, or in the least a very unlikely connection."

"Yes, it troubles me a little, "Lyle added. "With all the work into cultural sites I have done, I can't recall anything like it nor would I have really even conceived of it. We all know cultures interacted, but the Australian peoples seem far removed from those here where once the Silk Road was the connection from the eastern to the western world. I wonder why the obvious plan or deliberate relocation of the stone with the markings? It would also seem to have taken place a long time ago judging by the evidence around the midden. It defies any known contact with peoples from there."

Lyle continued, "Perhaps it was relocated away from the grottoes here at Dunhuang. The Silk Road was the lifeline between vastly different cultures all along its' route. As time passed, more and more traders came and more and more trouble followed. People in those times were often confronted with more change than we ourselves experience. Still…I am baffled as to the connection, and how it came to be in Australia long before European settlement or any recorded travels there from Asia. And…the stone has similar markings but we don't know why. It could be a marker or clue of some type."

"Well, the markings would indicate it may be just so," Raynie said. "The information we seek unravels like some type of puzzle requiring a particular understanding to decipher meaning. These pieces or relics are not instruments but I suggest, are more in place to assist understanding."

"Yes, but what meaning?" Jenna asked a little frustrated. "We have no real indications other than the torus and the feelings in the lower chamber."

"Synchronicity," Raynie said.

They fell silent for a few moments thinking of the events and of synchronicity without effort.

"So why does it mean we are involved?" Jake asked.

"Maybe we are simply meant to. Look at our backgrounds, and we are being told of how we can be trusted. Think for a moment. All of this is based on intentions. Our own, those of Chan and others. Perhaps it is simple."

"What do you mean Raynie?"

"Well, the mudras were an essential clue to discovery of the lower chamber. They indicated intentions and from within these intentions, a field of energy is realized. They combined to energize the lower chamber, I am sure of it. Any person with a sense of a higher self would have detected something beneath the caves long ago. So…I am thinking the access to the chamber was its' activation as well."

"So who discovered it?" Jenna asked.

The other three looked at her and she knew what they were going to say. "Chan," they replied together.

Jenna was the most technical professional of the group who at times struggled with the notions based on synchronicity.

"And next you are probably thinking Chan knew of our intentions and our backgrounds and somehow sensed we were the ones to help him."

"Probably," Lyle replied. "I suspect his life is devoted to this and his work has probably gone on for a long time, particularly in finding those who can help him. It can be reasonable to think he may have researched and cased out some candidates, including ourselves."

"Still a lot of mystery and things unexplained though. Maybe Chan knew of you two before he came up to you at Fongs?" Jake said.

"And so there shall be more for you, yes," the restaurant owner said as he stood at the door to the room. "Sorry to sneak up, I did not mean to, but you were all so involved I had to listen. I have brought you tea. No doubt you can see I too am part of this helping. My understanding does not go far past the torus for it is likely this knowledge is my only part to play. But…I have news for you. My most regular customer has left the city and also he has left another note for you to read."

"On there is written some advice for you. I have been told there is no direction, only advice. From this you must determine what you are to do. But please, continue to help us. Do not leave us at this time please."

He was almost pleading with them. They were unsure of what they were doing and where they were going, and with the added sense of danger, he was concerned they might decide to discard this journey and return to their normal lives.

"We are not leaving. I still have a few weeks before my lunar mission so there is a lot of time."

"You may think time is there for you Lyle, but be assured there are those who move against this, and those who do the same yet are unaware they are doing so. Urgency is important. No delay. Life is about to change so very much long before we thought it would. Those detonations you recently saw in your news are mere diversions and are a false threat to influence the minds of the many. This is bad indeed as it caught us un-prepared and so we have to move quickly."

"With all of this, I had overlooked the situation at home," Jake said. "John and Tobias. We should contact them. Surely they will have something to add."

"Yes, yes, contact your friends. I know what they are doing and we thank them."

"You know?"

"Of course. You know Chan, well so do I. Take this paper and study it. I will return later with supper. I ask you leave tonight just after the golden hour. This way you can have some cover of twilight."

"Leave? We cannot stay?"

"You don't need to."

"What about your customer?"

"He has his own path to follow. I will hear from him and so perhaps will you. Remain open to the connections building. Stay alert and look for intuition. It is often said in your ways to go with your gut feeling. Some call it the Wu Wei – to achieve without trying through thought. Do this."

He then left them to discuss the latest developments and to study the piece of paper. When he returned a couple of hours later, the four were still speculating on the piece of paper. Markings showed similar mudras to those they had seen in the cave, but additional markings were still eluding them in meaning.

"We cannot determine much beyond these mudras," Jake said.

"Yes similar to those in the cave. What else do you see?"

"We cannot work it out," Jenna replied, "They almost look like diagrams."

"You are correct, but what are they for?"

"We were hoping you could tell us."

"Um," he laughed a moment, "Me. I am not aware enough to interpret such work. They are beyond me. You need to trust your intuitions."

"And these," Lyle said, "I have seen something a little similar before but these are different. It is almost as if they are indicators or directions. Old maps I have seen of this part of the world have similar items indicating a path to follow. Those old maps were not just traveling maps for a journey by foot or horse - they were more like paths to discovery. I studied them some years ago and I learned they were used to guide young people to places for higher understanding and appreciation of the self, yet they would also indicate physical locations as if they were on a map."

"And how do you use your intuition when considering such things?" the owner asked.

"Um…as if the place indicated when you see it as a physical map, is a representation based on the place to go, based on the psychological map."

"But are they actual locations?" Raynie asked.

"Most certainly," the owner replied, "As you can see this is a map but it does not show a path to follow like a trail or a highway."

Lyle then expressed a self realization, "It is a path of self actualization, or a guide to show people where to go based on how aware they are and to interpret these indications as directions."

"Precisely. We all are on a journey of self-enlightenment regardless of what we do or where we are. Study this during your travels. You must leave this evening. I have word of people here other than locals and tourists."

"But we don't know where to go."

"Trust you will by the time you need to depart. I will return in an hour when you must leave."

He left them to eat supper offering them nothing else to understand the puzzle before them.

"Well, looking at this, it would seem the grottos are marked here. See these mudras and their proximity to what must be a city on the fringe of the desert. I can tell from these converging lines this is a city," Lyle said pointing to an area on the page. "To be given this at this time must only mean the journey is from this point onward."

"Then we go further west?" Jenna asked.

"Yes."

"But from here, there is a lot of remoteness with hardly any settlements."

"I know," Jake added, "I have been scanning geo-spatial information. Heading west from here will take us towards the wilderness of northwestern Tibet."

An hour later, the owner returned, "Farewell friends and many blessings for your journey. Take these supplies of food and drink I have prepared. You will not come across many vendors to help you west of here. Travel safe and remember to trust your intuitions."

The four of them thanked him for his hospitality, each embracing him warmly, and then they departed taking the old ways to the outskirts of the city. They drove in silence heading west away from Dunhuang under a vivid evening sky of dark hues and the first glimpses of stars.

"Remember back at the springs when we visited after the pagoda?" Raynie said. "Consider the event similarly. I mean, we were not exactly sure on what it meant at the time, but now with this additional information, those images and the feelings we had at the springs, mean something more."

"It helps," Jenna added. She had been struggling more than the others with the concepts they had been given. Her scientific mind still edged towards analysis of the events and to proportion them into some basis in science, but she was failing. This type of thinking or approach was relatively new to her, though not entirely. Whilst able to grasp concepts beyond those strictly scientific, her senses often returned to the orthodox thinking coming with the majority of science endeavor. She felt keen to overcome this and had been discussing it quietly with Raynie on several occasions.

"Think then Jenna. We are encouraged during this time to trust intuitions, our gut feelings. The owner also told us to look for events or information becoming apparent as a result of this trust. Maybe you could see it scientifically. Imagine there are energies or forces, or whatever…at play. Whilst we cannot exactly pinpoint their origins in a scientific way, perhaps they are scientific in the sense of deriving from a source we have been unable to detect in a measurable mathematical method."

"When we were in the caves, the mudras indicated a sense of awareness required to decipher the method to open the door to the lower chamber."

"Precisely. Also, think of faster than light, you know the science. Until you had the methods to detect material or energy beyond light speed, it was seen as a fantasy of science fiction writers and the few theoretical scientists of the time."

"Yes. But then we opened our minds to new possibilities and set about trying to prove them. String theory and extra dimensional theory are examples. Also, when quantum physics looks at the underlying energies, they see a reactive process with results corresponding to how they are being analyzed. So therein lies the potential for a state of flux, ready to be changed or realigned or…so you are saying these energetic resonance of consciousness are linked to our projected intentions."

"Yes, well at least it is what I have come up with. Perhaps this venture of ours, this entire thing, is emanating from those intentions. All people involved so far have been enacting this, making it happen without the confines associated with focusing on how. It is more a case of just is, without the need to consciously scope it in our brains. Even the eye detail on the stone Jake and I found in Australia indicates a resonance with insight."

"Like projecting a field of energy tied to your intentions based on your feelings?"

"Well, think of an old analogy. Those with guns are more likely to meet some trouble or their end by way of a gun, or a person who incessantly projects worry into their lives, can often experience the very event they are so concerned over, thus bringing it into their life. Positive people achieving success project their intentions towards achieving success, meaning they experience those things or events coinciding with fulfilling their expectations based on their intentions. This can happen in all instances whether one chooses good or bad."

"When I think of all the events so far since Lyle and I were at the Space Station, I can see there is a link. It is as if there are workings going on without any conscious effort or decision to make them happen. Coincidences often occur and we can be too casual in our acceptance of them often just putting them down to chance. But, if you look at the word co...incidence, then one could easily read it as co being cooperative, and incidence being incident. Put them together for a cooperative incidence."

"A step for you," Raynie giggled a little jabbing Jenna in the ribs.

"Yeah...I am learning to go outside the confines of orthodox scientific approach. Now I can see a similarity with this and my work on the protein strings where a catalyst enables them to transform by themselves without my instructions."

"Don't worry," Lyle added in an assuring tone, "We can all go outside the confines together. Now...the mudras linked to the statue and the images we could see in ultra violet light in the lower chamber, tie in with this even more strongly now. Our study of the images we took inside the chamber, correlate with what was on the paper the owner gave us. The gestures are to stimulate a response not a reaction. The very nature of this information is based on intentions and through these, simply allowing yourself without thinking or analyzing to see them connect, is the response through your gut feeling. I have studied several culturally significant historic sites aligning with this way of thinking. I might add, in several different continents as well."

All four of them were standing outside the vehicle in the middle of the road marveling at the majesty of the panorama surrounding them and confronted with a decision to follow their heart feelings to the peaks of the world, or continue on towards the unknown along the highway. To the south lay the great expanse of the Himalayan Mountains with an open highway stretching into the distance to be engulfed by the towering peaks of Tibet. To the west lay the desert highway, skirting the Altun Shan and Kunlun Shan mountains, passing through remote settlements on its way to Hotan and further to Kashgar at the outer western reaches of China.

Each of them went into their own world, dreaming of the scenes to the south as they entered a semi meditation state feeling the welcoming from there and how it spoke to them beyond their mind.

Finally when they had rested without intent, it was thirty minutes later and they all felt the authentic presence for continuing west along the highway to save their wanderings within the mystique of the Himalayas to another time.

Chapter 19

It was eleven at night as Steve McCray stood patiently watching the HAARP installation power up. Standing patiently had become rare for him even when in full command, and now as he was not in control of proceedings, it was an even more distant state of mind. He had been informed well enough in this instance to quell his usual anger with this issue. The team had arrived from Anchorage, linking up with those already present, and all were now testing whatever it was they had built. He still did not have precise details and this irked him, but he was now under direct orders to keep his mouth shut and command his side of the operation. Until this time he was unaccustomed to such blatant orders as he had often considered himself at least on the fringes of those in higher office who made the big decisions. This time though, he had felt the full weight of their influence and without remorse, those in high office saw him as just another field operative.

The hum of the antenna array began to build as its' transmitter wave generators came on line. It created a type of vibration in the air and all present stopped for a moment when they felt this. Five minutes later, the antenna array was operating at one hundred percent with a projection vector restricted to one thousand feet. The projections could be sent out over thousands of miles, but now it was limited to a short incursion for testing purposes.

"HAARP Alaska communications, this is HAARP Norway here. We are monitoring your situation and advise all is nominal."

This was a standard procedure for both HAARP installations where one would monitor and advise the other during all operations.

"Okay Norway," Steve responded. "Standby for power up of the booster systems."

It was his best description for the cache of weaponry the specialized team had deployed. Whilst not apparent as a weapon in appearance, it was specially designed to be exactly a weapon - unbeknown to most of the scientists who had been involved with its development and who were now carrying out deployment.

Mark Bolden and his first officer had been brought along, though neither of them really had a part to play in this latest objective. The authorities had included them in order to maintain surveillance and ensure they could not leak any information about the cargo they had brought from Japan to Alaska.

"Steve?"

"Yeah Mark?"

"What do you think of this? I mean personally not officially?"

"I think it stinks…a lot. They are up to something I am sure all of us will not like regardless of service or science or citizen. This type of thing cannot be good for any of us."

"Yes. I am in agreement there. Some of the components were developed from discoveries they made using the Hadron collider. Even a large portion of the general public knows there is some very high end work going on there. Further, I can imagine there is some unrest back home and it worries me."

"Yeah. I hate it. There is always an element of undesirable conditions attached to these operations."

"A downside to the service and to science. The powers to be don't want any information leaking out. They think the masses of consumers should go on relatively and blissfully unaware. Personally, I think there is always an element of inherent danger with blind faith in anything."

"Too right…" Steve trailed off thinking of his official position and how he himself had been blindly holding faith for officials in higher office regarding him as anything more than a field commander operative.

"This is special operations team leader to Steve McCray. We are engaging our booster system. Stand by for further advice."

Steve immediately snapped out of his thoughts, into officer mode, "Acknowledged team leader, standing by."

The area around HAARP was already aglow with the antenna array at one hundred percent. As the booster system came on line, the glow intensified to fill the entire valley surrounding the installation. At its' center, the array was too bright to look directly at with the naked eye, so all present donned their protective goggles. The glare then rose to a steady intensity as the system was extended to one hundred and fifty percent."

"This is team leader. We have established booster equilibrium and will now proceed to three hundred percent. Stand by."

A loud winding noise similar to a large electric motor rapidly increasing in pitch took over the base startling nearly all personnel. In an instant the system was taken to three hundred percent resulting in a massive lightening type spike erupting from within the glare accompanied by a sound like thunder as if matter was tearing apart. Seconds later, the glare subsided and the test was over.

"Team leader here. Test complete. Return to nominal operations."

Immediately Steve flicked a switch bypassing the booster systems and returned the array to its' regular hum and glow.

"What now?" Mark asked him as they both removed their goggles.

"Analysis of results and more secrecy I suspect."

"Scientific approach, test and analyze. How about some coffee? My shout."

"Yeah, it would be great," Steve said relaxing a little at Mark's poor joke about it being his shout. The installation was equipped with the latest human service devices and Mark's shout would be to simply speak his request to the machine and out came the coffee.

****

"One thing puzzles me," Raynie said as they drove on through the night under a brilliant starry sky. "If Chan opened up the lower chamber then I wonder why he allowed others in to examine the chamber."

"I too have thought similar," Lyle responded. "He alluded to the danger of this information in San Francisco, yet he has been instrumental into opening up this to a lot of other people. Sure, it is not been advised to the authorities yet, but those scientists back at the caves will surely say something to someone. Perhaps there are others Chan sees as worthy for seeing this information?"

"Mis-informing as well maybe." Jenna added. "There is a lot of it going on in scientific circles. With the general ignorance for the public being the policy of the authorities, we have released inaccurate information merely as a gesture to keep the masses placated."

"Yes, I thought along those lines too, Raynie said leaning towards Lyle from the rear to the front seats, "Do you think we are still being followed?" She suddenly felt angst at the prospect of this - something they had all lost a little sight of during their conversations over the meaning behind the information they had been given.

"You can count on it. I suppose Chan could be looking out for us wherever he is. He is playing two parts in this I think. One to help us help him, and the other to distract those who know some of this information. The danger he spoke of is real. From his perspective those who seek to do wrong are appreciating some of the wealth this information provides and no doubt they will strive to use it for manipulation. If he can lead them down the wrong path convincingly enough, he may be buying the time we need. By opening up the lower chamber to others, maybe he was acknowledging the awareness some have of this information. There are bound to be others like us in some ways at least. Maybe he had to calculate the risk so we could enter the chamber. Otherwise it could have remained inaccessible."

"These guns we have." Raynie still felt troubled, "When you said before about the intentions and those with guns could likely meet an end by gun I became uneasy. I know they are for our protection but they scare me."

"Well, think of it this way. A lot of people hold guns as they come from a sense of worry or even paranoia they will need to defend themselves. In this sense you could be attracting the very need. We however…well I would like to think, would only use them as a last resort. I don't feel paranoid and neither should any of us. There is an element of chance also operating here. We need to keep focus on what we are learning to guide us in conjunction with decisions we make based on our feelings. Think less of the weapons and more of what our intentions are, as hazy as they seem at the moment."

As dawn began to break, they approached the desert city of Ruoqiang. Located on the edge of the flat expanse of Taklimakan Desert, their view stretched away to the foothills of the Altun Shan Mountains. The city lights of Ruoqiang twinkled, with the distant snow laden peaks shining brilliantly in contrast to the grey and amber colors of the morning. They entered the city and found an establishment where they could buy a meal and some coffee.

"John?" Jenna was calling using her holographic phone.

"Yeah. How are you? And the others? We thought we would hear from you by now. What's going on?"

"Sorry. We have been so caught up in all this, we overlooked a few things, including calling you and Tobias."

"No problem. I figured you must be onto something. Are you looking after yourselves? Not too much action?"

"Yes and no. Yes we are looking after ourselves, and no, there has been some action. All has been mostly good but for an incident on the way to Dunhuang." She went on to describe their journey so far.

"Interesting how you mention this state of flux in respect to understanding concept," John said. "A bit un-scientific for you."

"I am getting my head...and heart around it. So how is it going?

"Good. Tobias and I have made significant progress and..."

"And what?"

"We have met two others, Asper and Lorraine. They have been helping us. It turns out they are from a group who oppose this technology overdose into everyone's lives like we do."

John went on to explain how Tobias and him had met he two women, their conversations and their trip to the high rise.

"Seems like you have been very busy...um..."

"Yeah," John interrupted. "There is a bit of a thing going on. Tobias and Asper..."

"And Lorraine?"

"Hmm...maybe," he trailed off laughing knowing Jenna was alluding to potential relations between them. "Where are you going or don't you know?"

"We don't know exactly, but we feel as if we are heading in the right direction."

"No doubt. I have always seen you as a person with direction Jenna."

"We are going to work on researching and our journey ahead a bit more today. Our stay here will be for at least twenty four hours so we can work on it."

"Okay. Anything else?"

"No, not really. Just keep your head up. We are being followed so we will contact you again next as we have our holographic phones switched off when we travel."

"You know me. Always alert. Make sure you all stay safe."

Jenna returned to the others who were seated in the café booth where Lyle and Raynie were sipping on green tea and Jake was being brought a coffee. The smells perked up her senses and she greeted them asking why they had started without her.

"The smell was too good to wait," Jake said looking up as Raynie and Lyle continued to drink.

"Well let me have some," Jenna said taking an empty cup and pouring herself some tea from the pot on the table.

"Let's go to the city gardens after this place," Jake said when they had nearly finished.

They paid their bill shortly after and left for the short walk down the street to the gardens. The view to the mountains was visible throughout the city and during their walk, their minds returned to thinking of what lay beyond in amongst the peaks and higher, upon the Plateau of Tibet.

Seated on a bench under a sprawling tree they felt a degree of relaxation amongst the setting – the first they had felt for some time.

"What a beautiful stark contrast," Raynie said breaking a temporary silence.

"A reflection of the world we live in. Such beauty at times can be in stark contrast to the goings on around," Jenna replied.

"Reflection!" Lyle exclaimed. "Jake where is the piece of paper?"

"Right here," he said taking it out of his pocket.

He handed the paper over and Lyle examined it for a moment.

"See this symbol?" He pointed to one appearing to be on the left hand side in a border surrounding a central symbol. "The symbol in the middle represents the torus surely. But…if you look at it as infinite then there is no left or right side. This depends on your natural inclination on how to hold the piece of paper. Turn it a little and presto, it appears as if it is on the bottom."

"So?"

"Well look. We thought the imagery looked like two eights side by side, an eighty-eight, just with additional lines curving off them. Until now it meant almost nothing we could determine. But looking at it now, it appears as two infinity symbols with the lines curving away. Think about this in the context of what we discussed earlier of other dimensions, including string theory and the rest."

Suddenly what he was meaning became apparent to the others. They leaned in close together and Raynie gave Jake a quick kiss on the cheek.

"Back to this," Lyle said. "See those curves as strings, links if you will between dimensions. There is infinity there and another in parallel with those lines apparently leading off to nowhere. If you see them as connections beyond what can be illustrated on a page, then you might get your mind around it."

"Why two though?" Raynie asked.

"I figure there are two because one leads to another and the other is infinity within our grasp. Our paradigm is dualistic in nature. Perhaps there are two in a dualistic balance within consciousness…black and white, good and bad, positive and negative. Beyond this a non-dual we might see the underlying energy or consciousness giving impetus to reality and actions."

"Okay so what does it mean to us now?"

"Well beyond our range of concept there could exist energies we are unable to harness. We are likely required to see existence in a different paradigm or way more attuned to the natural flow of consciousness rather than an egocentric dualism approach of definition to suit the self rather than non-dualism…if you will."

"I suppose it backs up most of what we have discussed in relation to intentions and going with gut feelings," Jake added.

"Yes, and more. We are on a journey of discovery of those energies or fields…whatever they are. This symbol is a motivation. See how the mudra here indicates motivation to seek higher understanding and to apply this learning?"

"Yeah, but you said reflection," Jenna stated feeling a little confused.

"I am getting to it. The reflection is where the other dimensions are affected by our intentions and thus set up the energies to allow them to manifest in our physical reality. So they reflect back at us similarly to how we discussed quantum physics where the particles react to being analyzed or examined."

"It is wise to say such things yet unwise to make them apparent to others who you do not know." A middle-aged man spoke gently them, and despite his quiet nature, they were all startled. "I am sorry to startle you but I can tell you are not of the mind to be concerned."

"Who are you?" Raynie asked voicing the concerns of the others. The man had come upon them silently, much to their disappointment considering their earlier vigil to remain alert.

"Only a messenger. People are watching you and watching out for you. I am of the latter." This advice immediately brought them all to a much more alert awareness of their surroundings.

"How do you know we are those whom you are watching?"

"Oh you are. I know for certain. I am here to say but one brief thing. You must keep moving. Those who oppose you…and oppose us are closer than you think. They are watching you but not so interfering as far as I can see at this moment, yet they may interfere at any time. They want you to lead them, and to inform them. You must leave this city now, this morning. Staying any longer will only strengthen their will."

"What do you mean?"

"They seek to learn how to activate energies from you. They can sense when you become more and more aware of what it is you are doing. Be assured what you are doing is of much more importance than perhaps you have considered. These people were able to track you from Dunhuang, always remaining in the background, but always there. Our efforts to stop this have proved futile."

"How did they know us?"

"They have been watching and waiting since before you left San Francisco."

"But what about the chase in the desert near Dunhuang?"

"Ah, one of their failures. Those who oppose us do not always employ the smartest individuals. It was their mistake, but still they linger. You have learned more since you arrived this morning. Take knowledge and continue west. You must reach Hotan as soon as possible. I cannot say more other than to go to Hotan and seek the Melikawat Ruins. There you will realize a great reckoning within yourselves and much more of why you are doing this."

They left the gardens immediately acting upon this advice. The drive to Hotan would be over one thousand miles and from the strangers' words, they deemed it necessary to get there as fast as possible.

The next eight hours were spent on the road as they sped along the open highway into the high sandy desert. The great Kunlun Shan Mountains gradually came into view as the road swung south towards the edge of the desert passing through the town of Minfeng. When they arrived at Keriyan Town, they decided to rest for a short time.

Stopping in the center of the town by the Keriya River, they noticed several features alluding to the distant past of the historic location. A place known for artifacts dating back over two thousand years, Lyle filled the others in about Keriyan.

"Han Dynasty artifacts are from a distant troubled past where once the talk of this region was the amount of arms and weapons its' citizens held in defense against incursion from the west and east. Also, it is rumored Marco Polo stopped here on his journey east so many centuries ago from his home in Genoa Italy - opening up the first regular contacts between east and west."

As they looked around they found a sign indicating directions towards a location featuring some of the oldest murals found anywhere. In an instant they all looked at each other. Nobody could resist the idea of a visit to a place featuring such temptation, given the information they were conceptualizing and feeling on this journey.

After a short time, they arrived at the location where they immediately set about looking at the almost ancient images. The murals though faded from the passage of time, awe struck the group as they appreciated their age, and now with their insights into such murals, they also could understand more of their meaning.

Familiar mudra gestures became apparent after only a short search. Each of them in turn took time to study the gestures, evoking a sense of remembering within them. Feelings from the lowest chamber back at the Mogao Caves arose as they stood viewing. They were more like memories of the feeling rather than the actual energy all people who had been to the lowest chamber had experienced.

Back on the road, the Kunlun Shan was now on show with many peaks to the south rising beyond six thousand meters. Jagged angles erupted into the sky from the backbone of the range, their ice clad spires piercing the deep blue of the day. Their journey traversed these mountains where spectacular scenery struck awe in each of them. By nightfall they had reached Hotan where they first went about seeking to find accommodation.

They awoke early in the morning as the sun caressed the nearby mountains with colors of orange and purple, as the last stars lingered in the western sky. Well rested, they all felt a renewed sense of purpose now having reached their next destination. After breakfast they took the short journey to the Melikawat Ruins eighteen miles south of the city. The drive through the city took them over the rivers for which Hotan was renown - the Karakash River known as the Black Jade River, and the Yurungkash known as the White Jade River. Both rivers were the lifeblood of this oasis city and for centuries had drawn desert travelers from far and wide.

The road then took them out amongst the sands, which by this time had begun to catch the early light of the day. A spectacular ochre contrast with the sand dunes radiated against the backdrop of the steep snow clad mountains further to the south, lured them on as they drew closer to their destination. Upon arrival they noticed one other group of travelers. Feeling inspired as they were, they offered warm greetings and conversed with the other group who were following the route of the old Silk Road. In the tradition of the old ways, they bade the other group safe and interesting travels and then moved on to explore.

"We too are travelers of the Silk Road," Raynie said caught in the mystery and aura of the moment.

"Indeed. We travel seeking surety as did those many centuries ago who had struggled across the wide expanses to arrive at this oasis," Jake replied. "Let us explore and discover as have many who have come before us."

As they toured the city amongst the old cascading walls, some with the remnants of ancient art representing times long since passed and others embedded with glass ornaments, they talked in earnest about what it was they were here to discover. Their directions were to proceed to the ruins and there they would learn something significant, but at this time they still were almost entirely unaware of what it might be.

At the farthest corner of the ruined city, they came across a small doorway, its' wooden door long gone. In contrast to many of the other buildings at the site, this one still had its' roof intact and so beyond the doorway was darkness except for a little light coming in through a narrow window to the rear.

Immediately upon entering, they were thrust into darkness prompting them to use personal flashlights. The air inside was surprisingly cool with an aged sandy musty aroma. Their beams flickered around the interior, across stone walls and upon the uneven floor as they looked for anything of interest. Lyle rested on something appearing to his eye in a flash, prompting him to call the others over.

Embedded in the wall just a few inches up from the floor was a round piece of green glass. As they examined it, a glow from within gradually became visible, intensifying as each second passed.

"Strange. Perhaps it has been cut into facets for the purpose of catching sunlight to make this glow," he said.

Without warning, the light suddenly intensified temporarily blinding them like a camera flash. When the flash receded with light from the sun strong enough to create a bright inner glow, an image had become visible within the core of the glass. Immediately they recognized the image as being similar to one of the images illuminated by the ultra violet light in the lowest chamber at the Mogao cave.

"This actually looks more like a mineral rather than glass. Early settlers to this area were known for their glasswork...I read it via a holographic phone query. But this could be jade, a stone revered in these parts," Lyle said thinking of the white and black jade rivers. "Dark jade known as Nephrite Jade, was very much sought after."

"Yes," Jake added. "Look closer and you can see its' crystalline form."

They all leant in to get a much closer look, the jade at once revealing its' inner form to them.

"This type of crystalline form is monoclinic, meaning it is characterized by three unequal axis with a pair of them not at right angles to the other. In a way, it is similar to our thoughts about angulations concerned with dimensional theories."

"Nephrite... derived from the old Greek word nephros meaning kidney. Hmm, how does it tie in with..." Lyle trailed off thinking more of the subject.

"I have it!" Jenna exclaimed taking over from Lyle's previous sudden outbursts. "The kidney is used to filter and cleanse and then form waste for expelling from the body."

"So you are saying?"

"Well, suggesting really. The nephrite is concerned with cleansing and filtering. Maybe in old times people saw this jade as medicinal and could have used it for kidney related problems."

"Then this room may well have been used for healing, perhaps a physicians' room."

"But the image?" Raynie interjected. "We were unable to determine its' nature back at Dunhuang and this one being almost identical."

"Then the image surely must be concerned with filtering and healing. See how it contains what looks like a human body with several intertwining lines running though it, and how it is slightly fragmented due to the crystalline structure of the jade?"

They all examined the image for a minute in silence, each one of them trying to determine some type of meaning from what they saw.

"If it is healing and cleansing then for our purposes it may be revealing something to indicate healing at a deeper level beyond just for the purpose of healthy kidneys. And...the fragments could be showing fragmented reality or positioning of the body."

"So...this could be something for eradicating, um... filtering out unhealthy elements of one's life or being," Raynie said taking over from Jenna.

"It falls in line with almost everything we have looked at so far over the past couple of weeks. All of it points to eradicating energy unhealthy for growth in awareness and intuitively going with your feelings to link up circumstances healthy for growth in awareness. This jade is a metaphor for our allowance and to cleanse the remnants of our own ills to permit the intentions to be realized through this healing."

A noise outside suddenly brought the group out of their deliberations and they quickly focused their flashlights on other parts of the room. The other group with whom they had conversed with earlier had found this part of the ruins and was endeavoring to satiate their own hunger for discovery.

"We'll just exit before you come in," Jake said aloud. "There is not much space in here."

"Okay," came a reply as the four of them began to leave.

Brilliant sunlight strained their eyes as they exited, causing them to look away from those standing outside waiting. When their sight had come around, two of the three people in the group had already entered the room, the third lingering at the doorway. Jake turned to see the man and apologized for not having made eye contact as they exited.

"Anything to see?" the man asked.

"Not much really. Just a room but interesting to see it is one of the last few in these ruins relatively still intact."

"Oh," he said losing interest in the conversation as he was keen to go inside himself.

"Do you think they will see what we saw?" Raynie asked as they walked away.

"Perhaps. Perhaps not," Jake replied. "The jade has been there a long time and I figure many people would have seen it over the centuries. I suppose it could look similar to any other relic, or maybe like these images, you need to be free in the mind to see the meaning. I suppose, with all the glass embedded in the walls about this place, one could easily overlook it as being just another piece of glass."

"Let's hope so," Lyle said. "We were warned of being watched, let's hope those watching us are not them."

About half way through the city on the way back to their vehicle, they saw another group who had recently arrived to explore.

"This place is getting crowded, let's go back to Hotan and think about all this," Jenna suggested.

"Yes I agree," Raynie replied. "I have a sense or feeling of something after we saw the jade back there."

"Me too," Jake added. "It was or should I say is, something like a slight elevation similar to what we felt in the chamber, but slightly different in a way I cannot describe."

Half an hour later they sat by the White Jade River under a tree enjoying some light refreshments. With the heat of the day upon them and even though they had rested well after the long drive to get to the city, the heat still drained them a little. They were all eager to relay their individual concepts about the feelings they had experienced when viewing the jade, but soon were lost to distraction from being tired. As their conversation waned, they began to relax, enjoying the romance of being in a desert oasis and to spend some time as couples do.

"Jake!" Raynie called out to him from the shade of the tree as he sat by the riverbank.

"Yeah?"

"Come on. Lyle and Jenna are going to take a walking tour around the city. Take some time out from this and do a bit of a tourist thing. Let's join them."

"Can't it wait? I am feeling the driving stint a bit still. Can we catch up with them?"

"What's wrong?"

"Nothing really. I just feel like day dreaming for a while."

"Oh…okay, I'll tell them."

An hour later, Raynie and Jake were walking along the riverbank on their way to meeting the others at a pre-arranged place.

"The cultural museum is just up here a little way," Raynie said as they walked holding hands.

"Cool. I'm feeling hot from this walking."

"Are you sure you are alright?"

"Yeah...well sort of. It feels like I could be coming down with something."

"Really darling. You should have told me earlier."

"I didn't know. I mean I just thought it was a bit of fatigue. Now I am not so sure."

A moment later he fainted and nearly pulled Raynie to the ground with him.

"Oh no! Jake are you alright?" For a moment there was no response and Raynie became very concerned.

"I am here, but it feels like I am getting a hellish fever."

"I'll call the others." They had decided to switch their holographic phones on when separated. "Jenna. It's Jake. He has fainted. Can you meet us by the river? Come quickly!"

She took both of Jakes hands and helped him to his feet before leading him to some shade out of the midday sun. Five minutes later Lyle and Jenna arrived. They both set about immediately tending Jake to assess his condition.

"I don't know what it is," he replied to their inquiries. "Suddenly it seemed to sweep over me. I felt a little run down prior, but this just came on in a rush."

Over the fifteen minutes the three others watched over Jake as his condition began to worsen. The moment they agreed Jake needed medical attention, Lyle left them to bring their vehicle so they could take Jake to a doctor.

"You have been poisoned," the doctor said after having examined and then stabilized Jake's condition.

"Poisoned?" Raynie replied, "But how?"

"It is a slow release poison taking affect over a few days and then begins to come on strong in a short period of time. You might have had a drink, or something to eat. Not to worry so much, as it is not a fatal poison. It is just something to keep you out of action for a day or so."

"Where could it have happened?" Raynie thought out aloud. For was while they sat next to Jake's bed after the doctor had left to attend other patients. "I cannot figure out where Jake was poisoned because we are not affected."

"What about the coffee in Ruoqiang? You two were having green tea and when I returned after calling John and Tobias, Jake was drinking a cup of coffee. I joined you two in having a cup of tea," Jenna suggested.

"But why poison Jake? We were told to move on quickly from Ruoqiang as there were people watching us. The man told us they were only watching us."

"Maybe they thought they could slow us down by making just one of us fall ill," Lyle proposed. "It would seem to be a fever or the like and arouse little suspicion. Perhaps they were losing track of us and needed to stall us, and if so, it worked alright. The doctor said it would stall Jake for a day or two. We are going to have to stay here longer than we anticipated."

"What do you mean?" Raynie asked him. "We did not have any specific direction or place to go anyway."

"Yes we did."

"Huh?"

"Jenna and I came across something woven into an old carpet at the cultural museum and lo and behold, there was Ch… No wait, I think we should discuss this somewhere else."

Raynie said she would stay with Jake overnight during his recovery and the others agreed, deciding to work on the information they had learned at the museum, and then catch up the next morning.

During the evening in Hotan, there was a traditional festival celebrating the history of the Silk Road. Hotan was a city influenced by different cultures through time, settled by Buddhists in its' earliest period, then by Muslims, and then Chinese in the later period. The festival combined the riches of all these cultures in a celebration of diversity and of resilience against the harsh desert surrounding the oasis. Traditional costumes, art works, and dancing filled the main streets casting a shimmering aura over the rivers meeting at the city center. Food vendors bestowed their wares for all to try as tourists and locals joined in the atmosphere of dancing, singing, and eating. Jenna and Lyle took this opportunity to lose themselves in the crowd, enjoying each other's company as they joined in with the festival atmosphere. Despite their elated mood, they remained vigilant for anything suspicious, and of course thought of Jake's recovery.

By midnight they were tired and slightly intoxicated from the party, so they decided to return to their motel room. With their minds full of swirling images they embraced and spent some hours expressing their affections.

Early next morning they returned to the hospital to find Raynie and Jake eating breakfast with Jake appearing in much better health.

"Looking much better today," Jenna said as they entered the room.

"Oh yes. Jake is getting back to his usual self. The doctor said he can be discharged today as the poison does was not as strong as he initially thought," Raynie replied.

"Mmm," Jake added through a mouthful of food.

"Good to see. Lyle and I have some news concerning Chan to discuss. So as soon as you can, let's leave this place and get moving."

"Good news?" Jake asked having finished his meal.

"Very good news," Lyle replied. "But I'll do the driving. Even with the automatics, the nature of these roads means it is best we continue on driving manually."

"This place is really a step back in time," Jenna said when they were on their way an hour and a half later. "Sure, they have some technology, but this place is far away from the big cities. It is as if people here still live as they have done for many centuries."

"Well at least some old world charm can still be found," Raynie replied, her love for the character of the past never ceasing. "Um, where are we going?"

"Kashi or Kashgar depending on where you are from. And from there we fly," Lyle announced. The trip ahead to their final destination in China was around four hundred miles, a distance they could easily cover during the day.

"Kashgar is the most western city of any size in China," Jake said as he studied a holographic image. West from there is Kyrgyzstan then onto the Middle East."

"Not so far," Jenna replied keen to get the conversation going about what she and Lyle had discovered at the cultural museum the day before. "We will almost make it there but not quite."

"So tell us about yesterday, ours was awful."

"Well, after arriving at the museum we went in just to look around casually, like tourists do. Lyle was concerned about maintaining some type of cover, so we went in as a couple appearing as if they had recently fallen in love…"

"Insufficient cover," Raynie said with a giggle. "Jake and I have noticed how you two feel. You look in love."

"Really. I thought with our journey and its' events, we would have looked otherwise a bit pre-occupied."

"Your eyes and how you look at each other is the tell-all sign. So what was Chan doing there?"

"Yeah, back on topic," Lyle interjected feeling a little bashful at this discussion.

"We went to the museum and came across an old hand woven carpet. The Hotan province aside from its' jade, is also known for intricate woven carpets. Anyway, we saw an image in the carpet…not at first, but after a little while. Gradually it became apparent to us as if we were staring through the entire carpet or staying just out of focus. I wondered if it was just from staring at it for a while, but no, there was the image."

"Of?"

"A mudra with giving hands. These clues do indicate a cleansing or healing in a holistic sense where it is given in the human spirit. I say spirit meaning our intentions or feelings, except this time the image stood out with such reverence we were slightly taken aback. It was telling us how to activate this cleansing as a way of being able to be even more in touch with our intentions as authentic consciousness. Similar to the mudras we have seen, it was a gesture, a nuance as if to light the way before us. As confusing as it may seem, we immediately related it back to trusting your gut feeling."

"And Chan?"

"Typical to his usual ways, he suddenly arrived on the scene out of nowhere. He had been following us and had seen Jenna and I go to the museum. These coincidental meetings are determined by our intentions and our actions he said. You have done well to make these connections here in Hotan by seeing the image before you, as many others could not. He said it was important for us to feel the effects from the jade and to again see and sense feeling from the imagery woven into the carpet. We were right he told us – it did take a sense of detachment from our own selves where we were authentically in the moment. Then he asked where you two were, so we told him the full story. He was alarmed at this and again took to us urgently of our need to travel and continue this journey. It was only those seeing what we saw, who could in turn help activate something. He was unclear other than to say it is important for us as we have the capacity to then go on to share this activation…whatever it is."

"Well, we did want to talk about how we felt at the ruins. So I guess it sums it up." The others exchanged looks as if to confirm Raynie's thoughts. "So why are we going to Kashgar?" she asked.

"He told us to go there and to then take flight out of China," Jenna replied. "Again and much to my amusement, he gave us some paper with information. It has the image we saw in the carpet so you two can see it. Chan gave us this as he told us to keep viewing the image to retain it very much at the forefront of our minds and expectations as we travel to Europe. It will also help our feelings and how we align these through our intentions and then actions."

"Are the directions ambiguous as per usual?" Jake asked.

"See for yourself," Jenna replied handing the paper to Jake.

"Hmm, somewhat, but at least it indicates a city."

China's western gateway of Kashgar had become a shining example of their nation to the world of the Middle-East. In contrast to the sparse environment the travelers had encountered since before journeying to Dunhuang, this city featured many of the latest technological advances. Its' centerpiece was a spectacular high-rise of nine towers linked together and reaching over one hundred stories set in contrast amongst the remnants of the old city from times past.

Adorned with features similar to those the travelers had seen in the capital, it sparkled with lights and ornamental fixtures bewildering them at first when they arrived at the city fringe after driving without stopping most of the day.

Entranced with the sight, they stared at the sheer beauty of what appeared like a city from a fantasy story, with the old diverse historic buildings surrounding the city giving way to the jewel-like cluster at the center.

Lyle drove them to the airport without delay and purchased tickets for the next available HyperJet flight. He had been driving all day as Jake needed more time to recover properly. Two hours later they were comfortably seated cruising at mach four and an altitude of seventy thousand feet on their way to Vienna, Austria.

Chapter 20

The Agent of the authorities looked on in disgust. He was never one to think kindly of people in general, and seeing John, Tobias, Asper, and Lorraine enjoying themselves drinking at the wharves, made him hate them. Was it jealousy? Did he have a bad moment in his history making him feel this way? There was no reason for hatred aside from his own feelings he generally carried around. There was no history, no jealousy, nothing. He had always been in the service and the service had always been in him. Not a day went by where he would long for another life - he was committed, or so he thought.

He considered hate as part of his job and he was an expert at forming strong dislikes towards people, objects, and places. San Francisco with its' checkered history was far from the sterility found at authority central and he actively went about the streets looking for faces he could hate.

He hated the smiling couples in love strolling along the foreshore. He hated China Town with its' colorful adornments and exotic foods. He hated the way people went about their business blissfully unaware people like him were there to make their lives difficult should the need arise. He wanted people to fear him and for what he stood for, but times had not been right for his way of thinking, until now.

He could feel, something rare for him, where soon his presence and those of his superiors would bear down upon the public and institute a new way of life. Soon those distasteful frivolous ways of this city would become sterile like it was at headquarters. Then they would taste it. Taste the bland formal way of life concerned only with order and compliance. Taste the brunt of being forced to submit which would make them all cry. Yes. He wanted them to cry.

Cry for what they would lose and cry for their separation from what they revered as being individual. He even wanted most of the lights to change. Sick of the colour - the cold grey lights from the deepest passageways underground at headquarters made him feel in control. No distraction from obligation and duty. He had no sense other than to be a part of the great machine soon to be planet Earth.

Despite his hatred for most technology used for pathetic services like providing entertainment and comfort, he wanted to roll out the technology machine the world would soon become. His place in the machine was yet to be decided but he knew he would reach a suitable controlling place where he would make others beg for his forgiveness, cry as they would at the brutality of his actions, and despair at the outlook and future in store for them. He would break them.

His eyes never faltered as he looked for any sign providing him with information. He had become an expert at reading people's faces. He could tell when they were lying and especially when they were frightened. Though not a naturally aggressive man due to his small physical stature, he knew how people would react at the wrong end of a weapon and this made him smirk. 'Screw them,' he thought seeing the two couples kiss.

He was getting pissed. Angry at the ambivalence between his situation and their apparent happiness, he vowed he would make it especially hard for them if ever he were to get them into interrogation.

The hard line of interrogation excited him. To-date it had only been practice, setting everything up for real life situations and he often salivated at the prospect of seeing people collapse into emotional disarray whenever he wanted.

'Bloody do something,' he thought.

Impatience was not a virtue for him - it was part of life. His concerns were to get people and get them fast. He sought revenge for nothing specific, but he wanted revenge on everyone who was not like him - on anyone who could not see the hard line of authority to which he was committed.

He continued to watch relentlessly never taking his eyes away for a second. They could not see him, nor would they ever know of his presence, and this he cherished for he had become diligent at concealment and maintaining a suitable cover for any operation. This was his second mission. The first had ended up at a dead end and this pissed him greatly. Now he sought to make up for the useless mission through doubling his efforts to ensure a convincing victory over these people. He had followed them into the high-rise and through the city after, and now watched them wanting to close in for a kill.

Little did this Agent know through his warped sense of smugness, he too was being watched. Little did he know he had also been tracked across the city.

A few hours passed by as he watched the four of them become inebriated with the more they drank.

'Stupid bloody alcohol!' He hated drinking too.

Anything to distract away from service and compliance was worthy of his hate, especially the inane rants and laugher of intoxicated people. His only distraction was to voice regular status update reports through to headquarters via secret communications, in order to file a complete history of his movements, actions, and any information relevant to the case.

He was filing the latest update when he noticed something on John's face. It was a look in defiance of the man's appearance. As stout and well built he was, John suddenly appeared to become soft and emotional. The Agent especially hated such things. Why should a strong man ever become weak enough to have and then show emotion?

"I will break you, you soft bastard," he whispered to himself. "I will bring you to your knees and you will tell me all I need to know." He smiled but only on one side of his mouth. He was incapable of a real smile - the only time he came close was when he thought of breaking people.

He stayed on until the two couples left the bar and departed for the wooden house where they were staying - following them was easy. The many people about the streets on a night like this gave him plenty of cover and to complete the picture, he acted a little drunk himself. Others would only see him as a single person probably making their way home drunk. But the person who watched him knew otherwise.

Trained to be an expert at covert operations he kept a good distance from the Agent. His mission was to see John and Tobias were not interfered with. Asper had informed him about their residence, their contacts, almost everything she knew outside personal information. He was part of the same group as the two women and he himself had prepared for the Agent.

The Agent skulked around the garden outside the house for a minute or two after the couples had gone inside. He was getting tired of this. Nothing had really happened providing any more to work on than he already had, making him more and more pissed as the night went on. Barely able to contain his anger, he moved on from the house but hid not far away so he could be in surveillance should anyone appear outside. He would track them to the ends of the Earth if necessary.

As dawn approached he was feeling a little tired yet still determined to maintain surveillance, when the two women suddenly appeared at the front door. They were carrying something.

'What do you have there?' he thought. 'I'll find out.'

He saw the two women depart and head to the AeroTram station just down the street. He decided to follow them and at least see the destination for the tram they would catch. After, he would return to stake out the house. Little did he realize his error.

Before he could take a dozen steps a man was upon him and punched him so hard he was knocked out.

"Do you have no respect for ladies or people in general? Bloody peeping Tom," the man said as he gazed at the Agent out cold on the edge of the pavement.

He left the scene and approached the wooden house, leaving the Agent lying askew on the ground. A few people passing by glanced momentarily at him, but to them he appeared as if he was a drunk who just could not make it home from the night before.

"Who is it?" John said after he had heard knocking three times.

"Someone you need to talk to," was the reply.

John came to the door and looked at the image on the monitor - he did not recognize the man. "What is it?"

"I know Asper and Lorraine."

"Oh. Then come in." John opened the door to meet the man. He was at least six feet eight inches tall, a few inches taller than John. "Gee mate, you're a mountain, come in."

The man laughed at John's remark, "Thank you, I have some news." He went inside with John who introduced Tobias. "Nice to talk to you…after watching you for the past week, I'm Mike."

"What!" John immediately became highly suspicious.

"Relax. I've been looking after you."

"What do you mean?"

"Yeah. We are pretty good at it ourselves," Tobias added.

"As I said, I know Asper and Lorraine. We work for the same group."

This immediately eased the situation so he continued.

"When Asper and Lorraine found you two, they immediately requested I get on the case, as backup you could say. So…after they knew enough about you, my situation changed from following you, to keeping an eye out for you. No doubt you are taking measures to be secure, considering what you are doing. Well despite your efforts there are Agents out there also watching what you are doing. Your visit the other day to see Raman. Well, there was one tracking you then."

"The passerby when we were at his door," John said, confident he was right.

"The exact person. Well I just took a little care of him no more than ten minutes ago. In fact, he had been watching you all last night down at the wharves."

"Gee…"

"Yeah, there is more. He managed to follow you back here and now they are going to know a lot more about you. Those bastards report in every ten minutes or so."

"We have to move, and now!"

"What about the others?" Tobias asked.

"They already know. I called them just before I took the Agent out. They are on standby at…"

"Don't say. Tell us on the way there."

Tobias set about packing all they needed as supplies and John packed up all his tech gear. Within ten minutes all three men were ready and then left the house locked, before they made their way onto the streets.

"No vehicle, we are on foot. See there?" Mike pointed at a person lying still on the ground behind a hedge. "It's the Agent. He'll be okay. I just knocked him out. We should go in the opposite direction. From what I could see, he was working alone, but will still need to be very alert. If he doesn't report in within an hour, the authorities will send someone after him."

"But you said he reports in every ten minutes."

"They also have a window where if an Agent does not report, they give them an hour before any alarm bells ring. They figure an Agent could be onto something and they allow some flexibility, but not much. We need to be clear of the city as soon as possible."

"Where will we go?"

"Way out of the city to Lake Tahoe. I have a friend with a cabin in the Sierra Nevada Mountains on the east side. He knows we are coming sometime. I'll call him as we walk and tell him it is today."

They walked on taking a roundabout route towards the city center. At California Avenue they stopped a moment to discuss what had been said about arriving at Lake Tahoe today.

"He's good. Security is his thing and he advised we are good to go. Just to make sure we are careful leaving San Francisco."

By the time they reached the city center they had decided to take the public tube to Sacramento where Mike knew of a vehicle they could use for the rest of the journey. Public transport was one of the fastest ways for land-based travel. Most suspended roadways linking cities also included separate lanes for public carriages. Each being cylindrical in shape, they operated on a levitation track where speeds of three hundred miles per hour were common. The trip to Sacramento took less than an hour, giving the three men time to discuss the situation and what they could do at Tahoe.

"So we meet up with Asper and Lorraine in South Lake and then we continue east to my friends' cabin," Mike said as they disembarked the carriage.

"What is his name?" John asked.

"Ryan. We call him the little king…of security. If there is something to know, he knows it."

"I wonder why we haven't met him previously."

"Cannot say other than he has only been in contact with our group. He is a reclusive type of person. You will like him John. I am sure you two can work on this and get results."

"Yeah, after telling us about the Agent, a lot of new ideas and worries have entered my mind."

"Hmm…a lot more work ahead of you. Any ideas yet?"

"Well it seems as though there are systems completely outside of the chip thing. We are going to need information from the inside on what they are and their capacity."

After arriving at the South Lake Tahoe commercial center, they made a quick holographic phone call to confirm a meeting point to reconnect with Asper and Lorraine.

"We'll take the turn off to Jackson, then it is about another hour through the forest from there," Mike said when they had met up with the two women. "When we arrive, I suggest we just take it easy, relax for a while, and then we can get down to business. The forest will have a good effect on you, and with long views to the ranges, you can take it in. Soak up some energy."

"Sounds great," both Asper and Lorraine said together.

"I am going to have to leave you there. I cannot stay. There are still too many Agents out there for my liking. In fact, one is too many. I'll be going back to the coast to see if I can find some."

Ryan was waiting outside for them, appearing to be in a meditative like state. "Just soaking it in," he said getting up. "You want to do this type of thing up here. Not much else around here than your own self, which is how I like it. Gives me the room to focus on what I need to do."

He was right as the effect became immediately apparent - first the smell of pine in the summer sun, and then the clarity of the air and sky. With introductions out of the way, and after a farewell to Mike, the four of them decided to relax around the cabin leaving Ryan to do what he did.

****

The Caspian Sea glittered in the sunlight offering an amazing view for the travelers as the HyperJet continued towards Europe. On an indirect route, the flight path took them over the northern end of the inland sea after crossing the sparsely populated area of southeast Kazakhstan. They were just over an hour into the flight and had been talking earnestly about what they might find in Vienna, when the spectacle brought a hush to their conversation. Other passengers also disengaged from chatting to gaze out the windows at the water sixty thousand feet below.

"It is so beautiful and so steeped in history," Raynie said finally breaking their silence.

"It is Raynie," Lyle replied. "There is a long history of many conflicts through the centuries in these places. Keep watching. We will soon fly into Russian airspace."

The others leaned closer to the windows wondering what Lyle was referring to. Within a few minutes they saw a bright flash.

"What was it?" Raynie asked.

"It is the beacon of the Russian Federation. The Russian authorities installed the beacon to be seen by all on the ground and in the air. When you see the flash, you know you are now in Russia."

"But it is just a light isn't it?"

"Well yes and no. If you see it at ground level, the light is only a small part. The center of the city is like Kashgar and the light is atop a grand central complex of eleven interlinked towers."

Within an hour, their flight was flying over the Black Sea.

"Ladies and Gentlemen, this is your captain speaking. We are preparing for deceleration from mach four in twenty minutes. Please be returned to your seats and engage restraining devices by this time."

Deceleration for the HyperJet commenced as scheduled gradually losing altitude over Romania and Hungary in preparation for landing in eastern Austria. As the jet descended, two sonic booms sounded as it went sub-sonic on approach to Vienna International Airport.

****

Emotion cut deep, very deep. Witnessing the crushing of his son's spirit hurt him to the very core. He was not someone who would normally let such emotions flow, but this time, he could not hold it back. Breathing in gasps, his mind took him to images where his son's enthusiasm for life was often met with bluntness, negating it for him and making his own plight as a child even more difficult. How it hurt to see the innocence of his son taken away through the anger and disdain brought upon him.

Such adult concepts, as useless as they are, were nevertheless action…forced upon him and thus his innocence was stolen. His right to be an inquiring learning child, his right to express himself as himself, his right to feel validated and thus be encouraged, taken away so very often through hurt and through selfishness. The look of sadness on his son's face hurt him again, and again with each grasping breath.

How cruel… His heart was almost beating out of his chest as if it was reaching out to his son itself, all those miles distant. It strained against his ribs wanting to be there, to protect and to love, yet it was bound inside its' own cage and he would have to rely purely on its' signal covering the tyranny of distance and reaching out to his son. To give, to give was all he could think. What else could he do? So apart yet in his own heart always connected. His feelings subsided a little as he started to think of ways to at least minimize this for good. It was time to change tactics and make a move to see this put right. His son had everything to live for and he wanted to show him this.

Then, as if to start again, the memories of their times together and the spirit they share welled up, shortening his breath. He knew he was strong, as he had been to this place before. Quelling the expression of his feelings, he struggled between giving them all they deserved and retaining some composure. He knew there was strength in expression and never any shame, so he held his head high as they gave strength to him. Such strength goes beyond anything thrown at his son to crush his son's spirit, and he could feel it. He would change this - he would have to break through. The essence in him, is essence in me, we are one.

John awoke from his dream struggling with what had just happened. More than a dream, it was almost identical to an experience he had some years before. He had witnessed the suppression and attempts at submission exerted on his only son. He had gone through the tearing emotion because he cared for him and loved him so much. He had acted, and it was successful. The bond they shared was strengthened even further as his son progressed towards adulthood. Showing him, teaching him, and helping him find himself without such negative incursions stealing his son's rights to himself, was his focus and he felt honored to give to his son what he could...from respect as well as love.

But why this, now? As he awoke further, he remembered where he was. He was lying under a shady pine outside a cabin in the Sierra Nevada Mountains on a fine late spring day. He drew a deep breath to steady himself, feeling clarity coming from the pine scent and the freshness of the air. He looked around to see he was alone. His companions were sitting inside the cabin having a meal with Ryan. Another breath and he could smell what it was they were eating. Realizing his own deep hunger at this time, the smell motivated him to get up and go inside.

"Hi sleepy," Lorraine said as he walked in.

"Hmm. Yeah...hungry."

"Come eat," Ryan offered him a place at the table by indicating with his hand.

"Strange dreams," he said gathering food onto his plate from several dishes in the center of the table.

"You too."

"And us," added Tobias and Asper together.

"It's this place," Ryan added. "It does things to you."

"Yeah, must be. I had a dream about my son. It felt real enough and was basically a recollection of an experience I had. The dream and the experience were both a very emotional time."

"Me too," Lorraine added. "Except mine was to do with my mother and a health scare she had a few years back. She fully recovered though. Where is your son?"

"Living in London."

"They seem like they were very emotionally charged dreams. Tobias and I discussed ours, which were both very similar and emotional." Asper had always been one to take dreams quite seriously, thinking they could often be connections to the truly conscious mind.

"It sounds like they may have been key emotional and insightful times for you," Ryan said. "I do a lot of meditation here at the cabin. Like you, I have gone through similar experiences during these past few years since I moved here. Cannot say there is anything remarkable about the place, other than the obvious serenity and beauty of the mountains and forests. They might contribute to opening the mind and clearing away thoughts, thus revealing emotions and feelings. I have often thought it is about a recollection within where you gained strength and vision about solving difficult situations."

"Hmm...we need some now with this security tech," John said changing the topic.

"Yeah. I thought we could do some of work tonight. I have some gear here you will like John," Ryan said to him with a calm smiling face.

After dinner, they all adjourned to Ryan's workshop.

"Here is the latest I have on the identification chip authentication thing to deal with..."

"Look!" Asper exclaimed interrupting him and pointing to the only window in the workshop. The others turned to see what it was gaining her attention. Sitting in a tree immediately outside the window was a large Owl. Considered in some cultures as being a creature of wisdom, the Owl was staring at them through its' large round eyes. Its gaze did not even falter when they moved - remaining directly fixed on them.

"Is it a real Owl? Tobias asked.

"What do you mean?"

"Sure it is not a robotic surveillance Owl?"

The others except Ryan laughed at his joke. "Whilst I know it isn't, don't dismiss the possibility," he said.

"Really?"

"Yeah really. The authorities have some decent robotics at their disposal. So much so, I have taken steps to install automatic scanning equipment for such a thing. They could easily disguise the tech with any type of animal they chose, but an Owl would be a better choice than a Coyote for instance, purely based on their nature."

"So then perhaps the Owl could be confirming a bit of wisdom taking place. It is said in the Native American cultures and others, when you see an animal, you should take notice of its presence and what it could mean for you by the type of animal you see," Lorraine said.

"Let's hope so. It seems as though we are increasingly coming up against some pretty tough issues to overcome, so some wisdom would be a reassuring thing."

"Not to mention those dreams we had this afternoon."

"Um…yes mention them," Ryan said. "And remember them for they can be a metaphor of your mind where free of ego, truth comes without effort."

Chapter 21

The Agent had awoken on the street, coming to in the heat of the midday sun. After clearing away his grogginess, his anger and hatred returned. He began to hate himself for having made such a simple mistake resulting in him losing contact with those he was tracking. His thoughts then turned to reporting in to headquarters. As he was about to engage his communicator, two other Agents were upon him, gaining his attention with a tap on the shoulder from behind. He knew what it meant. He would have to report contact had been lost and such failures were looked upon with scorn. There would be no punishment, but if he did it again, he was sure there would be.

"Come with us," one of them said, beginning to lead him away from the scene. The two other Agents took him to nearby vehicle and they drove off. An onboard automatic notification system told all other vehicles on the road to get out of the way, ensuring it priority amongst the city traffic.

As he rode along, his saw the faces of those on the street turn to see the vehicle as it drove by. He felt a little more at ease after his failure as his hatred returned and he thought of what was to come. They would all notice him and other Agents soon enough. They would not be able to avoid it.

He spoke to the other two, "See them?"

"Mm," was the only reply.

"They will be ours soon."

"Yes, but no more screw-ups on your part," one of them said. "Your mistake is a lot bigger than you think. Your failure means there are people operating out there who are onto us. Only an idiot would allow such a thing to occur."

'Screw you,' the Agent thought, his hatred turning to the other Agent who had just chided him, 'I'll be your boss some day and then we will see who is so smug.'

Upon arrival at headquarters, the vehicle descended twenty stories underground via an elevator equipped for the task of moving machines and people. Inside there were personnel everywhere at monitoring stations, having strategy meetings, and others housed in extravagant offices - obviously the superiors. The authorities had ramped up their efforts, sparing no cost in resources and people. They were determined all should proceed as planned and the unassuming public would fit into place.

Yet uncertainty was building and little did the public know events had been carefully orchestrated for the very purpose of distraction away from what was actually happening.

The Agent was escorted to Superior Officer One who was sitting at a desk going though some holographic data.

"Sit," was all she said.

She continued to analyze the information for another minute before speaking again.

"Lucky for you all hope is not lost. It seems as though your earlier reports from last night, have given us sufficient information to continue tracking these potential fugitives. Thus, you will remain on this case. Take this data and analyze every aspect. It contains some leads on the types this group would associate with. Don't fail this time."

She dismissed him without any further words, and he left the office returning to his desk to see what he could do.

His desk was located amongst a hundred others, all busy with other Agents. He passed the canteen and despite his hunger, he decided to focus on the work he had to do, his swelling hatred providing the sustenance he required.

'How bloody dare they put him through such indignation,' he thought. Condescendence was something he dished out. To be addressed in such a way humiliated him and this made him determined more than ever to track the dissidents down and have them submit to his brand of humiliation. Agent Eight was his designation and hatred was his constitution. Agent Eight was a megalomaniac.

****

The second full test of the HAARP booster system was about to take place. This time, the specialized team had set up a mock system on which they would directly apply the new booster settings. Steve was on standby, keen to get underway and let them finish so he could return to overall command of the installation, or so he thought.

He would soon be replaced, as it was standard practice now for senior officers to be discharged from duties once they had reached a certain level of knowledge about what was going on.

Steve watched as the system came on line with the flash and accompanying sound. He saw operatives from the team busily tending to the mock system projected as a gigantic holographic image coming from a large round base.

Mark was again beside him.

"They can create a network mimicking any component of central systems," he told Steve noticing his puzzled look.

"Oh. What does it do?"

"Basically it is an over ride. This setup has the capacity to take over and run normal operations or block them."

"But why?"

"Mystery to me. I only know of the component we brought here on the Enceladus. Initially it was developed as an emergency responder for use if a natural disaster occurs and systems need to be brought back online immediately. My team was testing it along the coast of Japan where they are earthquake prone. Aside, I can only imagine how they are using it here. Definitely some modifications have been made though."

"Why do you say so?"

"My hunch is it will be used on a much larger scale and with it hooked up to the HAARP antenna array, it could have affect over a large area both physically and in virtual space."

"Sounds like crap to me, sorry. But what reason do they have to align it with this semi-military antenna? This thing is used for atmospheric harmonics creating pattern stability for affecting the weather. I don't see any sense in boosting it, no need as the system has been working fine for years."

"We are both pretty much in the dark on this and I don't count on it being anything but secretive. I was not allowed to know about any details until I arrived here at the installation."

"Yeah, those bastards over there have only just kept me in the loop too. Like I am only told enough to keep this place operating, but really know very little."

A minute later the test was finished and operations returned to normal. Mark left Steve to his duties, deciding to take a walk and think about what he was doing, or not doing, and how long he would be stationed at HAARP. His duties had tapered off almost completely, where his only responsibility now was being there as backup should anything go wrong with the responder. Walking along the perimeter of the array, he noticed there was another much smaller team doing something to the main connections in place for the booster system. Until now he had been unaware of their presence, so he took a moment to watch what they were doing. It appeared as though they were upgrading the actual hardware links, something he thought was un-necessary. 'Why the much larger capacity?' he thought.

One of the team suddenly turned, as if he knew someone was watching them. Immediately he was on his communicator telling his superior officer of what was going on. Mark now knew too much. The smaller team had been working under the cover of an operating array normally off limits to all personnel. Responding to the communications from the field, a small unit immediately dispatched for Mark's location.

When they reached him, he had walked to the opposite corner of the array to the operations buildings, so they were able to take him off the site without anyone else knowing it had happened. They escorted him directly to an waiting fully automated vehicle for a ride to Anchorage and subsequent re-assignment.

****

Since arriving in Vienna, the four travelers had been taking in the tourist sites around the city, again uncertain about what they should do next. On the second day after a meal of traditional Austrian cuisine, they decided to visit the museum dedicated to the city's renowned musical genius Mozart - a prolific eighteenth century composer. Recognition of Mozart's genius was displayed throughout the museum interior via audiovisual holographic installations with one featuring a life-sized rendition of the composer at work, and another showing concerts where his works wooed audiences. Traditional art pieces of busts, paintings, and original musical scores were also available for visitors.

Whilst at the section displaying the original scores of Mozart's hand written masterpieces, Lyle spoke about the significance music had played across all cultures from the ancient to the modern, "It is within the harmonic frequencies and vibrations where a lot of mystery resides."

"What do you mean?" Jake asked.

"Consider the effect music has on all people and think of their attributes as hypnotic in some instances, joyous, painful, expressive of cultural values, and messages some sent as a means of communication. These are all harmonic nuances yet with a common theme – feeling. The expression of feeling and of the sub-conscious, either one or the other, or both, are always a centerpiece behind the motivation to create music. Mozart, along with other composers of the era were projecting this. As European civilization moved beyond the renaissance period and began to develop more complex structures, so too did their music. Prior to these composers coming onto the scene, music had been bereft of structure approaching anything like we see here in these historical pieces, and was mostly created to please those in royalty and high office."

"Amongst the general population, there had been little need for music to appeal to the senses, as most were too busy with the struggle of survival. And, what makes Mozart and other geniuses like Beethoven who was deaf stand out so much, is the fact they were amongst the first to really explore the properties of a musical score to the effect where it would be complimentary to people's lives. Through delivery of such well-attuned works, these composers established the standard on which a lot of music has been based on since, hence their reverence now as genius."

"There has even been scientific studies into the fields of harmonics and the effects not only on people but on the vibration of matter itself," Jenna added. "Sound is attributed now to much more than previously considered and so we in the scientific world, have taken this into account during the development of new mechanics, devices and the like. It all began with the early research into Cymatics - the study of visual sound and corresponding vibrations."

"Precisely. Since the beginning of this century a lot of advances have been made in this area and so it has provided a fresh insight into the significance of music in all cultures. Vienna was one of the centers for this during Mozart's time as it was a hub of cultural development and refinement in the day."

"There was the period during the late twentieth and early this century where the world largely overlooked the value of sound on everyday life and on the world. During the years of struggle when it became evident oil was no longer a long-term energy option from both a reserves and pollution perspective, people and companies were very reluctant to consider this, as they were all too concerned with how it might impact upon the convenience factor in daily life."

"One side espoused machines to make life easier, and the other were not interested in taking them up in mass consumption. Can you believe there was so much noise in the first three decades of the twenty first century, pioneers of this research looked upon society in disgust at how there was a machine to do everything, and all running on a very finite polluting energy source. These machines were very noisy amongst the growing throng of vehicle, media, and industrial noise. People were being affected but they were not even considering how it could influence their lives and thinking. Thankfully the research prevailed and we moved into the quieter times shortly thereafter, thus reconstituting an element of harmony back into society, but only an element. The notion of truly harmonious societies is still as distant as it ever was."

Lyle continued speaking seeing the others retaining a high level of interest, "With this renaissance of a type, the masters like Mozart gained recognition for the value of their works. The science on this type of thing is very solid. We take it very seriously, so much in fact, entire scientific divisions were established to continue research into the properties of sound and how it affects nearly everything we see…or hear."

"Maybe it is why I often like the soft sounds associated with the solitude I sometimes seek," Raynie added. "It is not like I am a loner, I just appreciate the aspect of how relative silence is in fact not so at all, for if you take the time to listen when all seems quiet, it has an effect something like putting you in touch with the very essence of reality around you."

"So very true…" spoke a voice from behind the group. "And now with this in mind, you need to study the other information I provided on the last piece of paper I gave you."

"Chan!"

All four of them turned to see him standing behind them looking at the same original musical score stimulating their conversation.

"Be aware of all you have learned so far, to trust your intuition for it has brought you to this point. Do not focus away from this if ever you can help it."

"But why this…this thing with sound?" Raynie asked him.

"It is not complete your endeavor and sound is so much a vital part of your understanding. It is why I sent you here to Vienna, to encounter the genius who once was at work here and in many respects, he continues to be. Again, to feel the essence of this where it occurs, is why you travel. This is not then always the way, but at this time it is for our mannerisms and feelings tuning to your heart being the reason why we must take these steps now. Time is pressure now. Additionally and far removed from the music studied here, one should consider the underlying principles music has to offer from an ancient sense and see the grand expression there and here – both are examples of this creativity seemingly taken for granted and not seen equally and justly."

"Think of the tribal rhythms created by many indigenous peoples and the sensations coupled with feeling one may experience from a tribal drumming pattern, and the soulful harmonies created using the voice. These attributes tie in directly even with this European style of music as you call it. The harmony within sound is one so very relevant to the existence and feelings inside humanity. And further, consider the properties of the information you have seen and felt. Think too of the effects chanting has for these peoples and the way in which it is used to clarify the mind to connect with the heart in their philosophy of authentic presence – being in truth with oneself and realizing this as the elemental condition of a human being."

"Do you have anything else to say?"

"Rely not upon me, but upon yourself. I am merely a guide to you, someone who is assisting you. What I give to you is mostly for your own sakes, not at all is it a thing for dependence. See it as you have seen it. Mostly this information is an awakening within you. An awakening to appreciate values underpinning all life, all existence. You have chosen this and so it is your choice to define it however far it goes. Largely the people of Earth have forgotten these values in their forward thinking, yet sub-consciously they remain, for life comes upon them bringing this essence. You are re-activating this resonance or memory within for it to become at the fore of your thoughts, your actions, and your feelings. With this you build the energy and at the right time, you will send it out freely to the world. Yes, the human instrument is ever so much more powerful than you realize and yet it really is nothing of mystery for it already exists."

"Also, the field of your heart is strong, extending much further than your eyes could ever see. It is upon this basis true progress will be made. Come, we should leave here now, we have much to discuss away from where there are ears and minds not ready for such matters."

"How did you know we were at the museum?" Lyle asked as they walked along an historic paved street of the inner city.

"Much you know and yet much you do not. Since you left China, I have kept watch on your movements. It was prudent to allow you a day or so of respite, to relax. Too much information would burden you at these times and so it was best I keep an eye in your direction until the timing was right. Pressure is high upon us yet we must not succumb to it through improper choices. I knew your intuitions would take you to the museum eventually and if they did not, I was ready to prompt you."

"How?"

"Hmm…as best I can say is just to trust me. You do don't you?"

"Of course," all four of them replied.

"Here," Chan stopped them outside a nineteenth century apartment building a few minutes later.

It was a fairly non-descript building which did not stand out from any of the others lining the narrow street. "This place we can talk and we will."

He led them inside to the cool dark passageway of the interior hall leading to an apartment furnished mostly from historical pieces and appearing to be free of any technology.

"There must be no distractions so please do not use your holographic devices. We are here to focus on knowledge and feelings. Each step of your journey including this one is elemental in opening yourselves to the tasks ahead. This is not only a journey in body. Remember this."

Jenna decided to switch her holographic phone on for a moment and see if she had any waiting messages.

"Look, John has tried to contact me. I had better see this message."

She selected the message and a holographic image of John appeared. He was sitting under a tree in what looked like a pine forest.

'Strange,' she thought considering for all her knowledge, both John and Tobias were at her wooden house in San Francisco.

"I have some bad news I am afraid. Tobias and I have been looking into some additional tech stuff we are going to need. This identification chip problem just up scaled. We are going to have to construct some masking algorithms to counteract the security…so I am working hard at it now, well about to. Tobias and I, along with Asper and Lorraine have left your house Jenna. Don't worry as we locked up, so it should be secure. Our position has been compromised and so we are now in the Sierra Nevada Mountains staying at a cabin an associate of Lorraine put us on to. It turns out there are Agents following people like us. This guy Mike had to take one out who had tracked us to your house. It became dangerous to stay in San Francisco any longer. It seems safe here."

"We are staying with a security expert. His name is Ryan. Anyway, I hope you are all doing well. Don't worry about our contact either. I have created a mask so the authorities cannot trace this call."

"We have had some strange feelings since we arrived here. This guy Ryan spends a lot of time meditating - he says the cabin where we are at is in a place doing something to you. I am not sure what other than to say we have all had some weird dreams connected to past events where we had to rely heavily on our intuition to correct a wrong or bad situation. Ryan said it was the effect this place has on people as he has had similar experiences himself. Anyway, keep safe and let us know what you are up to. I'll be in touch again when I have more information for you...this is a real nice place."

The view then swept around the scene showing the cabin where four people sitting at a table were visible through a window. Then it showed the immediate forest around the site and concluded with a sweeping view of the distant mountain peaks.

Chan had been watching the holographic message along with the others as they all stood just inside of the apartment, "I see your friends are beginning to understand this as you do. I have been waiting for them to realize why they are taking these steps to protect you from the authorities. It appears as they are now treading a similar path."

"Do you know them? How?" Jenna asked.

"Oh yes I know them. They are nearly as much a part of this as you four are. Essentially they are going to support you in your future intuitions, mostly by providing the security you need to be able to move, um, travel where you need to awaken what you are awakening. You may not be so aware of this, but the liberties so many across the world are currently enjoying, are about to be taken away. This is why I am here with you now. This mission if you call it such is urgent and of the utmost of importance in preventing the instituting of measures the authorities deem necessary to fulfill their own agenda."

"And most important is why they must not become sufficiently aware of what it is you are revealing, for such people would view it as a tool, a device, even a weapon to influence and control the minds of many."

"But surely they can do so with technology."

"Oh yes they will try, however the measure of the heart and the intentions based inside will always be much stronger. The best they can do is to distract people from this and unfortunately human beings are prone to quickly forget things, and so they will rely upon this to bring about a new way of life. If they are able to activate what it is you are activating, then human beings will be subjugated for many decades, if not centuries, by their negative powers. It is now when strength of heart and of intentions must prevail or many human beings will lose sight of the true expectations required for balanced life. This manifests as dis-easement within and thus they offer technology to sustain health and so-called well being whilst all the time building a stronger and stronger dependency."

"And this type of dependency, as you said just before, is not the way of natural life for people."

"No it is not. We depend on some things in an elemental way. Now turn off the device and get the last paper message out I gave you, we have much work to do."

They spent the next two hours discussing the images Chan had drawn on the paper. Each image depicted a basic meaning of the mudras they had studied, along with a rendition of the torus seen at the restaurant in Dunhuang.

"Within the torus is the essence of eternity," Chan said. "See how these curved lines interact with each other yet they are not connected directly? This is vital to your understanding. It is not a lineal passage of one event linking to another, but more a lateral vision for how realities and energies can interact given the opportunity."

Jenna had noticed a mathematical construction within the torus, "I can see the interaction as if it was a formula for the building of momentum. These equations, so I will call them, indicate the passage of time and yet not. They almost appear as though there are instances in parallel as indicated by those curving lines, yet those instances interact."

"Yes, a very good analogy. Much of the information contained within the torus can be interpreted in this way and so to people who do not properly understand, reason with it as if it is a lineal process. Thus…they do not see the meaning of how intuitions can open up knowledge and activate other equations within the torus without seeming to give them direct attention."

"So it is not a puzzle where one thing leads to the next, then onto the next and so forth. It is more of a guide and if understood correctly then the others perhaps just fall into place though natural progression."

"Very good. You are getting much closer to the meaning behind this image. Your conversation about parallel infinity whilst seeming impossible to the lineal mind, is actually an indication of the premise by which activation of the true harmonic heart energies can interact and play out to create realities or situation on levels you do not normally see. It is this type of energy the authorities fear most, and it is through their modes of constructing dependency where they influence and manipulate the minds of many hoping people will forget or not even consider anything other than the prescribed life they have in store for them."

"But what I don't understand is how we are going to do anything with this," Jake interjected. "I can understand the potential here, but how can it be applied in the material world we see around us?"

"There is no need to apply it in such a way. Seeing as such too is a lineal approach. The essence here is what counts for the results in activation of this torus. It is through its nature where its resonance travels like a wave, yet the wave is always there. Such interpretation is difficult to describe as our words are mostly centered on the lineal approach but look at it this way if you will. It is a memory. A memory from within you since before your birth. It is within the very construct of reality and has been there since your atoms were born in the stars. Does this help? Picture a field of intention, much like the burgeoning technology being developed using tachyons and teleport. Yes I know of these things. They are but a reflection of the intentions and discoveries the human race is making. A reflection of more understanding and as they study them, the energies reflect their intent."

"Human beings invent and discover technology for two reasons. One is to explore as many pioneers have done previously - it is within our nature and as we explore our consciousness, we construct representations of our inner discoveries. But the other…it is not so great. In recent times over the past century or so, technology has developed at an astounding rate. And along with this has also been a strengthening desire among the few who control the technology, to build dependency on it for the masses and so their intentions are not reflecting intuition other than how to manipulate people through technology for the sake of economics and other power struggles. We are now at a time where the human race will have to decide and many seem to be making poor decisions."

"Is it why this is so urgent now? You mentioned there will be a loss of liberties for people," Jake asked.

"Indeed. The movement on this is of very strong will. People are at risk of losing this contact with their true authentic selves."

"But why? People seem content and the authorities appear to be in control."

"Yes they are but there remains too much uncertainty for those in power to continue this way. Also, this is why I met you at the Mozart museum, as there is still too much individual genius seen as dissent in their minds. Geniuses have always stood out from the majority and have often been ridiculed for their ideas many times throughout history, only to later be understood and often revered for their insights. You are amongst those who are geniuses, in fact most people are - they just do not realize this."

"Genius is seen in the sense where an individual makes accomplishments based on their strongest intuitions of who they are, and then they go about acting upon them or responding to them from an inner sense for the cause of many. This in turn fulfills their expectations of what they see as their role or place in life. It is what they have to do, without any sense of doubt raised primarily through learned ways shaped often by manipulation and the strength of ego. This doubt is very much associated with ego and so too is the struggle for power this world has endured for many centuries."

"Egotistical struggle is at the foundation of many failures and serves to make known, insecurities to others. There is no need for this insecurity. No need to worry and no need to have power over another. Such things separate people from each other and create competition. Look at the great cities now, full of people trying to outdo each other for the sake of status. This is not progress - it is repetition of the same mistakes made so often…" Chan trailed off appearing for a moment to be lost to his own thoughts.

"In a way, this negative ego thing is disharmonious to the good of the world," Jenna said breaking the temporary silence.

"Yes, so see why I have helped you to understand the place of sound. Sound is part of the harmony of existence and you…people need to understand all the energies at work for real progress."

"Back in San Francisco you mentioned the moon demon and the statue in Fong's restaurant," Lyle said, his mind taken to his up and coming mission, now only a few weeks away.

"Ah Fong," Chan smiled. "He has guarded the statue for a long time. His customers just see it as another piece of traditional Chinese art culture, but it is much more."

"What significance does it have? And also the springs we stopped at after visiting the White Pagoda on our way to Dunhuang? I am going to the Moon in a few weeks…"

"Yes of it I know also. Your mission there is very much a part of this as anything. I cannot say why for again it is up to your intuitions to determine and respond. But I will say to think of how the Moon is seen in Chinese culture and in many others. This common thread associates the moon with divine powers and has been worshipped through time from ancient to the present. Often the moon is seen as an entity giving way to the birth of the sun and this light in turn gives birth to life. And our intuitions are often mistaken as myth or dreams, missing the possible subtleties indicating our intentions. So much has been overlooked in not seeing any metaphorical representation linked to the emotional presence of a human being where energies then create outcomes not easily seen or considered, but still of effect to the heart."

"Within each of us resides iron, so elementally affected by the force of gravity. It is in our blood, what we create, and in our food. Thus the affect of the Moon is very great as an attractor magnetically. This attraction is a balancing act in a way and so without our conscious thought, the Moon maintains an element of balance within us and all around us. You must know how it seems people tune into the cycles of the Moon and how it correlates with the cycle giving rise to birth and creation."

"Which is what we seek...to activate?"

"Yes, you are understanding this well. With such balance as key to our intuitions away from ego control, we require a steadiness in order to be able to focus and yet not focus for to lose focus is the key elemental of understanding loss of ego. Whenever I speak of focus it is of this for the focus is the authentic self present in truth without the mind's effort. Now imagine if such energies were highly erratic. People of the Earth may well reflect this with erratic behavior..."

"But they do," Raynie interrupted him. "Sorry Chan."

"No need for apology, you are correct and this is where I round off this point of understanding. As human kind has moved away from intuition and reacted to their world, they have become very much out of balance, mostly due to this ego control, which in turn generates fear and toxic invasion of the organic human experience. But do remember, the projection of self is perfectly appropriate through all life and this is not to say to live among the wild things. It is to be the genuine self."

"We see some cultures regarding the Moon as evil or the like," Lyle said.

"Again yes. So now perhaps you see the significance of the statue at Fong's restaurant. The demon is telling people there is evil involved with the Moon and so is a distraction away from the balance it offers. For those aware of these things, the statue Demon is a stimulus into recollection of their true nature. This is not a purely physical thing, for much of human psychology revolves around the consequences of the Moon, and the demon is not what people might consider in respect to it being evil. The guidance in legends attained through encounters with such entities, have always been to provide wisdom in overcoming."

"So the relevance of the Moon is merely concerning understanding balance of humanity within the picture of...reality or awareness, um...or consciousness? But why is my mission important? It seems like we are getting this as we talk here in Vienna. The need to travel there seems as part of this seems irrelevant."

"It is most relevant and will become apparent to you in time as your travels now have allowed you to explore the recollection of your feelings."

"Um, back to the torus. What actually is it? Is it a thing, a relic? Is it on the Moon?"

"It is a thing, but not how you would imagine. Consider life as a torus, and also the Earth and the entire universe of existence. Study of its' shape reveals the eternal cycle where there is no beginning or end. Also, you were given information in Dunhuang about it being eternal. Well it is what it is. More I cannot say for even I only know of it as an intention. No person has ever seen such a thing as an instrument or as a relic, but knowledge of it is very strong. Perhaps you may find it in a physical sense, I cannot be certain. But I do know this. You are instrumental in its activation for its energies have largely remained dormant for a long time as it is a reflection of the will and way of humanity."

"Volition?" Raynie asked.

"Yes, the will or volition. It is now in these recent decades where we have felt a sense of its presence, or…its' will to be felt. It is as if it is sending an unconscious request."

"What you say is pretty hard to grasp. I thought we were going to find an actual physical thing."

"You may, but once again, you are seeing it in a lineal sense."

"Well how would the authorities use it to manipulate people Chan?"

"The answer is something I cannot give other than to say if they become sufficiently aware of torus energies in a capacity beyond their current knowledge, then they will react to such a discovery and this may lead to them developing a means to utilize the energies for their purposes or goals using a vortex amplifier. Such a device could open vortexes providing almost endless energies for them to manipulate."

"A vortex amplifier? I have heard of such ideas, but only as speculation," Jenna said.

"Be aware of these possibilities Jenna. For now our work is done, there is nothing more we can align here with in Vienna for this meeting. It is imperative for you to have travelled to experience this, otherwise it may well have just been a sense of cognition, a thought somewhat bereft of the feeling. This feeling is energy and you are so very able to connect it yourselves, though you have probably been mostly unaware of this in your lives until now. Stay and go when you know it feels right, but leave no time to waste. More will come to light as you travel. Take your energy, and your intuitions with you."

"Where?"

"A most unlikely destination. You must travel to Africa and visit the ancient town of Timbuktu in Mali. Information can be found there showing the very reason for trouble in the second decade of this century. Some people knew of its significance and they did what they could to suppress this information, even to destroy it in their plight against enlightenment. But fortunately they did not prevail. Enquire of the Dogon people. They sought a harmonious way of being despite their internal struggles. From this experience you will gain more feeling and insight vital to your engagement of clarifying the egocentric self identity. Be mindful of how this may not be clear to you. To be aware of subtleties."

"Are you going there? It seems as though you have been following or traveling with us."

"You may need me…I will determine through the passage of time. You must trust yourselves. One last thought to help you on your way. Consider the notion of intentional spirit setting the path for light to follow. These are your intentions and light is traveling behind them. All light is a vision from the past, no matter how small amount of time in the past it can seem to be."

The following day they arranged for the next available HyperJet flight from Vienna to Nigeria, due to depart two days later. From there a connecting flight in conventional aircraft would take them to the desert town in Mali.

After two days spent enjoying the charm of Vienna, they boarded their flight to Nigeria, left the majestic mountains behind, first crossing Italy and then the Mediterranean, before continuing on over the Sahara Desert to the West African nation. From such a high altitude the patterns of sand dunes were a spectacular sight as they flowed along the lines the desert winds traveled. In the evening as their connecting flight touched down in Timbuktu, they marveled at the ochre light cast across the seemingly endless sea of sand. A porter met them outside the airport terminal requesting they use his services to find the best accommodation in town, and by dinner they were comfortably seated in a restaurant sampling the local cuisine.

Chapter 22

"What do you think Chan meant when he said human spirit sets the path for light to follow?" Jenna asked as they enjoyed coffee after their meal. "Sounds something like tachyons to me."

"Maybe it is," Lyle replied. "Remember when he said what we create is an expression of our awareness? If you look at what he said and align it for a moment, then you can see the similarity. Being true to our spirit as in who we actually are when in the moment free of ego control, we naturally express human spirit through our intentions. Often enough, we are distracted by thoughts of self in the world or what we have to do and this is not always of our best choosing, rather it feels forced somehow."

"I get it. There is something happening and an energy setting it up for the manifestation of what the intention of the energy is. With light appearing always from the past, then what is in place for the light to be sent on the intended course?"

"Each moment the construct of everything draws from source energy consciousness as presence then in the phenomenal plane of reality…the physical plane. Whether it is something a person decides to do, or the birth of a star, there is something beyond what we perceive as the speed of light. Light is a limitation to this dimension. How can infinity be held within a limited spectrum? Those two definitions defy each other in plausibility."

"Gee, what's in this coffee? You two are having a brainstorm," Raynie said jokingly as she looked into her cup.

"Makes sense to me,' Jake added. "I bet John could tell us a bit about this. He is working with flux mechanics and is likely to have some thoughts."

"Yeah…I wonder how they are getting on there at the cabin. It sounds like Ryan knows security. My mission is less than three weeks, so it means I really only have less than two, and I will need something for the identification data before then."

The remainder of the night was spent researching the Dogon Tribe of Mali. It was true when Chan had said on how they sought a harmonious life, despite having some traditions seen as barbaric. Dogon tribes worshipped two stars located near Sirius B - Po Tolo a male star, and Emme Ya a female star. During the late twentieth century when knowledge of their traditions became more widespread, there was debate about their capacity for astronomy, as both stars were not visible to the naked eye. Conjecture on how this came about continued for years, until there was no convincing resolution for or against some unknown or lost knowledge of the stars.

Next morning they awoke to a rare day of light rain in the town. "It looks like a day to experience this place as it hardly ever is. Walking the streets of

Timbuktu in the rain. Come on sleepy head," Jake prodded Raynie. "You have to see this."

The four of them walked the slippery streets for a few hours during the morning, until the sun began to make an appearance. "Let's eat and talk about what we should do," Raynie suggested feeling a surge of hunger.

"What information do you think Chan was thinking of when he described this place?"

"Not sure Jenna," Jake replied. "Raynie and I talked a little about it last night as we were falling asleep and could not work it out."

"I looked into any historical sites and we are pretty well there already. No outstanding places or ruins. I think the desert environment was just too harsh all around this town," Lyle added.

"Anything like the mudras Lyle, or ancient images?"

"Not a lot really. There is some art and craft dating back a long time, some traditional masks, but not much else. Oh…and there is the Spirit festival held each year in worship of Nommo. It is the festival we have seen advised as just three days away. The festival is about the stars of Sirius B."

"Well Chan knows his timing. Rain and festival in Timbuktu," Raynie added.

For the next two days Timbuktu prepared for its' annual festival. The streets were adorned with elaborate decorations, lights, and masks. Food stalls worked over time preparing traditional feast for festival goers, and an air of anticipation was building amongst the people. On festival eve it was ready and so the busy streets became calmer.

When the sun began rising over the sand dunes, the festival then came to life. Those up early were open for business or busily preparing for the day of activities as people already began filling the streets, dogs barked, and livestock scrambled over the ancient cobbled pavement. The atmosphere about the town was a splendid indulgence of positive harmony, and this feeling in the air was embraced by the four travelers. Never had they witnessed such an event so unique in its own character and in particular, the deities so vividly shown through costume, dance and art.

They stood on a corner as the sacred snake Sewa wound its way along the street - its' arrival during the night said to cleanse the spiritual leader Nommo and transfer wisdom. Children danced around the snake dressed as stars, and there was one dressed as the moon. As the snake approached Nommo, a stream of dancers appeared as if they were the bad energy being cleansed from Nommo, and then another stream of dancers flowed to the leader from Sewa, bringing with them the transfer of wisdom.

The scene enchanted the four of them, and at once they knew why Chan had sent them here. It was not for any relic or for any image, it was to experience the festival and feel this essence of harmony and spirit through people coming together with elementally intentions free of the persona. Together they formed an entity in a way – devoted to acknowledging place within the grand scale of the cosmos, through to the feelings and emotions emanating together as people.

They discussed how similar this cleansing was in meaning to the Nephrite Jade at Hotan seeing the transfer of wisdom to the cleansed spirit like the cleansing properties and crystalline structure of the jade. When prompted, they had no hesitation in joining others who followed the snake as the scene was repeated around the town. All of them danced as the spirit was cleansed and wisdom transferred at nearly every intersection of the old streets where the air teamed with a sense of the occasion as a mixture of spicy aromas and sounds of the festival.

Afterwards as the afternoon lengthened, they joined in the lavish feast, with the town still a melee of harmonious celebration. Stars seemed to be shining brighter when the night sky emerged, reflecting the festival below. The four travelers made no mistake about where Sirius B was, with many of the locals pointing it out to them whenever the opportunity arose.

Over the next three days they continued to look for anything else they thought Chan might want them to see. They toured the museums again, visited the oldest of the buildings searching for any clues, and spoke to some of the elders in the town asking for stories of the old traditions and the harmony they sought in life. Nothing further came to them and at the end of the third day they were convinced Chan had sent them here to see the festival and to appreciate the local's vision of harmony for life in an environment drawing upon both the resilience and the fortitude of people just to survive. Very much locked into history, Timbuktu was a town steeped in tradition appearing almost unchanged despite the times.

"Where shall we go next?' Raynie asked, now a familiar question amongst the group.

"There has been no sign of Chan or anyone else these past five days. I can only imagine he had not traveled here and so were are in fact alone and the next move is entirely up to us," Lyle replied. "I suppose our only option is to return home and thus our little world tour comes to an end."

This brought a hint of sadness for a moment to all of them as they realized their impasse. They had been so caught up in this journey, most thoughts of home aside from those of John and the others, had eluded them. Now with the reckoning of going back to California without anywhere else to go, they felt resolute with one thing - they would take their heightened sense of intuition and all they had learned back with them. This aided their recovery from the brief sadness, as they knew the activation Chan spoke of was the onus of why they had even commenced these travels.

His words of coincidence still figured prominently and were all they had to go on. It was an open book for them all. They had definitive destination, yet inside they each knew the energy of their experiences had set them on a course beyond anything they could liken to normal travel, be it for discovery or associated with their profession.

Jake and Raynie spent some time together discussing what they had found beneath the snow. What Chan meant by the activation, was still an issue eluding definite clarity within them.

Despite their optimism, they could feel a sense of deflation accompanied by confusion. What had Chan meant by an urgency now seemingly forgotten?

"Perhaps see how we interpret what he told us," Raynie suggested. "Obviously he wanted us to help him immediately, but perhaps his perspective is actually to start sooner to be ready for later."

"Ready for what Raynie?" Jenna asked.

"I would tell you if I could."

Next day they organized a flight back to Nigeria and a connecting HyperJet flight back to the east coast of North America. They had chosen the east coast after lengthy discussion based on the news John had told them about the Agent in San Francisco. Jenna's house was far too risky, but she knew an associate scientist who owned a house near Boston. She contacted him the night before their departure telling nothing of their journey other than the need to locate somewhere in the Boston area so she and her colleagues do some work. He agreed they could use the house for a short time.

"I am going to call John and tell him we are back and where we are. I expect he is probably wondering what we are up to," Jenna said a short time after they arrived in Boston.

Upon returning she had news to tell them John and Ryan had made a lot of progress developing the technology, including a device for Lyle.

Later in the evening, Jenna received a holographic call from the head of her office at Berkley.

"How are you Jenna? And how was your break. It is busy here."

"I'm fine thanks Gary. I could come in a little earlier…"

"You still have some time to go. You're going to need it. We have a new job for you. Well, they do."

"What is it Gary? And what do mean by 'they'?"

"I have been instructed to prepare you for this job by the authorities. They want you to work with the protein strings to help them assess a situation. No other information was given aside from this being more an order than a request."

"An order? I suppose we can expect this with the sensitive work we do. Where and when is this job?"

"It will come as a surprise. They want you to go to the Moon."

"The Moon! Oh, great. Wow. I am surprised. When?

"In a week. You will have to check in six days before. I reckon you could stretch it from a couple of days after today. Sorry, but they came in here appearing and sounding urgent."

"Anything else?"

"Just report in. I'll see you when you get back. Good luck Jenna."

"Thanks Gary, bye."

"Lyle!" She shouted to him before entering the library where he was seated reading a book on quantum physics, "I'm coming with you."

"What?"

"Yes it is true. I have just taken a call and they want me as part of this Moon mission. They want me to help assess a situation using the protein strings. We can go together."

"These coincidences are becoming a bit crazy. Where are they leading to?"

"Maybe we don't know or feel enough of what it is Chan is indicating where events line up and seem unreal. But then, how else do they actually happen to anyone. Otherwise anything could be seen in the old sense of con-incidence. I'm so excited to go Lyle."

"We will need to leave tomorrow for Kennedy Space in Florida."

"What about us?' Jake asked as he and Raynie came into the room wondering why there was excitement. "Can we stay here?"

"Um…you can but I only have this house for a few more days and both Lyle and I will be away for two weeks. What about joining the others at the cabin, in the mountains?"

"Sounds like a good idea," Lyle said. "Take some time out in the mountain air whilst Jenna and I breathe the manufactured stuff. You can get to know Asper and Lorraine and from what I hear, Ryan might have something to add to what we have learned recently."

"Hmm…sounds alright in fact," Raynie said looking towards Jake thinking of just spending some quiet tome together in relative solitude. "It will be a good opportunity for Jake and I to continue the discussion we began back in Australia, though I think its' relevance is much clearer now. Getting to know the others will be nice in such a setting. We'll be thinking of you as we smell the fresh pine and look into the sky at night knowing you are watching over us."

They all laughed losing the serious edge to the conversation.

John had sent the necessary devices for both of them to use in masking the identification chip the day before via a courier network only he and Ryan knew about. When the devices arrived, they provided some much needed relief to the space faring couple. Ryan made an additional security algorithm break through just prior to John sending the devices and they were confident the two Moon travelers would be secure.

"See you in two weeks," Jake and Raynie yelled to Lyle and Jenna as they entered the boarding area for their HyperJet flight to Florida the next day. They waved back leaving them with a broad smile before turning a corner to be lost from sight. For a moment Raynie and Jake felt alone, as this was the first time the group of four had all been apart for weeks.

"Let's go,' Raynie said breaking the moment and tugging on Jake's arm.

She moved her hand down to his and they walked together holding hands out of the terminal. The next two days were spent relaxing at the house in Boston and preparing for the trip back to California. Their flight was uneventful aside from the views at fifty thousand feet and before they had time to soak it all in, they had arrived in Las Vegas for the drive up towards the mountains. Jake was again in his driving element and took to manual control of the vehicle they had hired taking Raynie on a roller coaster type ride at high speed up through the mountains.

At Monitor Pass they stopped for a while to rest and take in the view.

"We should come back later in the year and go skiing at Tahoe," Jake said as they stood under the wide-open blue sky.

"Yeah sounds great. I cannot wait. And look, Alpine County, we are in snow country."

They turned left at the intersection lower down in the valley, taking the road towards Jackson. After about ten miles, they made their way up the small dirt road Jake described as a track, towards the cabin in the forest. Warm and heartfelt greetings were in store for them. Both John and Tobias instantly felt at ease and after introductions, Asper, Lorraine, and Ryan felt similar.

"Welcome to my little piece of paradise," Ryan said to them as they walked inside to have a round of coffees. "I am sure you have lots to tell us and we are all ears."

"I…um we do have a lot to tell you. With this little black out in communications we have been enduring, I have almost burst at the seams wanting to spill the beans to you guys," Raynie replied.

"Well I sure hope I don't…um, spill coffee beans I mean."

Chapter 23

'I wonder where Mark is,' Steve thought, as he was about to witness the third and final testing phase of the booster systems attached to the HAARP array. 'He has always been here well before tests began.'

He had not seen Mark in over two weeks and thought he must have been assigned to some support duties for the responder, but now with his absence at the test, he became a little suspicious.

"Standby," was the call from the specialized team leader.

Thirty seconds later the now familiar hum, flash, and crack of thunder indicated the booster system had been brought fully on-line. This test lasted longer than the two previous - continuing for ten minutes before it was powered down. Again, the holographic virtual systems were abuzz with technicians analyzing the results.

Steve could not relax even though the test had concluded. He felt troubled in a way different to his previous misgivings of losing ultimate command over the installation. Something he could not pinpoint bothered him. Such an imprecision was simply not his professional way - now it had become personal. Never previously had he been affected like this.

'Devotion to work always…' his thoughts were interrupted as two officers he had never laid eyes on before, appeared at main control.

Only one of them spoke, "Steve McCray, you are hereby relieved of your duties at HAARP. You are now under orders come with us for re-assignment. Gather your personal belongings for departure in fifteen minutes."

"What the f…?"

"Strict orders have been issued for you are to comply with our demands without question. Failure to comply will result in your arrest."

The two officers indicated for Steve to leave the operations center and be escorted to his quarters.

"Why are they doing this?" he asked as they walked between buildings.

"Again, no questions. Any more questions will be seen as dissent on your part. Dissent will only bring about your arrest."

They watched him carefully as he packed his belongings into a single bag. When he finished, one of the officers requested the bag be handed to him, "You will get this back in time. Until then, the authorities will meet all of your requirements."

The three men then walked out to the aircraft hanger where one of the authority HyperJets was already warming up. Steve could not think of why he had been re-assigned. There were no problems with his command at HAARP, as all operations since his posting had run smoothly from his perspective, and additionally his military record was impeccable.

'Something is happening. It is probably the bloody booster system,' he thought as he boarded the jet.

The two officers accompanied him on board and once given the all clear, the jet soared into the sky on a southerly heading. Normally Steve enjoyed flights on authority HyperJets, as he never ceased to marvel at the sheer technological might of the machines. Each jet was equipped with laser canons, anti missile capabilities, and a payload of armaments dwarfing the capacity of the most advanced fighter jets from the recent decades. And then there were the carriers in the sky as he called them, those co-called mother ships by others.

Would he be sanctioned to now work in some bloody office stuck deep underground shuffling data? It pissed him. He hated the thought of spending his life stuck at a station and missing out on action. He was an operations man - one who often shone above the rest with his capacity to make things happen effectively and efficiently. He even thought he was at a stage in his career where they would give him higher responsibilities, but now with his re-assignment, it was clear he was not being promoted.

As the jet approached the authority base just outside of Seattle in Washington State, he forgot his worries for a few brief moments as he gazed out at the city to the west. Similar to other cities around the world, it too was a showpiece. Eight one hundred and twenty story towers all linked together, dominated the city center. Flanking them on all sides was a series of interlinked smaller towers of fifty stories, forming a band around the center. Most of the remainder of the city had been modernized in recent times leaving only remnants of older buildings on its outskirts where traders and the poorer residents were still housed amongst the poles and relics from the past.

Steve looked out towards those areas seeing the great lines of poles networking the old city. No longer in use and not seen as a priority to be dismantled, they formed an ugly perimeter to an otherwise spectacular city.

After landing, Steve was taken directly to see the regional superior officer who explained a little of his re-assignment to him.

"The authorities have decided to make your life a little easier Steve," the officer said. Steve knew he was lying. "You are going to California, now you can't complain there. Everyone loves California."

"Bull! I know people who hate the place."

"Now come on Steve, no need to get angry. You will like it there. We have an assignment for you at our base."

"Doing what?"

"I am getting to it. Central systems have decided they need good men to watch over operations there…"

"I am sure they already have good men working there."

"Yes they do, but they need you Steve."

"Why?"

"You are a good man Steve and they consider you will be an asset to them. Surely this sounds alright for you. After all, they believe in you Steve, they really do."

"Oh please, none of this mushy rubbish. Believe in me…do I get flowers too?"

"Now Steve no need for sarcasm. Officers at the base can see a path there for you. Look at this as an opportunity. I know you have been stationed in Alaska, so see this as a summer holiday. It is frigid cold up there. Surely you like warm sunshine."

"I don't really care whether it is hot or cold. What's this really about?"

"Okay, you are forcing my hand Steve but I can only tell you a little. When you get to the base, you will find out all you need to know…soon enough."

"Soon en…"

"Yeah. You are leaving immediately, today in fact, in about half an hour."

'Why so fast?' Steve thought.

"I read your thoughts Steve. They want you there now because they need you now. You are an asset to us Steve. Your record speaks to us."

"More mush. What is the real reason?"

"All I can say is space operations are stepping up a few gears and they figure you can be a key man to oversee this. You like space ops don't you? Surely as a boy, you looked up into the sky and wondered what it would be like."

"Yeah…I did, but this is a ground based job by the sounds of it. The chances of me getting to space…"

"Don't eliminate the possibility Steve. You cannot be sure where this assignment might take you."

"Anything else?"

"No. Nothing else I can tell you. Why even I don't know much more. Trust me Steve. This will be good for you. Maybe down in California, you could find someone. You know Steve. See it on the bright side. You must get lonely with all those years of service Steve. Now go with those officers waiting outside and get ready to leave."

The regional superior offered no other conversation indicating with his hand for Steve to leave the office.

****

Departure for Lyle and Jenna was imminent. They were seated inside the small automated shuttle for their flight to the Moon. HyperJet Space provided easy access to orbit and beyond using high altitude HyperJets carrying the shuttle to the edge of space where the shuttle then detached for rapid acceleration into orbit. Lyle recalled the time they met in space and realized their progress together now going back.

"Prepare for liftoff," the HyperJet captain advised. A slight jolt then indicated they were on their way, prompting them to grip each other's hand a little tighter.

Sudden acceleration pulled them back into their seats as the jet rapidly advanced down the runway to lift off in steep pitch towards four thousand feet. At the designated altitude, high altitude hypersonic engines engaged at twice normal gravity, forcing them further into their seats this time.

As they passed seventy thousand feet, they began to see the outline of space as blue changed to black. Casting their heads upward they could see the blue sky would soon rapidly disappear.

"Advising thirty seconds to detach," the captain announced.

"Do you know any details about your mission?" Jenna asked Lyle as he stared outward watching the underside of the HyperJet above.

"Not a lot other than they require my expertise to assess the impacts of some new mining venture about to start."

"Strange…what cultural significance could there be on the Moon?"

"None I know of. It seems a bit mysterious. But my work involves analysis at specific scientific levels applying to geology and substances. Every site I examine and report on has to be holistically looked at for environmental variables or contaminants, so I guess it is where the connection is."

"Fifteen seconds to detach."

"You do know the methods pretty well… for preservation. But the Moon is different. What possible effects or ramifications could there be considering no one had ever settled there until thirty years ago?"

"Your guess is as good as mine. What about you? They want you to oversee the testing of this new mining equipment."

"Reliability is the main objective. It uses a type of protein mechanics we have only just recently developed. I was unaware they would deploy it so soon. In fact, I have a lot of reservations over getting it going too early. There is just too much history of rushing into projects only to see the errors come up along the way. In my opinion it was still months away from this type of thing."

"What are protein mechanics?"

"Cannot say," Jenna replied.

"Five seconds to detach, Enjoy your ride."

They each counted down the end silently until the time when the craft was first released prior to engine start and the forces of motion gave a sense of it falling away from beneath them. In an instant then it was away, pinning them to their seats. By the time they had begun to gather their senses after the experience, the sky had faded, giving way to the depths of space with Earth as a planetary body.

For a time they gazed outward silently to the vast silent blackness they were so relatively immersed within. It conquered where it sought no offensive. It overwhelmed yet presented the human experience in such depth. And it cast them seemingly adrift as they always had been – to be amongst the stars, to see their home planet below, and to add dimension to experience.

Ahead of them was an eight hour journey alone in an automatic shuttle on route to the Moon. Their restrictive space suits were a hindrance. They felt close to each other now through their growing affections and through feeling the affect from the vastness around them where they sought each other instinctively. Physical touch was out of reach aside from a few kisses now and then and as restrictive as their suits were, anything else would be entirely out of the question due to their being monitored the entire time.

Out there halfway between Earth and the Moon they realized a feeling of being small among the vastness of space where up and down had ceased amongst the stars remote from home. From Earth to Moon as it was also from Earth to Mars for humanity…and beyond for those far flung workers mining asteroids, humanity had realized a sense of self seeing their part of the grand scheme unfolding as space. Within to the infinite and outside to the infinite – there was no real in and out, just infinite without possible discernible end. Their essence was but an arrangement within the vast field as all else was arranged…and moving, changing, progressing, and transforming. Their minds and hearts were also an arrangement and both served as transmitters for the expression of the cosmos through emotion, feeling, anticipation, and the momentary nuances of the human spirit.

As if prepared by their meeting with the others, with Chan, and their strange short trip around the planet now receding behind them, Jenna and Lyle came to these self actualizations. They found not only the knowledge, but also the impetus through motivation, allowing self to fall away where thought in respect to persona is no more and the moment is purely organic, even in a space suit onboard a Moon automatic transport craft.

"I wonder about the torus Lyle. From my work perspective I can see how energy in flux could be amplified using toroidal wave forms. The more I look at the Eternity image from Dunhuang, I see the relationship between the mathematical properties as if there is something needed to align the tachyons so they can connect to the sub-light energies."

"I guess John is looking into developing an algorithm for the flux connection."

"It is where the torus comes into it - somewhere in how matter is created and the resonant frequency of the matter and capacity to store other frequencies. Surely emotional frequencies are an example as being different. It makes we wonder how thoughts and emotions may create energy. They are electrical processes."

"Perhaps the worst thoughts and emotions like hate become some store of energy or they resonate back and forth to affect physical life."

"If you go around being angry, it affects you and therefore others around. You can't escape this cause and effect. Oh look!"

Jenna suddenly pointed out the window. Lyle leaned over as he was sitting in an aisle seat, to see an Earth bound spacecraft used for travel to Mars. It was a sleek design about two hundred feet long and barely viewable against the blackness of space. Parts of the craft were black and others featured highly polished metals reflecting the stars. A few red lights in the cockpit revealed three officers through the front screen of the craft.

"Amazing. I can imagine my protein strings powering craft like it soon Lyle. We are just about to make significant breakthroughs. It will be incredible compared to the existing technology we have."

"I'm looking forward to your type of technology. Am a bit hesitant about the others stuff going on though."

"More than hesitant."

"Absolutely."

As the Moon gradually grew larger, mountains, craters with shadow, great plains, and strange formations appearing as if they were electrically carved into the surface, appeared in more and more detail. It revealed more craters than possible to count, ranges higher than they had anticipated, and evidence of vast events of massive scale in the past. They were beginning to experience the Moon and not just see it. With the naked eye even through the best telescope, one could not appreciate the Moon until it loomed large blocking most of the view to space. The sun was to their left – brilliant in radiance and so obvious now as the light shining both upon the Moon and the distant Earth behind them. To see the Moon, Earth, and Sun in this way forever changed their perspective to embrace the wider revelation of systematic energies constructing…enabling reality both at a physical and emotional level. They felt a sense of respect for not only the vast system around them and within, but also a deeper sense of self respect knowing they were part of something larger. Chan had spoken of such things through his words, and now they realized more of what he had shown them to find within themselves and how this energy of respect can be shared with others.

"I'll always feel the warmth of the sun much better now Lyle."

"It's amazing seeing it like this. There is no way I could have anticipated these emotions and feelings. How can you even describe them?"

"I can't, but I love them Lyle."

They simply allowed themselves to watch, to stare, and to feel this presence where previous feelings of being small amongst the vastness of space, had changed to knowing their connection as relevant as any other within it all. There was no idea of separation seeing self against the greatness. It was all and was one and within resided their own character, their own emotions and feelings, their own imagination, and their understanding to always search looking to express definition endlessly as it was all around their small spacecraft.

"Fifteen minutes to lunar landing. Please ensure you are secured in the harness prior to the final landing sequence at one minute."

By the time of this automatic announcement came, the Moon dominated the entire view. Jenna and Lyle could see the lunar base as a small dot within a grey landscape – appearing so small and reminding them of their how confined their work would be. At least the base would give them hotel style accommodation prior to departure for the designated lunar site.

As they neared the base, a sprawling collection of buildings and spacecraft landing pads became evident. When they touched down gently on one of the four pads, a walkway then extended from the base building for their first experience on the lunar surface.

Chapter 24

"Attention citizens." A global wide announcement was being made. "Due to the recent events involving nuclear detonations, the authorities believe it is necessary for all citizens to be assigned personal identification chips for security purposes. Contrary to previous advice detailing the gradual phasing in of identification chips, it is now considered imperative for all citizens to have the identification technology now in the best interest of personal safety. Your local office of authorities will advise via holographic message when you are required to attend your local hospital for chip injection. Do not be alarmed, you can rely on the authorities to provide all you need to feel safe and comfortable as you go about your daily lives."

"What a load of propaganda rubbish! Who is going to buy it?" John was upset. "Lucky we sorted out Jenna and Lyle in time. I thought it was still too early but the authorities must be further ahead in this game than I realized."

Raynie and Jake had been at the cabin for a few days, spending their time relaxing and talking. This news quickly smothered most of comfort they had gained, now presenting them with the prospect of actually engaging the technology John and Ryan had built.

****

Agent Eight was happy. It was rare for him to be happy - so often fraught with anger as he was. Deep down inside he could feel it beginning to well up and dissipate his happiness, and he didn't care for a second. Soon he would disperse all the hatred he could muster and in his warped sense, it thrilled him. Part one of his plan was underway, and soon parts two and three would ensure his dreams of depravity would be realized.

His happiness had not been real though. It was not the happiness most people experienced and shared with each other, no, it was a false happiness he took as the real thing - more a passive aggression invoking his disingenuous half smile. His face was incapable of the expression like other people when they felt good about life. It was not a scarred face, quite the opposite, bland and mostly featureless, and the type of face one could quickly forget.

He felt buoyed to be ever more diligent in tracking down those bastards he had lost in San Francisco. And the bastard who knocked him out – well he would get special treatment. He rubbed his arm where his own identification chip was inserted - grateful in his own way it was there. Then he suddenly felt the urge to insert chips now in anyone he saw.'

"Agent Eight, report to your superior officer," was the call over the Broadcomm - the system developed for Agent communications.

'Bloody Broadcomm.' he was distracted from his thoughts, something he never took the slightest liking toward.

'What is it?' He left his station and made his way to Superior Officer One's office. When he arrived, she was also in what appeared to be some type of happy mood.

"Things are looking up," she said. "It appears as though what we have trained for will soon become a reality. Do you think you are ready Agent Eight?"

"Yes, I am ready. I have been ready for a long time."

"Hmm…I know. I have a new objective for you, as we have some information even you might find interesting." Again the condescendence, he hated it, and he hated her.

"What is it?"

"A lead."

"What lead?"

"Information we have only today obtained."

"About?"

"About your assailant."

This made him even angrier, "What about the fu…?"

"Now mind your language, you are speaking to a woman you know."

He gave her a cold glance. He saw her as a designation, a faceless designation who was merely a superior through rank but never of mind. He hated her purely because she was his superior and had been condescending to him. Regardless, he would hate any superior or any person, his malice not confined to determining sex, race, or status. Even those he pretended to like and who could help him service his own need for status were subjects of hate.

"You have been sent a data file, study it. Find out who it is we are dealing with. Do it properly this time or forget it. You know what is at stake and you had better control the situation with a lot more thinking…" she trailed off looking at him and infuriating him.

She wondered for a brief moment if he could carry out this objective without failure. "Go. I have had enough of this for now. There are many other issues to deal with."

'Incredible!' he thought as he left the office. His mind was trying to deal with the concept of how she had looked at him. He knew what she had been thinking. He was almost beside himself with total anger. His body felt it, and he was breathing it. He even began to sweat it and swear about it. It began to physically twist him, its' taste bitter in his mouth. At the edge of control he realized where he was going and calmed a little, instead just focusing again on hate. Drawing a deep breath, he walked directly out of the building and took an official vehicle before he drove away.

He drove fully on manual at speed taking the old streets. He continued on until he had reached the outer areas of the city, and then further up into the low hills giving way to the distant mountains. It was then more than two hours later when finally he decided to park, was his rage spent. He sat there hardly moving, staring at the reflection of the Moon in the lake. By morning he was asleep dreaming nightmares when the first light from the sun chased the stars away as South Lake Tahoe awoke to a grey dawn.

A few passersby looked at the vehicle parked by the lake. It was clearly unusual, with its striking design setting it aside from the types of vehicle the public could own. Slightly larger, it had similar features but additional panels indicated something else. It held a sense of power and mystery, and a formidable look where it was difficult to distinguish between window and solid panel. It had six wheels, not four, and they were larger than the average vehicle. Only the machines built for off road had larger wheels, and it looked like it too could go off road.

They could not tell if anyone was inside and perhaps they did not want to know. People left it behind moving on - its dull luster giving them an uneasy feeling. By midday it was gone. No one really saw it leave nor did anyone see where it went.

Raynie stood outside the cabin sipping a cup of coffee as she watched dark clouds gather over the distant high peaks of the Sierra Nevada Mountains. She knew a storm was coming by the way they were building and joining up so quickly. A sudden gust of chill wind made her shiver and she drew her free arm across her chest, the other holding her cup.

"Here," Jake said appearing beside her offering a small blanket which he draped over her shoulders. "Stormy weather ahead."

"Hmm, yes, thanks. How are you this morning?"

"Good, but a little concerned," he was thinking of the announcement made by the authorities the night before.

"Yeah me too. I have an uncomfortable feeling."

"I think we all feel a bit similar after last night."

The conversation went no further then as stood in silence until finishing their coffee.

"What do you think we should do? Any ideas?" Raynie asked.

"None really. I feel blank. For the first time in weeks I actually feel a little lost. Even our trip across China and the rest…"

"Was not like this?"

"Yes. Despite the ambiguity of Chan's directions, it did not feel like this."

"I know. I feel similar."

Ryan had been quietly walking up to them almost without sound.

"Good morning," he said as he reached their position surprising them.

"Good morning," Jake said first, then Raynie.

"We are in for a summer snow storm by the looks of it. We get them perhaps once or twice during the peak of summer, but this one looks bad. See how the clouds gather so quickly?"

"I felt a chill wind just before," Raynie added. The three of them fell silent for a time returning to look at the gathering weather until sounds from within the cabin brought them around.

"It looks like the others are awake. Let's have some breakfast and talk about what is going on. We need to make some decisions." Ryan said before returning inside leaving the other two alone.

Jake put his arm around Raynie as another gust of wind made her shiver. "Let's go in, perhaps a hot breakfast will help."

The others were busily preparing a substantial cooked breakfast as they returned to the cabin - its smell distracting them from their thoughts outside.

"Mm, smells great," Raynie said realizing her hunger. "Need any help?"

"No thanks, all under control here," Tobias replied. "Just about done anyway."

"It feels a bit strange without Lyle and Jenna here," Raynie said as the seven adults sat around the large wooden table eating breakfast. "I know we haven't seen them for a week, but I feel we are about to come up against something or find out something, and recently at such times they have been there with us."

A much stronger gust of wind suddenly battered the window behind them and they all turned to look outside.

"Gee the change was fast, it is already snowing," Ryan said getting up from the table, "I had better fetch some wood for the fire."

Jake, Tobias, and John also followed him outside.

"Quick, eat before it goes cold," Lorraine said as the men returned a few minutes later with fire wood.

As they finished the meal, they talked about the announcement with John's face gradually looked more and more concerned.

"Worried?" Asper asked him.

"Hmm…a bit. Judging by the advice of people being holographic messaged for identification chip insert, I am thinking about our own personal communications black out going on here. People are going to be contacted. If the systems tell those idiots in office certain holographic connections are not available, they are going to start wondering why. They are probably going to demand all holographic communications devices remain switched on and tell the public it is for security."

"Monitoring all the personal communications is a big job."

"Not for them. They can process data automatically with algorithms…"

"We have a whole new round of issues to deal with then?" Tobias both asked and proposed.

"Yeah, I was already thinking of them."

"What about Jenna and Lyle?" Raynie asked.

"Not sure. They have a standard personal communications black out with their Moon mission. I think they are going to need the gear Ryan and I built even though their mission is relatively short. This identification thing will come in fast…"

"Like this storm," Lorraine interjected indicating towards the window. This prompted them all again to look and see the snow was now much heavier.

"What about our own devices?" Tobias asked returning to the conversation.

"I can cover to an extent," Ryan replied. "It should not be a problem to set up a location masking algorithm, but as far as counteracting our own call up for the identification chip injection, I am at a bit of a loss."

"How about your inside contact? Can we get him to help us?" John proposed. "The central systems are going to record data as each person is chipped. We are going to need some fake data so they see us as having been done."

"Sounds like we are livestock," Asper said.

"Yeah. You can bet the authorities are progressively seeing a lot of people in such light. Think about it. You can rely on the authorities to provide all you need to feel safe and comfortable, and this mandatory urgent chip status. It sounds like they are herding people around."

"And injecting them for the prevention of…" Ryan paused mid sentence. "What is it? Why do they want to do this?"

"I expect it is about controlling the minds and lives of people. They are gearing up for something beyond just the identification chip. The chip is probably just the first part."

They all fell silent each having their own thoughts over Ryan's words about the authorities.

Lorraine spoke a minute or so later, "What is it Chan said? Trust your intuitions or gut feelings?"

"One and the same," Jake replied.

"We are going to need them," Raynie added.

"My experiences with meditation are similar." Ryan looked a little relieved as he recalled the state of mind. "Perhaps a little step back from all the questions could be in order. The questions can cloud our mind - let us not be reflecting the conditions outside, um…aside from the purity of the white snow. In contrast to the wind and dark clouds, see the snow as the odd thing out even though it is a product of both wind and cloud."

"Raynie, Jake, we all know how much you love snow skiing, well me too. Consider how a storm brings violence through wind and temperature, but often when it has passed, the landscape is brilliant with powder snow under clear and crisp blue skies."

Raynie and Jake laughed a little thinking of the joy when riding fresh untracked powder snow.

"Right. Now think of how there is happiness to be experienced as a result of the storm, a sense of vibrancy. This in turn, stirs your emotions, excites you and then you respond to your feelings through the actions of skiing, creating further momentum, more excitement. During these moments you are your unhindered self, purely in the moment expressing yourself. Then quite often at the end of the day, you will spend time talking about your daring, your excitement, and your mishaps as it often is with snow skiers."

"So you are saying if we let go of consternation in our minds, then our intuitions will lead us to answers?" Raynie said.

"Precisely. It is what Chan was saying to you on your travels."

"But answers still seem remote,' John said. He was also thinking of the technology he would have to build for overcoming the holographic communications issues.

"Indeed at this point they do seem remote, but… not to say they will not eventuate. My meditations have shown me a quiet mind can bring about enlightenment on any particular subject, or indeed just as a general way or feeling in life without any specific goal, free from the assessment and judgment often created when ego dominates. We need to trust ourselves for the answers to come. This is outside conventional lineal thinking where a starting point and ending point are set up and our experiences are about going from one to the other."

"But ego is not all bad," Asper added. "It is when the ego dominates reckoning the self as only the mind."

"Indeed, I speak mostly about the egocentric instances where it is a reflection of learned ways as a condition keeping us away from sudden intuitions or realizations. The ego looks for judgment in order to construct scope and define experience within certain terms or conditions and can have a dependency or habitual cycle. When we spend too much time in such places, we can miss other opportunities as we are in effect, blinkered or restricted into seeing mostly what the ego defines as the way things should be."

"Okay, but getting back to the original issue," John understood the conversation but he was still a little distracted with the logistical side of things. "We were asking about what it is the authorities are up to."

"Well John, what do you think?" Ryan asked.

"I think those bastards are going to try and steal away people's free will, to smother their lives in order for them to conform to the control they are instituting. They want to dominate the world, as they always have throughout history and this is just the latest iteration. And knowing what I do, it appears to be the most dangerous iteration yet. We should get back to work Ryan."

By nightfall, the storm had dumped eighteen inches of snow and the warm glow from inside the cabin was the only light for miles around, except for one other. Agent Eight was driving slowly along the road on a heading towards Monitor Pass, his vehicle unhindered by the conditions. He did not want to miss any road or track he considered worth investigating. His hatred had only slightly eased as he concentrated on his objective, as it was never far from the front of his mind. The data Superior Office One had given him was not specific aside from one thing. His assailant in San Francisco had traveled into the mountains, and the location of his holographic device had given the Agent a lead.

'Your mistake will be your undoing,' he thought as he struggled to see beyond the falling snow. 'You should have turned it off, but you didn't did you.'

He didn't care his information was over a week old. Time was irrelevant now - his main focus was on the task ahead. With the plans now under way, he felt an assurance of success, so time did not matter.

A deer suddenly appeared in the headlights, so he ran it over without any hint of remorse. The snow or the deer did not bother him, as his vehicle was more than capable of taking him where he wanted to go - all six wheels carving through its depths effortlessly. It was just he was a little uncertain of where precisely it was he was going.

Uncertainty was the opposite of certainty and this was his only disdain. Machines were never uncertain as their mechanics prescribed the way they behaved. He wanted this more than anything - for the Earth to become the machine he had always dreamed of. Only one thing rivaled this particular want. It was to find his assailant. Revenge had twisted him, made him even more bitter than what he naturally felt. He had tried to forget his own incompetence with the situation leading to him being knocked out, but Superior Officer One had reminded him through her smarmy condescendence.

'I'll show her,' he thought as he drove on, again thinking of his goal to surpass her in status.

Location readouts on the dashboard hologram showed him he was very close to the road leading to a cabin. He slowed down to make sure he would not miss the turnoff as the data only provided a general area in which to look. Another deer suddenly appeared, but he was traveling too slowly for it to be knocked down. It stared at him for a moment stunned by the headlights, and then it disappeared to his left through a gap in the trees. He turned to look as it disappeared from view and he saw a snow-laden track, barely discernible from the surrounding forest.

"There," he said aloud to himself. He turned to the left and followed marks left behind by the deer as it had used the track as a fast means to escape.

Ryan had calmly told the others to pack the gear they would need for the trip ahead. He had been alerted to the Agent's presence via a monitor device installed in a tree three miles before the turn off to the track leading up to the cabin. Now they were all ready and waiting as he warmed up the three snowmobiles in the machinery shed.

"Follow me as we go, don't do anything else. I have an escape route out of this area in case of a security situation. John, stash the tech gear on my machine. You are going to be cramped, but these mobiles will take three each despite being designed only for two. I will ride alone with the gear."

"Where will we go? There is a lot of wilderness about these parts." John asked.

"Don't worry, I can get us out. The vehicle will not be able to follow us through the trees so we have an advantage."

"Are you sure it won't?"

"Fairly sure. We are going to wind through some pretty rugged terrain."

"What about when the snow runs out? This summer storm is probably not dumping at lower elevations."

"If we can get safely out of here, I have a vehicle we can use. Just follow."

He boarded his own machine and the others crowded onto the remaining two.

"What about our tracks?" John said above the hum of the electric snowmobile engines.

"A risk we are going to have to take. Nothing I can do other than to hope the snowfall continues and covers them, but don't count on it. Anyway, the vehicle could be equipped with tracking hardware locking onto the remnant signal from the power source these mobiles have. At best we can really only buy a little time whilst whoever it is looks around here before finding nothing."

They all powered up and sped out of the machinery shed. Tree trunks dashed by barely visible as they kept the headlights at low radiance. The others followed Ryan on a hair raising high-speed trip through the forest with snow spraying behind them, kicked up by the snowmobile tracks. After a ten-minute ride, Ryan stopped and the others drew up alongside.

"They are at the cabin now,' he said pointing to a readout on the dashboard of his machine. "I set up a detector as we left. Let's keep going, time is of the essence."

They all powered up and were off again as before at high speed. Suddenly an explosion could be heard, accompanied by a brief flash from the direction of the cabin. They all stopped again.

"A fusion detonator I put in the workshop. Anything we left behind will be melted into one big lump. I could not risk anything back there. It will take them days to analyze it and then their results will be insufficient to get an accurate view of what we were working on. Let's hope whoever it was visiting, was also inside."

Unfortunately…the visitor was not inside the workshop during the explosion. The visitor, Agent Eight was closer than they could imagine.

"What the hell! Did you see Ryan?" Jake shouted as the snowmobile he was driving came along side Ryan's.

"Yeah. I don't have a clue what it was."

"I'm close now," Agent Eight said as his vehicle cut a swath through the forest. Twin laser beams were instantly vaporizing any trees or rocks standing in his way. He was actually enjoying the chase and felt his own brand of warmth at the efficiency of the machine he drove unfalteringly towards his target. He could see three snowmobiles were five hundred yards ahead of him and he was closing. Again, his distorted smile tried to express his feelings adding to his malice.

"Computer, lock onto those targets and prepare to fire," he said when he was within three hundred yards. He wanted to make sure he could take them out accurately. Not vaporize them, but simply stop them so he could apprehend them.

"Targets acquired," was the response. "Standing by."

A few seconds later he barked the command, "Fire!"

Three laser pulse missiles erupted from the vehicle, one for each snowmobile. In an instant they found their targets disrupting the mechanics of each bringing them to a standstill. Without any outward demonstration of celebrating his success, he continued on until he had reached the motionless vehicles. Each one was emitting a slight crackling sound as electrical currents in circumfluence held them stationary despite their engines continuing to rev.

It was then his anger erupted yet again. There was no one to be seen. The snowmobiles had been driving on automatics, their riders gone from sight. "Shit!" he yelled it as loud as he possibly could. "Shit, sh…" a light not far away caught his eye. "Oh I see you."

He turned his own vehicle in the direction of what was the garaged vehicle Ryan had, now being used to further the group's escape. He engaged maximum power vaporizing and speeding through the forest until he reached the same road the vehicle ahead was traveling along. He knew he was faster. He knew what he would do when he captured them. The restraining devices he had been issued with would make them whimper, and he would enjoy it. When he had them, he would always have them.

'Escape from deep underground where the authorities held dissidents was impossible,' he thought. 'I will have my time with you.'

Ryan engaged the automatics feeling confident they would do a better job during this chase than his own driving.

"We can't outrun it!" John shouted as they all saw the vehicle drawing closer, now about seven hundred yards behind.

"I have a trick," Ryan replied.

"Well you had better get onto it. There is something powering up on the front of the vehicle."

"A weapon I suspect. Okay, watch this."

Ryan entered a sequence on the holographic dashboard instruments. The rear of their vehicle flashed a blue laser beam directed at their pursuer. At the same time, a similar blue laser erupted from the front of the other vehicle. Almost simultaneously both vehicles came to halt.

"What's happening? What is the current we can see?" Jake asked. "And the engines are still going but we are not moving."

"Same for him. Look."

Agent Eight's vehicle appeared to be surrounded by the same type of current. "Something my friend on the inside obtained for me. This current in circumfluence stops the mechanics applying drive even though the engines are still running."

"Okay but we still have a problem. He is getting out."

"Just wait. You will feel a jolt in a moment."

Ryan was right as a moment later their vehicle began to move forward again, rapidly accelerating to the speed the engines on each wheel were revving at.

"I bet he didn't count on it."

"He's getting back in. He's following again."

"Yeah the one drawback. My counterpunch means releasing the energy used to hold him stationary."

They had gained a few precious seconds widening the gap between them.

"He's gaining again. What are we going to do?" Raynie sounded panicked. 'Stay calm,' she thought to herself.

"We can't outrun him. We will need to outsmart him. Unlikely he will use the blue laser weapon again and he is probably under orders not to destroy us."

"We need to split up then. As a single group, we are a single target. He will have to choose." Jake said.

"Good idea. Look, the snow is thinning right out."

Ryan then instructed the automatics to take the vehicle to full speed and they accelerated to one hundred and sixty miles per hour in just a few seconds. But the Agent continued to close the gap, now less than two hundred yards separated them.

"I have an idea. Ryan, take us to the main route between Reno and Carson City. Once we get inside the elevated roadway, the system will slot us in and him as well. If he follows us then he will not make any ground on us. We might have a chance to get onto the tube and have some vehicle allotments between him and us. Then we can take an exit suddenly by staying on manual destination. Afterwards we can split up. It will buy us more time and space. We will also need to ditch this vehicle as he will be tracking it."

"Okay, sounds like a good plan."

"I have a friend in Carson who could help us too. He restores vintage vehicles, mostly motorbikes," Ryan said as he took manual control and made a sudden right turn.

The Agent followed now less than one hundred yards behind.

Ryan made several other fast turns but the Agent immediately followed. "This is not working," he said. "Everyone, brace yourselves."

He put the vehicle into full reverse, its occupants holding on tight to prevent being injured due to the forces at play. Within a few seconds the vehicle stopped and reversed at a slight angle. Unable to respond in time, the Agent flew past them at one hundred and seventy miles per hour. Ryan then spun the vehicle completely around, took a sharp left turn, then another, and sped on at maximum power.

This bought them some vital time whilst the Agent responded, but not in the way they had anticipated. The Agent engaged his vaporizing weapon again and headed straight across the flat landscape in their direction. He was not angry about the chase - he liked it in fact. Such a chase was rare and he felt power and hatred mix together to give him the skills to keep going. He could see the objective for the dissidents. The elevated roadway was clearly in view illuminated brilliantly in the night. His objective was now to simply follow them onto the tube and apprehend them inside.

He watched them take the entry ramp from a distance, and he followed. It did not matter if there were vehicles allotted between his and theirs on the automated transit way. Where could they go once inside? There was nowhere as everyone was required to remain in their vehicles. He would just feign an excuse to have the roadway brought to halt. After all, he was an official Agent and he had such resources at his fingertips. Then he would simply walk up to them and restrain them, and hate them as they whimpered from the pain. This would entertain him, and oh the pleasure when he brought them into headquarters and showed the bitch he could do the job.

His vehicle took the ramp. He could see theirs being allotted as a space became available. He didn't care when he saw three other vehicles ahead of him as they were allotted spaces between him and the dissidents. A minute later he relaxed a little as the automated ride commenced. Shortly he would stop this thing and he would have them. It did not even matter if some of them escaped, he only need one. He would bleed them…any person until he had the information he required, and then he would apprehend the rest of them. By obtaining their profile data, their DNA scans and physical genetic profile, he would easily discover who they were by name. He would not use their names though when he interrogated them. He would never be kind enough to anyone to use their name.

Finally he decided it was time and so issued the command for the roadway to be stopped. Response to his command was instant and the roadway quickly brought all the vehicles to a halt. They had not escaped - he could see their vehicle just ahead. As he opened his door and began to walk towards them, he imagined from his limited imagination, the looks of fear on their faces. He wanted them to fear him and he would make those fears founded in truth. On final approach he drew his laser pulse pistol weapon. The occupants of the vehicle were still clearly visible to him.

He became angry, very angry. He blasted their vehicle with his pistol. He kept firing and firing. He blasted it with bolt after bolt of laser pulses until it began to become a wreck. He thought he had finally caught them, but he was wrong. When at last he had destroyed the systems generating the hologram of seven adults seated in the vehicle, he stopped. They had escaped.

Suddenly his Broadcomm sounded; the officer at the other end was requesting recommencement of travel for vehicles on the stationary transit. The Agent was forced to walk back to his own vehicle where he punched a holographic command for it to travel once again.

He took the first available exit and parked just a few minutes later, but this time he did not simply stare into thin air as he done by the lake. This time he went about analyzing the data he had collected during the chase. They had escaped but he could still catch them. He would not stop until he did. The thought of reporting any type of failure again, made him sick.

He decided not to report his status truthfully, instead filing some fake data about the chase and it still continuing. He hated lying but given the circumstance he was right at home with it. At least then he had more time. He would go it alone and he could excuse himself within the machine for this purpose.

The seven adults walked across the arid landscape near the outskirts of Carson City in the grey early morning light. They had successfully escaped the Agent by exiting their vehicle immediately prior to it being allotted upon the road transit. Ryan had managed to construct a hologram of them all during the chase, and so they slipped through an emergency door, and then took the metal stairs twenty meters to the ground below. They were still in a hurry but did not run. They had seen the Agent's vehicle enter the tube and speed away. Now, they made their way to see Ryan's friend.

"We'll stay there for a day whilst I work a bit more with John," he told them. "It will slow the Agent down a bit, but only a bit. My instruments detected a scanner in his vehicle. He will have other data on us, being mostly physical and the like, and use it to track us. We just need to make it as difficult as we can for him, including splitting up as we decided to earlier."

"When?" Lorraine asked.

"Tonight."

"Where will we go?"

"Trust your gut feelings there."

Chapter 25

People believed the message of security as the reason for mandatory identification chips, with many taking it upon themselves to have the chip injection prior to being told via holographic message. Fear was already in their hearts as news of the nuclear detonations was seen as a direct threat to their daily lives. Holograms had been running twenty-four hours per day since the very first advice, playing up the value of ensuring safety for all. Conversations in cafes, restaurants, at work and at home, served to heighten fear and the race was on to secure identifications.

The private companies offering personalization had been a cover. It was the authorities behind them, masquerading as private firms offering choice where choice was the very thing the authorities wanted to restrict. It was not a case of mass hysteria - more a general consensus of the chips being the right thing to do. Nobody wanted their luxuries taken away or even the slightest threat to maintaining their lives of product consumption. It was what they lived for, especially those in the high rise.

Prejudice was rampant where the trans-human population looked upon those not in the high rise, as either poor in status - not good enough to be trans-human, or as fringe dwellers who would eventually die out. They saw trans-humanism as the way ahead for human evolution. Being part human, part machine both excited and seduced them. Heightened experience and a long life of product consumption was appealing to those who basically knew of nothing else. Long gone were the days where the masses would exit the cities to go on annual holidays, or aspire to own land. The cities serviced all their requirements from being in the outdoors to providing products of comfort.

Many spent most of their lives using technology in both a work and social sense to meet these requirements or needs. Being needy brought dependency and this was the philosophy of the authorities.

Language had been re-constructed to fit in with life styles as many words were invented to aptly describe technology or express their limited range of feelings. The art of language was dying, replaced instead with acronyms and abbreviations in reflection of their awareness and of their laziness. It was a laziness stifling enquiry into the meaning of life, a laziness of attention, and a laziness in relations. Culture was retained, with it too being a cover though. The preservation of culture was a ploy, as was the work of people who were employed for this purpose. It was yet another cover designed to provide people with a sense of connection to their histories, yet they were being mostly lost.

Lost were the connections to the Earth in the pure sense of an organic living organism. With each new device, each new medical technology development, they increasingly built reliance on the trans-human way of life.

Even a lot of food stuffs were artificial despite the vast authority owned farms providing a produce market. Many foods were grown for the manufacture of proteins, vitamins, fibers, and mineral supplements added to base compounds digestible by humans. Foods grown in natural conditions were still available to buy and in restaurants and cafes, but the price was high and many prioritized wealth over food quality as the also relied on the nanotechnology within to keep them healthy.

The concepts of love, of family, and of friends remained, but in essence they were very much guided and smothered through technology. Many saw love as a part of life alongside products, work, and status. People in relationships were divided as technology intruded into the deepest personal experiences, often cultivating moods, emotions, thoughts, reactions, and outcomes derived from the existence of the technology. As each new product induced their allurement, so a fragment of human response through interaction began to be affected. Some even avoided the physical act of love, instead choosing technology for the process of creating offspring.

They censored the media as they owned the media, despite the public believing it was independent. Any news of dissent away from trans-human values was portrayed as scornful and non-progressive. The media singled out those who made bold statements or created groups to fight the progress of the human machine. Ridicule was their way and the general public became immersed into it thinking they were having their say or contributing their mind to the cause, only then to quickly lose interest as the next event or issue appeared through their devices and media.

Career was the main ideology featuring the most. Career brought status and status could afford the best technology and the highest apartments in the high rise at the center of many cities around the globe. Life on the top floors formed the aspirations for many and so they lived their lives trying to climb, to live, yet utterly they were at the will of the authorities. They were bound in most part to outsourcing their happiness. Seeking to contribute through work was their honorable intentions for contribution, yet so often this intention became an instrument for exploitation and smothering where over time, the origins of intent seemed lost.

Most were also in bondage to a common plight, the need for entertainment. An entertained mind is a consumed mind mostly devoid of creative free will. A mind free of creativity is also a conforming mind, and so the authorities provided the entertainment, as average and lacking in artistic values as it was. Their devices were a distraction whilst being a provider as their provisions cast synapses into turmoil to rewire brains in effect.

Billions of hearts beat giving life, yet those billions of hearts were also lacking in life. People were told to listen to their mind and to be practical, as the heart was merely an organ and the authorities could control its health through technology. Gradually most people of Earth were being deactivated, declining in real intellect as they dug deeper and deeper into false projections of life provided so strongly by the authorities.

Only those who still remained in far-flung places away from the imposing nature of technological development, or those who only used essential technology, bore a sense of remembering. They remembered and held a sense of the heart and mind connection to the Earth when a true sense of being was being forgotten, to then become hard and determined taking what one could in an inward sense of self.

****

Life on the Moon was arduous for some irrespective of how long it was for, or what tasks they were required to perform. At first, both Lyle and Jenna found this to be the way as they struggled inside confined rooms, airlocks and space suits. It was during their third Earth day at Luna One when they confronted this within themselves. Without any solid advice on where they would go or precisely what they would do, they were both feeling this angst. So far they had been assigned to acclimatizing tasks – jobs to help them get used to working in such an environment.

"I don't get it," Jenna said on the third night as they ate dinner together. "I have never been in a position such as this. Normally I am amongst the first to know details of any project, mission, or assignment, yet this time, just a vague notion to analyze data for the new mining machinery."

"Hmm…I feel for you. At least my job contains ambiguity by nature, often requiring my own investigations and research to define its purpose."

"And…nobody really knows me. I am used to being a major player, even directing some projects, yet this time all I have is the knowledge of what type of technology is being tested. Add all this feeling with adapting to the confines of this base, and I am getting a little headstrong. I want to do something about it but for the life of me cannot even come to any conclusion."

"Maybe we could talk about our trip and some of the infor…"

"Too risky, there is surveillance everywhere."

They finished their meal and decided to spend the evening at the data library and do some reading. On their way there they noticed a small team of operations personnel holding a casual meeting in one of the lounges. Jenna was confused as the small team appeared as if they were not a mining operations team. She thought she recognized one of them and was about to say something, when a feeling inside made her hold back.

She picked up her pace a little to catch up with Lyle who had made a few yards on her when she had paused.

"Something is going on here Lyle. I think I recognize someone from the group we just passed in the lounge."

"What do you mean? I would have thought there would be scientists here for the mining gear tests."

"There are, I saw them earlier. The person I saw is someone I met from central system weapons division only a few months ago. Apparently back then, the weapons division was assigned to scientific research study of the systems used for the mining gear. We were told it was purely as an information sharing exercise. The weird thing is at the end of the meeting, we were then told there would be nothing else the weapons people needed and it was true, they had everything we had."

"Perhaps they just want to see the mining…"

"Um no, sorry to cut you off. There are strict policies in place. Once a team is assigned, they are assigned purely for the length of the assignment. Another assignment would take months to organize as the logistics are huge and the levels of authorization are complicated. I directed the summary meeting with them, and I am absolutely certain all the information exchange was completed. They even advised the same from their perspective."

"Do you think they are going to deploy weapons on the Moon? There are none so far and with the trouble coming from the detonations and this identification chip suddenly coming in, maybe they think it is time to change."

"I can understand your reasoning and it sounds legitimate, but I have a feeling there is something else. Why am I not even being briefed about their presence? I have a lot of professional questions."

"And a particular feeling. Is it a gut feeling?"

"It sure is."

By now they had reached the data library and fell silent as they noticed a few others already inside.

When they were just about to enter, Jenna hesitated, "Hey, let's go for a walk instead. We can take a few of those connecting tubes and at least we can cover some distance. I am getting a bit sick of sitting around a lot."

"Okay, a bit of a leg work out sounds good to me. I am also feeling a little seized up. I could do with a bit of exercise aside from those machines in the gym."

The longest access tube in the Moon base complex was just over three hundred and fifty meters long, and as they walked through, they could see the

Earth clearly in full view. Central Asia was dominant including the Plateau of Tibet.

"Looks a lot further away than the other week," Lyle said. "Funny we get to see it now, from so far away. It would have been good to take the turn and head into the mountains then."

"Yeah, I thought about it for a long time afterwards. I have always had a fascination with the place but I am yet to go there."

"A bit unlikely for a scientist."

"Hey, we are not all just about numbers, equations, and formulae."

"Yeah, I know, I was just having a jibe at you."

They stopped at the midway point along the transparent tube for about ten minutes gazing out at the Earth and the stars - the surface of the Moon just inches away. It was like a dream with the barren lunar landscape and certain death just the thickness of the tube wall away from their faces. A few others passed by during this time, mostly on their way to a workstation, or to quarters for rest.

Shift change for general operations at Luna One was at nineteen hundred hours each Earth day. It was imperative for all Luna One officers to be punctual in both arriving and leaving for work to ensure efficiency. Resources for the base were counted to the very last morsel of food, droplet of water, and unit of oxygen, thus requiring all staff and visitors to apportion all activities on schedule and avoid any over runs or waste.

After their walk they felt like retiring for the night to their quarters – it seemed a little strange as the Moon was bathed in sunlight. Luna One had been in sunlight since their arrival and their sleeping patterns had been disrupted.

They lay together in bed looking out through the roof windows to the stars for a while before closing the blinds to darken the room. Surveillance was not present in their personal quarters in respect of people's privacy.

"So what about the chips? I wonder if they will bring it all online during our stay."

Jenna was lost in her own thoughts missing the content of Lyle's question. "What dear? Sorry I was miles away."

"I was wondering if they will bring the identification chip systems online during our time here at Luna One."

"I guess they will and they won't. Deployment on such a large scale is going to take some time. I expect it will take at least a couple of months by the time everyone has been done. But the systems will be in place - they probably are up and running already. And we have to be alert to this. They might take the initiative for all science and military personnel and do them straight away. Working with or for the authorities can sometimes be very limiting where people, officers, and the like can be the first in line for such things."

****

Superior Officer One had just received her latest assignment as head of authentication analysis.

'Why me?' she thought. 'As if I don't have enough to do already.'

The holographic data floating in front of her contained the necessary codes and files she would need to carry out this role, along with a list of designated officers to support her. She read through the file hoping she would not see Agent Eight listed. Her hopes were realized, as he was not there. It had been twenty-four hours since the global announcement and the system would be fully functional forty-eight hours from now.

'Well at least I have a couple of days to get ahead with my work...except for useless Agent Eight.'

He had not sent a report for two days and she was not pleased. She held back though, unwilling to send anyone after him yet. She was too busy to deal with his failures and she knew he would contact her in time. His job and his life depended on it and she knew the little weasel loved his job. She turned off the holographic data and decided it was time to finish work for the day and go home.

Going home was a release for her, with the views from her top floor apartment offering respite from the days she spent deep underground. Although all the other officers saw her as hard and uncompromising, she did have a softer side but she would never show any softness with anyone at headquarters. She was a consummate professional superior officer and like Agent Eight, her life depended very much on her maintaining this front. She had made it to the top floor after years of hard work and sacrifice, almost of her very soul. Determination to never go back was her main motivation to keep all other officers in their place, including Agent Eight. She did not really despise him, although she knew he hated her. She was simply after status as he was, and there could never be any compromises.

Five minutes later she rode the transit tube for officials located underground away from public scrutiny and to retain secrecy for officer identification. As she traveled and began to feel a bit dazed, she forgot her work and instead thought about her one real passion, music. It soothed her after a day of relentless intrusions and taking a hard line at staff, reminding her of days now long past. Nobody ever knew anything of this though, except the very few friends she had on the outside. They were officers too and she did not trust them so they were not close friends, more like associates. Her life as an officer was mostly bland, almost as bland as the face of Agent Eight.

****

"Finally," Jenna said to Lyle the next Earth day as they were both on their way to the office of Luna One Commander. They had received a call to advise their mission duties would commence today. "Now we are getting somewhere."

"Welcome. I trust you have been comfortable," the Commander said when they entered his office.

"Thank you, yes," they replied in unison.

"I see you have successfully completed the acclimatization tasks assigned to you. Sorry for this, I know you both must be wondering what your assignment here at Luna One is to be."

"We do know a little," Lyle replied. "But yes, we have been wondering."

"Good, then I have some news for you. Your official assignments begin on this Earth day, and by chance, or stroke of luck for you as a couple, your assignments will have you working alongside each other. Now what can be better?"

Luna One Commander was an openly generous man in dispensing an air of optimism whenever the chance arose. Both Jenna and Lyle had felt at ease the moment they met him shortly after arrival at the base. He had a manner where everyone he met immediately felt comfortable in his presence. Jenna and Lyle had discussed this on their first Earth night, remarking how similar he was to Chan. The Commander was so very similar, even in appearance to Chan – leading them to speculate if it could actually be Chan in one of various disguises.

"I have some data files being sent to your holographic devices for you to study. Each file contains an overview of your assignment, a mission brief if you will, and data detailing the logistics involved with carrying out your duties. You are indeed lucky in a way. Both of you will be traveling to a sector of the Moon only recently explored, so you will be pioneers for the development of the sector."

"You are most kind Commander, and both Lyle and I are grateful for your wonderful hospitality and the respect you give to us," Jenna said smiling to him and relieved they were finally on their way, to somewhere.

"Oh thanks to you Jenna. You too are of similar ilk and I must say I am very much looking forward to seeing the results of your assignments."

"Commander?"

"Yes Lyle."

"Jenna and I were wondering if it is at all possible for us to contact some friends we have on Earth. They were about to embark on a journey, a holiday, and we are very interested in hearing any news from them."

"Hmm, normally I would grant such a request without a second thought. But do understand there is something afoot here at Luna One and I myself have been instructed on maintaining a communications black out with Earth, except for official matters only, until I am advised to do otherwise. I am sorry, but I cannot allow it."

"I understand your position Commander, please excuse my asking."

"No excusing necessary. You both present as entirely trustworthy and as people of admirable character, for which I too am grateful. It is not often I meet people like you two. So many officials and others so secretive, it almost becomes a burden to my natural ways. Anyway, I am sure you will both be very busy over the next nine days, and…your friends on Earth will likely have plenty of stories in store to tell you when you go home. Oh, and one last thing. Please do not hesitate to contact me should you have any questions or requirements I can help you with." He rose from his seat offering his hand for them to shake in turn. "And the best of success for your assignments."

"Thank you," they said, again in unison as they left his office.

"What do you think he meant when he said 'secretive'?" Lyle asked as they walked the passageway from the Commander's office back to their quarters.

"I can only imagine," Jenna was a little concerned. "It is likely something to do with those authority personnel I saw last night."

As soon as they arrived back at their quarters, they engaged their holographic devices to study the mission data the Commander had given them, and were immediately very much surprised.

"The Leibnitz Mountains, I have never heard of them," Jenna said as they both reviewed their data. "Located almost at the southern pole of the Moon."

"The Malapert Crater," Lyle added. "Situated at eighty eight degrees south. We will be at the fringe of where between the Earth side face and the far side. This is exciting."

"And we get to ride in a Luna Lander."

"Sounds a bit like the days of the first Moon flights over one hundred years ago. I think they loosely called the landing craft of the first Moon landings, Landers. I bet the craft we get to ride in will be a lot more sophisticated though."

"In fact the Luna Lander craft of this time are significantly more technologically advanced than those pioneering craft, which were little more than tin cans fitted with thrusters and instruments," Jenna responded. "I have a good knowledge on the history of propulsion and space craft."

"They are looking for rare Earth…or Moon elements," Jenna said as they both continued to analyze their data, reading through mission specifications and objectives. "I was sure they had already found enough large deposits of these on the Moon, and in the Asteroids. It is the main reason they are mining in the asteroids. It says here I am to supervise the testing of new mining equipment and to report on its efficiencies, dependencies, and any anomalies encountered during the test. One big thing…" her eyes suddenly widened.

"What?"

"They are going to use the protein mechanics I have been working on."

"Wow. I can only imagine what it means for you. You could go down in history."

"Don't be silly, silly. I don't want to be the subject of notoriety. I just like doing this work."

"Okay sorry," Lyle was joking because he knew he did not need to apologize to Jenna.

"What about you Lyle? What is your objective?"

"It appears as though I am there to assess the immediate impact to the surrounding Moonscape as I thought. There is not much more detail other than the experiments I need to carry out to do this. It also says my expertise in conducting these experiments is required as I am apparently a leader in this area for disseminating results then worked into feasibility reports. Still a bit vague though. Maybe they need my knowledge of containment for avoiding contamination or the like."

"Now you have me thinking. The protein mechanics have to be contained in a very specific field; otherwise any contamination could affect organic matter and mineral matter. We are looking at nano protein strings."

"How do they work?"

"Um, similar to nanotechnology. Their strength is where the strings naturally at the microscopic nano level have a very high conductive capacity and operate more or less at human body temperature. My previous work with the cooling of fusion propulsion was the foundation of this protein string work. It was through those experiments where we became aware of how to manipulate the strings and then apply conductivity testing. Some scientists had theorized about the idea but the protein banks always went beyond the normal organic body temperature. There is a certain range where organic proteins can function. Too hot and they fuse together and too cold, they shut down. But the big breakthrough I made was to get fusion to occur at the much lower temperatures than anyone had previously."

"I can only begin to understand what you say."

"It is all you need believe me. If I were to detail the entire process behind the fusion propulsion systems, we would need about a week."

They both now felt a lot more at ease with their situation and excited to be going to a region of the Moon far beyond the normal reaches of Luna One. The first lunar base was located on the fringes of Mare Tranquillitatis, commonly known as the Sea of Tranquility. In honor of the first human visitors to the Moon, the base had been built just a few miles away from their historic Apollo

Eleven landing site. Another base had been constructed at the northern end of Mare Serenitatis...the Sea of Serenity adjacent to the foothills of the Caucasus Mountains. This base operated by Russia, had been constructed in honor of the first Russian manned lunar landing. The third base was more of a remote scientific outpost located on the Rumker Plateau far to the west and distantly remote to the other two bases.

"Okay, we have two hours before departure. Let's get a bit of relaxing done and chat for a while," Jenna proposed. "We are going to be in and out of airlocks and spacesuits, and will be confined to the space inside the Luna Lander and the mining machinery when we get there. The Landers do have small recreation rooms, but really it will be like living aboard a small ocean research vessel on Earth."

Lyle opened a channel to Luna One catering and ordered meals for both of them to be delivered to their quarters so they could talk without surveillance.

As they ate, Lyle was viewing some holographic data on the origins of the naming for regions of the Moon, specifically the Leibnitz Mountains. He almost choked on a mouthful, and then regained composure, "You are not going to believe it! Hmm, maybe you will. Look at this." With a swipe of his hand, he rotated the orientation of the data so Jenna could take a look.

"Oh my."

"Indeed. I immediately thought of Chan when I read it. These coincidences are becoming uncanny."

Jenna read the information out loud, "Gottfried Wilhelm Leibnitz, a German mathematician and philosopher who discovered differential calculus. In his philosophical writings he regarded matter as a multitude of monads, each a microcosm of the universe and assumed an established harmony between spirit and matter as a perfect exemplar of the human soul. Wow. And a man clearly of two minds. The differential calculus determines both maximum and minimal points used to determine variables in between, and yet this philosophical edge is very much ambiguous with the harmony between spirit and matter.'

"Sounds a bit like Chan's statement of spirit setting the path for light to follow."

"With all light in the past no matter how small the past is. He also said he knew about your mission to the Moon. I wondered how, but with this, I am beginning to establish some type of connection."

"And...look there," Lyle indicated a smaller section of holographic data.

"Malapert means bold behavior sometimes seen as impudent showing lack of respect. Now I am really seeing a connection. Boldness can be seen favorably or not, as can the interpretation of lack of respect. I am sure Chan would not espouse to showing anything a lack of respect, nor do we. Ha, even the Luna Commander told us so."

"Yes. There are some values in the world for intended purposes calling for respect, but in essence the respect can be ill placed where those values accepted as normal, are in fact negative and detrimental."

"And so those values do not deserve such respect. Some people are bold enough to challenge them. There have been many examples throughout history and they are still occurring. Think of this identification chip and the propaganda used to convince people they should respect the authorities for looking after them, when in fact the authorities want to control them."

"I could not agree more, and..." Jenna gave Lyle a wide smile, "I love you."

The Lunar Lander spacecraft stood on the launch pad with just its pilot as the sole occupant. He was busily carrying out pre-flight checks and bringing systems online. As his two passengers walked along the tube connecting the craft to the departure room, he watched them carefully trying to assess their character. He was not a suspicious man by nature, but with the secretive exploits of the authorities fresh in his mind, he was uncertain now about most things going on at the base. He was a civilian pilot who had realized his dreams of flying spacecraft on the Moon and he was proud of this achievement. Billed as the best pilot in situation on the lunar surface, he never failed to live up to these expectations, due to both his skill and his attention to detail.

"Permission to come aboard," Lyle said through the intercom.

The pilot stood at the door to the craft smiling broadly. He looked a bit of a rough and ready type and when he spoke, they knew he was Australian, "Permission granted. Welcome aboard, I am Jacques Offener, just call me Jack."

Lyle and Jenna shook hands with Jack, both doing their best to hold back a laugh.

"We are going to spend the next nine days together so it is best we get to know each other on a first name basis."

"Hi...Jack. I am Lyle, pleased to meet you."

"Jenna. Nice to meet you Jack."

"Okay, there are the formalities done. Now we can get down to business. I'll fill you in on our flight plan once you have stashed your gear. Your sleeping quarters are at the rear, to the left of the recreation room. Galley is to the right."

"What about work space?" Jenna asked.

"It is in the passageway with holographic banks on either side. You will pass through it on your way."

The couple followed Jack's directions, stashed their gear and returned, pausing at the holographic banks on their way back.

"Looks pretty good," Jenna said approving of the array of holographic computers.

"Okay, here is our flight plan," Jack said as they sat down in two of the four available seats in the flight control section. "We leave in five minutes, so do those harnesses up while you listen. Our flight will take ten hours from Luna One to the Leibnitz Mountains. We don't rush these things. Our only course deviation will be as we pass over the Sea of Nectar, Mare Nectaris. We do this for reconnaissance purposes as it has been selected for research and every flight to and from Luna One on a heading south, is required to gather data on each pass. Additionally if there are any problems during the flight, a small depot has been established there for emergency purposes.

"Sea of Nectar sounds very sweet," Jenna said.

"Ha, you'll be buzzing by the time we get there. The views during our flight are spectacular to say the least. Firstly we will pass by Theophilus to our right, a huge crater some one hundred kilometers in diameter with surrounding peaks rising to over four thousand meters. It is often regarded as one of the most superb features of the Moon. Then we will pass by the Pyrenees Mountains to the east of Nectaris. They catch the sunlight beautifully and you will notice some of the orange colored lunar sub surface showing through. From there, we veer slightly west for a straight line approach to the south."

"Sounds like an interesting ride,' Lyle said.

"It is. Now, our cruising altitude will be at three hundred feet so you will get a nice close up view of the terrain as we travel. You can take those harnesses off once we reach cruising altitude but they must remain on until then. And lastly, as we leave Luna One we will pass almost directly over the historic Apollo Eleven site, so I'll take her down to one hundred feet for you to get a good up close view."

"Cool," said Jenna thrilled at the prospect of seeing the site. "I have always longed to see it."

"Then long no longer," Jack replied in a jovial way.

Liftoff was as per schedule, the Lunar Lander rising effortlessly before engaging forward thrusters.

A short distance later, Jack brought the craft in low over the Apollo Eleven site and slowed to three meters per second. "Nobody is allowed to go in," he said as they looked at the transparent dome covering the site. "The dome was erected to protect it from debris, radiation, space rocks and to keep people out. They want it preserved as it was left back then."

Indeed, aside from the dome, the landing site appeared as though the pioneering astronauts had just left it, with their footprints still clearly visible.

"Reminds me of Scott's Hut in Antarctica," Lyle said. "The cold temperatures have preserved it so well leaving it to look the same as when they left it over one hundred and seventy years ago."

Jenna was busily looking around the entire site taking in the historical values. "See there," she was pointing at the seismometer left behind by the astronauts as part of the instrument package they had deployed. "Readouts from the instrument continued well after its use by date. And there," she pointed at another object a little further away and just outside the dome. "A laser reflector. It still is used to calculate the Earth to Moon distance, though mostly for astrophysics students as we have a lot of much newer technology in place now." She was clearly excited about the site and Lyle noticed her youthful exuberance.

"Okay, we need to go to three hundred and get going," Jack said. "Sorry to interrupt your time."

A minute later they were at cruising altitude, "Right, we are at three hundred, you can unbuckle."

They traveled through relatively featureless terrain until Theophilus Crater came into view.

"We need to skirt around it to our left and go between it and the Madler Crater."

"Sounds good," Lyle replied as Jenna gave him an excited look.

Towering peaks gave the impression they were a mountain range rather than the walls of the crater. It was a remarkable sight as they reached into space contrasted against the black sky. Jenna and Lyle were used to seeing mountains on Earth reaching into an atmosphere, but here on the Moon with none, they took on an entirely different perspective illuminated by the sun with the blackness of space in the background.

"Good isn't it," Jack said noticing the looks of awe on their faces.

"Sure is," they replied together, their view not faltering. The Lunar Lander had a mostly unobstructed view with a transparent flight control cabin aside from some hardware located in the floor and in a dashboard for the pilot.

"Now we are about to traverse along the side of Mare Nectaris," Jack told them as the peaks began to recede. "It is pretty flat except for the other side where we will approach the Pyrenees Mountains to pass over our reconnaissance point."

He swung the Lander a little to the left to align with the point. As they traveled along over flat terrain, the distant mountains gradually came into view.

"More like a clump of hills really," he said when they were close enough to see some detail. "In a moment you might notice some of the lunar sub surface. Once the sun hits it, the orange will be very evident."

As if on cue, they reached a point where the sunlight on the hills illuminated the orange lunar soil, creating a vivid contrast against both the blackness of space, and with the gray found on most of the lunar surface.

"Beautiful," Jenna said.

"Like you," Lyle whispered to her.

"I heard you," Jack added. They all laughed.

A short time later, Jack turned the craft to their right for the heading straight to the Leibnitz Mountains. The Lander followed the course of the terrain maintaining an altitude of three hundred feet, meaning it had to go up and over, and down and over at times.

"I suggest you get some food and some rest," Jack said two hours later, interrupting them as they analyzed data at the holographic banks. "We still have a bit to go and you might need to rest up a bit before we land. The galley is fully stocked so just take your pick."

"What about you?" Lyle asked.

"I need to remain in the flight control cabin to monitor our flight even though we are on automatics. I'll grab some food later."

Lyle and Jenna left the holographic banks, fixed some food, and then sat in the recreation room to eat and talk.

"What a trip," Jenna said.

"Yeah, one I will never forget. We have done a lot of traveling lately and seen some amazing things. This counts as up there amongst the best despite the Moon being lifeless."

"Hey, not entirely lifeless. I am here, and you."

After finishing the meal, they took Jack's advice and rested for the next few hours.

"Hey sleepy heads, time to wake up. Only half an hour until we land," Jack said waking them a while later. They had both slept longer than they had anticipated.

"Did we miss anything?" Jenna asked through a yawn.

"Just a lot of craters."

Half an hour later they touched down at their destination. The only signs of life were another two Lunar Landers, and the mining outpost. This consisted of a small service building used to house personnel and machinery, about one hundred feet square.

"Gee, not much living space here," Lyle said looking concerned.

"No, there never is at these outpost locations. You need to get used to cramped conditions pretty fast. Stay here whilst I go over and arrange some room."

"What, they don't know we are coming?"

"Oh yeah, they know but they just think you will cram in with everyone else. My orders are to get you some space though. Just wait for a bit." Jack put on his spacesuit and then proceeded to the airlock on board the Lander. "Back in twenty," he said through the helmet communication system.

Jenna and Lyle watched him take the steps across to the mining building in typical lunar style where each one would carry him a little through space in the same bouncing way people had become familiar with since those first Moon pioneers.

He returned in the same way twenty minutes later with good news, "I told them you would need some extra space for your work. They were reluctant at first as space out here is such a premium, but I talked them round. You are lucky as you get an entire room to yourselves."

After donning their own spacesuits and taking the bounce-like walk to the building, Jenna and Lyle were shown inside to their room which both of them thought was more like the size of a cupboard.

Chapter 26

Raynie was tired. She and Jake had been traveling on foot for hours since splitting up from the others. After meeting Ryan's friend in Carson City, they had gone their separate ways the next day - his friend had been unable to supply them with any transport. Jake was feeling similar as they walked the last few miles into Reno.

As a security measure they had not taken public transport with the systems requiring all passengers to register their details and destination prior to travel since the identification chip announcement was made. John and Tobias had taken Lorraine and Asper with them and were heading south towards Las Vegas, with Ryan deciding to remain in Carson City with his friend. Their plans were to split up and meet again in two weeks at a house Jake's parents owned near Lassen Volcanic National Park in northern California. The decision to do this would allow Lyle and Jenna enough time to return from space and report, as they were required to do, and then be able to connect up with the group. They had all taken the technology John and Ryan had built, and were confident it would enable them to remain secure.

Reno had never been much of an attractive city in the recent past with significant crime statistics, and nor was it attractive in the present. There was very little evidence of any recent development other than a few holographic projectors here and there, and other technology deployed to control its citizens and visitors. It continued as it always had, riding on the back of chance where one could lose or gain fortune. Those in central authority secretly hoped it would just go away, so they left it to its own device, and to run its own affairs, until now.

Seizing upon the opportunity of the security announcement, the authorities went busily about the city rounding up anyone who could easily be injected and therefore, made to conform. They saw it as an experimental ground, testing the new technology and testing their ways of both interrogation and deprivation.

In contrast its sister city to the south, was shown all the consideration they considered it worthy of despite its shortcomings. Facades were taken to an extreme where the old palaces of money laundering were revamped into glittering towers, and a person could spend a life above ground working and then gambling their lives away. The authorities saw this as a perfect medium to disguise their motives of conforming. Playing with those embattled souls who sought escapism from their embattled lives through a quick win or a quick sleaze, they promoted it to anyone who was foolish enough to want it.

The group had decided to split up and immerse themselves in to the two cities considering them a mire of circumstance making it more difficult for them to be tracked. In contrast to this assumption, the authorities were in both cities in force, and so they had made a mistake.

Agent Eight had enough information on them and he could find them anywhere as long as they were in the vicinity. And his success was imminent as he watched the couple struggle the last few miles into Reno. He watched them as they entered the shabby looking restaurant. He saw them embrace each other in a kiss just after they left and he hated it. He watched them walk through the park in the city center holding hands as lovers, and he hated them for doing it. Then he watched them take lodgings in a motel on the old strip, and so decided it would be there where he would make a move.

As he started the engine of concealed six wheeled vehicle, the low hum of its' six engines made him feel even better, more powerful. By punching a holographic switch on the dashboard he took it out of covert mode where its' very material construct refracted light from the vehicle's surroundings thus rendering it invisible. He barked a command - it was on full automatics and so during the short drive over to the shabby motel he positioned his weapon.

The vehicle surged ahead and within a few seconds, stopped again immediately outside the motel. Agent Eight immediately went inside. The clerk at the desk looked at him and began to speak, so he shot him. Not to kill, his weapon was set on stun. Then he went upstairs and began his final search. Nearly every room was occupied and so each of them bore the brunt of his weapon. Door after door, stun after stun. He had done it at least two dozen times before he reached them.

They were lying on a bed together almost asleep. He did not shoot them as it would be inconvenient to have to carry them to his vehicle. He just spoke, "You two are coming with me and don't resist."

Raynie and Jake could not resist anyway, as they were outgunned and simply too weary.

He led them downstairs amongst the din caused after he had begun shooting. People were screaming, others trying to assail him, whom he shot. He took the couple to his vehicle. They were already in handcuffs and were whimpering at the pain. His half smile returned, looking as bad as ever. He would show Superior One bitch.

They could not protest, only whimper. The pain had them and so did he. Then he drove away without remorse when he struck pedestrians a few times. He was an Agent and no one could stand in his way…except the bitch back at headquarters. He kept driving but became sick of their whimpering, so he shot them telling them to 'shut the hell up!'

****

John and Tobias were inside buying some supplies at the store while Asper and Lorraine waited outside. They were standing beside the highway outside a road stop located on route three nine five heading south towards Mono Lake.

"What are you thinking of?" Lorraine asked Asper.

"Calling Raynie and Jake."

"Maybe we should see how they are getting on in Reno. It has been quite a few hours since they were dropped off and they did have to walk the rest of the way."

"Okay, we'll call them." Asper said touching a device positioned behind her ear. "Jake, Raynie?" There was no answer. "Their device is on. I'll try again. Jake, Raynie? Maybe they are sleeping or something. I'll try again later."

"I spoke to the store owner," Tobias said when he and John returned outside. "He knows where we can get a vehicle. The place is about ten miles from here. We'll have to walk unless we can hitch a ride again."

They had made it this far from Carson City by hitching a ride with one of the large cargo vehicles travelling the route. But it was not continuing any further and so now they had to organize another ride somehow.

"How do we get this vehicle?" Lorraine asked.

"Buy it. The store owner said the person is selling for a good price."

"But walk ten miles?"

"Yeah. I don't like the idea either, but we have to. John and I cased out vehicles at the store here and there are none available, despite the parking lot being almost full. None for sale and I won't steal one…not a good idea."

"Yeah I guess you are right. Well, let's get going then, we have quite a walk ahead of us, but…um, maybe if we call them to come and get us and we can buy it then."

"Thought of it. Apparently this guy is pretty paranoid. The storeowner phoned him when we were inside and the guy just said no. He told him, if we want it then come and get it."

"Not good for sales."

"It didn't seem to matter. He said he didn't need the money, hence the price."

They covered the distance to the seller's house over the next two hours, and when they arrived the house looked deserted.

"I hope he hasn't gone out," John said.

"Nope. I'm here.' They turned to see the seller standing behind them pointing a laser rifle. "What do you want?"

"We are the people who want to buy your car."

"Oh you are, are you?" he said lowering the rifle. "Well you better come with me out back and I'll show you. No funny business though, the price stands."

"We have enough money."

After a quick check of the vehicle, they bought it and drove away.

"The guy is a history piece," Lorraine said looking out the rear window, but the seller had already disappeared back inside the shed out of sight.

"Hey, should we try Jake and Raynie again?" Asper asked.

"Good idea." John tried his small communicator and this time there was an answer, though in a very low voice.

"We've been caught, going to San…"

"What did you say?" Agent Eight barked.

"I just said we should have fought this man…to my friend," Raynie replied.

"Ha, as if it would have done you any good. Just shut up. We'll be arriving at headquarters soon."

Tobias stopped the car, a look of shock on everyone's face. Everything both Raynie and Agent Eight said had come through clearly.

"Turn around," John said. Tobias did and hit the accelerator taking the car to maximum speed within a few seconds, on a heading back to San Francisco.

Chapter 27

Jenna was working with a holographic projection inside the 'cupboard'. Lyle and her were attending to their individual tasks, analyzing data and preparing for their first venture into the prospective mining zone. Lyle could see the protein strings clearly and became fascinated. Each string appeared to look very similar to a DNA strand except they were single strings and not intertwined as DNA appears to be. He could see the image change as Jenna entered algorithms and equations.

"What does it do?"

"These equations are part of an algorithm I use to prepare the protein strings for conductivity. Watch this."

She entered further information and suddenly the projection increased in radiance. "See this one?" she said putting her finger through the projected image. "This one is almost ready. They take a little to warm up, for want of a better word, and then they are good to go."

The remaining strings began to take on the same radiance as the one she had indicated. Within a few seconds the entire projection was glowing like a strand of lights in a way.

After entering a further sequence, the strings changed again where it appeared as though they were comprised of many individual light sources rather than just a general radiance.

"Next I initiate quantum phasing. This allows each string to accept quantum mechanical manipulation, which is basically where they get ready take information on board. You can imagine how many channels it opens up. The phasing is merely a state of semi flux – we are dealing with speeds just below light speed here. When the information load commences, the phasing amount increases according to the amount of information sent along each string. At the quantum levels there is no overcrowding…simply as there is not enough data to create crowding, despite there being a large amount of data. The huge availability of quantum particles is a natural characteristic of the proteins. They don't heat up and remain at the same temperature. No chances of over powering them."

She entered another sequence sending more data to the strings, which responded by appearing to move.

"Don't be deceived as they are not actually moving, it is just the data passing along the string as the quantum phasing increases and decreases, giving them an appearance of movement."

"This is an enlarged view isn't it?"

"Yes. You could call this organic nano mechanics just to get an idea of the size of the strings."

"So in effect, with so many channels all the data arrives or is conducted simultaneously, or almost."

"More or less…very tiny fractions of time."

"And the phasing is also the transmitter?"

"Hmm…transmitter. Somewhat. Not actually a transmitter but you could say so. Aside from enabling the information load, it also works as the interface between the strings and whatever is receiving the information."

"I can see an application for this as a test bed scenario for the work I do."

"Oh yes. Propulsion is merely one of the many things this technology could be applied to."

****

Steve had been at the base far too long for his liking. He had not been given any specific commission, rather appointed to oversee small internal operations at a level he considered to be much lower than his previous role at HAARP. His thoughts were mostly about his re-assignment, baffling him into asking why over and over again. It was easy for him to assume operations at HAARP were part of some type of action, but what confused him was why he was removed. Every assignment he had ever led saw him in charge from beginning to end.

He had not done anything wrong, nor had he failed in any of his duties of command. There was no issue of compliance as he followed orders every time and he could not remember one instance where he might have asked or said anything his superiors would see as insurrection.

Steve looked up to the Moon in the dusky sky as he walked along, and thought about what he had been told in Seattle.

'What did he mean when he said don't eliminate the possibility? This bloody place has been nothing but routine boring crap since I arrived here. They need you Steve. What for?'

His workday had finished just a few minutes earlier and he was on his way back to his own private quarters - his only respite from the otherwise dull existence his professional life had become. As the path meandered through the base, it passed by the small museum dedicated to the early Space Shuttle tests and landings taking place there just over a century before. He stopped for a moment and considered having a look, his first since arriving at the base, but decided to move on. He was tired, not from hard work but from boredom and from not having enough to do, and now it was over for the day. When he arrived back to his quarters, he ate and relaxed, and then fell asleep early as if there was nothing better to do.

****

The vehicle was going down a long way. It was in a tube, a square tube and not a tunnel as it was vertical. The lights outside were flashing by at regular, very regular intervals. They were almost hypnotic and it seemed to be taking forever. When at last the lights slowed and the vehicle came to a stop, it was twenty stories below street level. Nothing but light was visible, blocking vision and senses. They had never been this low…in their hearts. They had never been beneath the city. Nothing was over as it had all just begun. Now, they found it hard to feel, despite their times with the others and with Chan. They knew they would prevail, somewhere in their sub conscious, but they did not feel it yet. They felt lost and confused. How had Agent Eight found them? John and Ryan's gear was good and it was still working. Would they find it?

"I suppose you are wondering how Agent Eight found you. Well, let's just say you left some samples behind at the cabin," was the first thing Superior Officer One said to them after they had been made to wait for an hour.

Agent Eight was also in the room, sitting perpendicular to his superior and to Jake and Raynie. He showed no expression as he would not dare to appear as anything else but bland in this instance, yet inside he was as maniacal as ever. There was nothing he wanted to give his superior indicating any idea he was trying to please her. And these bastards, oh the pleasure he felt at having tracked them down so efficiently using the DNA scanner installed into his vehicle. He was impressed. It had worked so well and over such a long range. He thought of the chase from the cabin. It had thrilled him almost every inch of the way.

"All we need are names and locations. Nothing else. Provide those and most of your troubles are over, but…we will have to keep you detained for a time. Then, you are free to return to your lives."

Raynie and Jake said nothing.

"I see the look of worry on your faces. We will look after you as the authorities are always there for the citizens," Superior Officer One continued. "Simple, yes?"

Agent Eight was almost bursting at the seams, yet held his composure. The sheer malice of his intentions was the driving force behind him now, but he remained steadying his outward expression of self as it twisted his inner conflict even further. He wanted to interrogate them his way. The Superior Officer was being too soft, far too soft. She was almost being nice and it sickened him.

"For now, you are to be taken to holding cells for some rest. It looks like you need it. With a fresh mind and a good meal, you will be in the best condition to give us all of the information we need. And congratulations. You two are the very first dissidents we have captured. You are fortunate as I have chosen to personally witness the very first and you are the first. For those who will follow, I am sorry to say they will be left to our Agents alone and their methods are not so as dignified as mine.

The last sentence stirred Agent Eight a little and his warped smile began to appear. Superior Officer One immediately noticed this.

'Yes I bet you think you will have a place in history,' she thought with a touch of sarcasm.

"Anyway, no more for now. Agent Eight, take them to the facility. You may do your work there where I will be watching."

The Agent escorted Raynie and Jake out of the office towards the access door leading to the square tube. They had remained silent the entire time, feeling no need to speak or really listen. They knew what the Superior Officer meant when they could go free after detainment. It would be after the system came on line and they would have had chips injected at the facility. Mostly they thought of each other and of their friends, and these relationships gave them strength with continued growth in knowledge and bonding.

"Wait," the Agent told them.

He made a request for his vehicle and a minute later it was positioned on the platform.

"Get in."

The ride up the tube was much clearer than the ride down. Rather than being hypnotized by the lights, this time they counted them. They had been in pain during their arrival and now they had emerged out of the groggy state it had induced. It had been a strange pain. Not an electrical pain, or pressure, it was like an internal itching, and without any means to scratch the itch, it felt like they were going mad. Its' severity had fluctuated once in response to something the Agent did via the holograms on the dashboard of his vehicle, so they knew its level could be controlled.

As the Agent drove them through the city on the way to the facility, they noticed how other vehicles automatically moved out of the way. By the time they had stopped, both of them estimated the journey to have ended somewhere to the northeast, across the Bay Bridge, and along the automatic tube road for about fifteen minutes after, meaning a rough distance of thirty to forty miles. Both of the devices John and Ryan had built were still on. This gave rise to some certainty and a deal of uncertainty when they wondered if the devices would be detected.

Upon arrival they were taken to separate cells, each equipped with their own private washroom. Then a meal was brought to them and nothing else. They were made to just sit there and wait. There had been no sign of Agent Eight since their arrival either and this puzzled them. Both of them had been preparing for a much harder time when they had been left in the custody of this man.

"Raynie. Jake. It's John. We heard everything. We are back in San Francisco."

Neither of them dared to respond directly as they knew high intensity audio surveillance would be in place at the facility. The devices they had been given were only a few millimeters square and stuck to their skin behind the ear. They could hear John's voice being sent as waves directly to their brain, by-passing their eardrums entirely. It was amazing how John was able to synthesize the synaptic conversions occurring during the interpretation of sound waves by the brain in real time.

"They took us over the Bay Bridge and on for a little while afterwards Jake!" Raynie shouted.

Three cells inside the massive detainment block separated them from each other, and she shouted this to Jake as if to speak to him.

A voice came from nowhere, "Keep it down in there. You and your friend will not be able to determine this location. Anyhow, it doesn't matter, you are here now." None of the officers at the guard station took any more notice, completely unaware Raynie was telling John where she thought they had been taken.

John replied, "Raynie. Jake. I am going to remotely deactivate your devices now. I am worried the authorities will discover them when they search you, and if they have some type of scanning to detect them. Take them off and destroy them. I am sorry you will be on your own after but only for a while. Don't worry as we are on your case."

A moment later they both removed their devices and then flushed them away in the washroom.

"How are you?' Jake called out to Raynie a moment later, thinking a little normal conversation was okay now.

"I'm fine. How are you?"

"Same. I guess we just wait and see."

"Yeah. They will be able to analyze our responses and see if we are lying. It frightens me."

"It has me worried too. It's going to depend on their line of questioning I suppose."

"Yeah."

"Get some rest. I'm going to. Help us relax away from all of this for a while. We need it."

"Alright Jake. Talk soon."

They both lay down in their respective beds and eventually fell into a restless sleep. Since leaving Carson City, it had been a long walk and then the Agent had arrested them, so they had not yet rested.

Agent Eight woke them three hours later, himself having been asleep after the long chase the day before.

"Get up. We are about to begin. I hope you are well rested because you will need it."

He felt sarcasm and malice as he spoke. If he had his way, they would need all the strength they could muster to endure his methods of interrogation. His only anger stemmed from the knowledge Superior Officer One would be watching. He would have to gain her approval and he hated it.

Holographic handcuffs were again placed around Raynie and Jake's wrists as they were escorted from their cells. An issuing officer or Agent controlled the cuffs via a small device on their belt, or wherever they chose to stash it, and they worked by attaching themselves to the individuals' DNA patterns obtained via scan immediately prior to use. Agent Eight had them at their lowest setting, making his two prisoners feel the anticipation of the coming itch, without actually getting the itch.

"Do you want to scratch yet? Perhaps you need to feel like scratching? I can make you itch so bad you feel like you are burning from your very soul. Would you like it? Do you want to feel your soul burn? I can make it so in a second." He increased power on the cuffs for a second, causing them both to flinch.

"You see people like you are not what the machine needs. The machine needs people to live their lives conforming. After all, how can a machine operate if all its parts do not perform what they are required to perform? The machine will break down, and this machine is never going to break down...once it gets fully operational." He lost his composure for half a second.

"Agent Eight. Keep your mouth shut. Stick to the questions," Superior Officer One barked over his Broadcomm.

"What do you mean fully operational?" Jake asked.

"Shut up! I ask questions!" Agent Eight was angered by more condescendence from his superior. "Tell me the full names of all seven of you who were in the cabin, starting with your own."

Raynie and Jake gave them their full names.

"And the others?"

"Asper, John, Tobias, Lorraine, and Ryan," Raynie replied and Jake repeated this.

"Oh, bloody smart now eh!" Agent Eight made them itch for ten seconds, at a more intense level than they had felt previously. It was horrible and they began to know what he meant by burning. It was as if hell was rising up from within. He took the level back down.

"I said full names."

"They are," Jake replied. "We only know their first names." Agent Eight checked the readouts from the lie scanner – Jake appeared to be telling the truth.

"Where are they?"

"Somewhere in California. We don't know where."

"Are they at the house?"

"I don't know. I don't think so."

"Do you know how they made it to the cabin?" he began thinking of his assailant.

"We were told it was Mike," Raynie replied. "Only Mike."

The Agent saw she was speaking the truth.

"Did they tell you about me being assaulted?"

"No."

Nobody at the cabin had mentioned Mike's assault on the Agent, and Raynie and Jake were now grateful for not knowing anything about the incident, feeling certain Agent Eight would likely try anything to extract some type of revenge.

"Did they tell you about their visit to the high rise?"

"Yes."

"What about it?"

"They said they went there to see an old friend of John."

"What does this 'old friend' do?"

"They didn't say. Just he was an old friend and they had taken the trip to see him."

This was all John had said about going to see Raman. He had only mentioned it briefly without going into any details, or giving Raman's name.

"What are your friends doing?"

"They are looking into ways to avoid getting identification chips."

"You know nobody can avoid the chips – they are mandatory. How are they going to do this?"

"I don't know exactly but they are working on technology."

"What technology?"

"I don't know what it is called."

"What about you?" he looked at Jake.

"I don't know either."

"How does it work?"

"Something to do with creating a false signature."

"How can they? They don't even know how the identification systems work."

"Again, we don't know," Raynie replied this time.

"Do you two have anything? Any of these false signatures?"

"No." She was thankful they had disposed of them as she could now tell this as the truth.

"What do you think is about to happen on Earth?"

"We think the authorities are going to take away people's freedom," Jake answered.

"And?"

"And…um, turn people into emotionless slaves to service this machine you so highly regard."

There was still no evidence of lying on the scanner.

"Anything else?"

"No…for now."

"What do you mean 'for now'?"

The Agent was becoming tired of the interrogation as he was obviously not obtaining any tangible information he could work with. He decided to give Jake an itch for a couple of seconds, making him whimper a little in anguish. "Don't get smart with me. For now, what?"

"It is all we know. But I guess we will know more as time passes."

"Know more!" He laughed at them. "You will only know compliance. You and your friends are powerless to stop any of this with your little pathetic efforts at dissidence." He gave them both another itch. "Remember what I can do to you."

"Are you finished playing the fool Agent Eight?" his superior bellowed. "We need to get information, and not play your silly little games of self-indulgent nastiness. Get on with it!"

More condescendence. He was now very impatient with the whole thing and had just about had enough from Superior Officer One.

"You know we are going to hold you here until the identification systems come on line don't you?"

"We had guessed," Jake replied.

"Well you guessed correct. And you know what? I am going to take great pleasure in giving you your injections myself!"

"Keep to the questions. I don't have time for your little fantasies," his superior was herself growing tired of this interrogation method and was beginning to doubt her Agent's abilities again.

"Do you know why we are going to release you instead of keeping you here permanently, or killing you?"

"Yes," was all Jake said.

"Yes what?"

"Yes sir!"

"Don't get bloody smart again,' he gave Jake a two second itch. "Yes, what?"

"We figure you are going to track us so we might lead you to our friends."

"How very perceptive of you. Again you are correct. But this time, you will not have a choice in the matter. Do you hear me? You will not have a choice!"

The interrogation concluded and Agent Eight instructed a guard to take them back to their cells. He then turned to the holographic projection of his superior officer.

"Do you have further instructions?" He wanted to keep her satisfied but only to the extent where she might decide to end her involvement in this case. He was wrong.

"Yes I do Agent Eight. You are to report everything you learn about these people to me. You will keep me informed every single step of the way. Do you understand this? And…you had better get more than this pathetic interrogation session gleaned out of them!"

She shut down her projection.

Suddenly he was alone in the cold light of the interrogation room. He liked this. It was one of the few things he did like, but it was based on hate. He liked to be alone, as he hated any stupid minds interfering with his work and his manic thoughts.

****

Jenna was in a spacesuit inside a tunnel one hundred yards beneath the lunar surface powering up the holographic bank she would use to analyze results from the mining equipment testing.

"I am ready to commence real time analysis," she said through her helmet communicator to the mining team leader.

Testing commenced on schedule and she began to see the results coming in. Figures looked nominal on the holographic display as the protein strings floated in mid air directly in front of her – a sight almost artistic in a way.

By the third day, all had proceeded according to her expectations, without any occurrence requiring her expertise. She decided to talk about it later with Lyle.

"How did it go?' he asked her when they were both back in the cupboard a few hours later.

"Same as yesterday, and the day before, and… Lyle?"

"Yes?"

"I cannot for the life of me understand why they have brought me to the Moon if all I am going to do is report nominal results day after day – something one of my associates or even a student of protein mechanics could do."

Lyle sensed her frustration and his eyes indicated to the surveillance device inside the cupboard, "I guess they wanted the very best here to make sure everything works."

"Yeah, you are probably right,' she replied picking up on his cue. "How are your results coming along?"

"Very similar. I have analyzed all of the mineral and radiation properties in this location and there appears no cause for concern due to the mining tests."

"No contamination?"

"No, none."

"Hmm…during the earliest days of the protein research and I mean earliest, contamination was definitely an issue."

"How do you mean?"

"Well the first work was done on Earth. During some of the first tests, proteins were accidentally released into the atmosphere. This was bad for human beings. As they are organic proteins, they were able to lodge inside human bodies and attach to the existing proteins and grow."

"Sounds ugly. What did they grow into?"

"Oh nothing life threatening, more disfiguring."

"Disfiguring?"

"Yeah. They grew into lesions and cystic type growths. Human bodies proved to be the perfect hosts actually. Whilst the proteins could attach, the human immune system was put into overdrive to fight them."

"But if they can attach, wouldn't the body accept them?"

"Yes and no. Due to their synthesis and therefore being artificial, the endocrine system had a hard time dealing with them."

"I see."

"There were the natural elements of protein integration missing. They were too perfect and so overloaded the system, with the resulting growths. Basically they confused the white blood cells."

"Did they decontaminate people?"

"Mostly. Some will struggle with the effects for the remainder of their lives, and others were able to make full recoveries. Tests showed it depended on the strength of a person's DNA gene endings, or Telomeres, and the amount of exposure to the proteins. The body was effective in slowing the protein duplication processes but it could not stop them. And from this discovery, they invented the nanotechnology now widely used to maintain Telomeres where cells are reproduced."

Chapter 28

The next three days passed without incident for Raynie and Jake as the time to system startup for the identification chips drew nearer. Agent Eight did not come to see them at any time, and so the guards who delivered meals were the only people they saw. Their conversations were limited by their physical separation, so they kept to shouting out short checks asking each other how they were feeling.

On the fourth day Agent Eight paid them as visit.

"Only two days now," he told Jake with a freely expressed look of hate on his face. His superior officer was not watching him now so he felt able to be himself. "How do you like needles? Personally, I see myself as a poor physician, so I guess it is going to hurt when I carelessly shove it into your arm. You can scream. Oh yes, scream all you like. The pleasure will be all mine."

"You are a hateful man," Raynie said from a few cells down.

"And you are a pathetic woman," the Agent replied as he walked towards her cell. "It is a pity you are not in handcuffs. Perhaps you would like to? Any more crap and I won't hesitate to make you itch." He was now looking into her cell as she sat on the thin mattress atop a steel platform. "How is your bed? Looks comfortable."

"You don't." Raynie felt a similar condescendence towards the man as his superior did.

"What do you mean?"

"You don't look comfortable. You haven't since the first time we saw you."

"What the hell do you know? I am the one calling proceedings here aren't I?"

"No."

"What?"

"I get a feeling it is your superior who is calling proceedings and you...you are just her little lap dog." Raynie couldn't help herself. She was not in hatred of the Agent but she knew he would react to her.

Agent Eight drew his weapon and pointed it straight at her through the holographic cell bars. "You like being smart don't you..."

"Leave her alone," Jake yelled imagining what was going on.

"Oh, your little friend here wants to protect you. But he can't can he. He is useless in there like an animal."

"You are the animal."

Agent Eight lost control and fired, the shot hitting Raynie in the leg.

" Now see who is the animal. Look at you crying and flailing about in pain. Do you need to be put down? Should I do the humane thing?"

Raynie was wincing, as the pain from the shot radiated throughout her leg. "Lucky for you it was a localized stun. Your poor little leg will be better

232

tomorrow. After all, we need you to walk to the clinic so I can give you an injection, don't we?"

He left the cellblock, laughing at the sounds coming from Raynie's cell and at Jake calling out to see if she was alright.

****

Jenna and Lyle had continued with their work on the Moon and both of them were feeling a bit flat. Their results had not yielded anything out of the ordinary so far and the initial excitement at being on the lunar surface was long over. Also troubling their minds were the impending identification chip systems coming online in two days.

"I'm worried Lyle. Do you know what I mean?"

The surveillance system was operating.

"Focus on the results of your work. I am sure you need not worry - it appears as though you have what they need."

"Could I turn the system off?"

"Possibly…" Lyle knew she was talking about disengaging the devices John had given them. They were both worried they had been over cautious. By having a live authentication for someone who had not been identified as having had the chip injected, could raise suspicions. And, with all data to and from the Moon passing through an analyzing filter, there was no way for John to disengage them remotely from Earth without creating a big security risk. "How do they filter the data anyway?"

"It is like a net catching any data. Nothing can escape aside from a faster than light transmission and the authorities are still in the process of refining the technology, so it does not really exist as yet."

"Flux mechanics?"

"Yes." Jenna replied knowing Lyle was referring to John's recent data teleport work. "They are not strong enough to send over distance outside of the atmosphere yet. It has something to do with gamma radiation. Someday soon though I expect they will get past it."

They awoke the next Earth day and saw an additional Lunar Lander had arrived during their sleep period. When Jenna looked to see who it was so far from Luna One, she immediately recognized the same authority person she had seen at the base. This aroused her suspicions and Lyle's when she told him the news. Aside for the extra craft, operations at the site appeared to be continuing normally.

As per usual, they worked at their respective holographic banks analyzing data and filing reports. The mining had been progressing successfully with the protein strings increasing its capacity tenfold over the previous systems. This enabled much faster drilling into the bedrock and was proving to be exactly what those who were in charge were seeking. Lyle was going through real time environmental data as the mining drills sent information back to him at a constant rate. He could see the holographic readouts showing the rare elements and minerals as they had previously, along with data analyzing the immediate effects for contamination from both the protein strings and the physical drilling itself. All looked nominal.

Jenna was herself, carrying out the tasks in situation at the mining face as she had done on all the previous occasions. No indications of any rogue string anomalies were found, and the drive systems were performing as expected, again.

'They really want these elements fast,' she thought as the drilling continued. 'I wonder why?'

There was nothing she could think of as a reason for the urgency in this operation. Her scientific knowledge of the latest developments in technology gave her no further insight than her own personal curiosity.

Lyle's mind began to drift a little away from his work the more it became routine like Jenna's. His thoughts turned to Chan and how he had known he was traveling to the Moon. Further to this, he recalled the discussion with Chan about how the Moon was seen in many cultures as a giver of life as it gave way to the sun each day.

'It seems a long way from there to here,' he thought. 'This place is so remote...I can't think of anything to do with Chan from all of this.' An alarm then sounded and he immediately returned to his work.

The readout was showing something unusual so he entered a sequence to see if it was real data or some error in the system. He checked it again and again. The results were all the same. Something else was there in the rock. The data showed a definite feedback from an unexpected substance. As each scanning wave bounced back and forth, it appeared to be getting stronger. He adjusted the settings on the holographic readout to encompass a wider variety of elements, minerals, and radiation. There was no change, other than the constantly and exponentially growing feedback of data outside of the parameters he had established. He made a few more adjustments to include crystalline forms and precious metals. As he did so, something even stranger appeared in the data. It was if the data itself was taking shape.

At the same time, Jenna had also begun to receive strange readouts. Thinking it was some type of error building, she entered some equations in a hope to stabilize the readouts coming through, but it did not work.

'Very weird,' she thought as she tried yet another sequence.

There appeared to be an unknown crystalline structure coming through in the data. She then made some further adjustments to detect hexagon and octagon differentials, seeking to observe any infinitesimal changes resulting from the variables now showing in the hologram.

No change occurred - in fact the circular definition became even clearer. Then another circle became evident and according to the data, it appeared to be rotating about the same plane as the first circle, yet not intersecting the first circle. The mathematical off spin then begun exploding with enormous amounts of data becoming evident as hundred of equations emerged and kept coming.

Jenna, like Lyle, then thought of radiation and made some other adjustments to investigate. As the holographic image intensified, so too did the shape she was beginning to see. There were no radiation readouts other than the nominal readouts she had seen. It baffled her…until she had a sudden realization. The data was showing her there was a torus shaped construct to the crystal within the rock and the mathematics were now evident in the hologram, confirming her intuition.

Simultaneously Lyle could see the crystal torus forms, prompting him to increase the spectrum analyzer to focus on crystalline particles. The emergence of the torus data continued.

Jenna's excitement was almost too much to hold back, but she kept composure, instead focusing on scanning as much information as she could. Within a few seconds she had a clear image, similar to Lyle's. In a flash, she tried to make more sense of the data, her mind racing. Then after entering some more sequences, she detected additional information including what appeared as a torsion wave.

Then she saw it and knew what they had found – it was of a crystalline torus character and it looked similar to the image they had seen in Dunhuang. Within a second of realizing this, her entire holographic bank shut down, leaving her standing there in front of a blank control unit. Simultaneously, Lyle experienced the same event and he stood there aghast for a moment, until Jenna contacted him, "I assume you saw it too?"

"I did." They spoke no further to avoid surveillance.

Jack had been routinely checking his Lunar Lander as he did each day to ensure it was at optimal status for flight, when he received the call, "Please report to the control room for orders."

Aside from the 'please' he knew it was a command rather than a request. He exited through the vehicle airlock after donning his suit and took the bounce walk over to the control room where the commanding military officer at the site met him.

"You are instructed to take Jenna Atkinson and Lyle Shrewsbury to Luna One as soon as possible. Their work at this site is complete and the authorities deem it necessary for them to finish here and return to the base."

"Okay, understood."

He had never taken authority orders previously and thought it a little odd it was happening now. With his craft already prepped for flight he did not rush back immediately, instead choosing to find Lyle and Jenna himself and tell them the news. He need not have for they were already packing under escort from a military officer. "I am coming with you," the officer said.

The journey back to Luna One was nothing like the journey from there to the mine site. All passengers sat in silence and Jack was not sure why.

Jenna and Lyle were brooding as their imaginations fought against what they knew deep inside. As soon as they had confirmed the existence of the torus, all of their work had immediately ceased and they were now being removed from the site, now in full command of the authorities.

Ten hours later as they approached the base, they could see HyperJet Space Earth to Moon transit shuttles taking up all four landing pads. Upon arrival inside, there was no greeting party and no sign of the friendly Luna One Commander. The entire base had taken on an edge. Within an hour, they had been assigned passage on the next available shuttle craft transport back to Earth, scheduled to depart in thirty minutes. After liftoff and for the entire return journey to Earth it was similar to the trip back to Luna One from the mine site – mostly in silence, as they felt apprehensive about what would happen when they arrived. They spoke only briefly a few times to confirm each other was alright.

As the craft made final approach towards Earth, they noticed dawn was breaking on the North American east coast, and it was the scheduled time for the identification chip systems to come on line. Lyle and Jenna knew their own devices would have now registered from outside the atmosphere. Moments later they watched as the heat shield on its' under side radiated with a bright orange glow as the shuttle craft commenced re-entry into Earth's atmosphere.

****

Agent Eight was up early long before dawn. When the systems were about to come on line, he already had Raynie and Jake strapped into chairs and prepared for their injections. He had decided to do theirs at the same time as the systems became available. With a holographic countdown showing, he counted out loud to them as the few remaining seconds wore off the clock. At two seconds to go, he injected Jake, taking pleasure in seeing his discomfort due to his imprecise method of injection. At five seconds after, he injected Raynie, she too wincing at the pain. He had not been able to inject them at the same time or at the precise time the systems starting operating, but close enough was good enough for him now. A steady blip sounded on his personal identifier – a small device all agents had been issued with the previous day. The blip pleased him, as mundane as he was.

"You are free to go."

His sense of sarcasm also pleased him because in his mind, from this day forward freedom as a concept would be lost. He instructed a guard to take them up and out of the facility and then left the room without another word.

The cold grey light deep underground was kept at low levels as a way to psychologically tamper with the minds of inmates. After a few minutes through the dull passageways, Raynie and Jake were escorted to a waiting vehicle, taking them to a non-descript location.

They now had experience of what potentially lay ahead for many. Agent Eight had provided only a brief insight, and now with their own identification chips, they felt a heaviness of the burden to come. Both were determined to overcome any sense of depravity the Agent appeared to aspire to, so as they rode along in a vehicle after leaving the facility, they both thought of Chan and of the strengths they had gained from insights into energy and elemental intentions during their recent journey. When they were finally pushed out the vehicle by an officer, the dawn sunlight temporarily blinded them as they embraced and held each other not wanting to let go. It was their first physical contact since being arrested.

Chapter 29

Chan knew something had been discovered when his senses alerted him to a presence he felt as significant. Since the security announcement, he had kept a lower profile than ever, focusing his intuitions on finding Raynie, and Jake, knowing Jenna and Lyle would not have returned from the Moon as yet. Fong was giving him the best of service as he sat eating dinner.

The restaurant was almost full with people eating and talking. Some discussed their impending injection, whilst others eagerly showed their friends where they had already been injected. A few were somber, talking in low tones and he could not hear what they were saying. Looking at the faces around him, he felt sadness at those who appeared to be embracing the concept of the identification chip. He wanted to warn those who were yet to get theirs, and he felt a disturbing energy coming from the somber groups.

Two agents of the authorities were seated at a table near the door, having chosen the position so they could watch everyone inside, and also watch those who came and went. Chan was sure they were agents as their slight uneasiness was evident and his sense of intuition was speaking to his mind.

Holographic projections could be seen through the front windows of the establishment, repeating security messages over and over. 'Don't forget to be present for your injection on your prescribed date. Your safety depends on compliance to all conditions so the authorities can affect a safe and secure society.' The propaganda was sickening and persistent, not unlike the intentions behind the entire façade.

Chan felt urgency much greater than at the time of the first encounter in the restaurant. He remained calm though, as it was his disposition. More than ever, he sought solace in focusing on clearing his mind to stay alert for any sign or intuition, no matter how seemingly insignificant. Part of him hoped by chance, Raynie and Jake would appear at Fong's and his problem would be solved.

He noticed one of the agents take a device from his jacket and do something as he held it under the table away from view. The agent was scanning everyone in the restaurant for identification chips. Chan saw this out of the corner of his eye, confirming his intuitions on their identity as officers of the authorities. 'They are already up to their deviousness,' he thought, his mouthful of food sticking a little in his throat as he swallowed. Then in response to his thoughts, he reminded himself not to indulge in negativity, as it would lead to his own undoing.

Fong returned a moment later, "I have the best mangoes for pancakes. Would you like desert?"

"Your best mangoes...how can I refuse," Chan replied.

During this brief conversation, the agents had decided to leave, and now their absence had relieved the heaviness accompanying them. The general mood did seem lighter, conversation more spirited, and the somber groups even looked less burdened. Their presence in the restaurant had provided a sub-conscious sense of negativity, and to Chan, it was clear many people had unknowingly felt this.

Chan was later meditating in a room of an apartment overlooking the Sun Yat-sen Memorial within St Mary's Square, bordered by Grant Avenue and California Street. His mind was clear, now free from his earlier sense of urgency. Sun Yat-sen was an early twentieth century Chinese figure who had been seen as unifying, in a country emerging from its long era of dynasties. As he had entered the apartment, Chan had briefly stopped by the memorial, and considered the difficulties he personally faced as he thought of the celebrated figure who himself, had possessed the personal strength to overcome the struggle for unification of the Chinese people at the time.

Chan's life was similar, just very much more secretive and out of view of almost everyone. Now as he sat in this calm state, details on how he could affect unification were coming to him. Images of the torus, of people he knew, and images of the geometry of life and the universe, flashed through his mind.

Next morning he decided to take an early walk around the inner city and visit some of the places he thought Raynie and Jake might be. Chan had always been early to rise, embracing the clarity and relative quiet of those hours before the majority of the populace awoke. As he first walked the inner city, the towering mass of the central inter-linked high-rise blocks cast a long shadow over the western sector.

When passing the complex comprising of eight towers taking up eight inner city blocks, he noticed the pentagonal shape of each building. The irregularity of the pentagons within a large octagonal complex drew his attention. He noticed the conflict between the angles which then prompted him to consider their isotropic properties.

'There is a variation between these two geometries,' he thought. 'Their linear and solid angular structure exhibits conflict.'

He stopped and looked up as he considered this information further, noticing the angular elements of the building edges against the sky where clouds were slowly moving overhead. It was the same type of weather responsible for the famous foggy conditions to areas of the city. He watched the clouds for a few minutes as he thought about the geometric flow they followed on the invisible patterns of the wind.

He did notice such things as an observer and in a deeper sense for their establishment of the patterns and cycles at all levels of concept and creation.

'They fail to manifest a distinct meridian being so in conflict.'

He knew the importance of meridians in both the physical plane and the non-physical where they are the connecting points - his mind turning to the construct of the great pyramids of Egypt and their meridians meeting at the golden section.

'Geometrical progression is instrumental in building momentum…' his thoughts trailed off.

"I need to talk to Jenna on this," he said aloud, deciding he required the input of a scientist for him to better understand the images within his meditation the night before.

Half an hour later, Chan arrived at the vibrant Fisherman's Wharf area still hoping to find some sign of Raynie and Jake. Numerous couples and groups were at the various establishments he walked past. Some were eating breakfast al fresco style, others still lingering at bars after a long night. He reached the Hyde Street Pier without result and stood for a while gazing out across the water to Alcatraz, the historic island prison.

The sight reminded him of the struggle so much of humanity faced - imprisoned as they were within the confines of consumerism, working life, and their loss of connection with the very energies giving rise to their existence.

'So much taking place only in their brain,' he thought. 'Forgotten are many ways of the heart.'

He gazed out over the bay - his thoughts changing as he watched the motion of the waves across the surface of the water. Their momentum and formation was very much unseen beneath the surface where a few sea gulls in their own scavenging struggle for existence bobbed upon crests and troughs.

Sometime later he realized he had been standing there unaware the of the day's progression around him. Again he looked skyward and saw the increasing air traffic as JetCabs had begun to ferry people about the city. He thought of the minds of their occupants, largely consumed with their work they were traveling to seeking status in a seemingly endless repetition.

****

Arrival back at Kennedy Space for Lyle and Jenna was not quite the somber affair they had imagined. The authorities had removed them from the site as soon as the couple had become aware of why the authorities had also been in presence. People of high caliber seen as potentially valuable by the authorities, were given preferential treatment over those deemed as lesser value. Rather than immediately assigning them to other duties, they were greeted by an officer who immediately requested they come to his office.

Lyle and Jenna were still a bit mystified over this action, but felt they were out of any considerable danger. Fortunately for them, correspondence between the agents responsible for rounding up identification chip dissidents, and the military personnel at Kennedy Space, had not yet occurred.

"Come into my office and take a seat," he told them as they approached the doorway.

Once seated, the military officer began, "As you know, you have both been very instrumental in revealing the toroidal crystalline feature at the Leibnitz Mountains. Until now, the office of defense only had some quite vague spectrum analysis of the area obtained during the initial readings for the mining prospects at the site. We…they, felt it was imperative to unearth…hmm, un-moon this torus using the latest technology, ensuring it was removed intact and uncontaminated." Jenna and Lyle sat silently at ease listening, not knowing what to expect. The reason for their work on the Moon was now clearer than ever.

"However," the officer continued. "There is still work to do after the final extraction process, which is happening now as we speak. So, we are still in need of your services."

"In what way?" Lyle asked, thinking his job could not have any further involvement.

"Good question. First Lyle, we need your advice on maintaining the crystals in a stable condition after extraction, and Jenna, we are looking to attach some of your protein strings to the crystals in a laboratory situation in whatever way we can to see if it is part of a machine. As you know Jenna, nothing comes close to the protein strings and so we have decided the very best technology should be applied. Now I know you did not get a full look at the data coming in from…"

"We saw a hell of a lot," Jenna interrupted, a little confronted with the officer's assumption.

"Okay, you saw a lot. What we need is for you two to continue your work under very strict conditions."

"How strict?" Lyle was concerned they may in fact be swallowed up into the might of the authorities.

"Mainly secrecy."

"So why were we taken off site only a few minutes after discovering the first signs of the crystals?"

"Standard procedure these days. During your return to Earth, we debated about what to do with you. Some wanted you entirely out of the picture, and others argued for retaining your services, myself included. Basically you two are the best we have to look further into this."

"But how or what am I going to do?" Jenna asked again.

"It is up to you mostly. None of us here have any idea on what this thing is and we need your brain to try and work it out for us."

This horrified Jenna. The thought of giving them meaning and understanding was the last thing she wanted to do. Both she and Lyle had recognized the value of the crystals back on the Moon and they felt wary since.

"So again, Lyle we want you to continue in the same way but to work even more closely with Jenna on this. We need all the data you can muster because if this thing is dangerous, we don't want it interfering with the order of the things to come. If it is not dangerous, then we need to know all variables surrounding it so we know what we face if we are to use it."

"Things to come?"

"You are going to see things change a lot and very rapidly around here, around everywhere in fact. The authorities are sick of the state this place is in. They are tired of fighting against failures and the mess people can create for themselves, and so they are bringing in new laws to enhance the lives of people. Mostly to make them feel more secure, and to also structure some order in the world weeding out those who might come against this. Do you understand?"

"Sure," they said together.

"Is it why they have brought in the identification chip?" Lyle asked.

"Yes, but it is only one of the measures about to be taken. You will soon see the rest..."

"Oh."

"For now, there is no more. I suggest you both get some rest. We have quarters already waiting for you. You will find refreshments and clothing there. I must remind you to wear the official issue Geiga wear at all times as we cannot risk any human contaminations. Also, you are to report all findings directly to me. The officer outside will show you to your quarters...and welcome to Kennedy Space, I am sure we are going to have a fruitful working relationship together."

He ushered them out and the other officer took them through the main complex building to their quarters in an adjacent ten-story structure. Whilst surprised with their assignment, they were also concerned. They were about to become a part of this machine - something they were desperately trying to avoid.

"I wonder if we will be under constant surveillance in here." Lyle mentioned as they went in.

"I'll check," Jenna replied. She knew exactly what to look for and after a ten-minute search, came up with nothing.

"I wonder how the others are doing?" she said a short time later after they had showered and changed.

"Why don't we find out? Without surveillance we could call John."

"Good idea." She spoke softly after touching the small device behind her ear.

"Hi," John replied. I thought you two were still space bound."

"We came back early, or rather, we were brought back early.

"Why?"

"We found a toroidal type crystal."

"What!"

"Yeah, as soon as we found it, they brought us back. We are at Kennedy Space. They want us to keep working on it here on Earth. I imagine they are going to bring it back anytime soon."

"How is Lyle?"

"Fine." Her mood then quickly changed. "John, we are worried about the authentication devices you gave us."

"I can imagine. They would have sent authentication signals prior to your official records being marked as injected."

"Yes. What can we do?"

"I'm not sure. We are going to have to wait and see. I think we were a bit over cautious."

"Yeah, we thought so too. And now, they are keeping us here to work on this discovery. It means as soon as they discover our blip, they are going to come after us."

"A problem. Can you get away?"

"Unsure. They have assigned duties for us but have given no indication of our liberties…if we can travel."

"They'll want secrecy."

"Hmm…if they get us, they'll take us in and…"

"Interrogate you and ask about us."

"Precisely. We are very worried about it."

"We are too and a lot more than you know."

"What do you mean?"

"It's Raynie and Jake. Some agent arrested them. We don't know where they are."

"Oh my. How can we get around this…um, situation?"

"We are working on it in San Francisco." John then told her about the chase from the cabin in the mountains and details they heard when Raynie and Jake were arrested. "I contacted Ryan, he is still in Carson City and he is trying to help us. We are building an algorithm to upgrade these devices."

"In what way?"

"Well, until now, the synaptic audio conversion has been incoming only. We have just about finished making it a two-way thing. I'll remotely send it to your devices when we have finished. Then, you will only need to think what to say and it will work."

"What about the others?"

"I told them to get rid of theirs before they were interrogated. They are on their own for the moment and have likely been chipped already."

"So they will have real identification chips?"

"Yeah. But if we find them, we can get them out. Tobias and I had our service chips removed when we left Alaska. I just need to get hold of The Fixture again...hopefully."

"Any ideas on where they are?"

"San Francisco somewhere. We are looking for them now."

"How are the others? Are you all together?"

"Yes, and they are fine if not for the shock of hearing about Raynie and Jake."

"What next then?"

"Sit tight and do your work, but look for any opportunities or ways to escape – you want to avoid them finding out about your authentication devices. Have they searched or scanned you?"

"Not physically, but I am sure they will have scanned us when we arrived back."

"Don't worry too much yet then. There is no way they can find the frequency the devices operate at. Ryan's insider friend has given us all the schematics for this security deployment. They are not even close...yet."

"Okay, we'll talk again soon. Give our best to the others."

"Will do, and same back to you. Will look forward to seeing you again."

"Us too, bye."

"Bye."

****

Raynie and Jake had been wandering around aimlessly for most of the day since they had been dropped off somewhere near Oakland. They had no idea where to go aside from just wandering about. Their minds were still reeling from their arrest and having identification chips inserted into their arms. They had both desperately scratched at the injection point in an effort to remove the chip, but it was useless. The injection had been deep passing through the layers of skin, into tissue and each contained an anti-removal mechanism.

Around noon, they decided to go to the wharf area in the city to lighten their mood, after having caught public transport back over the Bay Bridge. The authorities had given them all of their possessions back upon release including their money, and it was enough to see them by for at least a few days. They had even returned their holographic phones after analyzing all the data they held. Fortunately they had used the devices from John leaving no data of any use to the authorities. Whilst the authorities may find a total lack of data as odd, John had made some fake untraceable entries to avoid suspicion. This also meant there was no record of any communications with their friends for an Agent of the authorities to see as a lead.

By the time they reached pier forty-one, they were exhausted again feeling very hungry and decided to have a meal whilst discussing their next move. As they sat in full view of Alcatraz, they felt a little somber, thinking they had now become prisoners of the authorities, despite their release from the facility.

"Cheer up," Jake said to Raynie as he took her hand across the table "You know me…full of determination. I'll get us some help."

They had no way to contact the others, thinking using their holographic phones would be too risky, and they had no knowledge of Jenna and Lyle returning early from their Moon mission.

A sea gull suddenly appeared on the railing next to their table, its' familiar call distracting them from their somberness. It was persistent, waiting for any scraps they might leave behind and so it kept them company until they had finished their meal. As soon as they walked away, it flew down to ground level looking for bits and pieces. Jake turned back to see the gull now fighting with others over the very few remains of their meal and laughed - the first light-hearted moment since arrest in Reno.

"Scavenging for scraps eh? Go for it." He had seized on the vision as a way to try and joke about something to help lift their mood further, but it reminded them of the impending crack down by the authorities and so it fell flat.

"Yes they do struggle against each other for survival, like people."

The two of them turned to see Chan standing there but not looking at them. "Come with me," he said. "I have an apartment in China Town. We must go there, now. Don't do anything or talk to me, just walk along as though you do not know me. When we get to St Mary's Square, watch me, and then wait for at least half an hour before you go inside. I will be in apartment nine."

Within the hour, they had made it inside Chan's flat feeling sure they were not being followed. Apartment nine was sparsely finished with only a bed, a couch and a table with two chairs, and no sign of any technology at all.

"Chan. We were arrested. They gave us identification chips," Jake said. "They can track our movements now."

"Hmm…it is bad. We cannot stay here, no. You are being tracked even if you think you are not being followed."

"I guess we overlooked the tracking hey Raynie."

"We must move today. I will return in a minute." Chan left the apartment and returned a minute or so later. "I have made a quick enquiry, as there are people I know here in China Town. We can go now to another place…"

"But they will track us there too," Raynie interrupted him. Despite meeting Chan, she was nervous.

"We need to find your friends John and the others."

"Yes, they can help, but until then…"

Chan went over to the only window in the small apartment and looked out to the street below. "We must go now!" He had seen a suspicious looking six-wheeled vehicle parked on the other side of the square.

Without delay, they ran out of the door and took the fire escape stairs at the rear of the building. They continued running until they were all exhausted.

"My friend, he has a vehicle. We must keep going one more block." They ran again, all of them short on breath and their legs getting heavier.

Without word, Chan led them into an old disused looking warehouse, "Kim San! Kim San, where are you?"

"Here," Kim San emerged from a small alcove at the rear.

"Kim San, we need your vehicle."

"Yes Chan, it is ready…over there," Kim San pointed to a vehicle covered by a tarpaulin. "Take it, drive fast."

"Thank you Kim San, we are in your debt." Chan said as he tore away the tarpaulin cover.

"No debt. For you, anything Chan. Be safe, now drive away fast."

The vehicle was brand new, shining brilliantly despite the low interior light. Kim San then opened a large door for them as they entered. It was appointed with the latest technology and for a brief instant they were at a loss on how to control it.

Chan, unable to decide, just spoke in desperation, "Fremont!"

Immediately the vehicle came to life and drove outside on full automatics. It took the main link out of the city, across the Bay Bridge on then turned southward towards Fremont at full speed.

"What is at Fremont?" Jake asked as they sped along the eastern side of the bay past Oakland.

"Another friend. He can help you…a little. Your chips will give us away wherever we go, but he has something to buy us time."

Agent Eight was not far behind, smug in knowing he could find them wherever they went. Their vehicle took the off ramp from the elevated roadway and headed towards the address in Fremont Chan had instructed. Agent Eight followed and was closing, just two miles behind.

As soon as the three of them arrived, they rushed inside the building. Chan's friend was waiting and immediately seized Raynie and Jake by the arms – for an instant they were horrified.

Seeing their look Chan assured them, "He has something to scatter the authentication signal for your devices. It will stop the authorities being able to pin point your precise location, but they will still have knowledge of your general position."

They both relaxed a little as Chan's friend wrapped some material around their arms.

"This will generate a static scattering signal to confuse their tracking software," he said. "But you must keep moving as they can still track you to within a few hundred yards. This is new technology I have built to counteract the chips. There are others out here who don't like them as well."

"How do they work?" Jake asked after he had finished.

"Static field generator to scatter and create multiple signals, something I have been working on with a friend of mine, John."

"John?"

"Yeah, John Matheson."

Raynie was beginning to think another coincidence was again at play. Their meeting with Chan had initiated these intuitions for her.

"We have a friend called John, but we don't know his surname."

Raynie was struck then as her and Jake did not know John's surname.

"Well there are a lot of Johns in the world. Likely not to be the same guy."

"But it could," Chan said. "Tell John if you are in contact Raynie and Jake are with me. We are going to Chico in the north...at this address." He gave him a small piece of paper. "We must at least attempt to set up these connections," he said turning to Raynie and Jake.

"Thank you," Raynie and Jake said together.

"No problem. Anyone who is against the chips is welcome here."

The three of them left and immediately headed northeast, deciding to take a more inland route. Agent Eight was closing, his targets just five hundred yards away. He knew they had met up with someone and he was about to get more satisfaction. He prepared his weapon as his vehicle continued tracking and driving on automatics.

"What the hell! What the hell is wrong with you?" he was shouting at his vehicle. The tracking readouts suddenly showed a number of identical targets including the one programmed to zero in on the dissidents. "Stop!" he barked and the vehicle came to a halt.

He feverously entered a sequence in an attempt to fine-tune the scanner – it failed. The readout continued to show multiple targets. Then some reasoning came back to him as he noticed all of the targets seemed to be moving in the same general direction. He decided to follow, his anger not subsiding.

Chapter 30

"Finally!" Steve said after receiving notice of a data package detailing his first real assignment since being taken from HAARP. He brought his holographic station to life to view the details. "What the…?" was his reaction when he discovered his next assignment would take him to the mining outpost in the Asteroid Belt.

"They bloody well want me a long way away. You could not get any further away in fact." The mining operations in the asteroids were the furthest human occupied regions away from Earth.

As he read through the holographic data, he learned he was to supervise all authority operations stationed in the Asteroid Belt. Various maps and diagrams also appeared detailing the type of mining operations, their locations and the type of vessel he would be in charge of.

"I see what they meant," he said to himself, thinking of the conversation after he had been removed from command at HAARP.

A part of him was excited, as he would finally realize his dreams of space travel he had as a younger man. The other part was suspicious and a bit angry. The journey there would take around three months with a brief stopover at the Mars colony.

"Three bloody months of sitting in a tin can, and then only to sit in more tin cans."

He knew what they were doing to him – it was virtually a death sentence, or it might as well have been. The assignment was to last four and a half years, which meant he would be away at least nearly five years and he had no choice, other than to resign from the service.

He considered this for a while but decided he would take the assignment. Otherwise they would simply put him in jail. It was obvious he knew too much about HAARP, even though it was hardly anything. He had considered this over time since his departure from Alaska, and it being the only reason why he had been removed. Now, liftoff to space was scheduled for two days - they were sending him off immediately.

****

Central authority command was abuzz. Officers were everywhere and their superiors were holding meeting after meeting, working on strategies and logistics. The identification systems were now online and shortly the operations at HAARP would take effect. Firstly though, they had decided to carry out another nuclear detonation in order to further enforce the public's concern. They had chosen Reno.

In the early morning light on the fringes of the Nevada desert, the controlled delimited nuclear mushroom cloud grew steadily upward and outward. It destroyed the entire city in one great wave vaporizing buildings and all life. It made people scream for a mere second before they turned to ash. Dogs barked their last frantic breath, bird life simply disappeared, and horses bolted to nowhere. Life in Carson City was mostly obliterated, with many suffering burns and the after affect of radiation if they escaped the initial blast wave. Lake Tahoe was changed into an ashen landscape of mud - its' aqua blue waters and beautiful surrounding forests now ruined.

Ryan and his friend were dead – neither of them had more than a few seconds to realize what was coming.

Agent Eight watched it all on holographic projectors, his pleasure apparent. He saw the reports of destruction. He saw the reports of pain. He saw the reports of suffering. He was not angry this time. He was full of admiration. Admiration for the effective destruction wrought upon people. He admired the way the authorities had efficiently crushed so many spirits as he watched them act like fools, with their hysteria and their crying. And he admired himself. Soon he would be exactly where he thought he would and nobody could stand in his way.

He hated Reno and thought good riddance to the place wishing they had taken out Las Vegas as well. He hated the cabin where he had commenced his chase, thinking now it would be nothing but a ruin, and he hated Lake Tahoe with its gambling and holiday makers. Nothing suited him more than the blandness of nothingness, of grayness, and of coldness.

The authorities were full of lies. They filled people's minds with stories of false terrorists and false insurrection. They filled people's minds with paranoia. They filled people's minds with insecurity. They filled people's minds with false promises it would all would be alright. They would apprehend those responsible and they would serve justice to them so the population could see who to blame, could see who they could hate, and could see why compliance with everything they were told, would keep them safe. Already choice was disappearing fast.

A state of semi-martial law was immediately put into place, not only in North America, but also in nations and cities all around the world. From the great glittering jewel cities of Beijing, Moscow, and London, to the small centers and remote towns, authority control was served upon the people.

Many were almost unaffected, their self already given to the system. Some were concerned and so gathered to discuss if it was the right thing to do. Often many of these meetings were infused with officers of the authorities and so eventually consensus swayed towards supporting the new security measures.

Then…there were those who outright objected to such an intrusion into their lives, and into their souls. They could see visions where the simple freedoms of movement, of choice, and of human spirit, would be replaced with systems of ordinance and organized methods in pursuit of efficiency. They knew this was not the true elemental nature of human beings from their deepest selves beyond physical manifest. Technology was rapidly servicing the human instrument and through such service would come even deeper dependency.

Lights so beautifully ornamenting the buildings of the great cities were turned off and replaced with cold grey lighting rendering them featureless. Festivities and celebrations were cancelled. Cultural centers and museums had their doors locked. Alcohol and other indulgences were to be mostly outlawed, and private businesses were to be shut down in favor of system purchasing. Commerce would soon be cashless and conducted using the identification chips as payment. The authorities had convinced themselves they had thought of everything, and were now taking control of almost everything.

Inside the high rise, armed officers were stationed on every floor, and people everywhere were told they must be indoors no later than nine at night. In coalition, authorities everywhere created an order where populations were forced to comply. It was an order of insurrection against human values and ethics.

Steve McCray departed the next day for the trip into space. He was not piloting the spacecraft, but rather, was considered as a VIP passenger and thus was given all the privileges of such a position. He still felt bad though, not only because of where he was going, but how his life would take on a lonely existence far flung from most of human kind.

Gradually throughout the course of recent events, Steve was becoming softer and easier going - his feelings of being a staunch commander receding. Even though he had nobody to call family, no lover or partner, and what appeared to be no role on Earth, he felt deeply saddened when he heard of the atomic event in Reno. Steve had spent years of his life presenting a front as an officer to maintain order, but underneath he was sensitive to nuances of life.

As the spacecraft lifted further and further into the atmosphere, he feared he was abandoning ship and this upset him. He never abandoned a post, never abandoned a mission or let anyone come up short under his command. Now in some way now he felt he was needed more than ever on Earth, but there was nothing he could do about it. Then, at the time when the craft initiated atmospheric exit thrust, he was pushed back into his seat with the forces making it hard to move, and at this moment he felt helpless, pinned, and unable to do anything.

Chapter 31

Jenna and Lyle had watched the events unfold at Reno with disgust, knowing the authorities were behind the destruction of so many lives. Jenna openly wept so Lyle held her tightly, softly stroking her hair. When the news was too much to bear, Lyle turned off the holographic vision and they just held each other for a time.

Operations at Kennedy Space had increased with the influx of military personnel and machinery to the base. When they left the living quarters building the next day, a military officer was waiting for them to take them to their assigned workstations. A heightened state of security was in place with all employees now assigned officers to escort them whenever they were required to travel about the massive space complex. Upon arrival at their workstation, they discovered new orders had been issued for all personnel to be given the identification chips as a matter of urgency.

"Security level is at red," sounded over loudspeakers throughout the space center at regular intervals.

Their approach to their work was slow as they both felt uninterested and too preoccupied with thinking about the events in Nevada. Their mood hardly changed until the officer who had instructed them when they first arrived, suddenly appeared at their door. He was carrying a small metal box about twelve inches square.

"Well, here it is."

"What is it?" Jenna asked.

"The crystals."

"In there?"

"Yes."

"Oh of course." For a moment Jenna had forgotten her visions of the toroidal crystals on the holographic bank had been magnified, and so she had expected something much larger.

"We need to get to work on this immediately. Anything you require, do not hesitate to ask." He handed her the box and left.

Lyle had stepped out when the officer delivered the box and returned just after he left. He noticed the box straightaway upon return, "It is the crystal isn't it?"

"Yes. The officer told me that we need to get to work on this fast, but you know what?"

"What?"

"I feel like stealing them and running away. Far far away."

"I know. There is not one cell inside my body wanting to deliver any type of knowledge about what the crystals can do."

"Oh it can. Think about what Chan…" She stopped herself remembering they were under surveillance. "I hope they missed…"

"Me too," said Lyle, in the same hushed tone, frustrated he had forgotten such a rudimentary thing.

Jenna opened the box and they both looked inside. The crystals appeared to be very hard and they thought was diamond.

"I will place them inside this resonance chamber here. Just keep on eye on the variables as I power up the chamber Lyle. I am going to do a carbon isotope scan first." She entered a sequence via the holographic controls resulting in a very low hum from the chamber.

Lyle monitored the resulting data, "All looks nominal for diamond."

"Okay. I'll increase the power and scan the neutron quantum spectrum. It will give us a lot more detail on its purity." She made the required adjustments and the crystals began to glow a little pink. "It's beautiful."

"Now I'll see what sort of conductivity it has…"

"Wait! I am getting some silica readouts here."

"Silica?"

"Yeah. Adjust the spectrometer a little and see if we can detect the level of silica particles. Also give it some unshielded ultrasonic waves and some waves in the upper spectrum – I want to see if there is a vibration we can get going here between the carbon and silica."

Jenna responded to Lyle's request thinking it a little strange as she had not considered there would be silica, and about intensive ultrasonic waves to make the crystals vibrate. Immediately after entering the sequence required for the test, they began to respond. At first they both thought it was just going to repeat the pink glow again. But the glow kept intensifying and as Lyle had thought, it also began to vibrate. They both just gazed at it for a few moments forgetting to watch the resulting data exploding on the holographic banks similarly to when they were discovering the crystals on the Moon. Then without warning, the crystals flashed a blinding flash for an instant and then stabilized to a regular glowing and vibrating state.

Without word, they both knew what they had to do next, but they had no idea how they were going to do it.

Jenna shut down the test so they could think for a while about how to steal the crystals and get out of the space center. Neither of them were pilots so an aircraft was out of the question. For a moment she thought they would not be able to simply walk out of the base with the crystals, then she reconsidered - they needed a plan.

Returning to look as if they were still working for the sake of the surveillance, they pretended to be analyzing the test results, whilst still thinking of ways they could escape with the diamond like crystals.

Then suddenly, Jenna heard John's voice inside her head, "Jenna, are you with Lyle?"

"Um…yes," she said softly.

"Stand by. I am going to remotely reconfigure your devices."

"Okay."

Twenty seconds later John's voice came again, "Try thinking something to say to me."

'Okay,' she thought. 'It is toroidal crystal, we are certain.'

"Good, it works. Amazing. What will you do?"

"We are trying to work out how to steal it. It will be difficult though, as this place is teeming with authority personnel."

"Um…wait a bit." Their communication fell silent.

"Lyle?"

"Yes?" he said softly.

"Try thinking a communication to me." He did and it too worked. "Good. Jenna said you have found crystals but you cannot think of a way to steal them."

"None," he responded as a thought.

"I have a way…I think might work. Listen. Tell me the spectrum results you have, I need to know the vibration frequency of the crystals."

"Um…it varies slightly, increasing with each moment."

"I thought it might. It may be linked into the Schumann planetary resonance exponentially increasing each second. I am going to send a masking frequency to your device. You will need to take it off and attach it to the container of crystals. Don't worry about your security authentication, it will still work."

"Okay," Lyle took his device from behind his ear and gave it to Jenna who placed it on the box of torus crystals.

"Jenna?"

"Yes?"

"I am going to set the frequency to match the Schumann Resonance…including its variations."

"Alright."

"Now. All you need to do is take it and leave the base. The scanners will not detect it as they too are calibrated using the Schumann resonance, so in effect, anything showing up on their readouts will be masked."

"Alright, but it is going to be nerve wracking."

"I know. There is a lot of nervousness about now with all this stuff going on. Trust yourselves. Nearly everyone is nervous after Reno, so get out quickly as you can."

"Where will we go? There are bound to be travel restrictions in place."

"There are. I suggest you commandeer a vehicle or buy one or something. Avoid air travel."

"Okay."

"And best of luck. We are heading towards Chico in northern California. My friend in Oakland told me he had met Raynie, Jake, and Chan."

"How?"

"I'll tell you when you get here. Also, avoid coming in through Nevada. Take a more northern route. The authorities have devastated the northern end of the state and some of California, but it is safe. They used a delimitated nuclear explosion and so the effects were limited to a specific area…even the fallout."

"How?"

"They are able to manipulate the radioactive isotopes using some type of nano-tech to breakdown at a very fast rate after a specific time instead of the normal half life we are used to. Don't know much more, but if they have the capacity, who knows what else they have up their sleeve. Travel safe."

"Well, we need to get going Lyle. We must whisper to each other in close hoping to avoid audio surveillance. I am thinking of a way we can get out of here without raising suspicion immediately, but they will find out what has happened in a short time after we leave."

"What's the plan?"

"I am going to set up a resonance field based on the data we received during the testing. It will make it appear as though the crystals are still here in situation under test conditions. You need to leave first. I suggest you go straight from here to our quarters and pack a few things we will need. I will follow, but after about thirty minutes. Then we are not observed as leaving together."

"But what about the chip injection? We are both scheduled for two this afternoon."

"It is part of it. Tell them you need to go now, as there is some testing you need to do taking most of the afternoon and you thought about getting the injection early so you can return to your work. We are dealing with authority here and they like an eagerness to comply."

"Okay, and then?"

"When you are gone, I will request a personal meeting with the officer who we report to. I will take the crystals with me in my pocket as the container is small enough…thankfully."

"Right."

"Then, at the penultimate moment when I arrive outside the office, I will request passage to quarters. I'll use a feminine excuse…they cannot refuse."

"Sure."

"The injections are being carried out at the space center hospital which by a stroke of luck is on the northern perimeter of the base, are you following?"

"Yes."

"When I get to our quarters, I will request the same as you after staying inside for a few minutes. I'll fake a reason based on something I have just realized. I am sure whoever escorts me will not be smart enough to think much more than his authority duties…to escort us wherever we need to go. I will tell him to wait whilst I have my injection. By this time we will both be in the same location at the northern perimeter."

"And from there?"

"It is a tricky part. The escorts will not be waiting right outside the injecting room as they will know there are other officers inside the hospital. This is where we need to make a move."

"We ask for transit outside the base?"

"I was thinking the same. We have been given rights to go outside."

"But what about the injection?"

"Those officers won't know if we have had it or not if we allow a suitable amount of time for the injections. So we use the devices John gave us to provide us access outside the base. The chips are now a pre-requisite for access to leave this place. I will still have mine behind my ear and yours will still be on the torus in close enough proximity to register authentication."

"So we walk right out of the base."

"Precisely!"

"One thing though. With authentication occurring just prior to our re-entry into the atmosphere, surely they will be tracking the signal?"

"I can imagine they will, but as we have had no questioning or been arrested as yet, I can only imagine they haven't yet made the connection. I'm going on my gut feeling."

"Sounds good enough for me," Lyle looked into her eyes and gave her a quick kiss.

"Huh?"

"Luck, and because I love you."

Jenna's plan was precise and so too was its execution. An hour later, they stood waiting at the main access gate outside the space center hospital as an authority officer confirmed their identification and then opened the gate for them to freely walk through. Five minutes later, they were on the public transit system used by the many visitors to Kennedy Space for public viewing of spacecraft launches, but on this day there were none and so they had the transit carriage entirely to themselves.

They disembarked the transit at Tampa and immediately went about looking for a vehicle for the long drive across the continent to California. Within an hour they had purchased an older second hand model and were traveling on the east coast elevated transit network. The network on this side of the country was an immense collection of tubes servicing the vast populations. One could drive at high speed from Florida to Massachusetts and west to Alabama and Kentucky without having to leave the elevated roads or the need to engage manual driving.

A while later as they drove north through Georgia, they mapped out their route to the west - first deciding to leave the main transit in Atlanta, then proceed via Tennessee and Illinois before turning left through Iowa, South Dakota and Montana. Then they were to head due west through Wyoming and Idaho, and onto Oregon, before changing to a southerly direction taking them to northern California.

By the time they had reached the halfway point through Georgia en route to Atlanta, the authorities at Kennedy Space were on full alert to their absence and to the missing crystals. Not long after, the authorities had communication with Kennedy Space about fraudulent identification signals.

Just before nine, Lyle and Jenna stopped at a motel on one of the old roads just outside of Springfield, Illinois.

"Lyle?" John was contacting them a short while later. "How did you go?"

"Like clockwork...thanks to Jenna. We are in Illinois."

"I think we should turn your devices off. The authentications might give them a way to track you. When you get to California, give us a call. Even if I don't answer straight away, I will get a message. How's Jenna?"

"Fine...sleeping, she is exhausted."

"Tell her the news. We'll talk when you get here."

"Alright, until then."

****

Agent Eight was in a usual angry mood as he drove around northern California looking for Raynie and Jake. He had tracked them along the lonely road leading from Lassen Volcanic National Park into the lower altitudes towards the west. He was now relying on a rough idea they were in the area near Chico. As he entered the town from the east, the familiar scattered signal again showed they were moving and he realized he would need to maintain a vigilant chase if he was to apprehend them.

He turned northwards, skirting the town, on an intercept course. His efforts to de-scramble their signal had proven useless, but his determination made him resolute in finding them.

He tracked them further north, passing through Siskiyou County, then further as they traveled on into Oregon. Onward relentlessly he followed them into Washington State and then saw the scattered signal approach the border with Canada.

"I'll get you there," he said aloud, and he immediately contacted border authorities to give them orders to apprehend the two fugitives. Unbeknown to him, John had contacted The Fixture to arrange a meeting just south of the border inside the United States.

He watched the signal continuously with growing hatred, leaving his vehicle to drive itself. This time there would be not even a morsel of remorse. If he found them and they led him to others, he would then kill them. They were of no more use anyway. All he wanted was to find the leaders of their organization or whatever it was, so he could claim a grand prize.

The Fixture had no trouble crossing through the border controls. He had sufficient technology to pass through using a dummy chip with fake credentials. He had been waiting for the others at a café just a few miles over the border for ten minutes when John, Raynie, and Jake arrived.

"Nice to see you again," he said shaking John's hand. "Ah, you must be Raynie," he shook her hand. "And Jake. Nice to meet you. Let's not waste any time."

The Fixture led them outside to his vehicle, parked at the rear of the café. "Get in."

All four adults entered and sat down in his vehicle.

"This is going to hurt a bit," he said as he prepared the same instrument he had used to remove the chips from Tobias and John. "But…I'm sure a little bit of pain is worth it to you."

"Sure is, we hate these bloody things," Jake replied. "Do Raynie first."

The Fixture positioned the extraction instrument and slowly inserted the end of it into her arm. She winced and let out a small cry as the instrument dug into her tissue and pulled the chip out.

"There it is," he said showing her the tiny chip held by the claw like end of the instrument. "Now Jake." He did the same for Jake, who also winced but remained silent. "Okay, you are now free, but we have one more thing to. Now I need to destroy these little bastards." He took out the small kiln he used to destroy the chips, and powered it up. "We can only kill them with high heat. Say bye bye to your chips."

They both said 'bye bye and good riddance' as The Fixture placed them inside and shut the cover. Within a few seconds, the chips were dead.

"You can relax now." Raynie and Jake both had a little laugh, as they now felt happy to be free of the chips and of the dreaded Agent Eight who was now eight miles away.

As the signal disappeared completely from the holographic readout, Agent Eight did exactly the opposite to Raynie and Jake. He almost had them and now all evidence of them was gone. He exploded unable to control himself as he saw his dreams smashed. He swore and swore as his mind twisted and his body did the same. His vehicle continued to drive on until it stopped at border control. He was out in seconds, unable to contain himself continuing his cursing and attracting the attention of others at the location. They watched as he lost his composure more and more. They saw him end up on the ground twisting and rolling about like a madman. They saw him finally get up seething. An officer approached him to see what the problem was, and Agent Eight shot him dead. He began shooting at others indiscriminately, sending them dashing for cover, and then he turned the weapon on himself, for a brief moment wanting to blast his own head into oblivion.

He hesitated and as he did so, four authority officers who had rushed to the scene, took the opportunity to seize him. He had now become a prisoner of the system, and so they took him away to be detained and to be charged with murder. Agent Eight had lost, his megalomania being his downfall.

****

When they reached Chico, Lyle tried his holographic phone to contact John, and by chance, he answered, "Hello Lyle, where are you?"

"In Chico, where are you?

"Same."

"Good. Come to the Northern Café in the center of town. As soon as we finish this talk, reset your device and wipe everything."

"See you soon."

"See you soon. We have quite a tale to tell you."

Chapter 32

He watched her looking at him with a look of utter contempt on her face. Agent Eight sat there with a bland face free from any expression, his natural way of being anyway. Superior Officer One could barely speak, so enraged she was with his failure. All she had were four names, and they would do everything they could to avoid identification. They were basically at square one and this infuriated her.

She did not care for Agent Eight in the past, and she cared even less now. He looked like a pathetic little man whose dreams had been shattered and she wanted to make sure it was true. She herself had superiors to report to and Agent Eight's failure was in part, her responsibility. She despised him for this as she considered how it might affect her own status, fearing she might be relocated lower down within the high rise.

For a moment she reconsidered her position, longing for the sanctity at home when she listened to music, but she quickly was past this and began shouting at him, "What a bloody useless waste of space you are. In fact, I have a good mind to send you there and open the airlocks. Then I will be utterly free of you forever."

"You have been charged with murdering an officer of the authorities, and whilst your pathetic little dreams of power may have enabled you to consider murder as just part of your work, when it comes to the authorities, you are very much mistaken. What to do with you? I am at a loss. You are to face charges for your major stuff up, and personally, I hope they give you the longest prison sentence they can think of." She fell silent for a few minutes to consider what she could do.

"I have no reason to come to your defense. None! And…nor will I. I am going to recommend you serve your sentence as far away from me, from this…as possible."

"What do you...?" Agent Eight began.

"Shut up. I do the talking now. Only me. Let me think about what I can do to get rid of you." She fell silent again, this time for longer.

"I am going to recommend you serve your sentence a long way from here. Fortunately for you there is a little flexibility in how you are to be treated, but just a little. What use are you sitting in prison wasting time and money? None. In fact, you are barely any use at all. But…you can be assigned for rehabilitation." This last statement weighed heavily on Agent Eight. He had never seen himself in need of rehabilitation.

"The authorities have no room, no space, and no use for little idiots like you. But…there is one option, just one." Agent Eight knew what was coming.

"Yes. Space. I will send you there. Far far away into space. Then I can be free of your smarmy little mouth and free of you pathetic little brain. You don't deserve it. If I had my way entirely I would just throw you away, but I cannot. The authorities in their ever vigilant view of efficient practice would not like you wasting away in jail and wasting money, so space it is. Get yourself ready you bastard. You are going in two days. Yes two days until I am rid of you for good. I'm sending you to the Asteroid Belt – the furthest asteroid I can find will be your new home. Do you like it? Your pathetic inability to carry out such a simple job has earned you desolation. And don't think you will be in charge of anything when you get there, because you won't. We have just the job for you…if you can manage not to screw it up as well. How does the sound of being a guard appeal to you? Now get out of my sight – I don't ever want to see you again. Guards, take this pathetic piece of rubbish and throw him on a spacecraft."

Agent Eight hated her for immensely barely able to control himself. He hated her almost more than he could imagine hatred, and he immediately began planning his escape from the asteroids. The guards then seized his arms and took Agent Eight away as ordered. Within forty-eight hours he would be beyond Earth's atmosphere on his way beyond Mars.

****

Finally, they were all together again. The adversity of recent weeks had taken a toll on their spirit – Chan had told them it was a test of their tenacity. As they discussed the Reno event and its repercussions, they fell silent for a few minutes thinking of Ryan. He had given them his undivided commitment to aiding their cause and his death weighed heavy on their hearts. Despite only having known him for a short time, they had connected with him and his insights through his meditations.

Chan was the only person present who had never met Ryan, but he too felt saddened at his passing. "We must understand in life, many are given as to aid the growth of others. We should show him the respect so deserving for his positive affirmations and commitment to the progression of awareness, and not let his passing go un-noticed in our spirits."

They all had dinner together on the first evening of reunion, part as a celebration of Ryan's life – they at least owed him something, and in part as a way to reconnect.

When the dawn came, Chan said they might focus on the remnant energies from Ryan – the energies he had given them. They all decided it was best not to watch of any news, not to think of the recent devastations wrought upon so many innocent people, and not to think of what might happen in the future.

"It will give us energy to be in the now moment, to be in our present hearts and minds, and to focus more on anything we see or feel as an intuition," he said.

Then he turned to Jenna and told her she must show them the crystals. "It is time. We were not of mind to discuss this last night for our focus on Ryan was a requirement for our further intuitions."

Jenna revealed the crystals to all present. They just stared at them. It was then when Chan was forthcoming. Reaching into his pocket he then revealed the actual Torus of Eternity. The magnificence of it being a diamond fashioned into a perfectly smooth object with inscriptions seeming to be just below its' exterior surface, began to have an impact immediately. Even in this relatively benign state, they could feel and sense some type of energy or presence.

"Chan. You told us in China, you were unaware of the torus being an actual object and we felt you were referring to it as something we each hold within us."

"Indeed. It is now after your proving to me of your intentions, character, commitment, and motivations away from egocentric self identity, I reveal the torus. Your understanding at the time meant it was best you did not see it as an object for it could then have tempted you into thinking of it as an object of affection. It is not an object of affection. It is beautiful and ever so pleasing to the eye, and my intuitions then told me for you to see it as an object of meaning, of activation, and so much part of all of you. Since then, you have all experienced events bringing you to this place where you are able to view the torus. The torus represents dimensional cycles in life...in existence. Do you understand?"

"Um...a little," Lorraine said being the first to reply. The others agreed.

"When I speak to you John, and you Tobias, and to you Asper, and to you Lorraine, I am of the heart even though you were not involved with the journey like the others, I am feeling you have been brought here to this time based on your expectations and on your hearts' intentions. Do you understand?"

They all nodded in agreement. "Now we must continue and we have much to do."

"But the torus looks...um, deactivated if anything," Lorraine said.

"Believe me, it is not. Its' very discovery is part of the activation process so commenced by your friends here."

Chan looked at Raynie, Lyle, Jenna, and Jake in turn with a look on his face reminiscent of similar times where he advised them during travel along the Silk Road route. They each had a feeling Chan was saying a lot more to them than his words indicated.

"It is important for us all to understand now very much more needs to be done." Without giving anyone a chance to ask why, he continued. "Those who also seek the torus do not really know why, and fortunate for us, they found it for us. They appear to have a limited knowledge and this was sufficient for them to play a part in its activation through its' discovery. From there, they have no idea what it really means or how it works, but…they do know it is significant. And…such minds residing in limited understanding are still affected greatly by the negative ego traits and so they would try to manipulate the torus for their own ends."

"Can the torus stop them?" John asked

"No. It is not the place for the torus to choose. Negativity is the way of their egos. Such a view is not correct. They can though, use it to enhance their power, but in a limited sense. Think if you will of the saying human beings only use a certain percentage or part of their brain. Well this is often true, for many who are afflicted with this condition, are ruled by the brain, and so miss almost all of the connection it has with their heart."

"Ha," Chan laughed a little as he thought of what to say next. "You see…or feel it is not so difficult to understand if you consider intentions. Remember what I said to you when I told you to think about spirit sets the path for light to follow."

"Consider further what I just said a moment ago…sets the path. With this you may understand more." They again went to silence in contemplation of his words. "It is a thing of both dimension and of physical construct, yes?"

They agreed.

"Then consider the idea a person had the intuition of the dangers to be presented to the torus. Now do you understand? Human beings so much focused on their brains and on their egos, have forgotten their hearts and it is the hearts of humans setting the path…for light to follow. This is your connection to human spirit, an unseen energy binding all planes of conceptualization. Within this resides energy some people on Earth assimilate it into life with their brain controlled by egocentricity in the negative reaction state, effectively disconnecting the non-dualism connection to their elemental selves free in righteous alignment given by their creation as a being."

"I see…" Raynie began.

"Do you see or do you feel?"

"Um…feel I suppose."

For a few moments then, silence fell over them all.

"But why did we find the crystals? Why did all these events link together and end up with us here, with the torus?" Tobias asked.

"You just answered your question," Chan replied. "You said link together. This means connection and so it is the connected heart which is much more powerful than almost everyone who lives on Earth gives it credit for. It is not a power appealing to the ego, rather the connecting energy binding existence. The heart is also a torus of sorts reflecting this connection to the very basis of construct then enabling emotion and higher realizations."

"It was in the Leibnitz Mountains. Lyle and I researched who the mountains were named after and it turns out it was a German philosopher who was into the harmony between spirit and matter...intent and manifestation"

"It seems coincidental the torus crystals were located in mountains named after such a person, doesn't it?" Chan said. "Well, think of this as part of the activation process. This has been happening for some years now...since at least the time the name was dedicated to the area."

Everyone felt distinctly enlightened, this conversation giving them inspiration beyond any effect they had felt from the recent events and troubles.

Over dinner, Chan felt it was time to discuss more of this with them, "We have much work to do still."

"How do you mean?" Asper asked speaking the minds of the others too.

"We need to leave North America."

"Why?" Jenna asked. She was feeling a little tired from travel and all the authority check points. Both her and Lyle were now fugitives as well, so any travel would expose them.

"Go to further activate the torus. It is only the beginning. You and Lyle have seen just a little when you were at Kennedy Space. There is much more yet to unveil...um, activate."

"Where will we go?" John asked thinking of what he might have to build technology wise.

"Germany. Yes. There is more you need to feel and events thus to occur. Do not ask why at this moment. I will tell you at the right time."

"Why didn't you go there when you were so close in Austria?"

"There was no intention for a trip to Germany during those moments. It might have been just over the mountains, but think of those mountains as representing a climb all of you had to take to see beyond. This metaphor was laid out intentionally as part of the activation. There was no use for you visiting Germany when you would not have been able to feel the connection to be understood there. The journeys to Africa and to the Moon were requirements to be awakened prior to furthering your experiences by going to Germany."

"I need to get to work then."

"Yes John." Lorraine said herself excited at the prospect of travel.

"And quickly. We need to leave as soon as we can," Chan added.

"How do false identities sound?"

"Perfect," Asper replied.

Chapter 33

Passage into Canada was smooth via public transport, with their identities John had made checking out with the border controls. They had all decided to cross the border after confirming international passage out of Vancouver was not subject to strict waiting times. When they arrived in Vancouver, John took them on to The Fixture's place in the inner city. He would not let them in. He told them to split up and come back shortly after, as too many people looked suspicious. They did this, with John and Lorraine returning to see him - the others would meet up with the couple later.

The scene in Vancouver was more relaxed than any place they had recently been. People were about the streets, in cafes and restaurants, and everything seemed relatively normal. The only telling factors were the amount of official personnel everywhere and the dull light about the buildings.

During John and Lorraine's meeting, the others had organized the HyperJet flights to Germany, organized accommodation to ensure they were in by nine to beat curfew. They decided it was the right time then to relax in the park by the harbor. Military vessels docked on the other side of the harbor evoking particular interest for Tobias and Jenna. Neither of them had seen any design of such type previously – only Jenna had seen schematic holograms of the technology when it was still in a research phase.

"They look like they have some capacity for complete invisibility of both holograph and physically detection," Tobias said to her. "I have only seen similar fragments of material when they conducted a few tests at HAARP some months back. All I knew was something to do with the antenna frequency calibration."

"I know of similar materials testing to do with aligning systems frequencies with those produced at HAARP. What does concern me though is I have seen those vessels before, but only as proposed developments. I am pretty up to date with this, as recent as three months ago. I had no idea they had gone this far. I was involved because of my work with the protein strings used in propulsion systems."

The following day as the HyperJet powered up its engines for takeoff, Asper was almost beside herself with excitement. It was her very first flight anywhere in her life and she had been anticipating it all night. The views as it turned east over Vancouver harbor were her first thrill, only eclipsed when having reached the required altitude for hypersonic flight, the jet pulled her back into her seat on a rapid climb to seventy thousand feet.

"Whoosh," she said softly to Tobias. He smiled back at her, himself enjoying the same feeling as they could see the world below slip further away.

At cruising altitude, Asper simply gazed at the magnificence below and beyond. With the Earth's curve as a divider, she kept looking down to the mountains and the plains then becoming vast ocean below, and up to see the fringe of sky and space.

Three hours later on approach to Munich International HyperJet Terminal, she watched Paris pass underneath as the jet began slowing and descent, and then marveled at the great expanse of the restored Black Forest, just before landing.

"Now," John thought to the others via audio synapses. "Time to be alert, the Germans are likely to be pretty hot."

****

Superior Officer One was at her station in her office, as usual. It was not just another day at work for her - it was one she faced with a little nervousness. Today was the day where she had to explain Agent Eight's failures. She knew those above her regarded her, but since this entire security event, she remained cautious knowing anyone could quickly become someone else if it suited their need for status. 'Efficiency of the authorities' showed permanently at the top of her holographic bank, reminding her of how she had treated the Agent.

"I see you sent Agent Eight to the asteroids." Her superior kept looking at her, and at the holographic data floating in front of him. "My my, he has indeed been quite a nuisance, hasn't he?' She did not answer, as it was not a real question, rather a statement.

"Hmm…I would tend to agree with your decision to send Agent Eight to the asteroids. He is no use to us rotting in prison, wasting money. But, I am concerned with how I must decide on this from my position. As you know, I am compelled to take some action. Otherwise I would be seen as inefficient in doing nothing to enable the progress of the authorities. They don't stand for inefficiency you know, which means they don't stand for failure. I am sure you are well aware." He paused for a few seconds, was about to speak, but then fell silent for a few more.

"I see also you gave Agent Eight a second chance after the debacle in San Francisco. Why did you make this decision? It appears soft to me."

She answered, "I was prepared to let him prove himself. I thought then, he could make an efficient agent. It was only just after his induction."

"I see. And so what made you think he could have been an efficient Agent? I see here he was quite the opposite in fact. Large amounts of laser energy used to vaporize trees, stun shooting over twenty people in Reno…hmm," Recollection of Reno's destruction made him pause for a second. "Murder of all things. Murdering an officer of the authorities. I see how much this has cost, apprehending him, transporting him, holding him, and now sending him to the asteroids. Surely the authorities already had a sufficient number of guards at the asteroids. So much in-efficiency is what I see. No one really likes it. In my view even the death penalty could be considered. Such an efficient way to dispose of problems."

She remained silent – her superior had not really asked a question of what made her think of how she treated the Agent. Her superior was not interested in what made her think. All he considered was to merely be doing his job efficiently, as she did.

"I can only consider this. I must do something, and I will. You know like I do Superior Officer One, in order to maintain and even gain status, we in the service are not unlike what the population is to become. We need to take all necessary steps to eliminate any chance of inefficiency in order to prevent demise in status. But I also know you are relatively new to this business like me, so I am going to show you a hint of compassion. But don't get used to it, for it will not last. I have no desire other than to service the authorities, and when all evidence of emotion and empathy is gone from this planet, then all the better."

"Oh don't see me as a monster," he said noticing a slight look of disgust on her face. "I am nothing like your Agent Eight. Remember though, this is the last time I will give any leeway. For you I have decided to send you on an assignment, and your status could remain."

Superior Office One felt a tinge of relief. Upon seeing this, her superior continued, "I will further your relief and tell you we have a specific mission where your skills will fit in perfectly. I am sending you to Berlin. As you know, our authority friends in Europe do seek to further the efficiencies. I want you to do some investigation and then return after two weeks to report.

You will be issued with the appropriate holographic data. Study it well for you must bring something back, otherwise there will be inefficiencies noted. Oh this is not some do or die mission, but nearly. It is something I want looked into. When you return, you can have your job back, if…you are successful. Otherwise I am afraid I will have to take you down one level of status. Do you understand?"

"Yes. Thank you…"

"No need to thank me. You are dismissed."

****

Travel in Germany between major destinations required an application, where the local authorities would then confirm credentials during the one-day waiting period. Driving was relatively unaffected as was the pedestrian traffic about town and cities, despite the authorities present in almost all locations. Everyone was required to be indoors by nine though - the curfew was a global-wide agreement between nations.

The group had traveled the short distance from the Bavarian capital and found accommodation in a small motel located in Herrischried, a town at the edge of the Black Forest. The town retained much of its culture and architectural styles for which Bavaria was known and still had atmosphere and feeling.

"Soon these places will disappear. Not actually disappear, but the feeling in the air," Lorraine said.

"Perhaps not," replied Chan. "There is always a positive…as you know with electricity, positive and negative. The spirit of some people is strong. Don't despair…look for the positive in things. Focus your intentions there. Doubt is but a trick."

"Ah! Chan is in form," Raynie gave him a jab.

He laughed, pretending to do the same back "Ha. Watch out! Many form to come."

During the course of the evening and into the night they discussed the torus at length and it reminded them of the journey across China and into Africa. "Why did you not come to Africa Chan?" Jake asked.

"No reason. I only wanted you to go there and get a feeling for the festival."

"There was no danger for us as there was in China?"

"None I knew of. It was good when you left China, they had followed you much of the way, as you know with Jake being poisoned. But we were able to see ahead of them. We knew what they would do – it is the way for people who are being foolish, to make mistakes."

"So do you think those people are still following us?"

"Oh yes they surely would not give up until they get what they want. But they are not the authorities - no, they are a different group. Think of our earlier talk about the legends of evil creatures associated with the Moon. They are more like this."

"What?"

"No, not werewolves," Chan laughed briefly, seeing the look on Raynie's face. "They are a dark group. People who like to explore such a side of life."

"Side of life?"

"Way of life, call it what you will. They like these things."

"Do we need to be scared?" Lorraine asked.

Chan turned and looked her directly in the eye, and before concluding the sentence he scanned them all with his eyes, "Never be scared, or your ego will attract things to be scared about."

This brought them to silence for a moment, as the point felt a bit somber.

In the morning, they ended up at an institute for the study of movement in water, and its association with the related element of air - as Chan had intended.

"People who originally founded this institute were interested to study the wave forms and the rhythmical balance of the elements," Chan said as they stood outside before entering. "This is very relevant information to our understanding the activation."

"I think I know why," Jenna replied. "I have researched wave forms in the development of the protein strings. We looked into the interruption of circulatory systems being broken into a linear chain of cause and then effect. I was designing systems for maintaining the construct of organic laws attached to governing string behavior. Interestingly, when particular elements are interrupted, they always try to return to their original organic state."

"This was also very relevant to establishing fields in flux for the teleport, and for using matter and anti-matter frontier drive systems," John added. "Like you Jenna, maintaining a stable field or state is required, but in this sense, a state just outside the solid organic, or natural state. This is a fundamental requirement in establishing any type of flux mechanics, otherwise they will phase in and out of operation. This should be interesting."

"And so again, I remind you of how human beings create things to reflect their inner awareness," Chan added.

The first exhibition inside detailed the very thing they had discussed, focusing on how water always tries to return to its natural spherical shape when interrupted by gravity.

"See, water is essentially the element of circulatory systems in so many forms...or types. Think of the variations in matter where the flow of water comes into effect. Study this, for aside from a matter of science as it appears here in these holographic diagrams, it is also a matter of spirit. Spirit flows along similar forms. You will see more in time."

"Chan. I am thinking of this as an infinite cycle. If it is the basis for life and other forms, then surely it must not have either an end, or beginning...like a?" Lyle asked.

"Yes Lyle, you are somewhat correct, but we need to see more to understand this in a holistic way."

They moved on to another holographic image, "See here," Chan pointed at a section of the image, "Water flows or takes a meandering path. Many people...um, all people are of this. Consider the amount of water in your physical bodies. Now, notice this other information. Wherever water meanders, it also has inner currents. These are important as they belong to the life or spirit of the water flow and are as much a part of it as the main wave form."

"I am thinking of the talk about parallel infinities and the images we saw where it appears as though there are curved lines leading off the infinity images, "Raynie said.

"Indeed, those images of infinity are very closely aligned with your thinking and feeling now, in response to what I said of inner currents. Whilst those 'curved lines' as you call them appear to be going out and away from the symbol of infinity in the image you saw, they are also going within. And see here. Two currents spiraling as a natural form of flow. They mirror very much the DNA helixes as we understand them, yes?" They all agreed.

"The meanderings are very relevant. They can show you the loss of connection people experience when their egocentric sense of self leads them away from this natural connection. People say at times, 'meandering through life' and in this sense they have taken to losing their awareness of what this actually means. Here now, our intuitions are leading us to understand this connection in a proper way, but those who 'meander' through life, can often feel they are just riding this wave form wherever it takes them, winding along feeling lost within the ego struggle. This is a feeling also of loss of control, but such control is not from ego's desire to control things, it comes from a detachment and a feeling of being without direction. And so, those who suffer these times do not have expectations based on intuitions as their focus. Many of them in these situations want to feel these intuitions, but are without the awareness to see this connection."

The next holographic exhibition showed images of life forms and again the issue of flow patters featured. Raynie was observing some details on the construct of the human body, "See guys, look how inside bone structure, there are spiraling forms from the tiny fissures here," She enlarged the image so everyone could get a clear look.

"And consider the muscles where systems flow built around these bones," Chan said. "These systems, flowing as they do are of the spirit of matter. Your brain does not consciously think of making it this way, or keeping it this way. Where this occurs, it is more of the connection it has with your heart. Your heart too in physical form, is probably the best and most vivid example of this."

They all studied the images for a moment before Chan continued the tour he seemed to be guiding, "See how the heart is positioned mid-way between the organs of digestion and the upper sensory organs. It is a balance of the entire flow of the body, and a primal rhythm. And important too – see how the heart is a vortex?"

Without allowing time for an answer he continued, "This is most vital to understanding very much potentiality of the torus. The heart is a vortex center for the circulation throughout the body. Study this for a few minutes to see the heart as a vortex, and note the properties of how a vortex works."

"Now we must look also at the brain, for it requires our attention in our awareness of wisdom. The activity of thinking is actually a flowing movement, of water. See how the brain floats here?" he indicated toward an image of a human brain, floating inside cranial fluid. "This is the connection so many forget. The spirit nature of water aligns with true thought or intuition connected with the heart. When a person is ruled so much with egocentric thought and they have learned these ways through their lives, a disruption can occur. Water is foundation to this activity through its nature in linking it together as the nature of one is the spirit or energetic way of the other."

"I have been thinking of the harmony festival we went to in Timbuktu," Jake said. "The snake brought wisdom to Nommo through a flowing…"

"Yes, yes. See why I sent you there now?" Chan was eager to show them the connection. "The flow of water is also of the universe…consciousness. So see how they are…um, united? So when one thinks based on intuitions, it is the information of the universe forming the intuitions and so the brain is also connected when it decides on a response to these intuitions. In contrast where a degree of disconnection is involved, then the brain and ego reacts instead of responds as if the person is separated or enclosed."

For the next half hour they viewed several other exhibitions related to air and water. Many confirmed the earlier information on waveforms and vortexes, and also how life moves through both. They saw images on the flight of birds, how eagles ride the up drafts and down drafts, and how single birds join as a flock to fly as one, as do fish swim and act as one in schools.

"What I don't quite grasp, is the relationship of movement, as in simply walking along…"Asper began, but trailed off to consider what she was thinking about a little more.

"A good question. I will reply if you please? You think you are walking along the street in a linear way. You start at home and you go to a restaurant." This also drew the attention of the others. "Think then if you will of the water within you and around, and the air as well, being in this infinite wave pattern and torus shaped vortex deep within. So as you walk along, there are these occurring inside and outside. Your brain is in a way, creating rhythmical arrangements of vortices through the action of your walking. After all, you do also walk with a rhythm. Your brain has intentions whether they are from the heart or from the brain, and the act of walking is the response to these intentions. You might intend to go to a café, and so you walk there. But all this time, you are a vortex, you are within a vortex, and you are creating vortexes as reality is created each moment. Such a simple act…like walking is much more, as all things are more than they appear to be. We are just tuned into observations with our conscious mind – but the sub-conscious is always there."

"Sorry to diverge, but I am thinking of the many artificial things created on Earth," Jenna said.

"Yes, there are indeed a lot of these things, but they too are not so much artificial as you may think."

"How do you…?"

"Hmm…see them as formations of intentions. Similar to what we just discussed, a person can intend to do something, and in response they do it. See these creations in a similar way and understand how often their processes of creation are bound to the same waveforms and vortices. But, also there is geometry involved with this along with things seen as natural."

"But some are…or have been so toxic to life," Jenna responded thinking of humanities reliance so heavily on fossil fuels and chemicals in the past.

"Ah…simple analogy. Think of boiling water. By nature the water is spherical in its organic state. When we apply heat, we are in fact turning the water into steam and so this is breaking down the normal state of the water and trying to convert it to another natural state of steam. But, this water becomes toxic in a sense if we allow it to touch our skin, for it is very hot and it burns. So where we try to force natural elements together into a state where their waveforms are not compatible, then we get such toxicity. Some of the chemicals you may be thinking of are very much this way. There has been so much laboratory work to interrupt the natural states and to force them into other states."

Jenna turned to Chan, "I am very interested when you mentioned geometry Chan. Many things in nature exhibit geometric shapes, take hexagons for instance. They do not seem to appear as flowing…in the sense of what we have discussed today."

"Hmm…I was thinking in San Francisco of our need to discuss such things when I was looking at the high rise buildings. It is good you say this. But also understand these geometric shapes are also bound to the ways of the universe, and you will begin to understand how they flow. Now, I think we have seen enough here, for too much information at once can be difficult in understanding this relationship with intuitions."

As they left, there was a mixed feeling amongst them of some type of wisdom, and a feeling of some type of confusion. Many of the things they had learned were being re-shaped into patterns, flows, waves and vortexes, particularly the references to the heart. They definitely all took something from this visit otherwise unobtainable up to the time. It was a sense of knowing and of recollecting, in a fashion activating existing elements within they were mostly unaware of at the time.

"Oh, excuse me," Asper said as she opened the front door to the institute at the same time as a person from outside was about to enter.

"Not a problem," Superior Officer One said. "After you." She held the door open as the entire group of nine adults filed out onto the street. She saw all their faces, a few of them smiling at her, but she did not return any smiles. Inside though, she felt something a bit alien to her, reminding her of being at home and the pleasure she felt listening to music.

Superior Agent One had been sent to Berlin for a meeting with the authorities in the German capital, who then advised her on the trip to Bavaria. She was to investigate the properties of waveforms and vortexes herself, but not in the same way as Chan and the others, who connected it with intentions and intuitions. Her goal was to study this information for the purposes of the authorities in their development of technology to further trans-human existence. She was to report back to her superior so he in turn, could report to those who were building the algorithms for humanity's evolution in becoming part machine.

Understanding of elemental forces in life for their duplication in artificial life technology was one of many algorithms being designed to interact with organic matter. Others included stimulation of the sensory organs, refining the connection between nanotechnology and the endocrine system, and the conversion of data based life rhythms to the synaptic receptors in the brain.

She had wondered why the authorities had not simply looked up this information, but then realized her superior was actually doing her a favor by sending her there as measure of punishment for her failure with Agent Eight. Her superior has seemed amicable with her punishment for Agent Eight's failure, yet all the time he had been lying – setting her up to be his example to his superiors of how efficiently he could extract usefulness from personnel.

By the end of her visit, she was confident of having sufficient understanding of the information to be able to make a report to please him.

As she approached the exit, recollection of the strangers she had encountered earlier returned to her mind but she was not certain why – perhaps it was just because she was now exiting through the same door and simply recalled the previous event, or was it something else?

'And why did I think about being at home then?' she asked herself once outside. 'What a strange effect.'

She left the scene quickly forgetting the odd thoughts about her meeting earlier in the day – dismissing it as mere chance. She had a report to start working on, and there was still more investigations to come.

Later as she was working on her report, Superior Officer One stopped for a time, again thinking of the group she had seen earlier. Two of the people had seemed familiar to her, and then she realized. She had seen Raynie and Jake and remembered them from the time Agent Eight had interrogated them. She wondered why she had not recognized them earlier.

'It was a strange meeting,' she thought recalling her feelings at the time, where they seemed to glaze her mind and lulling her usual state of alertness. As she wrestled with trying to understand her oversight, she could draw no conclusions, but was resolute on finding them again. This prize would certainly allow her to keep her current status, and there was also a chance it could elevate her even higher.

Chapter 34

Holographic messages announcing further restrictions were shown in public places and sent to individual holographic devices in the evening as they all discussed their time at the institute. First would be the elimination of individual recognition of people by name via their identification chips. John was glad the files Ryan's contact had made for him, were complete. All people were now referred to as per their identification chip registration. For those who had taken the chip from the onset where personalization had been offered for a small payment, they too faced becoming a number.

Second, and perhaps the most intrusive issue to date, was the announcement the authorities now had access to all information about an individual and there were no restrictions in place to protect privacy. Until this time, people had been seeing the chips as merely an identification thing, a means to have your medical records available at all times, and as the future way for payment systems. They saw this as un-obtrusive, more along the convenience and safety lines, and so had not really considered them further. Now some people felt a little concerned the authorities might watch every move they made or thing they did, not knowing such a thing was already in place.

"Do not be alarmed. The authorities have designed this for your safety and your comfort. We want people to feel they are never inconvenienced. We want people to go about their day efficiently, and we want people to experience the best of life. These new measures will ensure we can deliver services to you most effectively – tailored to your individual style."

The message then repeated in German, "Du nicht sein beangsti..."

He turned it off, muttering, "Dezentrallsierung...."

"What was it?" Lorraine asked him – they had left the group and were sitting together alone in one of the bedrooms at the retreat.

"Devolution. Lorraine, I want to go to Britain. I know this information from Chan is important, but I want to see my son. I've been worried about him...a lot."

"Do you think he is safe?"

"Oh yeah...I suppose. It is just with this crackdown, I have felt uneasy being so far from him, and there was the dream I had at the cabin. Besides, this stuff today is still swirling around in my head."

"Like a vortex?"

"Hmm...my thing is more the technology. I am going to have to keep on top of this and stay alert to any new developments."

"But Chan said you were ready and we were ready like the others."

"Yeah I know, and perhaps I am, but it's just my..."

"What is his name?"

"Chris."

"Then go and see him. The others will understand, I'm sure. Um...can I come with you?"

"You don't need to."

"It's not about need. I want to come. It won't be for too long, and we are going to have to leave soon anyway. Where will we go then?"

"Yeah, no-one has mentioned it, not even Chan. I don't know how long I am going to be there yet. Who knows, they suddenly might make it illegal to travel between countries."

"Do you know where he is in London?"

"Not entirely sure, but I'll call him and find out." John contacted his son Chris in London via holographic phone and after he ended the call, he looked at Lorraine with a smile on his face.

"Good to talk to him then. Is he okay?"

"Yeah, he's fine. He said he would meet us at Heathrow."

"Well it's settled then. When should we go?"

"We need to apply – there is the twenty four hour waiting period. We'll apply tomorrow then."

John did not know Chris actually lived in the high rise in central London – a world unto its own comprising of twelve connected towers, each reaching to one hundred and fifty stories.

"Welches Gate hat der Flug nach London?" John asked the attendant.

"Gate elf."

"Vielen Dank."

"Danke. Auf Widersehen."

"Polite for an official during these times," John said as they walked to gate eleven to depart Munich for London.

"Maybe they think happy people make efficient people," Lorraine said, impressed with John's grip on the local language.

The others had said goodbye and they would be in contact to arrange the next place to meet John and Lorraine.

"I suggest a walk in this marvelous forest," Asper said grabbing Tobias by the hand. "I want to feel it – not just look at it. Well?"

"Very good idea," Raynie agreed doing the same with Jake.

"Yes, take a day in the forest. It will do you good. Tonight we need to talk of other things, so take in the forest energy and be refreshed. I will be about town today – I need to contact some people. I have seen..."

"What Chan?" Raynie expressed the thoughts of the others.

"Hmm...ha, ha," he laughed a moment. "I think I have seen some of your werewolves."

They knew he did not actually mean mythical beasts of the night – he was referring to the group who had followed them in China. His joke fell a little flat though as he saw looks of concern come across their faces.

"Oh, don't be concerned. We will take care of them, so enjoy the forest. But watch out for real wolves."

The forest had been accurately restored in the mid twenty first century as part of the recovery of natural wonders and the preservation of nature. Humanity had finally taken a turn away from the dirty energies they had used since the Industrial Revolution, realizing there was an inherent place for nature to be part of life on Earth. Corporations suffered the most from this as they were required to research and develop new energy sources, costing them so much money many had simply given up and gone out of production, This had played into the hands of the officials who had decided the authorities were to amalgamate and become owners of business, and of all energy supplies.

The trails within the forest were littered with rays of sunlight, permeating through the green leaves to the ground below. They were actually walking along a two-wheel track, giving them enough room to spread out and walk together side by side. Birds once absent from the forest, now sang to them from the trees as they took in deep breaths of the fresh natural air.

After listening to some tales of old Forest Lore from Raynie and Lyle, the sun had passed midday, its' heat bringing a hush to the forest around them. They sat there a while longer thinking of Raynie's tales and the simplicity of those times so many centuries ago. The times of recent past and what they saw as times ahead, seemed anything but simple and some part in them had a craving, to stop running, to stop fighting – but to keep learning.

"How do they know where we are?" Lyle asked Chan later in the evening when he had mentioned this other dark group. "Even the authorities find such a subject very difficult."

"Hmm…the authorities rely so much on data and technology to find you – these others do this through their intentions."

"How? I would have thought their intentions are fairly similar to the authorities based on our experiences so far."

"They are connected to a type of energy prevailing on Earth for a very long time. With each positive, there is a negative – as I said with electricity yesterday. You might see the authorities as the negative, and in many ways they are. But this other group are much more in touch with responding to their instincts – so well practiced in these dark ways. Today, you took a walk in the forest, I trust it was rewarding for you?"

"Yes," Asper replied before any of the others, "Raynie and Lyle told us some stories of mystery from times long ago."

"Then it was right for you all to listen. Think of this other group similarly. They have often been the founders of mystery and myth from those dark times in human history…"

"Not as dark as now," Jenna interrupted.

Chan looked at her slightly disappointed she felt such things, "It is dark Jenna, but there is always light as well. It is there to look, and feel."

"Did you see them again?"

"I did and I was able to distract them for a time, but I feel there are others and for this we must be wary. They will be relentless and if successful, they will expose a darker side to humanity so much more than those in the authorities are aware of."

****

Superior Officer One was scouting the town, looking for any signs of Raynie and Jake. She had taken to this extra self-appointed assignment with vigor, confident of her abilities to track them – motivated by thoughts of a successful apprehension seen positively by her superiors. Her day had been without success. There had been no sign of them at all, or of the others accompanying them. She wished there had been a way to have taken an image of the entire group, for she knew they were all together the previous day, and those others would make an even grander prize.

Still confusing her though, were the feelings she had during the encounter. She lacked the sheer malice of Agent Eight and instead she focused on career and improvement of her status – so the encounter had in some way, appealed to her sense as a human being.

The time was now approaching nine in the evening and she too was bound to the curfew, having not been given any special dispensation to be out any later. She resigned her feelings, and returned to her lodgings and the report. As she put the information together, the concepts and details she had gathered began to rekindle feelings though, and she was unable to put them aside. Her superior whilst giving her some leeway, had demonstrated the very essence of what the authorities wanted people to become – emotionless and purely efficient. His reassurance he was not a monster like Agent Eight, had done very little to comfort her as she saw a similar bland look in his eyes when he had spoken.

Status had been everything to her since she had entered the services.

Coming from an impoverished background, she had worked hard for many years to ensure she too would not end up like her parents – who were now long passed. She was alone, having never wed, and it had been so long since she had any type of affectionate relationship, she had almost entirely forgotten what it was like. It had been a long time since she had socialized at the wharf district in San Francisco and even longer since she had taken in any sense of culture or creativity – except for music.

She loved music and held it dear as it harmonized her and gave her a sense of emotion. It was such a contrast to her work and she had struggled with these two polarities at times, wondering if she had made the right decision to join the services. During the few times she had chosen to eat out in recent years, she had seen people go about their trade, at times envious of their simplicity and apparent lack of compliance to the rules so dominating in her life as an officer. With a mixture of emotions, feelings, and doubt in her mind, she decided she had had enough for this day and retired for the night. Her sleep was given to restlessness with dreams of Raynie and the others, and of perplexing life choices rising within her.

She awoke with the new morning feeling groggy, still embroiled in the aftermath of her dreams. As she ate breakfast, the appeal of being Superior Office One seemed to become less and less as she thought of her own superior, the look in his eyes, and the brutal methods of interrogation and detention she would need to supervise. Her thoughts then turned again to the Agent she had sent far away to the Asteroid Belt, and something in her made her glad he was currently in space traveling further and further away from her.

Despite this, she decided she must return to both her report and to tracking Raynie and Jake – her dedication to her work still strong. She was scheduled, according to her assignment, to make further investigations at the institute and she took it upon herself to conclude this during the morning, and then try to find Raynie and Jake in the afternoon.

When returning to the museum, she looked in earnest for anyone she might recognize from the day before, but all to no avail. Giving up on this, she went inside to continue her work.

She read a quotation aloud to herself as she viewed another holographic display at the institute, "O man, speak, and life of the universe shall be revealed through thee. Rudolph Steiner."

This moved her as she again, recalled the words at headquarters. The intention was to create efficiency within the authorities, efficiency within the population, and to remove sense of self, of emotion, to be replaced with compliance.

'Was this the way of the universe for humanity ahead?' she thought.

The idea of strict ongoing compliance to her authority superiors and in her own life began to taste bitter, feel bitter.

'Do I want to live a life bitter, just for the sake of status?' she asked herself. 'Do I want to be part of a universe of bitterness and compliance?' She left the institute, unable to focus on work any longer.

Despite her earlier intentions of finding the others, she walked the streets of Herrischried aimlessly. She did not stop for a meal, nor did she go back to her accommodation – she just walked on, thinking and feeling. She thought of her work and of her status - the appeal also rapidly loosening their grip on her. And she began to see what it really was the authorities were putting into place, and it began to horrify her.

She saw images of people suffering, and she saw images of a bland world strict with compliance and free of cultural and artistic values fearing she could lose touch with her own escapes through music. Normally she would walk with her head high and fully alert, but this time she barely even watched where she was going, only guided by inner senses to stop at the edge of a street to avoid vehicular traffic when required, or to take a turn to the left or right. She rounded one street corner with an ornate stone building and looked up at its character, feeling all this would soon be lost.

A collision with another pedestrian brought her back to her senses. Returning her gaze back to street level, she looked into the eyes of the other person who had recoiled a few steps.

"Hello Jake," was the first thing she said before she even really thought about it. Then she became an almost hopeless mix as duty and surprise conflicted in her mind…and heart.

Jake looked shocked, as did the other six adults with him. They were all unable to move, this meeting so unexpected because the person knew his name.

Superior Officer One then scanned the group looking for Raynie.

"Hello Raynie," she said her official composure returning a little.

"You must be mistaken," Jake said, thinking of their false identifications. He was about to give his name.

"I am Superior Officer One. I was watching when Agent Eight interrogated you and I was listening, but you could not see me."

The entire group of seven adults began to turn around as if to run away, but they were slow, a little hesitant. Something was almost holding them in place, holding back an utter sense of alarm and urgency to escape.

"We saw you at the institute," Chan said, the least affected out of the group.

"Yes you did, but I was not sent there to apprehend you. I did not even know you were in Germany – no idea where you were at all in fact. Now this. What a bonus for me. I could arrest you know. All I need to do is ask any of these officials about the streets to help."

Raynie and Jake could not help themselves and were about to run, "Don't run. There are officers everywhere. It would do you no good. And don't anyone else try anything either."

"A standoff then." Lyle said.

"No. Not a stand off. You really do not have any choice in the matter. I can take you from here now, and then back to the authorities by evening."

A look of resignation was coming across their faces. "But I won't."

Their looks turned to surprise.

"I want to talk. Let us go to the restaurant across the street there," she pointed to a traditional German establishment. The last sentence was more like an order rather than an invitation.

Chapter 35

John and Lorraine had met Chris in London at Heathrow International Hyperflight Terminal, after their brief flight from Munich. He was very glad to see his father for it had been over three years, and he returned John's parental embrace. After introducing Lorraine, they went into the central city for lunch.

Lorraine had taken a liking to Chris upon meeting him. He seemed to be a positive and generally likable person, reflecting some of his father's character she had grown to hold dear since their meeting in San Francisco.

As they sat in the traditional English hotel, John thought it might be good to finish their meal with a beer, but Chris refused. "I don't do any drinking dad, but thanks anyway."

For a second John faltered. The last time he and Chris had seen each other, was over a few beers in a hotel in Seattle and Chris had no objection to a drink or two then.

"Um…okay. Lorraine?"

"Yeah, I'll have a beer, thanks John."

"So how did you and my dad meet?"

"In San Francisco around a month ago."

"He didn't say why he was there. Last time I contacted him, he was still in Alaska. Too cold for me though."

"He was on a trip to see some friends. We met up one night and here we are."

"Does he still do things with technology or has he retired in old age?"

"Hey, he's not too old."

"Yeah I know, just he's my dad, I guess I see him as old sometimes."

"He does some tech stuff I think, mostly a hobby though. You know he left the services a while back."

"Yeah, he told me about it. Felt it was the right time to get out…shame."

"Why shame? He seems happy now. And the services are getting pretty strict about things recently with all this crack down."

"It's because of the nuclear detonations. I think it is a good measure. People need to be safe you know. Terrorists and insurgents don't really care who they kill or what they destroy."

The conversation fell silent as John returned with the drinks.

"Getting to know each other?" he said as he placed them on the table.

"Just a little," Lorraine replied. She had felt something strange about Chris after the short chat.

Chris had no idea of how Lorraine felt and turned to his father. "Dad? Do you want to stay with me at my place? I have enough room for you and Lorraine."

"Yeah. Sounds good. Where do you live?"

Chris replied with a slight sense of pride, "Eastern tower on level seventy six – in the high rise."

John was taking a sip and almost spat his beer back out into the glass.

"Are you okay dad?"

"Um, yeah, it just went down the wrong way a bit."

****

Superior Officer One had taken charge of the meeting as soon as the entire group had sat down and ordered drinks. "You know surely by now I have a pretty good idea of what you are up to." Without waiting for a response, she continued. "And you know it is my job to see the authorities continue their drive to efficiency and weed out anyone who might come up against such things." They all remained silent.

"You did give Agent Eight a run for his money didn't you," she said looking at Raynie and Jake. "And he failed me. Well he was useless anyway and he has the punishment he deserves…well, in part." She hoped the spacecraft Agent Eight was in, was increasing in speed so he could be taken farther away, faster.

"I myself have very little time for failure, and Agent Eight is best out of the way. He was a blemish on my record and my status."

"Why does status mean so much to you?" Chan asked.

"Doesn't it mean everything to every…um, most people? I can see it is not so important for any of you here and it puzzles me a little, but…" she trailed off thinking of her earlier feelings.

"It does mean nothing to me," Chan replied.

"Interesting. So what does mean anything to you?" She had not yet asked for his name.

"Many things," Chan replied.

"What about you?" It was a general question to Lyle, Jenna, Asper, and Tobias.

"Same," Tobias replied first, and then the others repeated his response.

"What does 'many things' mean? The authorities only want compliance and in return you get recognition of status. Surely it appeals to you, doesn't it? Your lives can be made so much better with the authorities on your side."

"I doubt it," Jake said. "Agent Eight did not seem to think so for Raynie and myself. I bet he really wanted to kill us when he found us. It was just process holding him back."

"Agent Eight failed to do his duty with the efficiency the authorities espouse to and so he is now being punished."

282

"About time," Raynie replied thinking of when she was shot in the leg.

"The authorities do not want people dead, unless they are of no use in the pursuit of efficiency. In fact, people are seen as valuable, so long as they comply with the objectives defined as efficient."

"Do you always just regurgitate propaganda?" Raynie asked. "Is it your way? Do you even breathe efficiently?"

"Um…" it was the first time Superior Office One had faltered. "No, I do not 'breathe' efficiently."

"It shows," Chan said without explaining any further.

"Are we of use?" Lyle asked.

"It depends if you object or agree with the new way of life being brought in around the world, and if you can contribute to the authorities' goals through compliance."

"What are these goals?" Chan asked.

"To rid people of in-efficiency they experience with non-compliance."

"To what?"

"To…" she was suddenly at a loss for a coherent answer. For a few moments she wondered precisely what the authorities wanted. "Um…compliance to the machine." The answer seemed a bit dumb to her as she said, but she was too late.

"What machine?" Jenna asked this time.

"The machine of economy, of working, and of status," her answers continued to falter.

"So why is this machine so important?"

"In order to manage people and make them see reason for compliance. After all, the authorities will soon provide absolutely everything anyone requires."

"Does it include feeling as a human? Does it include love? Does it include spontaneous happiness?"

"Those will be attended to…"

"You cannot attend to such things using a machine," Chan said. "They come as natural ways of being, in life, as feelings and responses to feelings."

Chan's words reminded her of her own internal conflict and she thought this man had a type of wisdom she could not describe, further adding to her confusion.

"Do you love anything?" he asked her.

"Um, yes. My job…and music."

"You love your job, but your job seems to be something taking love away from people if these issues of compliance are brought into effect. Do you want to do such things?"

"I cannot see why not."

"Can you see why though?"

"Yes, for the efficiency of society. Everyone will be happy with better lives through technology and through elevated status."

"But that does not answer the question. Why would you want to take love out of the world when you say you also love music? Music is harmony and wave forms. Your efficiencies seem to defy this."

"It is not a question of want anyway," Superior Officer One was getting a little frustrated. "It is only an issue of compliance. When the authorities control every aspect of people's lives, then people will see status is the most important."

"Do you actually believe so?" Raynie said in a cynical way.

"Um…I have to, it is my job."

"Again your job," Chan said. "It does seem to be your highest priority.

"It is."

"Really?"

"There are times where I want to listen to music. The authorities still permit this."

"But soon they won't. Am I right?"

"Yes…in a way. Some entertainment will be provided."

"So you will virtually lose this one sense of love you have too."

This sentence struck deep inside Superior Officer One. It was her most inner turmoil - her separation between work and the sanctity music gave her at the end of each day.

"How does music make you feel?" Chan asked.

"Um…good…look! I am not going to answer any more questions from you." She looked at Chan both studying his face, and feeling a little afraid. She fell silent for a few moments and considered what to do next.

"I am going to have to report you to my superior – I have no choice. But…lucky for you, I am just going to report a sighting as soon as I return to North America, so you had better get out of Germany. I can understand a little why you are doing this, but realize your efforts will be in vain. When the authorities unleash their lifestyles they have in store for people, you will soon see the futility in your resistance."

She had decided on this, as a sighting would stand her in good stead for retaining her status level. "I am cutting short my assignment and returning the day after tomorrow."

The look of relief was apparent on everyone's face, except for Chan who showed no reaction to this news. Without further words, Superior Officer One then left them alone in the restaurant.

****

John tentatively stepped into the elevator car to take Lorraine and him up to Chris's apartment on the seventy sixth floor. He was not concerned over any issues of identity and the threat of being caught by the authorities at this time - he just felt uncomfortable being in such places. But more so, he had been experiencing a great deal of inner turmoil since his son had told them where he lived. He watched as Chris led them in showing a slight hint of pride again on his face as he anticipated the impression he would give his dad. Chris had no knowledge of his father's outright objection to these places, thinking his father merely preferred the remote life of wild places such as Alaska.

Up and up they traveled. As each floor passed by in a flash, John felt a growing sense of dismay. He was trying to deal with how his only son had become a part of the high rise and he wondered a little scared, of how much Chris had taken to trans-human values in life.

"I think you will like it dad," Chris said as they stood outside his front door. He was thinking of his father's interests in technology and was sure he would be impressed with the inside of his apartment. When they went inside, John felt exactly the opposite.

Chris's apartment was lined with technology. Several holographic displays provided readouts of various kinds, and there was what looked like a dentist chair in one corner making John feel very uneasy. Several cables led from a holographic bank to the chair, with some having what appeared to be housings to accommodate syringes at the end. He had heard of such things before, and now upon seeing one in his son's apartment, he felt began to feel physically sick.

"How do you like it dad?"

"Um…impressive," John replied feeling entirely unimpressed.

"I thought you might like it."

"What is it?" Lorraine asked.

"Nano infusion chair," Chris replied. "I use it to maintain my inner workings. It keeps my nanotechnology running at high efficiency, and for adding updates to the software the authorities provide."

John was feeling like had had drunk over a dozen beers rather than just two. The sight of the chair was making him giddy. How could his own son be so opposite to himself? His giddiness began to take hold, his head swimming.

Chris noticed this, "Are you okay dad?"

"Yeah. Just need to sit down a bit. Maybe all the travel lately is catching up with me."

Lorraine knew why John was feeling this way after Chris had explained what the chair was for, and so she sat beside him comforting him a little by holding his hand.

"I'll get some refreshments," Chris said. "Maybe it will make you feel better dad."

"Yeah. Thanks son."

"John? What are you going to do?"

"I don't know Lorraine. I just don't know. I can talk to him, but with all this, he seems to be very committed to these nanotech…"

"Here you go dad," Chris had returned with three glasses of water. John drank the entire glass until it was finished.

After Chris had taken a few mouthfuls he offered to show his father how the chair operated, "See those cables dad? They are used to run a spectral analysis of my present nano health. When it is operating, they move over and around my body to carry out scans as I sit. And the syringes attaching in the others…well, you probably guessed. They inject new technology and also add the software upgrades."

"Do they work? Does it make you feel better son?"

"Oh yes. After the process I get a renewed sense of feeling. It is like I am stronger and clearer in my mind. They enable my body to operate efficiently."

Again, the word 'efficiently' played on his father's mind. Whilst John knew the value of efficient technical operations, he thought of it only in the sense of the type of technology he worked on – mostly to avoid the authorities.

"Do they help you to focus your attention…on your work?" Lorraine asked.

"Oh yes, more than ever. I work at my best immediately after an infusion. This gradually tapers off a bit and when I notice it, I just get in the chair for more renewal. Would you like me to show you? I have scheduled a session in the chair for tomorrow, but I could do it today. It only takes about five minutes."

"Yeah, why not?" Lorraine replied looking at John.

Every cell in John's body and every feeling in his heart were rejecting the idea, but he understood why Lorraine had agreed. He would not know his son fully until he saw him go to such low depths.

"Dad?"

"Yeah, go on show us."

Chris went over to the holographic bank beside the chair and entered a few sequences.

"It does an automatic scan for any software updates, and if there are any newly available, it downloads them directly to my cell walls without me having to do a thing."

He then sat in the chair and waited about ten seconds. Suddenly the cables took on a life of their own as the process began. First they did a thorough scan of his body. The underside of the chair was a netting type material and so the scans were uninterrupted. The sight was again making John feel sick, and Lorraine also began to feel why.

It was horrible to them both. Chris appeared to surrender himself to the machine as he sat there motionless. When the scans had finished, the other syringe cables moved to a store of new needles and automatically fitted one to each cable end – four in all. As they watched, they could both see the software upgrades appear as holographic images at first, which were then compressed into packets and passed into the electronic syringes. As each syringe moved into place over Chris's body they could see the upgrades waiting in the vessel above each needle.

John wanted to destroy them then, as he knew what was about to happen. He sickened further as each of them pushed through his son's skin deep into the tissue. He hated the sight of the machine intruding into his son – the person he had helped bring into this world now being given over to the ugly device. Suddenly a message appeared on the holographic bank, 'central systems now proceeding with software update,' and they saw the packets of data move down the translucent needles into Chris's body.

At first, Chris's face took on a slightly distorted appearance, something like a holographic image just out of focus. Then a few seconds later, it returned to a normal state, but his body didn't. His body appeared as though it was in flux just beyond a solid state and whilst this occurred, a slight smile appeared on his face. He looked as though he was an injecting drug user – John had seen a few of these people in Seattle.

The distortion of his body accompanied by a smile on his face did everything John feared. He was utterly repulsed and as Chris watched them, still motionless, John struggled with this internally. As the five minutes passed by, John wanted to get up and rip all of the syringes out and then take his son away from this, but he couldn't. Any sudden disengagement of the needles could actually prove dangerous.

When at last the time was up and Chris's appearance returned to normal, he felt slight relief, as did Lorraine who had been similarly horrified at the appearance Chris had taken on during the procedure. The needles then withdrew from Chris automatically and detached the syringes, disposing of them into a chute fixed into the wall beside the chair.

As he arose from the chair, Chris took a long deep breath just like the drug users John had seen did. "Well, there you go. Simple isn't it? Gee I feel good." John and Lorraine felt the opposite – they had never witnessed this procedure before and the thoughts of millions upon millions of people doing this regularly, made them both feel worse. Lorraine imagined great buildings full of people linked to these machine chairs and she realized some of her worst nightmares. John simply felt weakened by the entire thing.

Chris however, appeared quite the opposite, with a broad smile on his face, and standing more than upright. He looked for all the world like one of those amphetamine drug fuelled soldiers John knew existed in some parts of the authorities – powerful and indestructible.

Then he turned to face his father still smiling, "See here?" He pointed to a tiny spot on the underside of his forearm. "I have my ID chip now too. The authorities said with this new chip I would be able to monitor my nano-tech even more efficiently with a simple swipe over the holographic scanner, which means I don't even have to feel any loss of nano integrity at all. I really did not like those times when I began to feel less than I do now. They also said with the chip, I will soon be able get some updates without the inconvenience of going to the chair."

John then felt worse than ever, worse than in his dream at the cabin, and worse because he was watching his son become machine and it seemed Chris was slipping away from him. His heart was sinking as he saw the smile on his son's face not being one of happiness. It was a reaction to the infusion, and as such, was a smile devoid of any sense of emotion or feeling arising from his organic elemental self.

"Where do you work son?" John asked. They had never really discussed this in recent months.

"Central Systems here in London, for six months now. I am in middle management, looking after status allocation for anyone who makes mistakes and cost the authorities wasted money and resources. Soon I hope to progress to upper management and then I can also move up higher in the tower, and…if lucky, I might get the north tower where the latest technology is available."

"Oh…good for you then," John was resigning to losing his son to the machines and to the authorities, but he was not giving up yet.

'I must do something,' he thought looking at Lorraine who could tell what he was thinking by the expression on his face.

****

The people Chan had referred to as 'dark' were gathered for a meeting in one of the few remaining freestanding old houses on the fringe of the Black Forest. They discussed the group whom one had watched walk through the forest and they sought more. The setbacks they had encountered in China were behind them, and Chan's attempt at disruption was ineffective to their overall cause. In their seemingly never ending quest to satiate their hunger for their own type of power, they were gathered to work on what they could do to obtain the torus for their vortex amplifier.

Knowledge of it was tantalizing but this was in no way satisfying. Steeped in the traditions of their particular sect, they needed it as a means to power. Far from the type of power the authorities sought to institute, this dark gathering wanted the torus for their amplifier and as an object of worship. Study of the very few pieces of information they had found, had only enthused them to want it for themselves and to keep it secretly to themselves.

Secrecy was their method of being lived through their rituals – guarded as they were in allowing knowledge of their motives to almost everyone. To obtain the torus would mean they would become even more secretive, yet more powerful. They twisted the meaning of icons, of geometry, and of their role in life. The torus now was becoming their sole objective and they were preparing to do whatever it took to steal it from Chan and the others.

Openly they welcomed the concept of a technology-assisted life and used electrical weapons based on their rituals of ages past. In addition, practiced rituals on people were common enough as sacrifice to their deities or darkness in reality opposed to light.

As victims to their egos yearning in a quest for power, their path lead to nothing other than an eternal quest never finding and always lost as souls. Being so involved with distractions as realizations eluding them, any devious means necessary were of their nature to feed their blindness.

Now as they gathered at the edge of the forest, it too steeped in myth and ritual, they congregated as a means to amplify their power and to direct it at the others. Erratic chanting and movement, minds convinced of self in delusion, and a coming together in worship to face their epitaph of emotions, they all bore forward determined to evoke the spirits of their imaginings.

At the center of the room was a statue of a beast in representation of their actual quest – a beast of horns and a beast of hunger. Their energies were so ardently bestowed in the direction of the beast - their essence of intention would soon be born unto a life of service, not to the authorities, but to their master. Such as they were, their master would be one they saw with a sufficient affection of hate.

Chan was sensing this as he sat with the others who were discussing what they should do now the Superior Officer One would be notifying the authorities. He could feel their 'sphere' of influence, so in touch with the subtleties of energy he was. He knew they were close, but it did not scare him for he felt the strength of his intentions. He knew they must move and quickly for they were indeed very close. And he knew they knew the torus was almost at their fingertips and he must ensure it always remained so – out of reach.

"We must get far away…again. Yes, this must seem a little tiring by now – all this running. But those who seek us are near and strong, and we are up against not only the authorities, but also the ways of darkness even the authorities do not know of, or heed. We still have much to learn in activation of torus potentialities and we must do this in peace where we can feel our intentions and respond to them without angst. This is a key time for us…" he fell silent as too had the others listening to him speak.

"What about Australia?" Raynie asked, thinking longingly of the old house where she had met Jake. "It is a long way from anywhere and likely not to be so full of authority officials."

"Going in circles," Jake said.

Chan considered this, and Asper was suddenly excited at such a long HyperJet flight to the opposite side of the world, only then to be disappointed with what Chan told them. "Such is a good idea, but I think it is best we go separate ways for now. As a group this large we can attract too much attention. It is best for us to be two again. I will go with you for I have much to discuss with Jenna." She looked surprised. "But…the others must join up with Lorraine and John in London for now."

"Why?" Asper asked, her look of disappointment obvious.

"Despite the saying there is strength in numbers there is also weakness in these times. There are much harder times to come and you and Tobias will be needed in London. I do not know exactly why but it will become very clear very soon."

Chapter 36

The flight to Sydney touched down as scheduled in the cold grey light of dawn. It was mid winter now in the south, and whilst nothing like the frigidity so prevalent in the north during winter, there was a definite chill to the air. When they saw the harbor on approach to landing, one so revered for its many splendid vistas, it had appeared grey and listless, and Raynie hoped this was not a sign of things to come.

They had discussed this 'dark' group during the flight from Munich, where Chan told them more of their reason for seeking the torus. "It is a powerful thing and attracts those who view it as an object of affection for power. We must guard it carefully, even here so far away, for they will follow us wherever we go."

Now as they stood huddled together in the cold and deciding on where they could obtain a vehicle, they hoped relocation to this far-flung place, might restore positive feelings. When at last after taking the transit road and they had arrived at the old house southwest of Sydney, they began to relax with thoughts of the chase beginning to fade away.

****

The Earth – Moon system was clearly visible through the porthole type window in Steve's cabin. He had been watching it for days as it gradually slipped into the distance. Individual continents were no longer visible - instead, the Earth appeared as a blue sphere, and the Moon smaller and grayish brown. He was beginning to long for the planet as everyone who was away from Earth did when they saw the same view. Steve was among less than a thousand people who had ever made this flight, but he did not count himself amongst the lucky, or a member of an elite club.

The flight ahead would stop at Mars Station – a settlement of roughly two hundred people who oversaw mining operations on the planet and in the asteroids. Views of the red planet were nothing to note as yet – it was still a faint reddish spot, millions of miles away. He was about one third into the trip and there was still at least six weeks ahead before he would have some brief respite within the sealed buildings on the surface of Mars.

Out of boredom, he brought up a holographic display of spacecraft movements between Mars, Earth, and the Asteroid Belt. He saw a few craft moving about the asteroids, one just taking off from the surface of Mars, and one other on the same heading as him, about one week behind. His thoughts turned to the trailing ship and wondered if its occupants felt the same as he did.

As the ship behind displayed in full three dimensions, he noticed it was a different type to the craft to his. The bulky angular aspects of his transport were gone, replaced with a much smoother and rounded shape. Also it had no markings, whereas the registration number, the designated class of spacecraft, and the logo of the corporation affiliated with the mining operations, were mandatory for all transport ships. He was riding in a mining transport, and had no idea of the origins of the craft behind. Whilst the authorities were now sharing a global wide incentive for efficiency, they had not yet begun to share space technology. Steve continued to watch the image for a few more minutes before growing tired of looking at the hologram.

"Steve McCray, please come to the bridge immediately," came the voice of the ship's captain. It was the first such request made of him since he had departed Edwards Air Force Base.

Steve touched his communicator, "Okay, leaving now."

As he headed along the narrow passageway running the entire length of the spacecraft, he struggled to determine why he had suddenly been summoned as he was just a passenger on this voyage.

"Ah, Steve, how are you?" the captain asked as Steve arrived on the bridge.

"Um, fine thanks."

"Good. I have some news for you. We have a rendezvous in space in four days and we need your expertise."

"What for?"

"Well, there is a ship coming up behind us..."

"Yeah, I just saw it on holographic vision."

"We have been instructed to slow to eighty percent speed. The ship behind is capable of much faster speeds than us, but we are to slow down so it can catch up within four days."

"Why?"

"We are taking on a new passenger and the other ship is to return to Earth...where it is needed."

"Needed?"

"Yes, apparently something to do with official business."

"Who is the passenger?"

"Someone from the authorities. Apparently this person is being sent to the asteroids and we are now required to take him the rest of the way."

"I see. Is he important then?"

"Not to my knowledge. He has to go to the asteroids and we have been assigned to take him there. I just received word, so I thought I would tell you straight away so you can prepare."

"Prepare?"

"Yes. This person requires an escort all the way, for what I don't know, but they are sending some data through in a few minutes. It should give you a full run down. Once you have analyzed the data, I want to know."

"Will do. Anything else?"

"No more now, but please give me the details as soon as you have them. I like to run a tight ship here and I want to know anything of relevance well in advance."

"Okay. Um…do you want me to come back or will a holographic report do?"

"Just the report will do."

Steve arrived back at his cabin just as the data file reached the holographic bank. At first there were the details of the assignment and then an image of the passenger became visible, accompanied by his physical and personal details. Five feet four inches, thirty-one years of age, name George Smyth, designation Agent Eight.

'Designation,' Steve pondered this for a moment as he realized he was about to escort an Agent of the authorities and he knew they were unlikable and hard to work with types.

****

John and Lorraine had been staying at Chris's place and were getting restless. His son went off to work early in the morning and then was scheduled to return in the evening, leaving them to stay in his apartment during the day. They had not felt much like going about London, concerned as they were about Chris. As they were sitting out the day, they began to wonder about the others for the first time. There had been no word from them - John was used to this from previous experiences, but this time he decided to contact them. Before he could get a word out, Tobias was in his head, "John. It's Tobias here, I am with Asper and we are in London."

"Hi. Amazing mate, we must be connected or something. I was just about to contact you now."

"Where are you? We arrived here a couple of days ago and thought we would just leave you to spend time with your son. How is he?"

"Good." John was lying of sorts. "What about the others?"

"We have split. You would never believe it, but we were spotted in Germany and so we had to leave. They went to Australia."

"Australia, why?"

"Something Chan said. Anyway, it would be good to meet and talk."

"Sure, where are you? We'll meet you where you are." John did not consider inviting them to his son's apartment. He thought it somewhat embarrassing if they were to see what his son Chris was now like.

They discussed the events with Superior Officer One and why the others had chosen to go to Australia. John was reluctant to tell of any news about his son, but at last opened up a little when Lorraine prompted him seeing the questioning looks on the faces of the other two.

"He's fully into the trans-human thing. It makes me sick and I don't know what to do. He seems to almost be past the point of no return," John looked visibly upset.

"Can we convince him otherwise without letting him know what we are up to?" Tobias asked.

"I have thought about it…a lot. Believe me, the last thing I want is to lose my son to the system."

"What about just taking him. I mean, taking him away, and holding onto him."

"Thought of it too, but his identification chip will give us away."

"The Fixture?"

"We would need to get him to Vancouver. It could be difficult…"

"Yeah it would be dad. I'm sorry, so sorry, but the authorities contacted me just after you left Alaska. They knew who you were and have ordered me to do this. I had no choice. But if you comply then it will be easy and we can be together," Chris said this with three officials standing beside him. He had followed them and now they were to be arrested.

John had tears in his eyes - the torment of this very evident. He had dreamed of his son at the cabin and it had moved him so much. He thought he could prevent this type of thing then, but now his son was standing in front of him and handing him over to the authorities along with the others. Lorraine and Asper began to cry as well, for themselves and for what John was going through. Only Tobias remained silent as he internally dealt with the situation.

"Why son?"

"I had no choice dad, really I didn't," Chris looked upset and he was close to tears himself. "But it can be okay, really it can. We can be together and they have assured me they will only detain you to get information. Afterwards, you and the others here will be free to go. We can live together. Um…they said you could stay with me. Much better than living on the ground."

John thought told the others to remove their devices, and then he touched behind his ear and removed his own. The others discreetly did the same, making sure the officials did not see them. As they stood up, John was looking directly into his son's eyes when he dropped his own device to the floor, where it landed amongst his fallen tears.

Chapter 37

"Coincidences are great at this time," Chan said as they sat in the kitchen of the old house on the third night after they had arrived. "I can feel there is much to learn and to be also wary of." He paused for a moment as if distracted. "Jenna, I must talk with you…and the others on some matters I have been looking into." She had been curious since Chan had first indicated this in Germany and now felt at last he would tell her what it was about.

"We must work hard and fast. There are others of the dark sect also in this place. They do not yet know we are here, but they will soon enough, they will come."

"What is it Chan?" Jenna asked eager to get on with things.

"It is of mathematical and geometric designs also found in nature as elemental energies. We need this understanding, as it is some of the very foundation in understanding the activation of the torus itself and of the torus of ourselves."

"Does this sect have knowledge of these things?"

"Yes they do, but not in a similar way. Their intentions are bound by their beliefs. It is through unhindered intentions such as we share where torus activation in a real sense can be realized. And this must include an understanding of geometry for it plays a role in the underlying forces being accessed."

"So they don't understand the geometry?"

"They have an idea, but they twist it…like themselves. And so when it is twisted, activation potential is limited. With us, limits do not apply, as our intentions are infinite. The others do not see this infinity, they just see ends and if they were to meet such ends, they would become lost and fathomless on what to do."

"And so geometry plays a part in activation of the torus. When I saw the toroidal crystals on the moon, there were equations and sequences all over the holographic bank, they began to form the shape of the torus. They began forming non-interacting circles, and yet they were interacting."

"Yes precisely. They do not interact as they are formations of duality for the purpose of geometric harmony in the foundation of energies then shaped by intention. Recall our view of water and how it strives to return to its natural spherical shape. This also true for the geometry in life and things created. This is all superimposed by consciousness."

"Is this why the other group cannot properly understand the torus and just relish it as an icon or worship object?"

"Again true. Their intentions are against these natural ways of elemental being, and so they try to force apart things through their methods, but…whatever they affect, it is only temporary, for the entire time it is disrupted, it is striving to return, and so they do not activate the full potential energy."

Raynie returned then after she had gone over to the old stove and made a pot of tea. For a while they sat silently sipping tea, listening to the winter winds around the house.

"Listen to the winds," Chan said. "They are of such natural flows as those we studied looking at air. The winds carry on invisible waves, but those waves are there and all about due to these elemental relationships with spirit. It is not spirit of anything but the natural intentions of things and therefore, simply their way."

"So what are these elements of geometry you wanted to talk to Jenna about?" Lyle asked. "I am interested as I used geometry to calibrate readouts for obtaining elemental data during impact assessments and contamination testing. I have also researched cultures using geometric patterns in their beliefs - some see diamond shapes as most relevant, others see pyramids and…"

"And they are all correct. Each one is part of the human understanding and together they work to activate memories within the very cells of organic life, within stars, within water. It is the onus of human intention to work these geometries together without thinking for individually they only show part of the understanding. This has been awakening on Earth for many centuries, but it is only over the past one and a half centuries where they are truly beginning to be understood."

"Indeed as their potential was beginning to really be seen, there were times amongst the worst in human history. The wars of the twentieth century and the racial hatred came from the egos of those who felt threatened by this. It is then their way to have reacted as they did and cause so much suffering. And when they were defeated in these wars and their ways became of the past with only partial knowledge of these geometries. They were limited and inevitably given to loss, then the geometries began to interact…to activate. It is why in the times very close after these terrible histories, there were many advances in human awareness and understanding then reflected in their creations and technologies."

"It seems like those times are happening again with the way the authorities are trying to shut down personal identification of self – even now the identification chips will only see you as a registration number instead of a name," Raynie said.

"Yes Raynie, these measures are showing as similar because the human experience has not yet aligned with the intentions of natural flow, and as the times approach for great learning with this, once again we see egos trying to do what they can to overwhelm and control instead of align."

"Does it mean we can be sure they will not succeed?" Jake asked.

"I cannot answer precisely other than to say, we must not be complacent. To remain so would be to lose connection with true intention and so it would be very much like a repetitive cycle. This has happened many times in history. It may indeed be the way of the authorities to lose in the end, but there is no end, and this activation calls upon the intentions of humanity to meet the challenge and walk away from the loop it has been caught up in for so long where it sees an end as a state of finality where there can never really be."

"So it means nothing gets to perfection?"

"Yes, although something may seem perfect for an intention or befitting in the right time and place. There is continuation afterwards so in reality there is no perfect end, just a true intention aligned with the natural elemental energy of infinite resource. This resource is what I have spoken of previously as the energy of intention, waiting if you like for the human spirit connection to create and so we set the path set for light to follow."

"So this is the geometry information you wanted to talk about?" Jenna asked.

"Oh yes, but it is only a little. It is not the beginning, and as I have said, there is no end, but we need to understand these waves and patterns of geometry to grasp the construct of the torus for its activation. There is much more to attend and surely we will do this. I have questions of my own for you Jenna. It is prudent I am connecting with you now at this time for the sake of this learning as I have to understand myself if I am to guide my intentions as responses in this activation."

"What types of geometric designs did you have in mind?"

"All of them."

"All of them...hmm, it would take a very long conversation..."

"But necessary. Anyway, it would not be so long as you may think, for connection of these elements in patterns is the main thing we must grasp, and all of them share this connection. So, looking at all the patterns and forms is not so much the requirement, as to the feeling how they interact, and play out the creation of the universe."

"Based on the naturally flowing intentions?"

"Correct...for the real intended outcomes and not the conditioned ego conscious outcomes. All matter and energies of all types are of design geometrically at all levels."

"Jenna, you have no doubt looked deeply into this with your development of protein strings?'

"Yes."

"And you then understand how they interact in activating the energies naturally aligned to each form for the sake of connection and activation of these strings?"

"Yes."

"So if I was to mention the hexagon shape, you would understand how it relates to the creation of life cycles and the occurrence of proteins and other elemental substances.

"Yes I do. Um...think of bees for instance. They are intricately involved with the connection of life forces to fulfill the intentions and further the creation of new life. The bees pollinate the flowers giving birth to the seeds and so on. Also, the honey of bees is stored inside their hives in hexagons."

"And honey is such a product of this so it never goes bad or stale, and it is also been proven through science as very beneficial for healing and the realigning of the intended forms interrupted?"

"Absolutely. Science has tested and proven this."

"So the honey helps the water return to a sphere and it helps to balance the vortices again?" Raynie asked

"Yes it does," Chan replied. "This affect goes on as the heart restores to proper rhythm with this healing."

"You see these patterns in all life," Lyle added. "Many times I have come across life forms at sites where they exhibit vortexes and spirals, and they exist in places where they have been carried by wave forms."

Chan continued, "So the two geometries interact and connect for the purpose of fulfilling the intention. And such intentions, as I have said, are the foundations of existence and concept, for these patterns and waves are throughout...from the workings of your heart, your body, and your brain, to the workings of the cosmos."

"And Jake, you too align such things as you drive. I know you like this. It is your precision as a response to truth and clear intention projecting the course of your vehicle along any route, through corners and there is more. Even the dynamic construct of your vehicle plays a part as it too is aligned with the elemental forces of air and so it assists the clarity in execution of your intentions."

"Wow, I have never thought of it in such a way before, but it seems right."

"It is and it is part of the understanding which like infinity is beyond vast..." Chan broke off laughing, knowing to use the infinity and vast could be seen as a contradiction.

"I have seen vortexes take on geometric shapes in the study of planets. We always look at potential destinations for testing propulsion systems," Jenna said.

"I too have seen such things. I am thinking of the electrical hexagonal vortexes on Saturn. Electricity plays a vital role in all creation as atoms resonate electrically."

"Yeah, precisely what I was thinking of..." she said trailing off and wondering about her career path now changed forever.

"This is continuance of variations in intentions connecting. Not all planets are bound by the laws known here on Earth. This has been evident for many centuries. When I noticed angulations of geometric shapes in conflict when I looked at the buildings in San Francisco, this demonstrated the conflict within humans not recognizing alignment. This goes on further where people choose these trans-human values in mass consumption of offerings to mostly suit the ego's dominance over understanding clear and elemental intentions. Think of what happens inside these places and who are behind their construction, and then you will quickly align with understanding on this point. A state of confusion the world may often seem to be, and this is true for there are creations such as these to demonstrate this."

"And to think people consider them as beautiful and the nanotechnology as a life saver," Raynie added.

"Again there is understanding. You said 'saver' Raynie, and it is in this foundation where interruption takes place to give the conditioned ego enough potential over connection with clear intention. Confusion resides and a form of rescue is sought, whereas the intentions in alignment for natural response do not ever require any such rescue."

"And the status thing, where they try to out compete each other for jobs and material standing."

"Objects of affection and these are externalization from self based on the ego's uncertainty, and so the collection of these things and the desire to see oneself as better than another, is merely the ego demonstrating very little understanding in this application of intentions seeing life as finite. Common amongst this is the elusive ending sought as hunger rises again to seek novelty before it again wears thin. These things are but a loop and the authorities know this loop is a very tempting and safe place to be, and so they play on these souls who seem interrupted in the response to natural intention. They seek and they find, but then they need more to keep them focused and energized, and little do they see all energy is infinite and so this interruption does not connect with this infinity. Their desires lead them to suffering and so they seek new kinds of desires to overcome the suffering and yet they do not realize why. So they continue the suffering and even those who may live on the top floors of these places, need to reach higher. Within this need is the error, for it is the sense of need interrupting the intentions of themselves as natural elemental beings. This need is a form of disrespect for self when taken out of context to become a dependency."

"They fall out of the flow,' Jake said.

"Yes, many do. And many have done this to large effect only to bring about toxicity of the mind, heart, and body so often. It is not to say abandon all. There is perhaps a method better for all. We have seen in the histories of recent decades where humans sought to further their status without regard for the sustenance giving life. This was evidenced through destruction of natural places, and with the destruction of many natural foods, which then gives way to poor health and the need to use this nanotechnology as a life saver trying to fix errors best avoided in the beginning."

"They were just so blind to this in those days," Lyle added. "So many sites show massive ecological damage in the twentieth century according to dating procedures we use. Then it took almost too long for them to realize earlier this century. They just continued to waste away the planet, for the sake of power and money. They ignored it so they could feel good and powerful- they didn't seem to care at all. Sorry...I get a bit hot about this. It is hard to believe how ignorant people were and how short sighted."

"And now these 'efficiencies' – it is happening again," Chan said nodding in agreement with Lyle.

"They do it as a distraction, or interruption to the natural intentions of creation existing in humans where they really are responsible for what they create in life."

"It is true, as often what humans create is born from ill intentions of exploitation rather than stewardship through ways of power and wealth the ego sees as security."

"Then they go on to continue to mix this up, which then requires a new type of fix because their alignment is not natural and it causes uneasiness within."

"So the loop though seeming infinite is bound and not connecting with the parallel possibilities..." Chan said this leaving the sentence to fall away for the sake of a few moments of silent contemplation.

"There is one more thing I must discuss," Chan said. "It is the concept of an energy grid on Earth. They have been called lay lines in the past – call them what you will. But these lines are important for they are the geometric alignment for the Earth body...like a human body where it has meridians."

"Chinese use those in acupuncture," Lyle said.

"They do. These points are important again for this activation and it is why I have sent you to some and in those places and you experienced great things - of energy and harmony. Also there is awareness very much of these by the authorities and the other dark sect group. Both groups will view the torus as a method by which to amplify these energies."

"Are there any of these places in the Black Forest – it seemed to radiate an energy."

"It always has, so yes. There are others including Alaska."

"HAARP!"

"Yes Jenna and it is why they choose such a place for the antenna array. It has the power of amplifying energies. I suggest you research this – the information is common...um, available easily."

"Are there any here, in Australia?" Raynie asked.

"Oh yes. Most certainly they are here. For many centuries this place has been overlooked and populated mostly by indigenous peoples who passed this information by word of mouth, and through art. Australia is unique on the Earth as it is largely without writing, or relics, and the type of civilization here was as I said, passing their information by word. I know many other cultures did this, but here it is almost entirely the case. They call it 'dreaming' and it is not unlike this state of mind. It may feel like dreams, as it too has been a part of the entire elemental energies to be understood."

"And with the European settlement three hundred years ago and the terrible history afterwards, effectively was suppression of this knowledge..."

"And it was nearly lost. But as I say, human spirit prevails and so it remains."

"They went about systematically destroying the cultures here – there was little to no respect at all," Lyle continued. "It was like what happened to other native peoples, say the North American Tribes. I have seen images of people here chained together by the neck, used as slaves..."

"For the purposes of a very few to gain status, yes? This is the loop, which is also a bind where they are simply the same failures being repeated again and again."

"Failures are apparent this time in this same loop, and yet the authorities and their efficiency drive, punish people for failures..." Lyle broke off thinking for a moment.

"Yet their overall motivations based on ego driven intentions, are failing all the time. They do not realize this," Chan added seeing the look on Lyle's face.

"Then there were the early days of this century when they tried to repair this interruption." Lyle had studied their culture extensively. "They apologized to these people and yet it was mostly a mask. They remained largely outcast members of society in their homeland."

"That is true and so this place saw much ecological and cultural significance go to waste and to ruin. There was a time where Australia was such a vivid repeat of the mistakes made before in other countries."

"And so the loop continued."

"Yes."

"Are there any of these lay lines near this location, this house?" Raynie asked Chan.

"I am not certain, but it is worthwhile to try and find some considering you and Jake found the stone piece here. Try to reside upon them with focus on your intentions. There is electrical connectivity for energies to be had and most of the peoples on Earth are not experiencing this. A problem is then somewhere inside they want this experience but are lost at trying to feel it. This has been so very much the foundation of the modern world of consumption of things. It is worse now as many almost entirely direct themselves in this way, but they do not realize such consumption is again the loop and the requirement to connect will not be aligned through these acts of consumption feeding so much the ego. Even at times they are still within this loop when they take time to step away from what they think is a busy life. They are still stepping away to retreat from their life and this is still within the grasp of ego. This is a consumption too, where the life is lived needing this step away. It can be affective, yet when time taken out to have time out from mind occurs, this can be reliance rather than a way of life."

"It was a big mine back just over eighty years ago," Lyle said – the nation had been a focus of his work many times in the recent past. "Australia was seen as a vast resource for minerals and metals to meet the demand for consumption. They sold up great tracts of land and allowed mining and other similar ventures to destroy some prime agricultural land…and they had political people who would just argue about what to do. They would deny the destruction being brought into the place, and they would scramble for public support over pathetic polices concerning the ecological quality…the very quality supporting life. "

"And now we see such poor quality foods and those compound supplements," Jenna added. "Also they failed as in many places I guess…to realize their world around them was a reflection of their state of inner self. I suppose this led to the development of a lot of new medications as a way to counter balance this uneasiness - leading to where we are now with the nanotechnology people have injected."

"See the interruption here, for Australia is so very much a clear example in modern times where there is a much more detailed historical recording."

"And still they didn't learn – we are back to the beginning of the loop again now. It seems like objects of affection humans seek to define life and status, are controlled by restrictions and policies causing both strong desire for these things, yet it makes them difficult to acquire, and so they are in a loop…like their everyday jobs."

"Yes, humans are. It is why in this loop, there is the onus to escape the repetition. Activation of the torus is not just a thing about the object – it is about activation of it within all people. The torus is metaphoric and represents the connection of infinity, but it is not a loop though it appears as one. It is multi-dimensional. And like other things, activation of this object is a reflection of the activation within as people are also of many dimensions…at least in character."

"There is a long way to go, when you think of the trans-humans, the authorities, and the mining going on…they just don't seem to get it," Jake said. He had been mostly listening to this point, content in agreement with the others.

"No they don't get it. It is why we are gathered - to be part of the activation away from this. As human beings become part machines, the world will reflect this and it will lose sense of soul and connection to the intentions of the natural elemental energies. These times may be amongst the most difficult yet, as many humans are aware of much greater powers than even those tyrants of the twentieth century."

"And they play with the populations forcing in different directions as a way to manipulate them to an ends…"

"Of which, there are none. Think of your knowledge when money was such a driving force under pinning almost every decision and every motivational intention. This money was itself a part of the loop and so people in jobs were caught up in this and then provided entertainment through various artistic and physical mediums."

"Popular music and sports?"

"Yes things similar are again at the front of people's minds – just in different forms. But remember these distractions are again from the ego. You will see very much ego attached here then appropriated as part of a person's definition of self."

"So with this repeat in the loop, we are going back again to poor artistic values in nearly all its forms and people are being distracted into poor quality…"

"Of connection and therefore of intention. As I have said, where the conditioned ego drives the intention for awareness, so limited it is through its bind in definition of the finite and of perfection where it fails to activate the entire energies, so they do not get the full picture. Hence the poor artistic quality."

"Um, Chan?"

"Yes?"

"When Jake and I were interrogated, was it a result of our intentions?"

"Yes, again very much so Raynie. It is difficult to understand this, as it would seem absurd to intend to experience such things. One thing I can only say is your intentions resulted in actions taking you to such a place, but those intentions are not of being captured – it is just along the way to their intended place, the intentions experience physical events to help define those intentions as they occur. It is not a matter of intending something and then a point of finality. Intentions are made and set in motion so to say. Along the way or path they take is the shaping and definition of the intentions. Think back to the meeting with the officer in Germany. There is connection, as she demonstrated a change in awareness where she gave us the chance to get away. This in effect is her subconscious working with her conscious to continue the spread of these energies. It is like your arrest was the instigator of change within the individual. I know times like those are difficult to experience, but they have purpose and again, as the ego of the Agent brought on your arrest through its' interruption to elemental connection, this ego failed to keep you from continuing to spread these energies as you intend."

"Um…going back to the artistic values again, and music and sound in particular."

"Yes. It is why I sent you to Vienna. Music is very much a harmonious thing. And sound comes in waves of which there is also the relationship to connection of elemental energies."

"We did some research into the affects of sound waves at Berkeley," Jenna said.

"Then you are likely to understand this in depth. Sound waves are important as well in activation. The harmony of sound carries elemental connections within its waveforms and many of the machines used to produce things of consumption had created sounds interrupting this flow. These sounds affected much more than people realize when so many personal machines were so regularly used by many. They would affect wild life in the water, upon land, and in the air. And it also affected people because people are so much made of water, but they largely ignored sub-conscious effect sounds have on their very water molecules within, so concerned with consumption often…active in creating disharmony."

"The authorities are suppressing sound now through efficient devices and through limiting the range and quality of music. They appear in conflict. Surely as the machines are now much quieter, then there has been some change," Jenna said as she considered the impact sounds generated in the use of protein strings could change their water molecules to re-position and in effect be switches turning on and off.

"Yes – in ways they limit music. But there is a different intention with this. The suppression of sound is concerned with efficient machines and so the focus is not on harmony, but efficiency. And the suppression of music…think of the officer in Germany becoming uncomfortable when I asked her what she loved. Limiting the auditory sense of stimulation without the dynamic range to reflect back the dynamic range within people, is again a smothering and non activation of senses. Combined with constant bombarding of media, styles of sounds designed to gain sub-conscious attention, and the way entertainment becomes such a large part of time in life, there is a method to know where the people mostly are and mostly what they are doing."

"I see it re-enforced through media stories where news is made from products. It shows the blending yet people seem to keep watching it as if product news is really news compared to the origins as news where it was more of a community service," Lyle added.

"So you see there is the modification and the attempt to change the flow of what used to be for the people, into a medium of exploitation. It has become so much, many subscribe to living much time hearing music with their mind and not listening to their heart. It is a strong reliance on this product as a definition of the self…of the persona."

"Persona – ancient Greek for mask."

"Correct Lyle. It is an interrupted world where the mask is made, bought, sold, traded, and cherished. In part nature sees this as inevitable as life makes it definitions through the journey it takes. This is the journey chosen and so what becomes of choice is the intention all along. There is no other fault or blame – all comes from within for the definition takes place each moment through the experience of each moment. Distraction away is like the interrupted water flow in an eddy swirling to the side of the stream and going around where it can be caught and loses the flow to stagnate, or perhaps find again the flow to move on after a time."

"Is there any room left for ego?" Jake asked.

"Remember, ego is not entirely a thing to be discarded. There are instances where it makes connections to the elemental self as expression of an individual, and then in response it forms intentions to further this potential. The conditioned ego perhaps is a term I use to refer to a reactionary state rather than a responsive state, or where externalizations dominate over inner energy projected outward as is the natural flow, rather than being blocked."

"What about the expression of conditioned egocentric traits as a means of learning? Hmm, I suppose if they get the lesson…" Jenna asked and then murmured as she thought how often it seemed people could fail to learn lessons.

"Many times in history, the ego has also been suppressed by other egos. This is mostly from the insecurity one ego feels and what it manifests as in the individual when it is confronted with another ego aware of subtle energies and how to play them and thus be the most powerful. Think of a dominant person who sees the submission of the other and realizes this as a way to exert themselves. These instances of obvious lesson to some yet ignored by others, are the course of natural way created and so do not require more recognition for one who is unaffected. If one is affected, therein is an experience to learn as part of experience. To recognize more than required when one is unaffected surely is a poor way to spend precious time. Adding miseries or anxieties to your senses when they are not required through relevant direct experience, is a trick. This has happened through many times, not just now, and can bring in dense energy where life is heavy. Why be heavy? Being heavy is like complaining in life. What does it do for you other than becoming an addiction of sorts? Such focus on negative things serves this purpose of negativity one has chosen to express. Remedies to the issues creating the negativity rarely come from a negative mind. Positive solutions require the energy for their instinctive purpose."

"So when they talk about growth in times past as they do now, it is about the growth of efficiencies and the growth of technology as progress. There is no real obvious development of positive change – more a meandering around the course of where the river of life could go."

"Yes. What they call growth, is growth apportioned into the world through the intentions mostly from negative ego. During those times not so many decades ago, growth of economies was the focus. It was then a lot of devastation continued to be put into the world and into people - then through their measures of control and manipulation, they convinced growth was for the good and advances in technology could then treat any of the interruptions coming. We are seeing this again with the nanotechnology people use in most instances. Whilst there is good, there is also bad. But this growth is from the intention to control and provide from a foundation of negative ego desires…bound with insecurity. This insecurity exists with those in control – it is the reason for their control. And…they place this onto the peoples of Earth at large. There is no elemental growth when these distractions cause the interruptions. There is some, but it comes in small amounts and so is easily consumed through the intentions furthering the experience of the loop so much of humanity has resided in for so very long."

"And this is all geometry?" Raynie asked looking a little puzzled.

"Yes. Geometry is central to the connection of communication for this is not just with words or images, but it is with the elemental energies. There is the geometry in the body communicating with these, and when it is not entirely seen because of negative addicted dependent needy aggressive ego, then the communication is interrupted. There is so much subtle communication from people's sub-conscious and this forms most communication between them. If you disrupt their elemental sub-conscious by operating from the conscious ego, then this suppression of true self will lead to uneasiness and can become real in toxic behaviors. It is all energy exchange and so indirectly behavior can lead to actions resulting in energy patterns, waveforms, and atomic resonance going out of alignment and so the geometric relationships are interrupted."

"Some cultures actively try to communicate using waveforms. Not just the waves created using technology, but with the elemental forms in nature," Lyle said. "I was thinking then of Tibetan prayer flags when we were at the cross roads for the Plateau of Tibet or to continue west through China."

"Indeed Lyle. Peoples of Tibet do set their intentions upon the winds. Their use of these flags is where they are connecting their intentions of wisdom and other things, to be cast out for all people and all of the Earth itself."

"Somewhat like the festival in Timbuktu. There was the flow of wisdom…"

"Set upon the geometry of elements in natural flow. This again is another part of the activation and is to be understood. These intentions are free from the ego desire for control and power, and they are not to be confused with assimilating them into how they apply using the ego either. They are in giving as opposed to the taking. Taking is so much a part of the loop humanity has repeated so many times now. Once free from the constraints in thoughts and feelings, these meanings become apparent themselves as new ideas and intentions develop based on this state of presence being open to potential positively rather than being weighed down and dense in the negative. People can enjoy more liberation from the burden of worry and so much analysis to live rather than exist and cope."

"There are times when we need to cope though Chan," Raynie stated.

"By nature these times occur and it is our nature of intention defining how we cope with such situations. At the foundation comes the appreciation of self respect allowing us to be true rather than to live compromised where time is spent poorly and so often people can let themselves down. We cannot be certain on anything other than to be certain as self in the time rather than distracted out of time. And yet this certainty of self is precisely the opposite for there is no certainty of self as everything constantly changes and freedom is allowed and not defined.

Chapter 38

Jenna was walking with Lyle out in the frosty fields where Raynie and Jake had found the stone two months before. They strolled amongst the tiny fine white crystals feeling much more at peace than they had for some time. The chance just to wander in the open, without hindrance and without any sense of concern had sunk in for all of them at the old house and on this morning, the couple felt a strong sense of connection. Stopping in the same place as Raynie and Jake, they noticed a feeling about the grove. Although it too was coated in white, they agreed there was a warm feeling. For some reason, Jenna thought of the torus, which she always carried in her pocket. She took it out and as she did so, she dropped it into the frost. Lyle leaned over at the same time as her to pick it up and they both noticed something.

There it lay in the heavy white frost, but there was now a faint tinge of pink colour to the torus. They had expected the torus to look almost invisible in the frost, except for its defining shape, but now with such a white background, they were certain the torus was showing a slight pink.

Instead of picking it up instantly, they continued to gaze at the torus, wondering why it had this pink hue. It was a pleasing feeling to look at the faint pink diamond ring about two inches in diameter. They could not help but stare at it for a lot longer than they thought, until when finally Jenna picked it up and held it in her open palm. The pink colour disappeared against the skin of her hand, and for a moment they thought it had gone away, until Lyle stretched out a white T-shirt he was wearing from under his jacket. Jenna placed it against the shirt and the faint colour returned.

"So beautiful," is all Jenna said. She thought of how Chan had given it to her for contemplating geometries. Then they both decided at once to go back and show the others. It was Chan who was looking directly at them as they walked towards the kitchen door.

As they entered, they simply did not attempt to close it behind them, so Raynie did so to keep out the cold, looking a bit mystified as to why they seemed a bit dreamy. Then the smells of breakfast brought Jenna and Lyle around, where they both looked around at the others smiling. Jake was curious and to asked about the smiles.

"The torus, it's beautiful," Jenna replied.

Chan knew why they said this as he could feel it.

"We know Jenna. Lyle, what is it with you two?" Raynie asked looking to them each in turn.

"It's the torus. It has a colour and it just...you just...feel good."

"Show me."

"Here," they were coming around even more now as Jenna took it out of her pocket. She placed it on the white tablecloth, and then everyone saw the faint pink colour.

Then like the others had, they gazed at in silence for about five minutes, until Chan spoke, "Feel how it is activated?"

Jenna then put the torus back in her pocket when she felt her stomach remind her she had not yet eaten today. "Where is the breakfast we saw you eating on the way back?"

"Here," Jake replied as he went over to the stove where it was keeping warm. "We saved you some."

For a few hours after breakfast, they sat in the kitchen discussing the torus and about how it had made them all feel. It was not physical warmth, they all agreed, it was a sense of warmth…and a sense of invigoration. Raynie had then gone to the library to bring back a dictionary from the shelves. She could have simply looked up words using her holographic phone, but she loved looking through old books and so had gone down the hallway, treading lightly and full of spirit.

She opened it on the kitchen table and went to 'invigorating', and then read the meaning aloud, "Filling somebody or something with energy or life."

"Ah, but can one ever be full?" Chan asked. He knew the others would respond with a 'no', so he continued. "It is a sense of perception for the intention to fully balance the natural elements leading to the next intention."

Over dinner, Jake raised the question of contacting John and the others in London, pointing out they would have to try the communicators vocally. John had told them the strength of signal for thinking words was not enough to extend much further than about five hundred miles. "John? Tobias? Lorraine?" he said. There was no response.

"Asper?" Raynie tried a split second later. Still no response. This was concerning, as John had assured them there would be no issues with global voice communications.

"Jenna, I'll go to the library and test my communicator," Lyle said as he rose up out of his seat and left the kitchen. Ten seconds later, she could hear his voice through her own device.

"Okay here," she replied.

"We'll leave it then until tomorrow. Perhaps they have them turned off."

Chan though it might be best to recall what they had been discussing, and to avoid being distracted with worry. "Always send to your friends and others, the intentions you want for them, and keep this focus."

For the remainder of the evening, they decided to sit in the library and read, chat, and relax. The weather outside had turned to strong southerly winds, bringing lower temperatures and rain, and as they sat, the first few flakes of snow began to fall.

Raynie and Jenna had fallen asleep on lounges in the Library when a sudden cracking sound woke then. Sitting up, they realized the others had all gone to bed for the night.

"It sounded like a tree branch," Raynie said as she walked to the window. "Yeah, it was. There's a bit of snow now, I think it couldn't take the weight and broke off."

"I'm going to bed," Jenna said.

"Goodnight then."

"Goodnight." It was well past midnight, around two. As Raynie stood there looking at the falling snow in the light cast out through the library window, she watched how some flakes would just fall, and others were caught in eddies and spirals, before breaking free to fall to the ground. Each gust of wind interrupting the steady waves of flakes, introduced these erratic patterns before moving on, and then the flakes would return to falling as a wave. She thought how similar their life had been recently, for a moment reminding her of the experience at the 'facility'. So adoring of places like the old house, the thought of a life in the cold grey world the authorities were creating, gave her a shudder, despite the room being warm.

Her mind drifted back to the flakes, once again going into a semi-trance state as she just stared at them. A few larger flakes landed on the glass in front of her eyes – they were large enough to see each of their own distinct geometric shapes.

'Every flake was different and yet connecting,' she thought. Then she tried to imagine the millions of different geometric patterns falling as flakes at the time. The numbers were beyond her, almost beyond perception, so she stepped back a little and went with the feeling of how millions upon millions of geometric shapes so intricately formed, were falling from the sky to her then.

She wished for a moment Jenna had stayed with her to share these thoughts – these feelings. 'I will tell her...'

She saw the snow in another way, as translucent, not white – the intricacies of each flake forming as patterns of light. In her mind, she was seeing millions of beautiful light patterns falling from the sky. She could imagine herself being covered in them, as her own light body welcomed the beauty and warming like they had all warmed to the torus. Then she thought of the flakes made of light, falling upon the trees made of light – their branches as fingers catching them.

She opened the window - unable to resist the urge, casting her own hand out the catch the snow. A star landed in her fingers and she held it there a few seconds before it melted away. She had caught a star.

'So much beauty...and mystery,' she thought.

Then she saw the entire scene with the trees and the house being covered in snow, and thought of how beautiful the house was to her. Not as an object of affection – it was the warmth it offered in feeling and character. She saw it with its sole light shining out into the snow as the only light for miles around.

"I heard Jenna go to bed and wondered if you were still here," Jake was beside her.

"It's so beautiful Jake. All those geometric patterns flowing on the waves of the winds."

"Just like you Raynie. It is one of the reasons I love you."

Raynie turned to Jake, looking deeply into his still sleepy eyes, "I know you do, and it is why you were so eager for us to meet here a couple of months back. Sure there was the research…but I could feel something when we saw each other before then. I knew we would connect."

"I am glad we did," Jake said embracing Raynie in his arms.

"Me too. I love you too Jake."

Next morning Raynie and Chan were the first to rise from bed. Raynie had spent the night dreaming geometries and was still buoyed by her experience watching the snowfall.

"Chan?"

"Yes Raynie?"

"I was watching the snow last night and thought of the millions of geometric flakes falling to the ground, and how some would be caught in little spirals before continuing their fall."

"Yes they are many wonderful patterns – I have always thought of the beauty in snow. They exhibit the sense of geometry all nature uses to coalesce, to further life, and for progression. It is a sense within us – we can only exist in such a way."

"Wish you were there Jenna," she said as Jenna entered the kitchen.

"Sounds wonderful. We did stay up late last night."

The day was only just beginning with a low gibbous moon in the western sky, giving way to a purple and pink dawn strewn with a few remaining clouds from the previous night's snow front. They all favored being early risers, and so a few minutes later they all stood talking as they watched the colors gradually wash into the newly fallen snow, and then the first rays of sun splash the tops of the surrounding hills. It had become a golden ring around the house as the pinks turned to oranges, reds, and yellows, with the first hint of blues low in the east. Then as the first light touched a small forest of pine trees down the hill - their green needles laden with snow, the sun had risen on a fine winter's day.

Chapter 39

Machine culture would be the emerging plethora of effective, efficient, and encumbered human experiences on offer. People inevitably had to accept this as evolution for the way ahead – encouraged to be a part of the machine and therefore of evolution in action. The means of the authorities would be swift – they already were. Systems were in place to far supersede the capacities of the present networks in use. What most people saw as the old technology wasting away on city fringes, lined with disused poles and endless wires, dormant power grids and communications networks, so too would be the way of their present technology sooner than many thought. Any move so great as this would require the utmost in stealth and ingenuity so as to lock down their intentions. It could not be a piece-by-piece gradual take over, although until now the events had been precisely this way.

The population had effectively helped them to easily make things happen. En-masse often without the slightest hesitation, they had turned to the technology offerings and welcomed the sense of security it offered in their individual quests for status. Status was not simply a work thing. It was also the accumulation of wealth seen as higher and higher quality – and of social credit progressing in life mirrored by residential level in the high rise.

Deployment of hardware was proceeding on schedule across all nations - managed by their individual authorities. Lock down of humanity was occurring where those few in authority who mandated decisions, would soon realize their desires of more status. Within days the deployment would be in place making apparent to the population, what was in store for them.

People would walk past machines already deployed every day, not realizing it was there at all concealed completely - regardless as many were already oblivious through distraction with their personal holographic devices. The authorities would stun the people with extraordinary machines to impress most through notions of efficient reason and begin a journey of a connected world accessing the ultimate in desire.

They would never be alone – they would be connected. They could do so many things for pleasure, for sex, for taking the human sensual experience beyond their minds. They were to access information deemed proper to fill their minds with knowledge seemingly. It would be alluring and provocative, seductive and regrettable.

"In two months, all payment systems will be online. Take your cash now to your closest registered bank for conversion to identification chip credits. No cash will be accepted for credit after this time."

This announcement was amongst the new measures put in place, with others announcing the conversion of insurance and investments to an assessed chip credits value.

"Private material property will not be affected. Own what you like, own what you can," was another.

Amongst this, Superior Officer One was feeling more and more unsure about the path ahead for her. She didn't much care for money itself - it was a by-product of her climb to status and entitlement. There were no elaborate possessions at her home as she was more of simple tastes, preferring those few objects of some meaning to her. She had no idea about the extent of change to come – she only knew there would be an onus to make people work hard and efficiently.

The depths of machinery standing motionless awaiting activation were not considered for she was entirely unaware of them. In fact, most officials were – even her superior only knew of something great about to appear. What it was precisely he did not know, but he did know it was tempting and despite his own apparent stance on emotion, he had desire, and his desire required temptation and the temptation would lead to even more desire.

She sat at her usual station, as the report from Germany was sufficient enough for her to keep her job, but the advice she had seen yet not apprehended Raynie and the others did nothing to elevate her status. This issue was immediately addressed upon her return, but it was not affecting her as much as she would have thought prior to going to Germany. She felt somewhat at a loss, lacking the motivation to be at her station and feeling a little like just getting away - even keeping her job had lost its luster. It too looked as cold and as grey as the lighting filling the cities now. She had liked the colors of the lights before, but now all looked flat, and so did her life.

****

John was becoming fed up with the torture.

"What do you know about flux mechanics?" The question came again and again, and each time he refused to answer, they would torture him with injected nanotechnology burning him at his nerve endings. He screamed each time the instant it came on, but nobody could hear – they had him in a locked space helmet.

Initially they offered him an easy way to comply with promises of a better life, but he would have none of it. So now, though he was a resilient man, he was being taken to new extremes. Deep in his spirit he remained vigilant, holding on for he would never give them what they wanted. He knew they would use flux technology to construct powerful vortex amplifiers to be used as weapons and as a means to draw in energies to manipulate atoms at will. John was about the only person alive to have sufficient knowledge for taking humanity to this level of technological evolution – he was the leader, the expert. The authorities knew this after tracking him and piecing his personal profile together. His stealth unit for masking his flight path from Alaska had been his biggest give away – though unknown to John himself. Its' mere presence had alluded them to his potential, and they already knew of his work in the services where he pioneered the first research into faster than light flux technology.

Pursuit of John and his companions was not a mere incident of tracking and reprimanding dissidents. John Matheson was the person they knew had their ability to help them realize even more than they were about to unleash upon people, and as such they would do anything to extract this information from him.

After each session when he was thrown into the cell where the others simply waited day by day, Lorraine would hold and comfort him during the time he took to recover from the brutal measures of torture they played out. Tobias, John, Lorraine, and Asper all had identification chips now, with each chip containing their correct identifications – it had been done moments after they were arrested in London.

This time though, they were not going so easy on him. They wound up the machines inside his body to release a pulse so searing it could take him to the verge of life and death. He could not scream this time - there simply was nothing inside him to express the torture. He began to slip into a void with images of his fears and emotions flashing around him. It was their way of literally torturing him to the edge of death with both pain of body and of heart. Then, when he felt like surrender to misery would be the only option, they switched them off and he was brought fully back to the grey light overhead.

"What do you know about flux mechanics?" He could not answer – he simply did not have the energy.

When he was taken back to the cell after this torture session, he was unconscious by the time he arrived into his friends waiting arms.

Next morning before any interrogation session could commence, they took him to a laboratory and inserted a device to probe his thoughts. It could be turned on and off at their will. He could feel the device searching his mind, and his memories – seeking the knowledge of flux mechanics. The authorities had information on flux but were missing vital components, and they feared vulnerability without all the information about the technology John possessed.

But John continued to resist. His mind strongly connected to his heart, fought the erratic stabbings into his thoughts. When these impulses came much stronger when he began to consider flux technology, he had to fight hard to resist their intrusion into the deepest areas of his knowledge. So strong and sudden the incursions were, he was startled by them and instantly had to redirect his mind elsewhere. He relied on his connection to his heart and thought of Chris. How sad it had been after all he had done for his son, but he never gave into sadness – determined there would always be a choice, or a response. Now those responses to his intentions and his feelings would be used to fight off the intruder.

****

A new announcement was broadcast via personal and public holographic devices, and to work station holographic banks everywhere. "Today is the final day to have your identification chip injection. Failure to have the injection at your prescribed time will result in your arrest and require the payment of heavy fines."

Superior Officer One read it to herself and rubbed her arm where she had her own device installed some months prior. To-date, it had not really concerned her and she had noticed no change in her life. As soon as she was injected, her entire data file became available and she was allocated payment only by chip credits.

This announcement also meant operations at the facility would increase due to the inevitable numerous arrests about to take place. It would be a lot of hard work processing and interrogation people, overseeing Agents, and managing the entire affair according to the policies of efficiency her superiors wanted from her. And its appeal seemed even flatter than before, if such a thing was possible.

Her life had become empty now as she realized how empty it was, and also how empty it had been for years. Her music was her sole solace against it, and now she saw herself as a lonely person who sought one thing of harmony amongst all this. Work had effectively driven most of the life out of her as she saw the truth in her ways of the daily job acting with the façade barking orders - it all seemed futile and lacking. All it gave her was some comfort at home being higher than most others, therefore having a view – but it was a view to a suppressed and suffering city, so it was not a good view. Over years she would repeat the same thing over and over where a little part of her wanted variety from the act of such repetition.

When she thought of herself many years ahead, she was old and no longer in the service and therefore would no longer be seen as efficient. She would lose any position in the struggle for higher status, instead left lonely to hopefully quickly leave this world in the least pain after spending her twilight years consuming what she could.

It was not good enough. She could feel a fire had become alight inside and now she could see the flame. She had let the others go in Germany and she had been feeling all of this since the chance meeting at the institute. She was not losing all hope for in fact, she was being given some. It was invigorating in the sense it made her question and wonder as she felt a sense of exuberance – a feeling from memory not of time but of self seemingly allowed again to be expressed.

When at last her day at work was over, she took time to walk the public passageways on her way home. She stopped at times to watch people moving about, distracted with their destinations and passing by the many small wonders even to be found at the hearts of cities. She could hear the holographic broadcast advertising the latest technology upgrades with their messages of assurance to the fear based people. She could see fear on some of their faces – not the fear of danger, but the fear of losing status, the fear coming from dependency. It was in their eyes for their faces were not lined with the wrinkles of experience – the nanotechnology took care of any such disfigurement.

When she did finally arrive home, she just went to the window and sat, staring at the view. The city did not sparkle in the dusky light. It was dying in a way with a silhouette now dull and flat against the distant horizon over the ocean to the west. It was becoming a remnant of what it was - a shadowy memory and a shadowy beginning.

As the time of nine passed and the city became still, she wondered if there were any other faces behind the many windows she could see, and if they too were seeing the same. But something inside her told her there would not be so many as she would have liked and this would sadden her, so she looked away and realized what the sense of invigoration the others had given her in Germany actually was.

She could feel compassion for life, for things, for people. She could feel empathy about why the others had tried to avoid getting the identification chip. She could feel there was a connection, and it was nearly the first time ever – so far as she was from the innocent natural connections given during childhood to then be nurtured through the adult years. Memories were returning and they rekindled the fire as it burned brighter with each feeling, each recollection, and it invited her to seek more within its flame.

It was then when she decided there would be no more. No more of the daily grinding of her work now utterly pointless to her. No more pandering to the superiors condescending ways – she too had done this to Agent Eight, and whilst she had no regard for him, she felt a sense of regret in having acted this way. The power of position was flimsy, so dependent on compliance forced upon others for its immature ways. She would leave it all. She had no fears, as a simple resignation would be acceptable by those superior in office to her.

What she would do, she did not immediately know, and for a brief moment she felt a pang of excitement.

She did not care. Leaving the high-rise level she was on would not matter, as the view lacked appeal from any level to her now. Could she do anything for the others? She had been advised of the arrest in London only without any further details. She did not have an answer and she felt saddened at their plight, particularly the torture of John. Whatever it took though, she would try to do something, somewhere, somehow.

She resigned first thing in the morning. Notice was not applicable as the authorities could immediately fill her role. Her superior questioned her on why she was resigning, "I suppose you do not have the taste for what we are about to do?"

"No, it is not a taste, it is I feel I lack the will to be efficiently my best."

"A noble reason for the cause, but not your entire reason, if in fact, any part of your reason at all. I see fire in your eyes where I have not before. Not the fire of command. No, the fire of indifference where the flame flickers and your thoughts wander. Know such things will soon be compressed into limited experiences based on expectations brought on as a provision by the authorities."

"I know what is coming…of sorts."

"And do you object to it?"

"No." It was the truth, she had no actually felt objection, as she had instead focused on the flame. Her superior could see she was telling the truth.

"Then what will you do?"

"I have thought about it. Under this new way of life, it will still be possible to own a private dwelling…"

"For a while." She knew his interjection was correct and in a few years the authorities had scheduled the shutting down of private ownership rights.

"Um…I am thinking of a private dwelling in a smaller city, or town away from San Francisco. I have enough chip credits and I can get employment."

"You know you will still be bound to authority policy for retention of classified information…and you will be checked periodically for this."

"Yes I am. Don't bother yourselves though, I hardly know enough to be a security threat and nor would I want to be. I just want to leave the services quietly and peacefully."

"Hmm." He looked her face up and down. "I see no reason why we should be concerned but it does not mean we will not be doing surveillance on your movements and transactions."

"You'll be doing so anyway," She was right and he became a little annoyed at having been corrected in such a way.

"You can go. I will not wish you the best for your future, nor will I thank you for your service. I simply say one last thing to you, be very ready, for what is about to happen is much more than yourself or Agent Eight could have ever dreamed."

She left the office glad it was over. She had no personal items at her workstation so she just walked straight out of the building. She spent the remainder of the day sampling some of the city and did not go home until the evening.

She sampled foods she had not ever eaten previously, by chance stopping at Fongs' in China Town. She began to feel life how it was for others not in the services. She saw freedom in their faces, yet she saw the fear still in others. She felt intentions to do something if she could, to avoid losing this newly discovered feeling, this new vision of herself.

Chapter 40

Chan suggested they all take a field trip as the day wore on. Snow was beginning to melt in places, creating tributary flows of water joining to form larger streams. They noticed the elegance in the simplest of things with the droplets of water dripping from the edge of snow patches and seeing the momentum as it returned to its original shape. Shaded areas still holding snow, had vapors of mist rising and winding through the branches above. They noticed all these simple elemental intentions of air and water as they rode upon the invisible waveforms and geometries around them.

"These places and times feel good. They offer so much alignment and are all about us. It is in noticing these small and simple things where we can feel the connection. And they can respond to us…other life, and forces. See how intricate the connections are as this water gathers. There is always provision, always giving and always the intention for creation of life. These are showing us, though it may not appear so with just a glance, how we are much a part of this. It is with the interrupted ways of people, where most of this is overlooked, and so they experience things not aligned, bringing suffering and need instead of being able to be silent with self in such surroundings."

"Overcoming the interruption to the giving nature of elemental intentions is the key to aligning with these energies. This is not a belief - it is nothing of such things. It simply is allowance. It exists throughout, but many minds have conditioned forgetfulness interrupting this flow."

"What is very important to consider is the choices many have made at these times and in times past. They have lived lives of fear, as we have discussed. It is this fear as a choice, being most difficult to understand. A simple question is 'why would a human being choose a life of fear based on dependency?' There is so much giving happening at all times – it is this energy waiting to be re-activated within. Where there is uneasiness it is not easement and so it manifests in many forms."

"But can you take this to mean all illnesses humans can suffer?" Jenna asked.

"No, such is not the only understanding. There are things affecting life found in many different forms. These are part of the life processes in elemental intentions. Their natural energies are of these ways, and so you might see an animal afflicted with disease. This is the natural course of all of the waveforms involved with this manifestation. It is the way of being for this situation as a variation in nature. So too it is for all life. Where there can be uneasiness, is in the choices made when made under duress and to manipulate without consent. This leads to a simple un-balancing of intentions in many places and people, and this is often shown as an affliction."

"So a simple example would be a person who is suffering a mental illness and due to this suffering they do not eat the correct foods or do adequate exercise to maintain a healthy body."

"A good example. It is clear in many of these instances where it has been said some people can eat through boredom, and then they eat poor quality foods. This furthers the disruption even more. The perception of boredom and the reaction is not aligned with the giving nature of elemental understanding – where forces as waveforms and geometry respond."

"And so too is the connected ego a variation in nature as it manifests the elementally aligned intentions of an individual. Many times the ego can say to an individual all is well and perfect..." he thought about the word, but then continued considering they were likely to understand. "But it is reaction rather than response, when there is the affliction of power or manipulation. These things cause many interruptions to the happiness, to the health, and to the capacity of people to actually grow and take on further understanding as states of mind impede this. Such distractions are in place now as they have been, to divert people from such things as simple as the melting snow we have just observed."

"And divert them from being aware of the giving forces they are actually a part of."

"Yes. For without the need, then there is no power. There is no requirement for people to strive for status based wealth because such a system holds them...hostage. Life can be lived through experiences within a structured way where the motivation is complimentary. There is no need to have these fears of losing, for it also comes at a very high price. People see priorities in extreme amounts and so we now have this move by the authorities to further this with focus in place to continue suffering."

"Suffering has for so many cycles, been much a part of the human experience. It is said suffering can teach you what to value most, and for a lot, this can be true. But it is the human suffering going on almost unspoken. It is the suffering from the loss of connection to the elemental intentions inside and about them. They suffer the drawback...of these things they consume to feel good, and soon see they begin to want another then another. Yet, what they are bound to do and the very complex rules governing this existence cause much suffering."

"Parents spend time away from their children and leave them often in the care of strangers. These are times for children during this stage of life where bonding takes place and so in pursuit of status, they tender their children out and interrupt this bonding because of the conditions. And one must be alert to the variations in waveforms in these instances. There is joy to be felt in each instance where the parents are re-united with their children at the end of their working times each day. Do not overlook the surge in emotion here. This time it is their intentions speaking to them."

"This surge is both the elemental intentions doing what they can to align back to their proper forms after the interruption of the separation of child and parent. These are beautiful things and they bring much love and physical stimulation in touch and embrace. It is to remember the interruption for the sake of status, is the focus for this issue. They are failing also to see through the fear foundation intentions of the controlling egos, where giving is all around them and so they need not carry such fears…for safety, for comfort, for…something to do. This is a natural elemental intention based thing. It is a flow and when one is not living as such, it can be difficult for them to imagine and so they create an opinion. The allowance is waiting to simply be without need of respite as the conditions of mind then block this response to create a thought in reaction. And now as in times past, they seek reliance on machines more than they realize. This is opposition to machines being complimentary to life. And so the authorities through this can continue to herd people in their direction and what they want to see future human dependency become."

In the evening they gathered a stock of fire wood and tidied up around the house. A much stronger storm was forecast, and this time it would come as a near gale force with much more snow. After failing again to contact the others in London, they felt resilient to focusing on anything negative and decided yet another attempt the following day would be the best idea.

They were sitting in the library again reading where Raynie had found a title amongst the hundreds lining the walls and asked if the others might like to see.

It was an old book and looked like it had seen a lot of use since its first release in late in the twentieth century. She then turned it around to show them what was written on the back – water is a mirror reflecting our mind.

"Yes indeed," Chan said. "For our mind is the instrument to carry out our intentions."

Raynie flicked through some of the pages, looking for something to show when she came across an image catching her attention. They gathered around the table where they saw it was a series of images showing the reformation of the naturally elemental shape of water crystals. The water went from a highly disrupted form, to become aligned crystal patterns during the time people of the location determined the problem and then produced a remedy.

One interesting experiment detailed within the book, showed the disrupted state of water when it had been subjected to negative thoughts and sound waves.

Chan spoke on this, "See this inside of people who are experiencing negative. Elemental disruption is evident." He took control of the book, "See here? The water responds to music - there is a change to its crystal properties. And this." He showed them a water crystal subjected to audio of chant focusing on compassion. It had facet upon facet of hexagons forming an alignment.

****

Steve was ready to meet Agent Eight. Rendezvous with the ship was just seconds away as he strode the last yards to the docking port. His assignment detail was to imprison the Agent for the remaining flight. The big drawback would be Steve now had twelve duty hours per day guarding the Agent. Steve was dreading the long boring hours ahead – never had he been put in such a commission...at least since his early days in the service.

He heard the hiss of the docking port tunnel being pressurized for transfer without spacesuit as the Agent arrived. He heard the footsteps as Agent Eight walked the twenty-foot long tunnel, but there was no window into the walkway, so he really didn't know what Agent Eight looked like. Sure, the holographic banks could give you an idea, a projection, but they lacked the life experience of physical sight. Steve liked to get an impression of people when he first saw them - it had become his style during so many years of command. When the port door did open, he saw a man who immediately gave him a bad impression.

"Agent Eight. I am to refer to you as such as per my instructions. You are to be escorted to the brig where I have the unfortunate duty of guarding you until you are relocated via Mars Station, to the Asteroid Belt, then for service as a guard. In my official capacity as escort for your successful delivery to said destination, I am obliged to inform you I am not required to answer any of your questions in detail. You may ask them, but I probably will not answer."

Agent Eight remained silent – he had been this way almost entirely since lift off from Earth. His only words were forced out of him when his escort aboard the new official looking spaceship had ordered him to acknowledge his conditions of transit, rights, and facilities available. He walked a little in front of Steve now, his head down, and his hands in holographic handcuffs.

Steve felt no sympathy for how pathetic the man looked – a man who had committed murder. He watched the way he walked and it seemed like he barely knew how to do so. Every step looked like a step at the edge of something, but Steve would not catch him if he fell. Steve was not a cruel man in any instance - he could just not help a murderer.

He showed him to his cell and told him about what was available for his use...basically nothing. These ships were not equipped well for prisoners and the cells were fairly basic. He advised there would be two meals per twenty-four hours, and then left, engaging the holographic cell bars before disappearing into a small office where he could watch Agent Eight without being seen.

****

The dark group Chan had described was amongst many who held rituals over the two days of the injection deadline as it came into force around the entire Earth. People were rejecting it in their own way - some with age-old ritual, others in shamanism states of awareness dancing erratically, and people of beliefs holding ceremonies. Where native rhythms sounded deep in the forest and in cities, they held people to their rhythmic flow, compelling all present in earshot to join in effort against this invasion. They saw images of death, of destruction, of light, and of replenishment, but they were few in number as they had always been, with the majority of people only giving the passing deadline the slightest of notice. Those few who were outcasts roaming the remnants of the old streets with no established residence, would be eventually arrested and given chips if seen as efficient. Otherwise they would simply disappear.

"Authentication system has reached one hundred percent online." A computer voice made the announcement at headquarters as the final deadline passed west of Hawaii. The holographic monitoring banks were a huge array of projections featuring readouts, maps, and streaming commands. Periodically reports would flash alerts, with their contents showing details of people who had not received their injection. An entire team was set monitoring these reports and Agents were regularly dispatched when the people were arrested and taken to the facility.

The officer in charge went busily over the entire holographic bank – settling on a live street view. He could see people walking the streets, the majority appearing normal as they filed along in the left and right lanes the pavement was divided into. It was all quite mundane to him in comparison and he was about to look away, when he saw something he could hardly believe – nor could those in the street view.

As if from nowhere, a twenty foot tall robot had emerged from the wall of a building and seized an outcast person. It immediately apprehended the person, restraining them until the officers it had summoned, could attend the scene and take the person away. The appearance of a robot with a body of three sections like an ant walking on insect like hind legs and holding a man with fully dexterous insect like hands was not the most startling aspect of the event. It was its' appearance seemingly out of nowhere holding them aghast.

The robot had been positioned for weeks in fact, waiting ready to be fully activated. Until the deadline time, it had been in situation on the side of the building at minimum system status sufficient to maintain invisibility. As the systems came online, it remained invisible ready to apprehend any person confirmed as not having the injection. Fully automated systems were in place for real time updates and so it did not need to be operated by someone – it was autonomous.

Within its construct were the very protein strings Jenna had helped develop, now adapted as processors for the machine, and far from the intentions she ever had for the technology. It was equipped with regenerating nanotechnology and could last for years on a single internal and very small power cell. Operating on such power, it was uncompromising to its captive. As soon as the officers led the apprehended person away, the machine then went back to invisibility and nobody knew where it was.

The officer in charge returned his focus back to work after the shock of this vision. Located far from John and the others in the same facility, he was assigned the analysis and reporting of progress probing John's mind. They wanted the key elements to flux mechanics for transgressing beyond mere artificial intelligence to artificial sentience, and so they continued to probe push him, and he continued to fight.

He no longer had any interrogation sessions - instead he sat out each day with the others in the cell, focusing his mind to keep the probe at bay. Nobody came to see them except for the guard who brought them food twice per day, and they had no news of the outside world and of their friends in Australia. They had talked about them often, and about what they had experienced and learned before they had been apprehended. But it was in very low tones for they knew surveillance was in place. Their conversations however subdued, helped them retain calm minds in the bland cell bathed continuously in cold light.

When finally somebody else came to see them and advised they were to be given a holographic projector for viewing broadcasts, it offered very little to appease their situation. All they saw were regular messages based in propaganda thinly disguised as words of assurance for the population at large. The officer in charge had been given orders to provide this device as a means to distract John Matheson's resistance. He laughed when he told them how much they were sacrificing for a useless plight when he accompanied two other officers to install the projector.

Chapter 41

Agent Eight was neither making it difficult for Steve, nor easy. Steve was just bored and Agent Eight knew this. He also knew how when people get bored, they get distracted and so without Steve being aware, Agent Eight was watching him a lot more closely than he would have liked. There was no conversation from the Agent – just silence and watching. He could not actually see Steve in the office, but he knew when Steve had been there for long periods, and he took note of when Steve came and went. Then during the hours Steve was not on duty, he would consider any options he might have, under the gaze of only the security cameras. This was the weakness in the chain of guard over him, even more so than Steve's boredom. Whilst there were the eyes of the security cameras on him, there were often tired and bored people watching and looking away from the holographic images they produced, particularly during the hours when most people on board the ship were asleep.

Towards the end of Steve's fourth twelve-hour shift, Agent Eight spoke to him for the first time. "McCray?" His voice startled Steve, as he had never heard it previously.

"How do you know my name?"

"I heard it spoken by others."

"When?"

"Yesterday."

"What do you want?"

"Holographic projector. I need something to do. I like official broadcasts." He was lying.

"I didn't think you had any needs."

"None other than the projector."

"Why should I get it for you? Look at yourself." This was metaphoric as the cell had no mirror and the metals were dull, offering no reflection.

"You don't have to."

"I know that."

Agent Eight said nothing further, leaving Steve to think about the conversation and to think of what it was like to talk to him. Time was in place now for Steve to consider being startled by his first words, and to deal with his request. Behind the one-way glass, Steve was doing deliberating. He had been deprived of interactions and had grown bored on the long journey into space, so now the Agent's words sank into him further than he anticipated. His thoughts turned to thinking of the Agent, his mind processed the Agent, and his decisions were activated to consider giving to the Agent.

"Not now," Steve finally said.

Agent Eight did not reply. He had affected Steve as he had planned – for he too was aware of the human need for communication after long stretches of time almost alone. The Agent knew the other occupants of this vessel, of which there were six, would be busy at station or asleep, they too suffering the tediousness of space travel. And Steve said 'not now', which could mean later.

****

Not nearly as far away as the group in the old house would have liked, both the authorities and the dark sect were gathering. Unaware of each other, yet vaguely aligned, they were meeting in separate locations around Canberra, Australia's capital city under one hundred miles away. The sect had a long history of activity in and around this place, largely out of public view and away from awareness of the authorities. Since times going back over a century before, they had practiced rituals and even sacrifices to aid their cause. Mysterious disappearances of both people and animals, though not common, could mostly be attributed to them. Their motivation was strong and they saw the approaching snowstorm not for its amazing geometric forms, but as an onslaught and a time where life could perish.

The authorities were like the storm as they too were about to begin an onslaught. Their view contained the invisible machines, the dominance over how people spent their lives, and of the imminent technology to be deployed. And so it was these motivating factors superiors drew upon, ordering sub-ordinates out into the fierce weather to attend tasks for the sake only of efficiency.

"Soon people will begin to feel the torus when it is near," Chan said as the snow beat against the window, driven sideways at times. "But it must be kept on our persons at all times. It is imperative we do not lose sight of it now physically, or in feeling. We have seen it show us many facets yet appear to remain a stable glow. This is the activation in progress. Soon, it will increase at a much faster rate."

"How long will it take?" Jake asked.

"We do not know, as it is up to intention. But consider it has been activating for a long time and even if the speed of activation increases, we will feel it more than look at it as a point in time."

"How will we keep other people from feeling it?" Jenna asked.

"We must be alert to where we go and base this on our intentions. Those of positive heart will feel something and even if it is uncertainty, there is an activation commenced. Those of negative ways become aware of this something as our intentions are exposed. It will bring attention and with such attention there comes affection or desire to posses. The torus mirrors the material intentions as it is a pattern within the construct of energies where the energies are realized. It is not to be a prize and to be hoarded by a few, for the essence of the pattern it represents is a memory within all whether material or unseen."

"Are there other torus?"

"Infinite…it is not to focus on the number as such. This is a limitation in activation to reach a mind definition. One is the number in this instance as the torus is the catalyst to transition…"

"Sorry Chan. Like the flux John works with as the catalyst for data to then attach to the tachyon pathways beyond light speed he is working on. My protein strings are at this verge in part as well."

"Very much the same Jenna. The torus as a catalyst is materially required to manifest where application of intention can focus in this context instead of being an energy field unseen by the eye."

Raynie and Lyle returned then with armloads of wood, but Lyle tripped on the floor rug, sending him headlong towards the center of the kitchen. "Charging in like a bull there," Jenna said as she helped pick up a few logs he had dropped.

"Did I miss anything?"

Jenna did a quick scan, "Yes you missed everything." She filled him in on the conversation with Chan as they stacked the wood by the fireplace.

Raynie kept a close ear as she was doing the same with her logs. "Gee it's getting cold out there. Storms like this are rare in these parts. It normally only has two or three snowfalls per winter here. But two now since late autumn, with heavy snow?"

The wind took to howling around the house, its' unique old design making for wailing eddies, screaming currents, moaning beams, and the odd shudder now and then. The sect took to wailing as they huddled together in their group not so far away, with skin touching skin, fully naked. They screamed and they moaned, and some also took to howling. And as the superiors of the authorities ordered their operatives and sub-ordinates to go out into the storm, they prepared to engage new technology for deployment throughout the capital. Soon people would learn to scream, they would learn to moan, and they would learn wailing in ways they could never have imagined.

When the dawn arrived, they were up early again as the wind continued and so too did the snow, now piled two feet high against the house. The kitchen fire crackled smelling of burning wood and smoke – Raynie had stoked it well to burn hot and keep the icy winds at bay. She stared at it for a while watching flares reflected on the bottoms of cooking pots hanging to the side of the fireplace. The others were all sitting together around the large central table, huddled against the cold as in some way it brought them closer together for warmth, despite the heat from the fire.

Conversation was low, sometimes drowned out by the rush of a wind gust driving snow against the kitchen door - their only window to the world this day as the heavy snow rendered a white featureless scene. They had shuttered all the windows in the house, so it was left to the small windows in the doors as their only view to the outside. And then as the sun climbed higher beyond the heavy clouds overhead, there was only the perception of respite from the low light, for sunlight offered nothing else to see other than the white all around.

Jenna was still curious to discuss more of the geometry, "Are the authorities aware of the geometry around the Earth? You mentioned lay lines as places or meridians. These are connecting points…"

"Yes. Like all geometries there are such points where the elemental aspects in formation of the geometry intersect. These are the meridians where slight variations meet. Each variation also has focus in what some call the golden section."

"So the authorities could be aware of these sections where the focal point can then be amplified?"

"In effect, yes. They already use these types of energy points for instrument calibration."

"It must be the reason they have boosted HAARP. But I wonder why. The HAARP array has been used mostly for atmospheric testing and materials testing."

"Be aware the use of this array is the awareness within by these people, of the potential energies accessed using the meridian lines. It happens in the bodies of people and bodies of objects in space. They are fundamental constructs of the patterns and forms enabling elemental intentions to be projected…or transmitted. It is likely with HAARP, they are indeed of the energies and they are using them for their own intentions."

Jenna was calculating a few rough equations in her head as she considered what the HAARP array might be able to do. She was running through the waveforms in the theta spectrum, the beta, and others, but remained mystified as to their precise relationship to what the authorities are doing.

"Understand," Chan said seeing her thinking this through, "Such lines are the way of all creations and if attuned to, they can easily be accessed."

"I still cannot grasp why they would use HAARP."

"Oh it might be a simple thing as to expect they will use the array to amplify wave forms. Despite the infinite nature of elemental geometry, the vanity of ego for power creates projections to serve the finite desires of ego, and so the waves are created to affect things and life. Awareness of foundation to all things is recognized, but it is just the ego cannot accept this and so it manifests organization to deliver the projected intentions of itself."

"I am thinking of how reluctant human beings were when there was the first theories and research into faster than light speed. With this, subsequent detection and capacity to draw upon infinite energies is being realized. They have some way to go yet in order to fully accommodate it into their agenda."

"It is likely. From my own knowledge, I see humans reluctant to accept the simple notion of free and easy. It has been their way for so long where nothing comes as free and nothing comes as easy – yet it is all around them and within them. This is part of the limited scope of controlling ego intentions, and furthers what I have said in regards to the results of such things."

"What about the golden section you mentioned?" Lyle asked. "Several times I have seen this as a facet through different cultures."

"Interesting as this is often seen by those who espouse to the ways of ego, yet they do not fully understand. Some people of note have made clear their understandings of this potential throughout human history, but like many things, they have mostly been ignored."

"The golden section is involved significantly in visual art forms," Lyle said.

"It is also seen in algebraic and geometric properties," Jenna added. "It is a geometrical proportion, which like Pi, has an infinite progression due to ratios."

"And too this is found in the growth of organic things. Many instances in plants show this through formation of geometric similarities we have discussed. It enables the recurrence of proportions in the elemental intentions of all…um, creation, without failure. Human beings are so disrupted at times they too miss this connection and the all giving nature of things."

"And Lyle, it is so much the foundation of artistic properties for the perception of depth and the focus on the mind, eye, and connected heart. It establishes and follows a rhythm, and its artistic applications are not restricted to just visual art. It also enables the elemental intentions as a response to sound waves. This is part of the understanding from Vienna and why harmony of sound evokes something like a golden feeling. It can mesmerize some and often gives an uninterrupted sense of being. When it is this state, it is when the heart connects and the mind listens to make happen those actions in response. Artistic qualities are focused on the emotion they evoke – it is from the heart, these energies are aligned elementally for the elemental quality of the art can be somewhat…a channel, or a meridian within the geometries. This is where the connections are experienced and there are no deliberate egotistical manipulations. Art and music flow harmoniously and the authorities see this, which is why they are going to limit the exposure of people to artistic qualities, and so limit their exposure to these elemental waveforms and geometries."

"And a significant thought to contemplate is this – the golden section is intrinsically part of nature as evidenced by the angle of torsion within DNA and then for further feeling, the heart itself is an example of the golden section in how it works."

"Underpinning these desires to manipulate is no conspiracy as it is just their way and obvious to all where control of people is so very evident every day, in so many things, and brings the results they view as holographic broadcast for news and social status information. It is right out in open view."

"And this thinking clouds their view into many other things I suppose?" Raynie asked.

"Yes, it is a fog in their minds. They are manipulated over time to think and act certain ways, and so the nature then is to forget as humans have forgotten so much now over many centuries and habits can also easily be formed both in action and in thought."

"People are subscribing to machine based life and yet they wonder why after so many upgrades, they still often feel the same way."

"It is because they are expecting change but all they really do is the same thing time and time again. This is the loop in evidence, yet they are led to believe these machines are progress…"

"Some are progress," Jenna interrupted. "Sorry Chan."

"It is okay and you are correct. It is where I said previously when people see machines in these times as items of affection and dependency. Elemental flow is about seeing them as complementary. These machines can be used to enable alignment and to complement things, but they are largely used in ways by people who are not feeling this. We have discussed the toxic nature many machines of convenience have had over time through over using."

"And yet another way to consider this. Many machines have been created to make life easier. Life is easy in a pure organic sense outside of the mind measuring life's hardships as life simply flows as is the nature of all the cosmos on all scales. It is just the control ego sense of limited intentions interrupting this feeling and creating difficulty. Where the ego is abandoned, then it is complementary and it not from convenience, efficiency, or laziness. This too has been prevalent as dependency can lead to complacency, and such things are not the elemental nature of intentions. The elements are of constant flux, or state of change and emergence. It is when thoughts become lazy where this connection is lost and is a human construct of experience. This has often then reflected as uneasiness, as I have discussed. To have a psychology needing life to be easy does not easily accept when matters of life become difficult and this can contribute to making them even more difficult. Always searching for easy is relevant to natural inclinations but carries a burden when sought for means of complacency."

"Humanity seems to be caught in the past in ways," Raynie said. "They are simply doing the same thing again and again – they even look at the past and make it relevant for now."

"This is the disrupted state. Focus here means they are not feeling the elemental flows and so they miss the intricacies in their meridians for the exponential growth."

"What about the degree of pain? Not only physical but also emotion pain?"

"Once again, it reflects the disruptions. The affliction of pain is elemental in nature and also it is driven by desire. It can be of normal consequence for organic life to experience pain. Look at when a child learns if they touch something hot, it burns and causes pain. This is simply natural. Or see the pain of illness brought through age. Of course, this too has a natural element where we experience it to in essence learn the experience of pain. These are elemental conditions - often so much pain is resulting from the conditioned ego traits making decisions and actions leading people to experience pain in various ways. It is more when one is not authentic where they can create pain they could otherwise not experience. It is always individual and a sense of reckoning to see and then to feel this progress."

****

For John, pain was no longer an issue. He was training himself well in blocking out the rudimentary low capacity device in his mind. He had determined how it worked and the ways he could then limit its efficiency. It was simply re-directing base sugars found in synaptic pathways in a futile attempt to access or program his thoughts. John almost saw this as comical due to its in-efficiency, but he knew now why they needed the flux mechanics.

He was helped by the others through the sessions of torture and they had re-assured him as they watched him battle the mind-probing device. Without them he could have still made it through, but they made it much easier for him to reach this point of resistance.

One thing of interest did distract him for some time, to the point he was able to focus as much on it as he could. Tobias had turned the holographic projector on out of sheer boredom finding no relief through endless official broadcasts. To John, the device was of a benefit the officer in charge could never have imagined. As it showed the robot appearing and disappearing incident, he saw something. His time working with flux mechanics had trained his eyes to observe light as it transitioned the conduit laid down by the tachyons. At this frontier, the light waves distorted for a split second, and he had grown accustomed to seeing it during his data teleport work. This trained him to see tiny fluctuations in the light behind the officers as the machine was in the last split second of returning to its invisible state. To the normal eye, this would be un-noticeable, but John saw otherwise. It was then he began to think of a way to escape the facility.

He dared not discuss almost any of his planning to the others for the sake of avoiding surveillance. Instead he gave them snippets of information about his thoughts, by way of broken sentences at random times. He knew if the authorities put all the audio together they could listen in – the risk had to be taken. When he spoke, Lorraine, Asper, and Tobias all listened carefully.

"Tell…um, put the projector over there, Tobias." Tobias moved the projector to help their cover. "Reconfigure phasing capacity…it looks blurry." Jake did by first interrupting the projection signals then aligning them for a clear picture.

"Get rid of bars, it is still not focused. And duplicate codes - it might - the picture quality. Mask chip to change status for central processor recognition." Tobias entered a few sequences to increase the projector capacity as John instructed. John had effectively told them what he needed to do, and for once they took to being thankful for having received the projector.

****

Steve was reluctant to give Agent Eight a holographic projector, seeing no reason why a murderer should be given any comfort. Despite Agent Eight's hopes when Steve said 'not now' he had intended it to be 'not ever'. But here he was disengaging the holographic cell bars whilst two men stood by with pulse rifles pointed at the Agent. Steve had succumbed to Agent Eight mainly because of the ship's crew.

Agent Eight had taken to making a lot of noise of mostly incoherent babble at loud volume. He was worst during the hours when Steve was not on duty and unfortunately for Steve, regulations stipulated there must be audio contact and monitoring at all times. So the crew had asked Steve to give him the projector quite a few times because they were sick of hearing the Agent go on and on and on.

As Steve installed the device, Agent Eight did not watch, nor did he speak. He just sat there in silence thinking part one of his plan was now in place. He did not even thank Steve when the device was up and running, so Steve did not bother to speak to him and simply left the cell and re-engaged the holographic bars, before returning to the small office.

Chapter 42

People without identification chips were being arrested in large numbers – the facility had become a very busy place. The invisible insect-like machines were beginning to strike fear amongst some, and so they handed themselves in for injection as soon as they learned of them. Incidents involving the robots were taking place in most major cities, with an increasing number of Agents being deployed into the field to take care of arrests where no machines were present. Equipped now with hand held chip scanner devices, they could sweep through the population in any place or time and detect those who had not yet complied with the regulations.

Life on the lower streets had turned even uglier with disturbing scenes unfolding during the apprehension of those very reluctant to take orders from the authorities. Robots could attend any arrest and neutralize anyone who objected or resisted. Equipped with neural injectors, they could immediately access a person's brain and render them unconscious, involving a new concept in pain for those unfortunate enough to be taken this way. Horror entered the egocentric minds of people whenever someone witnessed a body being put into the lowest section of the robot before it disappeared.

Official vehicles were noticeable about the streets as Agents went to and from the facilities in many cities and towns picking up and escorting dissidents. Their six wheel vehicles were of particular interest to those who saw them as progress and without seeing them for what they really were, looked forward to a future purchase themselves. Vehicle design was sleek and they could disappear in the same way as the robots, but many officers chose to remain visible for the sake of intimidation.

For those who were unaffected and lived the trans-human life, the authorities met their needs with newly installed street side update stations. Regular holographic broadcasts showed, "Your chip device will notify you of any upgrades available to your nanotechnology. The authorities can take care of your needs with new street side stations. Look for them on most street corners and you need not to worry for you will have the latest available in personal and virtual security close by." It went on to show a case of a mother and son where the child could have caught a software virus during a daytime outing from the high-rise if he had not taken the latest updates whilst away from home.

Other messages displayed the horrors of contracting a software virus. "The authorities provide a real time update for software virus protection. Do not suffer the affliction of your inserts running at poor efficiency and prone to security violations. Ensure your health and safety now and remain at status alert in your life."

Status Alert had become a familiar term used by the population at large who lived with the inserts. It meant their inserts were operating at the intended level – to fall below 'alert' status would mean they required some attention due to inefficient processing of cellular information. Very quickly, the update stations became locations of affection for most who were eager to remain at 'alert' level, and they began to take on a social focal point where people would arrange to meet and even share social times.

As part of the identification measure, the authorities asked the population to answer a few simple questions for security. These questions would be used in a multi tier authentication process in protection of their rights should there ever be an instance of someone stealing their identity or registration number. Most did not mind so much how the system referred to them as numbers, as it was seen as a highly efficient method to organize their own personal data. The chip was now bringing with it new technology and personalized data for their holographic enjoyment, prompting them to think they were being looked after more than ever.

Deep inside, deep deep inside, the nano-tech was waiting. The satellites were positioned and the central systems stood as vast holographic banks. Machines of stealth had taken to the streets and many more were yet to come. Official aircraft were in place, as their mother ships kept to the clouds. An array of machines and antennas were on standby, and beyond the Earth there was control. The authorities were giving the people just enough time to get used to the chips…just. Then they would bring a calamity with such ferocity, the people would be powerless to stop them…when they had flux mechanics.

Flux mechanics were still the only thing on the agenda of those who had any level of control or decision surrounding the implant in John's mind. He could still regularly feel it push against him and he fought it off every time. He also knew it was getting them nowhere and soon they would grow tired of its inefficiency and look for some other method of information retrieval.

Work on his plan was proceeding well when he asked the others to help him trick the attending officers and guards whenever they came. He explained how they could prompt them to speak numbers through conversation and affirmation of their own conversation tricking the officers to repeat their words. John had reconfigured a small part of the holographic projector processor to record voices and configure wave forms to synthesize speaking.

His success had buoyed their spirits and they soon took no notice of their bland surroundings. It was not done yet, and success of the plan could not be guaranteed. Amongst all else at the facility, John knew escaping would be difficult, and then travel afterwards equally so as they all had been injected with identification chips.

They still had to work out a way of physically exiting the building and the external perimeter equipped with holographic shock wires able to stun anyone who touched them into unconscious. Asper and Lorraine had spent time on this issue, as Tobias remained attending to John's coded speech.

"See…chance, two…hmm for three, no four of you, and you take seventy hours to get there. He had given Tobias a sequence to discreetly enter via the holographic keypad he had made through reconfiguring projector resolution. By taking away some picture resolution, which would not be noticed, he could divert some algorithms to make the keypad. Now he was hacking into central systems to obtain the access codes through the doors of the building. Without any way to record the codes, it was imperative they all remembered them precisely, for a wrong code would bring an instant alarm. John had already hacked the algorithm for the holographic cell bars and so they could actually leave the cell, but there was no point until the plan was established for the best chance at clear passage away from the facility.

****

"See within the torus there appears a state of flux, yet when you concentrate on it, it seems to disappear? Jenna said as they were all looking at it again. "The pink hue seems to have depth but then it seems to be like a flat radiance from within. But what I am wondering about Chan is within mathematical circles as the torus is seen as a closed surface and the product of two circles."

"And so like water it is representation of the elemental intentions. This construct is for the sake of dimensional reality as you see it. Beyond this, other planes give rise to interaction of elemental energies and thus along these the intentions travel in waveforms as geometric shapes. The dimensions represented here are the gateway to these other planes. The torus is the means to accommodate other energy and also the energy of intent and emotion for these are energies at play affecting outcomes."

"This activation is brought through re-alignment with the elements and so natural progression takes place in a giving sense to enable insight into new patterns rather than repeating existing patterns almost entirely. You see, it is often the mistake of human beings to take and this is shown when they take for their own needs, when they take for desire, and when they take out of fear to feel personal security or satiating a want. They do this for fearing of missing what they think they require for happiness, yet they do not require such things to be happy. It is an illusion and illusion is in foundation of consumption and this also is the foundation of efficiency for the authorities.

"These energies do exist as elemental giving towards outcomes and ongoing change, whereas so much of these energies as they are expressed in the present way as a repetition of the loop, come as hardships or measures to form a secure version of reality for fear of the unknown."

"It is just those alignments are not yet in complete balance?" Lyle asked.

"Yes and no. They are not in alignment but there is no complete alignment. Alignment is an elemental energy in the giving nature and so it is progressive and not as finite as to be seen as complete. Feeling complete is not apparent either. Where one may feel complete they are feeling what it is like to attune to their elemental self for the time and so this does not bring on a hunger from emptiness, but rather an appetite for more. Rarely is it the case for such feelings to arise genuinely out of the negative ego traits for the negative is a hunger needing to feed. It is merely a perception of this. Another thing for your considerations is the saying in some cultures where it is wise to know one is always learning throughout life. Wisdom too is not a point of finality for to pursue or allow it, is feeling this appetite for more."

"How can people bring this into their daily lives though? It seems a world away from where many or most are now?" Jake asked this question, and Lyle had a bit of an idea of how Chan would respond, having researched alternative ways of life in various cultures.

"This is not specifically the way to view this. It does seem as if it is almost a polarity and quite the opposite – requiring people to give up so many things. They do not have to do this, for it is why they do things in life where they can find change. One can enjoy the many things life can offer through experience, emotion and even technology, but largely they are not sensing the giving nature of elemental intentions and so they think it is a removal from one way to another way. Simply, it is to align and allow with focus yet without focus. All those things can be complementary and life not put through such upheaval as many may think. Remember, it is the pursuit of many of the things in this present life leading to fear, leads to worry, and leads to need and dependence. Why would people not want to give up those things?"

It was not a question for them to answer, rather something to consider.

"And another thing I will say for now is consider the feelings when a person creates something by themselves and those feelings when it is acquired through purchase. There is understanding to see there, as creation by self is reflection of self, and acquisition is not as dear to a person and expressive of the self. Many work to acquire things and they easily can trade or on-sell them too making a purchase valid in this way, but those made with their hands, often hold a connection founded in sentimentality. This work is honorable and for the way of progression, yet for many it can be done where it seems all else is very confined and the person barely has time free from consumption and management of life to be themselves not meeting these their obligations and thinking of desires."

"What about the bracelet I bought Chan?" Raynie asked. "It could end up being sentimental to the journey through China."

"With such objects...of affection, they feel this way towards them because they remind them of their connections to elemental intention founded in their acquisition. This is a basis in love and so attachment for the recollection of fond times occurs even though it was in the past and there is progression now."

"It is not the way of a fallen leaf to reject progression. It does not sit upon a current of water being taken down stream, and want to go back to its attachment to the tree from which it fell. It simply progresses. And whilst human beings can be much more complex than the simple leaf, they are one and the same. They are both in natural progression based on the foundation of elemental intention in an organic sense."

"Then as the leaf carries on to the sea or to be snagged and be left high on the bank of the stream, it continues progression and changes form. The geometries within the leaf are a natural design to enable the elements to take it to another existence. Where it is seen to rot, this is simply the realignment of elements in a natural progression again in another way. Where it disappears and eventually becomes soil, the progress is the same. These properties exist too for human beings."

"There is so much they are forgetting. They have the elemental natural flows of giving and the additional capacity to move well beyond the leaf and use their minds to shape things and to create, to conceptualize and to wonder...yet they largely have their heads down or their minds distracted through their dependencies. They think they have it all, yet they are only seeing a small portion of the giving on offer. It is waiting for them...to be experienced."

Chapter 43

The dark sect had located themselves near the capital city for many years as they manifested their own internal struggles with the authorities over time. Their motivation was not unlike others, as they fought off the measures of control and the imposition to their type of life. It was their nature to strike back – the nature of the beast they worshipped. In these times, this choice served them well as they were able to obtain knowledge and details of the machines now being deployed in close proximity. They were as determined as the others to not become part machine – trans-humanism was for those losers in the majority. They certainly used machines though and they were busy at work making software viruses in an effort to strike back.

There were technical experts amongst their numbers and many of them had revenge in their minds, and their hearts – so they thought. As rejected outcasts, their ideas of technology had earned them dismissal from the services as their machines and algorithms were seen as inefficient. Now they could extract revenge and make people pay for contributing to this pathetic downfall.

They knew of the pain suffered by those who had been exposed to viruses in their DNA nanotechnology – they designed the pain. They knew of the suffering, both by individuals and by the authorities spending vast inefficient amounts of money to counteract their virtual offensives. And they knew of their power…growing. It was if their inner beast was about to break free of its imprisoning labyrinth, where its wanderings were lost in the underworld. They would soon become what they dreamed of – eternal in hatred and in sacrifice.

The sacrifice people were making in letting go of their freedoms as more and more systems came online to watch, to control, and to make offerings, was just the beginning. The sect too saw them as helpless, like lambs to the slaughter, and they would catch the meat as it fell. They would mince the emotions, the health, and the mindsets of individuals. They would carve them to pieces and stitch them back into whatever configuration they saw as necessary in order to vent their anguish, to force subjugation, and to compress authority based data into useless packets of distraction.

Viruses of unimaginable properties could now be created and the authorities were doing all they could to aid their own cause. As if lost in modern maze of catacombs residing beneath the world, the sect held weapons of ways based in ancient lore to be used now where darkness was to become their spectrum of light. With each attack, there came a reaction. Some might convulse and begin to froth, and others would bleed slowly until they died. Internal burning with its intensity unreachable caused slow agony, and the writhing of people was nothing to them. It was all part of their plan, their desire, to bring forth their essence founded in their beast, founded in themselves. These were but the first few of many to come.

Now, the torus still missing from their beast's crown was sought to complete an amplifier – their beast of infusion rendered as the bull deep in the underneath. They knew, and they wanted it so they could spread their dark wings across the planet, across the hearts, and across themselves, to bathe in their superfluous glorification of hate.

****

HAARP came fully on line with the booster system letting out a tremendous crack before leveling to nominal boost status. Simultaneously all who had identification chips felt the chips. It was hard to describe to each other as a feeling as it was more like a lack of feeling. Initially many thought it was something wrong, but soon the authorities waylaid fear.

"Today's update has been courtesy of the authorities in their best efforts to maintain efficient operation of all nanotechnology hardware and identification chip data security. Whilst you may feel a little different, be assured it is nothing of concern, and all will be normal. You can contact the authorities with any question via any one of the updating stations located near you."

What was to become normal was the way they felt now as soon they would forget how they had been.

Asper, Lorraine, Tobias, and John all felt it too. They immediately noticed how it seemed to make them listless to a degree – as if their cares slipped away a little. John immediately focused even harder on their escape knowing any weakness in his mind would let the implanted device do its work. He was almost finished and Tobias was no longer required for response to coded instructions.

The three of them watched him as he worked. They had nothing much to do and a lot of their conversations had lulled through exhaustion of a point or too much deliberation over an issue. When he looked up at them and took a deep breath, they knew he had finished. It would now be up to planning for the right time to escape.

Procedures at the facility had become standard due to the hectic state of the place now so many had been arrested.

"At least we are not the only ones against this," Asper said just to make conversation. "I heard a guard say there had been thousands."

"I bet they are many more who don't make it this far," Tobias added thinking of the remorselessness the authorities demonstrated. "And some who probably regret they did, judging by the screams we have heard."

The daily guard shift change was scheduled for one hour. This was a time they had considered for escape, but John pointed out it meant almost double the number of officials would be at operational status within the complex. He thought it might be best during the night shift after the guards had been at station for some hours and could lapse in attention for a moment or so. They would have to make a run for it – there was no other way. So long as the codes were remembered correctly, they could access the doors purely with speech overcoming the need to enter them manually. Normally, officers could pass throughout the facility based on a scan of their individual chip, but as a backup they could also speak the codes – the system would recognize their voice and the code, prior to permitting access.

Based on the prompts they had tricked attending officers who brought food and attended their requests. John had managed to synthesize several voice patterns of officers and guards speaking numbers near enough for recording. Fortunately the system security featured only this pattern based on capacity to recall for any officer or guard, and the confidence they had in their security measures. The voice patterns were identical and they would be transmitted via the voice recognition part they would take from the projector. He had tried it once and his voice was registered by the system as of one of the guards.

"Will data all patterns," he said in code, referring to the voice recognition processor.

****

The Fixture had removed his chip the same day he had been ordered to be given the injection. He had a device John had built to fool the systems and so was still able to function without an actual chip implant. Rather than destroying his own in the kiln, he tried connecting it to his holographic bank to see if he could find out more about its internal operations.

So far, he had been unsuccessful and at the third day, he became frustrated, 'Stuff it…I'll go for a walk to clear my head,' he thought.

As he walked around the inner city streets, he noticed several establishments had already closed. He decided to go to his favorite café, but it too was no longer, and wondered why his friend the owner had not come to him for chip removal. Whilst standing there deciding what to do, an apprehension robot appeared out of nowhere just three feet above him. It immediately jumped onto the pavement and stood there looking at him scanning. It was scanning for the chip hardware…it did not move. There was something going on. Normally these machines carried out this task in less than a few seconds, but now it had been five seconds…then six, then seven, then… In the same fashion, it disappeared and returned to its position on the wall of the building. Fortunately it chose to over ride the hardware scan because the software scan showed The Fixture had a chip identity.

He decided just to return home. He had not seen, but heard just a little about these machines and now he had just had one right in his face. It was a monster. The insect like limbs and tri-sectioned body gave it a most imposing look as it stood well above his height. The lowest section was at least ten feet in diameter, and the head, if you could call it so, projected holographic eyes as scanners linked to its processors. The mid section was its articulation point with arms of carbon nano composite much stronger than steel with telescopic extensions.

Later as he was again looking at ways to see how the chip worked, he thought he would contact John for some help, "John," he said aloud. There was no answer. 'Oh well. I'll try again later.'

****

Contact with John and the others could not be established and they began to feel a little concern now it had been so long. There was nothing they could do, for they had also tried holographic phone communications to no avail. They felt powerless, and so Chan reminded them again of their focus, "They are like the water trying to return to the sphere. This may seem abstract to you, but think of its intentions to return to its original state, and these are what I am sure, our friends are doing now. From our experiences previously, we are close enough in relations for them to know we would be thinking of them. It is where we should focus, for to feel powerless will bring powerless things. It is in their spirit to resist the forces applied to them and for their sakes we must recall this information as our own foundation of intentions and be confident for them to return."

It was the best he could offer to keep them from going into negativity.

"Understand there are the energies yet to have been discussed. These involve the intentions of accretion of elements."

"What are…?"

"They are gnomonic in growth where the surface energies remain similar to self. This is saying to you," they all looked a little confused with this language aside from Jenna who knew of such mathematical properties, so Chan changed his angle. "There are basic truths founded in the elemental intentions of our friends and these are the strengths building and adding up as the progress. There resides the place for our focus."

"Sounds like the Fibonacci equations," Jenna added.

"Ah this is no fib or nasty," Chan said, "It is in truth."

They all laughed at the speed of his wit.

Next morning the weather had mostly cleared, leaving five feet of snow around the house and across the fields. Jake and Raynie could not help themselves and so went for some cross-country skiing. The blanket of white extended across the landscape offering them vast areas of un-tracked snow awaiting their best efforts to carve lines.

It was easy for Raynie to see herself riding through the millions of geometric shapes, which were all in progression changing to another form – she had done this so many times before. She carved waveforms herself as she turned beautifully in the snow, taking the fall-line downhill with Jake close behind or beside her. Like the light snow still falling at times, they too felt light and energized, and their treks back uphill on the skis seemed easier than they had ever been, allowing them to talk without shortness of breath. Then back down again with each of them doing their best to find the sweetest line.

Chapter 44

All three space tracking dishes were engaged at the Tidbinbilla Space Center just south of Canberra, Australia. The authorities had them in full operational mode tracking movements above and far beyond the Earth. Since the early days when they were part of the network relaying the very first transmissions from the historic lunar landing, they had become an integral part of the burgeoning space industry. Now they were tracking craft and probes from Earth orbit, through the Asteroid Belt, and beyond the furthest reaches of the solar system. The space center had become a vital part of the latest logistical offensive being deployed by the authorities.

"Control here – tracking station forty three. We are aligning dish two for booster transmission and will advise."

As the HAARP array came fully online, so too had this center, along with many others dotted around the globe.

Dish two was being aligned to receive and transmit the signals it would soon receive from HAARP. Never previously had it been used as a transmitter, and so a technical team was busy monitoring all status updates as they engaged transmission technology for the first time. In parallel to its movements, the large radio telescope located two hundred miles away, was aligning its recently reconfigured dish to a coordinates setting for link up with Tidbinbilla.

The spacecraft transporting Agent Eight part of the way on his exile to the asteroids, had returned and was awaiting instruction eight hundred and sixty thousand miles away on the other side of the Moon.

Designed to reflect space, the almost unseen spacecraft took on a predatory appearance as it followed the space rock on a trajectory towards earth. Red lines of light within the craft's flowing and reflective design were the only evidence of it being there. It could easily match the asteroid's speed, and it did, following by just one mile.

"Asteroid on collision course with Earth. Stand by for updates from the authorities." It was a flash news bulletin on holographic devices everywhere, and people immediately listened and began to fear. They had no idea where it would strike, no idea on how big it was, and could imagine the many horrors it could bring.

The dark sect could see the ship on their own equipment and they were impressed with its design. Nobody amongst their groups in Australia or in other parts of the world had any knowledge at all of such a spaceship in existence. As one of them fine tuned the data stream hack into the central systems, of which nobody in the authorities had any knowledge of, he saw the asteroid would rush past the Moon, and then it would land somewhere in a region five hundred miles to the west of their location in Australia. At this moment, the dark sect were the only others to know where it would strike – the authorities had not yet advised the population at large.

Large holographic banks throughout the room dominated as a few of their members were watching and waiting. The asteroid featured as the main projection, with data streams, art and forms playing at the sides. Atop was their horned beast and it was there waiting for the torus. Its' two horns hummed and were encased in static charges erratically flowing over their surface. It eyes were red, standing by…longing to be brought to life. It wanted the torus and then it would be truly activated. The diamond would float in the air suspended by its horns – two horned torus. The ring would complete the circuit and the beast within them would emerge.

Now, they too were distracted by the ship. They wanted it now like they wanted the torus. It was of them, the design immediately reckoned with, and its intentions immediately read. Such a weapon was electric and so beautiful - they rushed and surged within, the desire to possess it growing exponentially.

Immediately they began to discuss ways to steal the spacecraft, driving each other into states of ecstasy and rising toward a crescendo at the thoughts of deviousness they shared.

****

Aboard the spacecraft, the captain responsible for redirecting the asteroid towards Earth, had been watching holographic status updates during the course of following the asteroid. Everything was proceeding well and he felt a hint of pride for his command – the very first command for a vessel of this type. He considered himself as making history, now he was captain of the first ever spaceship to be built on Mars and see action. The God of War planet had been chosen for its very secretive and distant location from Earth, and for its relative proximity as home to the development of a new wave of machines for war. It would not be a war of attrition where machines would float as wreckage amongst the stars, nor would it be a war of opposing forces battling across great tracts of land and sea. It would be a war of assertion, where the enemy was non compliance.

Now only two hours from striking the Earth, the first broadcasts came of where the asteroid would land. At first it was vague…somewhere in the southern hemisphere, but as people were glued to the holographic images, they slowly held them with minute-by-minute updates on precisely where. Relief turned to discussion about how unsafe the world was at the mercy of these space rocks, and many already began to consider what defense the authorities could provide for protection of the Earth and life itself.

The asteroid entered the atmosphere at incredible speed. It was two hundred feet long and one hundred wide. Heat began to sear its Earth facing edges, melting it and casting off fragments, causing what looked like sparks to fly, as millions watched on holographic vision. Then it exploded two miles up, sending a shower of hurtling meteors to the ground, and a shockwave for hundreds of miles. And then to most people, the event was over and they went back to what it was they were supposed to be doing.

But for some, it provided an opportunity and now opportunity was drawing nearer. News broadcasts covered the story again and again, and so the people did not forget about the asteroid. This prompted many people to continue thinking about what the authorities could do to in preventing another to keep them safe.

He ordered the vessel return to its designated coordinates and the pilot immediately turned the ship in a sweeping arc on a heading back towards Mars.

"Full acceleration," the captain said calmly.

The craft then sped on, quickly reaching its maximum speed of three hundred thousand miles per hour for a nine-day trip to the red planet. Cool ionic engines thrust a brilliant ring shaped glare outwards from behind the ship as they were engaged to full power – the protein strings proving to be one hundred per cent reliable. It looked like a star amongst the stars, again reflective of space.

****

"This thing is slow," Steve said to himself as he viewed another spacecraft movement hologram. He could see the other ship rapidly closing the distance as the numbers continuously changed. He was still five days out from Mars, where although it would still be inside tin cans, at least they would be bigger and there would be no little office and Agent Eight…for a time. He had received further advice on how to escort the Agent, and to where. They had designated Asteroid Seven Seven Nine as his destination. It was a small outpost with a small asteroid cluster about.

The mining operations there were only in their early stages and so Agent Eight had been assigned to guard this place. The cluster had a population of twenty-one – mostly mining personal and some support personnel. He would be one of two guards stationed at the control section for the cluster to ensure all operations were efficient and workers kept in check. Life at these outposts was a challenging affair, often leading to bouts of mental illness in some.

Asteroid clusters were tethered to a larger asteroid using carbon nano tubes – the larger asteroid then hosting a control center for the inhabitants who worked inside machines and space suits and were scattered across the smaller rocks positioned nearby. The combination of the tethers and the lights from the various mining operations, made each asteroid cluster appear like a spider web of activity floating in space.

Steve turned off the display and just sat there for a few moments in the small office. He could see Agent Eight if he bothered – as uninteresting as he was, so he did. He noticed he was watching the broadcast of the asteroid event on Earth over and over and took it as the Agent being his obsessive self again. 'Probably enjoying watching the looks of fear on people's faces,' he thought seeing the Agent lean in to the holographic image to get a closer look.

But Agent Eight was not actually doing this – he was thinking of the ship taking him to meet with this transport vessel. He was sure it had been used to steer the asteroid towards Earth, and he knew it was on a heading to its home base on Mars.

Steve did not know Agent Eight had done what he had done. Steve could not see what Agent Eight had done. And Steve did not see what Agent Eight did during those hours when he was away. The Agent had taken a little, just a little from the projector and configured a sensor device. He figured the ship's captain would not bother with a positioning scanner signal being so small it would be of no concern to him. But it was Agent Eight's signal, and to him it was becoming everything. He could see what was going on, but Steve just thought he was babbling on again as usual – instead it was the Agent's cover. He would do this at the times when he thought Steve would be most fatigued from boredom, and he was often right. Steve would momentarily give him attention see his babbling state, and then drift away, looking through the sensors monitoring the Agent, and not at them. And when Steve was absent, he would pretend to be asleep at times and watching the broadcast at other times in periods throughout the twelve-hours with those monitoring him being generally dis-interested.

Agent Eight knew what Mars Sector One base was like. He had researched it thoroughly – such information was privileged to Agents. There was a cluster of connected buildings for military research, spaceship building, mining operations, accommodation, and recreation. The cluster surrounded the central control building, which stood at five stories high. By far the largest though, was the spacecraft assembly building towering to over ten stories, and some five hundred meters square. Located at the southern end was the launch airlock. This was the largest airlock ever created at just over two hundred feet in diameter. Completed ships were first placed into the airlock with the inner door automatically closing behind them, and then the outer door opened so it could proceed out onto the planet's surface. From there, it was just a short flight across the base to the landing pads – eight in all, connected by long tunnels directly to the central control building. By this time, there had been three such launches of completed space ships.

Two other ships the same as the one on a heading back to base, stood silent on the pads. Only the red lighting was showing any status, otherwise they blended into the dark rust of the Martian hills to the distance behind them. The sun was low in the sky casting long shadows across the landscape, as it did for weeks at a time without much visible change.

****

Any communication between John and the others to the world outside had still not occurred. They were waiting in the cell longing to get out and longing for the right opportunity at the right time. So they continued to wait and at times watch some holographic broadcasts. They had seen all of the news about the asteroid but not much else other than more propaganda and advertising, "There is new issue standards in clothing for anyone who would like to purchase. Our new designs provide the best to you for wearing comfort and for efficiently keeping your body at optimal temperature. So get rid of your old and get the new. Try any style. Try any type. Feel sexy! The new Geiga Wear is waiting."

"Looks nice hey Lorraine?"

"Nice to entice…but I wonder what they might put into those clothes – you know, chip wise?"

"I will find out," John added. "They are going to issue it too all prisoners. Apparently it is more efficient to run this place with efficient bodies inside."

"How did you…?"

"Hacked the Broadcomm system using the projector. I have their conversations now. It's a bonus. I've been working on it while we wait."

Chapter 45

Carmel Madeleine was buying the latest in Geiga Wear from the local distributor in the small town one hour north of San Francisco. She loved the look, the feel, and the sensation it gave. She knew it would likely be sending data back to the authorities but she didn't care. It was Vandervals enabled meaning she could go places she hadn't been before.

"I'll have this one," she said jumping down off the wall. She had released the force enabling her to grip onto the smooth surface, simply by commanding it. The feature of the suit was a voice recognition processor trained by individual owners in only a few seconds to recognize only their distinct voice pattern. Upon request, Vandervals force could be engaged and disabled. It was marketed as a thrilling new dimension for clothing and was becoming very popular.

Carmel was happy today, happier than yesterday, and the day before. She was becoming happier and happier all of the time as she discovered the features of the town she was now living in. The people were about the streets and there was so much to do despite it being away from the big city. So much of it, almost all was entirely new to her and she loved the smells, the sounds... music to her ears. She was like she had never been – aside from those very early years of childhood one can barely remember. Now she was free again as each thing was new and present, entirely in the moment. There was no familiarity and she was convinced each day was new like this and would go on forever. It excited her to be tempted into making childish noises – the ones of the free spirit without care, without want, and at one in authentic presence.

Her walk along the main road to her house just over a mile away, was full of bounce and full of vigor. She noticed the flowers, the trees, the life around her, all busy and moving. She stopped for a moment looking high to the clouds above, watching them slowly drift towards the east. She could feel the faint breeze as it caressed the sweat on her cheek, and the taste was of nothing yet everything. She took deeper and deeper breaths...until she became a bit dizzy and calmed down a little.

As she walked on, her head still swimming, she felt like dancing and swirling on her way. It was all she had wanted, all she had dreamed, and all she felt she needed. The bees swarmed around her as she approached the flower laden front gate. Its' hinges were rusty and so they squeaked a little as she went through. She went along the pathway and under the arch, strewn with a grape vine bearing full yet green fruit. She loved the grape vine and the near ripe fruit would soon be good to eat. Then she went past the pond with a cricket sounding nearby, and further along the pathway to the door of her house.

She went inside, and the sun came in through the windows capturing some of her few ornaments in a contrasting light. She only had a few ornaments and they had been dear to her. She had never wanted many things. She went to the kitchen for refreshment, stopping to play some music from the holographic player on the way. And as she sipped a glass of fruit juice, she had never been happier to have forever put behind her – the days as Superior Officer One.

****

"Coming soon, the new Geiga Virtual Couple! Longing for embrace but away from your partner? Then long no more. With the latest in comfort wear, you can have the pleasure and the desires of being in the arms of your loved one with the new Virtual Couple software from Geiga. Take to the next dimension in compatibility and be together wherever you choose as your bodies respond to your partner's distinct bodily patterns. Your suit will help you feel the love! Get this anytime you choose with our newest innovation software download available at any update station. For a small price, you can have the comfort of being together whenever you like. The best in future wear, from Geiga."

"Do you think people will actually buy this stuff?" Lorraine said as they watched holographic vision out of boredom. They were sitting in the cell and John was still fighting off the device inside his head.

"Some will. Then it will probably catch on as a trend. More unwanted technology we can do without," John replied as he sat with his arm around Lorraine. "Or need."

Tobias turned off the projector as yet another advertisement began, "How would they do it? In those suits?"

"Relatively basic. They would be using the nanotechnology to stimulate nerves and sensory organs based on body patterns and scents they can synthesize with an algorithm, and then download into the nano-tech. They fail to mention in the ad where tech implants are required…a hidden necessity."

"Wouldn't most people in the big cities have them by now?"

"Hard to say. There has been a lot of take up since they were introduced a few years back. But if you consider the world at large, then you are probably only looking at twenty percent. They will get more in with these suits – people will want them and soon realize the only way to have them is to get the implants. It is the chip being the main concern, and how it can go out in massive numbers as a simple injection. You just don't know what it is capable of…yet. There is going to be more behind it than just security and convenience."

"And payment."

"I am worried about the payment aspect. It could force a lot of hardship, but I guess there will be an underground economy."

****

The dark sect was meeting to discuss how they could steal the spaceship. It had become a priority, though not as high as the torus. Their beast, a vortex amplifier, stood at the top of their holographic array still on standby, and they were growing impatient. No definite lead had been made since the sightings in Germany, yet little did they know the torus was so close. Without any solid plans, they grew even more restless – some took to sending out computer viruses to invade people's DNA nanotechnology, as a means to vent their growing anger. Others in the sect began to chant in the way they all would do, and the desperation in the voices was apparent. A few just stayed silent, conjuring in their minds, trying to feel the torus, sense its power, but they could not. Such things were figments - their imaginations carrying their desires no further than their minds.

What could they do? They even turned to their beast - it was an inner thing where its' darkness shed no light. When at last they almost gave in, they turned to their electric beast and it was in plain sight. They saw it happen as the horns flickered with electricity. The suggestion was all they would need, and soon they would have the torus and the people would begin to bleed.

Their leader entered a new pre-operations sequence he had developed from quantum entanglement, sending a signal to the beast. He realigned the algorithm to summon in the feast.

"Tor espial," he said as he sent it on its way, and so the beast did come to life to drain the life away.

Along the horns it traveled as a visible intention - the two horns each aside the place meant for the torus in suspension. It flickered forth and thither too, releasing what it might, to attract the torus unto it, for the coldest winter night. The signal sent across the plane unseen and all around. To find the response it would need, a signal in rebound. The place, the state the presence of where the torus did reside, for with the machine calibrated as such, there was nowhere it could hide.

The signal came back to greet them, it was astounding to them all. They began to dance and to celebrate at the misery they would install. Without question, without instruction, they all knew just what to do, and they set upon themselves to make their nightmares of dreams come true. It was a moment of reckoning in their own macabre way, of bringing pain to the Earth, onward from this day.

Their sense of joy was not such at all, they could never feel such things. The bells of the beast are the only ones tolling to those who hear its' rings. Despising as they were of the world, to them it did surround, so soon it would be coming to them and soon it would be found.

Their drive to muster in their hunger was ever oh so wild. They would take them all with them, every man, every woman, and every child.

Their beast had located the torus to within a twenty-mile radius, so they departed in teams and in vehicles to find their prize.

****

Carmel was busy about the house. Her new sense of life gave her things to do she could not have imagined before during the mundane repetition of service life. She wore the Geiga suit, as were many others about town. She had purchased seven of them and she had decided it was all she would wear. Others did the similar, the alluring clothing feeling sensual and so they were happy the authorities had given them this.

She had no nanotechnology implants herself having decided not to have them ever despite formerly being a superior officer. Yet her health was excellent for a thirty five year old. Now she felt good in a real sense for the first real time. She even admired the way the Geiga wear made her look as well as feel. It suited her – her new lease on life, her new buoyed enthusiasm for the discovery of so many simple things as her outward expression of self emerged. She had spent so long alone and in the service making her suspicious and inward, but now she was feeling the opposite without care for concerns such as those were.

The sun had meaning far beyond its' filtering through the city buildings, she had been used to. It was now warm on her skin, it was giving life to everything around her, and it simply was. Too often she had worked underground at the facility with its cold grey light, and now she realized how much she had been missing. Gone were her needs of status – she simply did not care. She had herself and she had her life. And despite the part of her knowing of the horrors ahead, she was determined to defeat them. Nothing in her heart would let this be taken away. She may not always be in the best places in her body, but in her heart she was now forever amongst these elements of life, amongst the progression, and she could never be anyone else.

"Hi," she said as a stranger walked by past the front of the house where she was tending to the garden.

"Hi yourself. I'm, The Fix…um, Timothy Collins." He had lost his head for a moment at her appearance, almost giving his cover name away.

"Hi Tim. Can I call you Tim?"

"Sure."

"Hi, I'm Carmel. Nice to meet you."

"Nice to meet you too. Very nice."

"Going into town?"

"Um, yeah. I am on my way through to San Francisco. Just been taking a break here overnight. Your place?"

"Yeah."

"Nice. Okay, I'd better go. I am hungry and feeling like some breakfast."

"Okay goodbye then. Maybe I'll see you in town?"

"Maybe. I'm leaving in a few hours though."

"Okay then, it's a maybe. Bye."

"Bye." The Fixture felt he could perhaps stay and talk to Carmel a bit longer – something in his gut feeling was trying to tell him to stop, but he went on...hesitantly, looking back once to see Carmel had returned to gardening. By the time he had walked the near mile into the center of town, he was keen to eat and took to the first café he saw. As he sat waiting for his meal, he looked out through the windows to the street beyond.

'Places like this seemed normal', he thought. 'But what's coming?'

The appearance of the robot on the street in Vancouver was still playing on his mind. After numerous attempts at contacting John, he decided to go to San Francisco and see if he could find him. It was a bit of a blind mission, but the chance was worth taking – he knew more technology would be needed in times to come.

"So what do you do Tim?" he looked around to see Carmel had come into the cafe. She had seen him staring out the window appearing to be in a daze, so he had not noticed her approach and enter.

"Um..." he stood up. "Sit down, I do electronics."

"What was it?"

"Electronics."

"Oh. Where? Just curious...I not an official," she saw a look of concern pass over his face.

"Um, Canada actually."

"I have never been there. What's it like?"

"Pretty nice. Um, what do you do?"

"Oh just things. I just moved here."

"Where from?"

"Where you are going."

"San Francisco?"

"Yeah nothing much else. I became sick of the city. It is nice in places," she thought of her day after quitting. "But I want to feel this…this real life, away from what the city is becoming."

"What did you do in San Francisco?"

"I was an officer in the services…" it pained her a little to recall this.

The Fixture was suspicious, "Um…what about, um, maybe I will go."

"No don't go Tim. Sit down please. You have nothing to worry about. I have left it behind for good. I don't hate anything, but the services sure come close."

He sat back down and gradually felt more at ease. He had been impressed with her the first moment they had spoken and a great part of him was telling him to talk to her now.

Carmel took his hand, and her touch electrified him for a moment like a pulse had shot through him, but a warm and pleasant pulse…like a heartbeat. "Please don't worry." Carmel looked him in the eyes and he felt a sense of being able to trust her. Gradually he was aligning with her – he could relax.

"Alright, but you can understand why. It's not like I am guilty of anything. I just have my suspicions about officials."

"Me too, it is one of the reasons why I left."

"Why else…did you leave?"

"I couldn't stand it. Something inside me was making me feel, making me think, and then I thought about what the authorities are actually up to and …" she trailed off thinking about the events inside the facility.

"What?"

"Um, what was, is…happening to people."

"What do you mean?"

Carmel was still wary about the lengths her ex-employer might go to for listening in, "Um, just being forced to comply."

"Comply to what?"

"To what they see as efficient, for the sake for them growing stronger in power and efficiency."

"Sounds pretty bland."

"It was." Inside she was experiencing a little turmoil about what she had witnessed being done to some to people at the deep underground complex. The nerve burning nanotechnology, the needles rendering them unconscious, the itching…the itching was bad, and how they were now taking people to places near death and mind manipulating them with images of misery. It was disgusting.

"What is it? You look upset."

"Oh, just how people were being treated."

"I know people who were arrested. Most of them are never seen again, and some they release with the chip after what they call rehabilitation, but only those they see can be efficient in the authorities meetings their goals…whatever they are."

"Do you have a chip Tim?"

"Yes," he was lying – he only had a device John had built.

"I do too. I don't know what is to become of me with it inside my arm, but I'm determined not to lose the life I have now… I left the life I really did not want."

He was struggling internally as he could help Carmel with her chip, but he could only get a device if John helped. She noticed his thinking, "What is it?"

"Just worried about the chips."

"Try not to. I'm not letting it get to me."

"Oh, it's not really about it getting to me."

The waiter arrived at then with his breakfast, and Carmel asked if she could have a coffee.

"There are uncertain times coming Tim."

"Yeah. I saw something I wish I had not seen."

"What was it?"

"A robot. It was about twenty feet tall."

"I have heard of those. They are used by Agents mostly, to round people up who don't have the chip."

"But what about when everyone has a chip Carmel? What will they do then?"

"Who knows, but it won't be good."

"I'm not feeling good about them at all. They are going to be a lot more than just police robots for chipping people."

"I don't really know – I don't think I want to." She was again reminded of the potential of a lot of suffering being forced onto people. She kept speaking as he ate, "I love it here Tim. I want to enjoy this place while I can. But I do know why I came here. It is to feel the way I do. I feel free Tim."

"But you have a chip."

"Yes I do. Perhaps freedom has a price. Perhaps it will not be so bad. People will still have to live, to be at home and to do things to even be balanced enough to remain efficient as workers. It cannot all be too bad."

"I guess so. It is just their focus. Working so hard for status. What does it mean anyway?"

"Not very much. I have tried it, and then I walked away. This is the way for me now Tim. I could never go back to the high-rise."

"You were in the high rise?"

"Yeah, all official staff live in the high-rise. There are members of the public too, the wealthiest ones. The rest are comfortable in the lower buildings, and others…they live on the fringes."

"I live in the lower buildings. Does it bother you?"

"Not at all. Think how low my house is. It is all at ground level." He thought about this for a moment, his trust of Carmel growing.

"Yes it is. A nice house too."

"I like it, but it is not everything. Life is what is important. Wherever you go you must have life. Buildings are not much without life."

"Plenty of life in the high-rise."

"Really? I think there is plenty of life forms, but not much life."

"I have never been inside one. What do people do?"

"They link up to their nano maintenance chairs, they watch holographic vision, they walk in parks in the middle of the buildings, and sometimes they go away and visit a restaurant, or take a planned trip to a tourist destination. Not much else. It is why I like it here Tim. It is real and not artificial."

"Like a holiday every day."

"You could say so. There is work here, but working in these places is not so difficult I believe. I don't work Tim. Not yet. I just arrived here."

He finished his meal and enjoyed a coffee with Carmel. They talked more about what life is like in the high-rise and on what could be lost when the authorities clamp down even harder. As they talked, he felt more and more at ease with Carmel. She had an effect on him nobody else ever had. There were plenty of good friends around him in Vancouver and in other places, but he felt something with her was beyond this.

"Are you leaving soon Tim?"

'Um, yeah. I was planning to go at eleven."

"You could stay longer. I could show you around the town. It's a nice town." He listened to his gut instincts this time "Okay, I'll take you up on your offer."

They enjoyed each other's company for the remainder of the day, and as time passed by they both felt calm and at peace. By early evening Tim had agreed to stay the night with Carmel, as it would be too risky to travel to San Francisco with the curfew in place. There were no excuses - if he was caught out after nine, he would be arrested.

Carmel went about her house lighting candles as the sun began to set over the low hills to the west. She loved their flickering flames dancing on the gentle breezes carried through the house. It was a cool summer evening and she took it all in – embracing her senses, so often deprived of such simple pleasures in the past. Tim was relaxing and watching her as she danced around showing him her vibrancy. He wondered how an official of the authorities could have ever been this woman, and how much she must have changed or simply released in her life. She was remarkable to him. Her effervescence was obvious in such a striking way he could not put word to it in his mind, but he could in his heart.

Sure, he admitted she was attractive, but the sense he was learning with her, was something beyond lust. She was compassionate, she loved simple forms as did he, and she loved to project and express herself. It was these forms, these patterns speaking to him.

He smiled to her when she smiled to him. For a second they averted each other's eyes, but then they returned for a second longer. They were speaking without words. They were feeling without trying. They began to know without asking. Then she left and went to the garden outside. He did not know what to do. Should he stay there or should he go out? Then she returned with some fresh herbs, and he felt a little silly.

"Take these for me please Tim," she said handing him the bunch of herbs. "Smell them. Feel them, aren't they great? Taste them."

"So fresh," he said chewing on a basil leaf – it was a bit strong.

"And alive. Here," she held her hand out wanting them back. He gave them to her and they touched for an instant. She quickly then went to the kitchen, and he waited, and he waited, and he waited, and then she returned. "Aren't you going to help me cook?"

Chapter 46

The house was found without anyone inside knowing, though Chan had felt uneasy all during the day. Now the five of them stood in the kitchen confronted by the leader of the dark sect.

He was not angry, appearing calm, yet resolute, "We know it is here. We have tracked it. You should have thought a bit wiser old man," he was looking at Chan. "I know you have been deceiving us for some time now, but your deception is over…ha, and ours is to begin. So if you please, give us the torus and it will be so much easier for all of you. But…if you make it difficult, it will not only be a futile measure on your part causing us to become…upset. Yes, upset is how best I can describe it for now. Who knows how upset we might be later."

"And…oh, we know it has been activated, otherwise our amplifier would not have detected it. And I am sorry, but despite your good intentions, I am afraid it is going to be used for our bad intentions. I understand its function well enough to know it can be used in this way. I think you do as well, otherwise I am certain you would have not been eager to put us off your trail, would you?"

"You can never…" Chan began.

"Don't utter never to me. I will do what it takes to please the wishes of my…um, let us say motivations. I know you old man - you will know what it is I speak of. You will feel it as you call it, but it is not a feeling. No. It is a knowing. A knowing our ways are the ways."

"You speak nonsense."

"And how do you reach such a conclusion?"

"Your ways. Your ways are nothing to do with anything but your ego quest for power. A knowing you say – you know nothing."

"Oh contraire old man, we know very much and soon you will too."

"I am not scared. You cannot feed on fear from me. Your dark ways are just silly games. There are no dark ways - there are just the ways. You speak nonsense as I said. I suppose you believe in evil versus good too. Ha! I knew you would."

"Oh, but such things exist old man and they are near."

"Near to what. To your flimsy imagination? To your ridiculous icon worship? To your unbalanced minds of hatred and anger? I do not accept you and neither do the others here." They nodded in agreement.

"But you will accept us. We can force you."

"I find it hard to believe. You are essentially powerless with or without your precious object."

"We are never powerless old man."

"How can you say so? I know of your rituals, your anger sending viruses out to the world, and your intentions."

"What are they?"

"Out of alignment and out of balance."

"Now you speak rubbish old man. We are never out of balance. We have the beast, our horned torus are ready, and we will prevail."

"Prevail against what? What is there to prevail against, your own imagined state of awareness? Your own imagined power struggle for status or supremacy? Supremacy over what? It is all in your head."

"There is nothing you can say or do to make any changes to this old man. It is the way. We must have the torus. Don't test my patience please. I do take ever so long to calm down again after raging."

Chan knew he was powerless to stop them taking the torus. They had no weapons and the sect weapons looked dangerous. He was testing them, trying to get them to think, but it was not working much, if at all. The sect was bent on obtaining the torus and powering up their vortex amplifier. This part concerned him greatly, for a vortex amplifier could do a lot of damage if in the hands of those who really could not control it properly.

"So what of us?"

"You will come with us. We cannot have you running around out here. You will be treated amicably so long as you behave in such a way. Otherwise you will not like what we have in store with our type of crack down. Those stupid authorities don't even know we exist…well, at least not to the extend we do. They too will soon see how powerful we can be. We want power more than them – they are just too bent on efficiency. So tell me where it is!" He was becoming impatient.

They looked at each other and resigned this as to be the next progress of the torus – they could not resist and they did not want to be tortured. "I have it," Jenna said taking it out of her pocket.

The sect leader did not grab for the torus. He just stared at for a few moments looking at the pink hue.

"So lovely," he said. "And thank you," he smiled as he gently took it from her hand. He held it up close to his eye to look into it, but then changed his mind and put it in a pocket in his long black coat. "Well, let's get going shall we. And see, we indeed have decorum, for we are not monsters." He indicated to one of the sect members, "Please make sure you lock up the house. We don't want to leave it open for just anyone."

****

Agent Eight watched as the other ship had overtaken the transport vessel and then continued onto Mars. He knew his arrival at the base was only a few days away and then he would act. He no longer had any of his babbling sessions, and so Steve and the others who watched him during the off shift hours, were taking no interest in him. All those aboard the ship were longing for the five days of respite on Mars, before departing again for their destination in the asteroids. He also knew there were three hundred and forty personnel at the base, and this figure was important to him.

He had secretly hacked into the systems on the transport and was able to access details on those who were stationed there. Although it lacked specifics, Agent Eight knew he could use the remaining data. He had already made his choice of who and where. It was now just a matter of when.

The thought of exile at a far-flung asteroid cluster left a bad taste in his mouth. He always considered himself as having good taste in everything he did, so he became ever more determined to make his plan succeed. After all his efforts, he had begun to feel sleepy and so left it to himself to fall asleep and enjoy the remainder of the ride with no need for the sleep interruptions as he had done previously. He lulled into sleep, a deep sleep and dreamed of the places Superior Officer One could never go.

He dreamed of his status beyond reach of almost everyone, and he dreamed of how he would bring it about. The authorities although his employer, earned no measure of respect from him – they were merely a means to an ends, his ends. And when he arrived back on Earth, it would be a very different place to when he left, and this played right into his hands. He could imagine the ease by which he could institute his brand of change, his brand of pain - in his dreams he laughed out loud. When he awoke after fifteen hours of sleep, arrival at Mars Sector One base was just over a day away.

Steve was feeling better, along with the crew. They were all only twenty-seven hours away from Mars now and soon they could get out of the tin can. The planet loomed large in the forward view as Steve stood on the bridge with the captain and the pilot. It was an impressive sight. He had seen large holographic images previously, but here now in space, it was real and Steve's dreams of space came back to him. They stood looking at Olympus Mons, the tallest mountain in the entire solar system over fifteen miles high. It appeared to rise as a great spot from the planet, dwarfing the similar volcano in Hawaii. Then he saw the great canyon cutting a huge swathe out of the planet and many times the size of the Grand Canyon on Earth. It was remarkable, and alien. He had never been on another planet, and now so close to Mars, he thought of this for the first time.

A day later and on approach he first saw the base appear when they flew over the hills to the west, its lights the first sign of human beings for millions of miles. As the lights grew larger, the contrast between sunlight shining on the base, and the powerful blinking landing lights, again brought a sense of alienation. The concept of stepping onto another world moved Steve then. His re-assignment had forced change in him and now this force was becoming a reckoning as he gazed down at the distant human outpost. Then the vessel came to a landing with a soft thud, and for the first time in weeks he was not flying in a ship but on the surface of a planet.

"Okay Steve. You know what to do," the captain brought him around from his dreamy state.

"Sure. I'll take care of escorting our prisoner to the holding cells inside the base immediately."

He was relieved because for the next five days, he would not have to watch Agent Eight. As he escorted the Agent through the long tube leading directly to the control building, he noticed the three spaceships standing on other landing pads. They were all the same, including the ship involved in the rendezvoused far back in space. Agent Eight noticed them too.

****

For Tim to have stayed with Carmel these last few days, he knew there must have been a connection worth pursuing. He was not given to casually being with someone from out of loneliness - he had spent many times alone over the years. He was not thinking of an affair – there had been no sex. He was thinking of something more long term and they were building a friendship. From there, it would be elemental to them both on where it may go, or flow.

They had just seen a holographic broadcast announcing the authorities had decided there was a need for a defense system against asteroids. There was general consensus it was a good idea and provided the impetus for the authorities to power up the grid systems again using the various radio telescopes around the globe. It was a stroke of deception and the public was advised the network of telescopes and the HAARP array were the instruments used to protect them. The antenna was now sending transmissions into the high terahertz frequencies – capable of affecting systems and people's feelings at their discretion.

Tim decided to switch it off as Carmel had left the room anyway.

"Come in here," she called from the kitchen. He responded by idling over to the corner so he could see through the door. "Well, come in."

"What is it?"

"I want to talk. I needed to get away from the projector. It was making me feel bad."

"What's wrong?"

"Ever since I was first thinking of leaving the services…and before come to think of it, I have, um, sort of regretted what I did as an officer."

"But you said you were only a supervisor – you didn't actually interrogate people."

"Yes, but I supervised those who did, and I am very sorry for this." She had begun to look quite upset.

"It was not your fault. You were just follow…"

"Yeah, orders. But it is difficult for me now and I chose to be there at the time through working for them. I cannot dismiss it simply because I feel happy with my choice to leave and be here. Tim, I feel sad for them. Sad for what is happening to them."

"Can I do anything?"

"You can hold me." He went to her and held her in embrace. "I have to do something Tim. I have to make some difference - it is part of me now. I don't want others to lose what I have."

"What can you do?"

"I don't know. I am at a loss to think of anything. When I think of Raynie…and John, if they get hold of him…"

"Raynie? Raynie O'Day?"

"Yes, Raynie O'Day. Jake Sinclair, Jenna Atkinson, Lyle Shrewsbury, John, Tobias, Asper…Lorraine."

"Are you kidding me?"

"No Tim, it is not a joke. I feel for them and others."

"I know them. John is the person I am looking for." He immediately felt as if he might have made a mistake, but then he recalled his trust in her.

After a few minutes like this, she broke away from him, "What can we do then?"

"Um, I would have to think about it."

"Then take as long as it takes. Thanks Tim."

"What for?"

"For being here…and now for making me feel there is hope I can do something."

"Anytime."

Later as they sat together on the couch discussing their options, Carmel had an idea. Tim had no knowledge of where John would be and she had not seen him admitted to the facility. Now she thought of something they could do.

"What if we went to the wooden house in San Francisco? You said John told you they had stayed there."

"It's a start. But he said they had to leave pretty quickly – some Agent had followed them to the house."

Carmel thought of Agent Eight, but only for an instant.

"I think it is worth it. If they get lost and have nowhere to go, then Jenna's house would seem logical, despite the risk. We don't have anything else."

"I suppose you are right. It was on my list of places to check anyway, come to think of it." Tim wondered why this idea had not occurred to him – putting it down to the three days he had spent with Carmel, and the very different way he was feeling now as compared to when he arrived in the town.

"Well?"

"Well…I think it is the only thing we can try, so let's do it…um, tomorrow. I have a vehicle."

"Oh good, I have not purchased one yet. I am not sure if I will actually."

"Tomorrow it is then."

They awoke next morning to a bright sunny day, and left as soon as they had eaten, packed a few things, and walked to Tim's vehicle parked hidden a short way down the road from Carmel's house. En route to San Francisco, they decided to stick to the older roads and enjoy the scenery at a much slower pace than the automatic driving or the transit road lines. Great forests of Sequoia Pines stood lining the Redwood Highway – the ground beneath them, a rusty red strewn with millions of old pine needles. For a while, they stopped at an old tourism spot to have some coffee. The old cafe looked seldom used these days.

It was an old wooden building of large pine logs featuring various displays and old tree samples. Nobody else was there, aside from the café owners who were an older couple concerned about what was changing now so rapidly in the world. Over coffee, they were eager to talk to Carmel and Tim as they told them there were very few tourists who stopped here anymore.

"We just don't see anyone like it used to be in recent years. We've been here all our lives," the husband said. "My parents passed this business on to me, and their parents to them. My great grandparents founded it mid last century. As a little boy they told me stories of what it was like then. People were happy, the Second World War was slipping into memory and they all had a new sense of life."

"It's true," his wife added. "My great grandparents owned a small business on the main highway near Placerville as you head towards Lake Tahoe. Oh the times then, with people going on holidays to the lake and the winters of snow when thousands would drive by on their way to skiing. It was very good for business. But now, everyone seems to be too busy with work and city life – we don't see days like they did so long ago."

"I wish we could have just ten percent of the customers they had back then. It would keep this place running. The transit lines killed it for us. People are in a rush these days to get wherever they are going. They just don't stop off along the way at places like this anymore. For many, the Redwood Forests are probably something they see on a hologram as they travel past at a hundred and fifty miles per hour. It is sad…" the husband trailed off thinking of what future may be in store for him and his wife.

"And these chips," she said rubbing her arm. "We don't like it, but we have no choice. You know, we only have about twenty years left in us and they said if we wanted to keep getting our supplement payment in old age, then we would have to get a chip. There will be no more cash, they told us. How we will survive? And, you know what they told us then? We would have to purchase chip payment hardware to be able to accept transactions. It costs far too much to for this business. Our returns are just not good enough to make it worthwhile."

"Yeah, you would think they would make it cheaper," Tim replied.

"It's about closing people down. They are aiming to restrict how much private business is out there. They say they are democratic as they look after public safety and comfort, but it is not true," Carmel added.

"Well it is how it looks for us. Jim and I here are just about beat. We can't survive paying off a huge debt to the authorities."

'What will you do?"

"I don't know Carmel. Just survive I hope. We might not have a lot of money, but we have each other…and this place."

The couple then left Carmel and Tim to their coffee. When they finished, they thought it was time to immediately continue on to San Francisco.

"Here," Carmel offered the couple some cash as payment for the coffee. "Take this and go and convert it into chip credits. Do it today. You never know when they might ban cash altogether." She had given them much more than the price of the coffee and for the price of chip payment technology. "Ah, don't say anything," she interjected when seeing the old woman about to graciously give thanks. "Let me…us, thank you."

"What…?"

"You have given us a moment we cannot forget, and we are grateful."

Tim sort of knew what Carmel meant and said a quiet thank you after she finished speaking.

"Best of luck to you," the old couple said as Tim started up their vehicle. "Whenever we take this highway, we…um, I will always stop here for coffee." Carmel could not speak for Tim in this instance, though she too felt they would be spending a lot of time together.

"Thank you," both the husband and wife said together, "You are always welcome."

"Thanks, bye."

"Well how was that Jim? You don't see the likes of people who are so kind and graceful much these days."

"No dear. Thankfully they are still out there in parts."

When they were traveling closer to San Francisco, they decided to take the road through the Napa Valley vineyards. Carmel had wanted to see it for herself and felt compelled as she was imagining the great fields of grapes still green with leaves and new fruits basking in the sun. As they entered the valley, they could see the transit road tube running through hills to the east. There was a regular stream of traffic flashing by at high speed - the occupants inside each vehicle likely focused on images and entertainment. Only a few would take a look at the valley and soon enough Carmel and Tim realized why there was probably not much interest. The former splendor of Spanish inspired vineyards settled with their stylish buildings amongst the shade of great Oak trees, was a shadow of its former self. Where a vineyard was still in production, it looked a sad affair – a mere silhouette of times past. Many vines in the valley were dying from a new disease. The authorities had announced they were working on a cure, but there would be no inefficient cure as it was simply a waste according to their objectives. People affected by alcohol and other forms of pleasure were too inefficient through behavioral, violence, and crime costs to society.

Carmel was very disappointed but would not let it get her down. She understood what she saw and she knew there would be others like this – sudden closures, farms bought out by the authorities, roadside businesses as mere ghostly remnants of their past days. The authorities were going to cater for all human needs. They were to control the food output, they were take care of any consumer need good or bad, and they were eliminating character in life. Like the bland architecture of the cities, they were going to match this with making people bland, whilst all the time believing they had choice. The authorities needed this control, but they were not evil, just greedy. And greed leads to all the manifestations required to secure the greed. Carmel had their messages atop her holographic display - this motto of efficiency really being much more of a mind control mechanism than was widely recognized. She vowed then to do her best to forget it from this time forward. Soon enough the Napa Valley slipped into their rear vision as they drove on without stopping.

The last leg of their trip took them over the Bay Bridge inside the transit line, and they both noticed how contrasting San Francisco looked to its former self. Whilst abuzz with JetCabs and HyperJet flights, there was a visible subdued state to the place. The towers stood at its center appearing mundane with a sense of numbness. People could be seen everywhere, their lives not much different, but they looked 'distracted', Carmel had said. Tim agreed with her as he pointed out people at update stations watching their holographic phones.

"They want them to be so dependent on technology to meet all of their needs," Carmel said as she too saw their faces. They seemed so far from where she was now. She felt alive – more than she had thought possible, and she felt determined.

When they arrived at the wooden house on the hill, the doors were locked and there were no lights visible from the inside. The time was seven, so without any access, they went to the fringe of the main city block, and found a cheap motel near The Tenderloin. By the time they had refreshed, eaten, and taken to spend time relaxing, the city was almost deserted. The streets were bare, except for an official vehicle now and then. Restaurants, cafes, and bars were all closed. There were no dogs barking, no cat fights in the alleyways as they had been banned from the city years before. It was silent…almost everywhere.

Beneath the oldest of the city buildings – warehouses long since disused, remained the last frontier of the underground movement in the city. Since the days stretching back to the beatnik era, San Francisco had become a hive of alternative approaches to life style. Through the decade of the hippies, the human rights movement, the cyberpunks at the beginning of the twenty first century, and the ecology based groups who were the first to call for restoration of the planet and to develop new energies to stop use of fossil fuels – the city was still playing host to the remnants of these movements. They had gathered not in the ways of a sect, nor as the elite secretively meeting. Their nature to gather was just inside them as they were of the type to be explorers in mind and spirit and so their gathering came from it being irrepressible to their natural intentions.

Each night at the underground venue, was an all night affair. People would enter by nine when the doors were locked, and then be able to leave after six, when the curfew lifted. The scene inside was of people dancing to music, groups and couples gathered at tables talking, and others sitting on couches exploring holographic art forms. Various states of dress determined the background scene for groups and individuals, some avant-garde – looking for a retro profile, some futuristic and others very much historic. But most wore the Geiga wear, and some had disabled the unwanted features installed by the authorities. They were a mix of people into technology, art, music, dance, and philosophy and they also were actively avoiding identification chip injections.

After finally falling asleep, Carmel and Tim dreamed of similar things and of each other. By the time they awoke, it was an hour after the curfew lifted, and the streets had gradually begun to fill with people again.

They needed to go out to eat and so they left as soon as they were ready, heading down Fourth Street towards the bay side. It was easy to tell all around, San Francisco was like other cities across the globe – it was shutting down. It was like there was an air of subdued life. It was if everything was attached to a specific purpose out of practicality rather than spontaneity. Like those other cities and the towns and settlements, it was becoming an efficient machine.

Some had imagined the horrors of massive machines striding about and ruling over their lives as they began to disappear amongst the endless cogs of machine society, and in part they were correct. It was not so much there would be a dramatic change to Earth, for it would happen over time and be far more subtle.

Carmel considered the price to pay as she looked across the bay towards Alcatraz. Loss of true spirit in seeing the elegant grace of what seemed the simplest of things, and the loss of humanity's connection to this grace as they embraced machines dependant on programming.

After walking further around the port, they found a small café set in the South of Market district amongst disused warehouses adjoined to some of the older wharves beneath the Bay Bridge. Carmel noticed the place was different to many of the cafes she had visited so far – aside from the stop off the day before. It was old. It had old framed printed artworks in places, and it had character. She was enthused with this and wanted to know more through feeling the place. Tim felt comfortable too, as the café reminded him of his favorite back in Vancouver.

"Nice place. Doesn't have a sterile feel to it."

"Yes. I like it Tim. It feels…there is something stirring you. The old couple's place was similar."

"Yeah. Um, this place reminds me of home," he felt a little sad for a moment. "But my favorite place has already been shut down."

"Part of the drive to get rid of a lot of business."

"Yeah. People are just accepting this and moving on. I agree with progression and moving on, but not at the loss of so much."

"It can be like the blind leading the blind."

"So much lack of vision…for the sake of efficiency."

"There are principles of efficiency Tim, which are okay. Think of how efficient life is. It is always in progression. I have noticed so much since I left this city."

"Hmm, true. It is just these efficiencies are really nothing more than to drive profit and profit is power."

"Because it can also build the machines Tim."

"Yeah. Profit can be good, as people can use it to better their lives. But who really makes the profit? All these things…of status. People think they are profiting from their work, their status, but are they? And what about the time in their life spent chasing elusive dreams?"

"It is why I left. I could see through it and I realized there was no point in giving my life to something I could not believe in. I like this place Tim. It is different and has an appeal to me."

"Me too. I like the stimulus it gives you. It allows you to really relax allowing you to open up to being more spontaneous. Some of those other expensive places seem too sterile to me and it is all a show…of status."

"It doesn't interest me Tim. I think status is a net, and the people are all the fish."

"Here we go. Two breakfast specials," the person working both the counter and the tables in the café, had brought them breakfast. The chef could be seen behind the counter, cleaning up after cooking their meal. They were alone – their meal, his first cooking task for the day.

"Pretty quiet in these parts," Tim said.

"Yeah. Business is slow, but we will stay open. There is no way the authorities will shutting this place down if we can help it."

"How long has it been here?"

"About eighty years, I'm not sure, I'll ask the owner," he turned around called out to the chef. "Hey Shaun! How long has this place been open?"

"Since two thousand and two."

"There you go. Eighty six years."

"Apparently back then, there was a scene around these old wharves," Shaun had come closer, wiping his hand with a towel.

"A scene?" Carmel asked.

"Yeah. One of those warehouse party scenes and art groups type of thing. You know, with live music and lots of people just enjoying themselves."

"Sounds great. What happened to this scene?"

"Shut down mostly. Like any place, some humans can get up to mischief, so they used it as the excuse to get rid of it…well most of it. There were some groups who adjusted."

"Are they still adjusting?"

"Yeah. You can still find a few about these parts now and then. But with all this crackdown by the authorities, they are getting harder and harder to find."

"Do you know of any art groups or musicians? I love music."

"Not really. I have seen a few people who look like they might know, but they keep a low profile."

"Are they dangerous?" Tim asked.

"No. They are not interested in power or manipulation or worshipping demons or the like. Generally they are peaceful, if not a bit strange at times."

"Oh great. Tell me, please, do you know of any?" Carmel asked seemingly buoyed by this news.

"It depends. I might, but I don't want to tell anyone, and you can't force it out of me either."

"Oh don't be concerned. I am not some official trying to get information. I just want to meet some of these people. I like what they do. I'm interested."

"Yeah me too," Tim added. "I was in a scene of sorts in Vancouver man."

He looked at them for a few seconds, and to Shaun who was just standing there watching. "I could tell you, but not directly. You will need to work on this contact."

"Um, okay," Tim replied seeing there was an identity cover in play not unlike the way people had to contact The Fixture.

"You have to meet at the update station on the corner of Townsend and Third Streets today at two. Now eat, I'll go and set up a contact."

Chapter 47

Waiting so long for a chance to escape had become boring. Doing their best to stay alert was a challenge, as was the ongoing battle John was fighting in his mind. As time passed, they noticed less and less new arrivals at the facility – it looked as if the crackdown on identification chips was working.

John had studied the movement of officials about the building as he continued to hack into their systems using the projector. When he decided the best option, he advised them without hesitation, "We need to go at six in the evening today. There is a periodic shift change over with officers going on two days leave after a twelve-day stint. During the handover process is our best shot. I know we settled on a later time, but this is the point we need to seize I think."

"The systems are automatic…alarms," Tobias said.

"We have the codes."

"I mean facial recognition. The systems will identify us."

"Yes, another issue. We are going to have to be careful…mostly to keep our heads down."

"But the Geiga wear? We can hide our face, but not the suit."

"I think I have an answer. See this?" he held a small amount of dusty material in his hand. "I made this from the projector. It uses old silica based chip technology. I guess they figure if it still works…for prisoners, then it is more efficient not to update."

"So what is with it?" Asper asked – they were in a tight group talking in low tones.

"Well, I can crush it with my boot into this dust and if I put the dust inside the projector and run a phased projection beam into it, then it picks up remnants of the phasing and holds onto them for about twenty minutes. We just need enough dust to rub on ourselves. This will, I hope, fool the system by masking the readout from visual suit identification. The cameras will effectively be blind registering only data sufficient to determine the suits."

"Well. Let's get cracking, um crushing,' Lorraine said.

"We must be careful not to waste any," John still looked serious. "The processors are small and we need a fair bit of dust. And do it…"

"Discreetly," the others interjected. It had become a familiar way during their imprisonment.

When they had all of the crushed silica dispensed to each and held in the palm of one hand, the projector would no longer work. There was no turning back. If the authorities caught them and saw what they had done with the holographic technology, they would be cast even deeper within the facility and would do whatever it took to extract information from John. He still fought the device, it was troubling at times, but he could handle it.

At one minute to six, they left the cell. They ran quietly towards the first of a sequence of holographic security shields. John gave the code and they were through. At the next, Tobias gave the code and they continued on. Two more and both Lorraine and Asper gave the code – they had remembered one each, as the codes were ten-digit numbers. The silica was working as camera scanners followed them but failed to identify them, the phasing residue still holding. At one corner they accidentally turned the wrong way – John had mapped their route. Fortunately the group of officials was all filing into a room and so had their backs to them.

At another corner, they encountered a robot of a type they had never seen before. They stopped concerned it would scan them and raise an alert. They waited, and the robot waited. Seconds went by before they just decided to run. Then the robot moved. It was a janitor robot – designed to stop until humans had been able to move around it.

The perimeter of the building was their biggest challenge, and then though not as difficult to get through, would come the perimeter fence. As they approached, the guard station was full of personnel.

"I have a plan for this bit," John said as they hid in a janitor robot hall closet. "You can hear the alarms, so they know we are out of our cell – they just don't know where. I have an answer. We enter the codes from here and add this extra code, which contains an algorithm I made. It is a simple open door instruction, so the guards will see the doors open but nobody there. It's going to be a risk, but we are going to have to take out as many as we can, using just our fists. Sounds a little pathetic hey. But…with some distracted, there will be others around not knowing what to do and so their reaction time may be affected. We need to charge them."

"But why?"

"So we can steal one of those little sensors they wear on their tunic. It is an auto sensor for opening the staff only doors around this place."

"Gee, you could have told us so before John," Tobias said thinking of what he would be about to do.

"Why? It is not like we could have made any other plan. But feel…you are pretty hyped up now with this escape – we all are. Use this and just go for it. It will give you an edge. You should know Tobias, they taught us in the services."

The two women looked at each other thinking 'yeah'.

"Okay, let's go. They burst out of the closet as two of the four guards were looking through the open doors, as John had described. They rushed headlong at the other two, punching and pushing them around until Tobias said he had a sensor. Immediately they broke off and followed him through the small staff door and onto stairs leading directly outside.

They were partially free in a sense, as there was still the perimeter fence. They ran. An apprehension robot appeared from off the wall and gave chase. It strode on metal legs, taking galloping leaps in pursuit. They were ten yards from the fence where guards without weapons drawn, were manning a gate ready to apprehend them if the robot failed.

The robot was only two yards behind them as they reached the gate – it could extend its arms and seize them, but not all of them at once. Dazed by their actual arrival to the gate and not having been seized by the robots, the guards, fresh to their shift, were knocked to the ground as the group ran straight at them. This made for a confusing scene as the robot extended its arms, probing for the right person to seize. It was programmed to apprehend dissidents only and so had to avoid the guards. Tobias finally made it to the gate and placed the sensor up to the reader device and the gate opened. Asper and Lorraine were attacking one guard, and John was dodging another and the robot. John saw the open gate and maneuvered towards it.

When he was close enough a few seconds later, he yelled, "Go!" and dashed through. The two women immediately let go of the guard and ran through the gate. But neither the guards nor the robot were ending it there. They immediately opened the gates, giving the robot a chance to make chase. It did, and so did the guards. Failure for them was not an option.

It ran, pounding the soil beneath it as it took huge strides in pursuit of them. The guards soon fell behind but did not give up. John told them to turn to the left and keep running. They ran and ran and the robot closed in – now just thirty yards behind. The ground beneath them became unstable and began to sink, but their determination to escape was as strong as ever. They ran on, their chests heaving. Their boots suddenly splashed into water and this slowed them down. "Swim," John yelled, so they did. The water was getting deep, but it saved them.

The robot stood at the water's edge – it was not equipped to pursue dissidents in water. Then the guards appeared, but only the robot could see the fugitives out in the dark waters. The guards upon seeing they were helpless were beside themselves when they thought about reporting this to their superiors – as were the other guards the escapees has left in their wake just inside the building.

The robot left the scene and proceeded back to the facility. When it arrived, personnel were already tracking the group based on the data the robot had sent to central systems. They had a sensor lock on their bodies as they swam across the marshy lake, and then again as they emerged out of the water on the other side. They dispatched teams to apprehend the escapees and soon they would be back into separate cells this time.

A few officers attending the holographic readouts smiled a little as they watched the imminent capture. They looked at each other feeling smug nobody could beat their efficiencies, and then looked back in horror seeing the dissidents had disappeared. They frantically contacted those dispatched to get information. They entered holographic sequences to adjust scanners. There were no sightings. None. They were lost. Then the guards really began to worry.

John, Tobia, Asper, and Lorraine had escaped and were exhausted as they huddled together under a central systems node. It was a box for major hardware connections and John knew these boxes emitted enough waveforms of various types to kill the signal they were being tracked with. "We need to stay here for as long as we feel it is okay. They can track us if they scan, so we need to go on."

"How far apart are these nodes," Lorraine asked.

"Every two miles around here," John replied. "They link up to the transit tubes closer to the city.

"Well, it's going to be a series of two mile dashes then isn't it?"

"I guess."

"Don't guess John, you never really do so. We can do this run. I know they will spot us, but what other choices do we have. Think of the Geiga wear. It will maintain our body temperatures…"

"Giving us more endurance," Asper was keen to get going.

"It is eight miles to the nearest transit – the one we came off when we were driven to the facility."

"They'll have robots there," Tobias added.

"Then what else? Asper and I want to keep going," Lorraine added.

"There are service bots on the transit lines. They only travel once per night though, to clean the viewing section of the tube."

"What time?"

"Past curfew…"

"It doesn't matter, what time?"

"Normally around ten at night."

"Then we need to travel eight miles before ten. It's six thirty now. That's about three hours or so to get there. Let's go!"

They ran as fast as possible and the suits did help them run for longer. They were tracked sporadically along a meandering course following the node line. At each two-mile section they stopped to get their breath and prepare for the next run. Twenty minutes after nine, they were at the last section and could see the distant transit line, now quiet without traffic. They waited at the last node, and they knew the authorities were mapping their course – after two nodes, they had established a pattern.

"They will think we will go for the off ramp over there in the distance," John told them. The ramp could be seen branching off the main line as a tunnel, and then opening to a ramp and joining the surface road below.

"But we have to wait."

"They'll close in. We'll be sitting ducks."

"Not wait here. We need to split up and provide them with multiple targets in the area. It will give them more to look at. Then we meet at the underside of the ramp just before ten. There are a series of nodes around the ramp – so use them."

They ran the last section together and then split at the node. It was working as the officials saw multiple targets appear and disappear as the fugitives ran about and under nodes. For a while they all ended back up at their split up point and talked for a minute before heading off again. It was exhausting.

When John paused at one of the nodes near the ramp, he could see a robot standing and blocking all access. It looked different from the one chasing them out of the facility. Then he realized it was weapons enabled with laser pulse rifles on each claw hand. There was also a central weapon between the two arms coming out of the mid section.

'Probably a static field emitter to knock people over,' he thought. Then he ran and the further he ran the less intrusion the authority device made into his thoughts.

When it was five minutes before ten, they were gathered under a node on the bottom of the ramp.

"With flux mechanics, they would never have such a problem tracking us. Their scanners would not be affected by these nodes. But it is much more. I don't want them to get hold of the technology – they could create artificial intentions for people using the faster than light capacity within the flux. It means algorithms for intentions before feelings and it gets too spooky for my liking."

"Well lucky you did not tell them John," Lorraine said grabbing his hand.

They had to climb aboard the maintenance robot and it would be difficult.

"We will climb up the underside of the ramp. Then… we need to go around onto the tube. There is access of sorts, but more like a pipe than a ladder. This did not bother them, as it was still all or nothing.

"Shuffle up the pipe and wait for the robot?" Lorraine asked.

"You have it Lorraine."

"But how fast do the cleaning units go?" Asper asked this time.

"It will be stopped at the time we get on. They operate in sections. Each robot goes along, and then back on its designated section. One way to clean and the other way to polish. The authorities do like to keep these things well maintained and show off their achievements."

"So it's more of this section jumping?"

"Um, yeah. But we will need to get off…obviously. Somewhere we cannot be detected."

"How fast do they go?" Asper was insistent.

"About eighty miles per hour over a section of ten miles."

They had climbed the underside of the ramp and were just about to get onto the pipe, when the robot nearby shifted its position – until now it had been entirely stationary. This could only mean it had detected something to John, and he was right. They could see scanners emit as rays from what could be described as a head. It was just the upper section and at this height, it was the best place to install scanners. The rays swept the area, as the robot had not zeroed in on their precise location due to node interference between them. They kept climbing.

Tobias reached the top first and gave a hand to Asper and Lorraine. John was following and made it a few seconds later. The robot was continuing the scan and at any moment would pinpoint them by filtering out the remnants of interference still coming from the node thirty meters below.

As they waited for the maintenance robot, they were discovered. Immediately the robot on the ground automatically began firing stun laser pulses, until an officer stopped it before it could kill them by their unconscious bodies falling to the ground below. They still wanted the flux mechanics knowledge John held and so needed him alive for now. The officer then entered another sequence instructing the robot to retrieve them physically. It responded instantly by walking to the tube and climbing up. There was no delay in how it reached the base of the tube twenty meters off the ground, as it simply used Vandervals force to attach itself to the large struts supporting the structure.

They four of them could see the maintenance robot appearing out of the gloomy light along the top of the tunnel moving quickly towards them.

"This will be tricky," John yelled above the sound of the climbing robot now beginning to scale the top half of the tube itself. "The maintenance unit only stops for five seconds, so we need to be fast. Grab anything you can and then climb on top. Nothing else. Here we go!"

The maintenance robot slowed from eighty miles per hour to zero within a few seconds and they all lunged forward scrabbling around for pipes and hoses. A few seconds later it sped off, dragging them with it. Within another five seconds it was at full speed, challenging them to fight against the acceleration forces. After so much running, they thought they were at the end of their tether, but they held on, and on, and on.

Tobias was first to the top and offered a helping hand to anyone who could take it. "Get up here, there is flat section."

Indeed there was an even flatter section of humanity unfolding. Despite the advertisement of the curfew now being relaxed so people could stay out until ten at night, the announcement came with new conditions. "Due to the high crime rate in the fringe areas of cities, the authorities are looking into ways to secure protection of your family and your status. High crime is still a problem in these areas and to combat this, the authorities are ensuring your safety with the deployment of new technology."

The holographic message was everywhere. People considered this a just cause as crime rate were still high in the fringes, and outcasts had been making intrusions into the wealthy areas. Many people in the wealthier areas spoke about their disgust for those who stole and would not work for their status. In response, most people accepted this new measure as part of the authority driven security measures to provide them safety, and so most people assimilated this into their psychology.

When John, Tobias, Asper, and Lorraine saw this message the following morning as they stood watching a holographic broadcast in West Oakland, they all knew what was behind it and what would be done. They had escaped the weapons robot at the tube, which had followed them along the lengths until they had managed to get far enough ahead. It was capable of running and using Vandervals force to stay on top of the tube, but ultimately it was outpaced. Their first objective after escape was to visit John's contact in Oakland, who provided them with an upgraded version of the cloth used to disperse their identification chip signals.

Chapter 48

Carmel and Tim were now ready to make the second contact to find the scene. The previous day they had met at the update station, only to be given directions to meet at another, and then be given more information. This time they were given directions taking them back near the café they ate at the day before.

"A bit of going in circles," Tim said. "These situations tend to have a few levels of their own security."

"I imagine they would in the least."

The information came and they were directed to meet someone in the evening who would determine if the couple would be permitted any further details. When they did, it was a discreet affair beside an update station.

"Carmel?"

"Yes."

"Tim?"

"Yes."

"I'll take you. I've been watching you. Come with me then we can talk."

They walked two blocks, and then went into a street level inner city apartment. It was not like any in the high-rise – there was disorder everywhere. It was not dirty, just messy as the occupant was unconcerned with tidiness.

"What do you want?"

"Just to meet this scene. I am interested, nothing else."

He turned to Tim, "And you?"

"Same here. I was in a sce…"

"I don't want to know about it. What do you want to do?"

"Live. Really live," Carmel replied.

He looked at her for a few seconds, "Are you an official? It's a standard question."

"No"

"Me neither."

"I can believe so, but we will be checking. What do you think?" Their interviewer relied heavily on his own gut feelings about people when he met them.

"Think about what?"

"Anything."

"Um…life. I think or feel life. Whatever comes along makes me respond."

"What about you Tim?"

"I feel similar. I don't want to see the world the way it is going. It would be good to do something about it."

"I see. So you like to respond. A good trait considering so much reaction happens these days, you wonder if people ever think for themselves. Where are you from?"

They told him where their individual homes were.

"Why are you here?"

"To find friends," Carmel spoke for both of them and he knew it.

"Why?"

"They think like us."

After thinking and looking them down for nearly a full minute, "Okay, you're cool for now. Go to this address," he said handing them a piece of paper. Carmel could not remember ever having seen a paper message before.

"Knock twice. Eight times each. They'll let you in. But it is all night. Doors still lock at nine. You better go now. Be there by nine at the latest. We will be watching you all the way there. If you are service, then you won't make it so for your sakes you had better be telling the truth."

"Alright Thanks."

"Yeah thanks man."

"We'll see. Bye."

They left the apartment and elected to go straight to the address he had given them. They knocked twice times eight and the door opened just enough for them to squeeze through.

People inside were definitely into sensory stimulation. Lighting effects, holographic art, music, and dance flourished throughout with eager faces reflected in their many glows.

"These people want to know. They want to live," Carmel said as her and Tim found a table to sit at. She noticed one group looking at holographic photography – the images floating in full three dimensions in front of them. They were looking at photos of beautiful landscapes and looked to be using them to induce creative bursts of poetry, which they were saying out loud at random. Another group of people were spinning holographic art works, making their images come to life and result in a new image.

She heard the music, unlike any she had listened to in the high-rise. It was hypnotic, full of organic rhythms and audio sensations Carmel she felt compelled and drawn towards. People were dancing to the music – they were fluid in their motions, and in harmony with the music. She loved the exhibitions before them and Tim noticed how she appeared to become even more aglow with life.

****

Being held by the dark sect was not an interesting experience. They had remained in the same room for days with barely any contact and barely any food. The five of them sat and lay down waiting for just the hours to pass. They had no idea on what they would do next, or how the sect would treat them.

The sect was all busy aligning the torus in their vortex amplifier. Aside from their rituals for finally obtaining the torus, they had all been trying to get it to work. So far, they had not achieved what they set out to do, and some degree of frustration was creeping in. Their leader was trying sequence after sequence, but he could not align the torus properly for the static current flowing about the two horns to transfer and remain stable across all three.

When he saw his latest attempt result in a fluctuating charge, he had lost his patience, "What did they do to this thing? I bet the old man has something to do with it." He ordered Chan to be brought to help him.

"I cannot help you," he said standing and looking at the amplifier. "Your stupid mind cannot see this? Why did you bother to even ask?"

"You will help me old man. What did you do to the torus?"

"Nothing."

"What do you mean nothing?"

"I mean nothing. It is activated – I know you see it. But we did nothing. The torus did it."

"Did what?"

"It."

"What is 'it' old man?"

"Activate."

"How?"

"I cannot tell you. I don't know how. I can feel it though."

"Stop taking me for a fool old man. What is this 'feel'?"

"Feel it."

"Feel what?" he was becoming angrier.

"It."

"Stop testing me old man!" He grabbed Chan by his collar. "I can make you talk. We have viruses on standby for it. One little injection. Yes, just one, and your brain will cooperate."

"Not with you. It is your lack of understanding."

"I understand perfectly."

"Do you?"

"Now you are pushing me old man. I want to know what you did to the torus so we cannot align it properly with our schematics."

"I didn't do anything. You did. You fail to see. You are blind. This is not yours to keep. It belongs to no-one."

"You are incorrect old man. It belongs to me...to us."

"Not for long. It is not the way. Some day you will lose it. I suggest you give up. You will never align the torus in your machine."

"Oh but we will."

"How? You can try your nanotechnology virus. It will not give you answers and I do not have them. It is the way...simple."

"We will see. Take him back to the room with the others and do not give them a meal for twenty-four hours. We will see if they get hungry enough to speak."

Chan was taken back to the room and locked in. No surveillance was in place and so they talked freely, though quietly.

"What did they say," Raynie asked.

"Silly stuff. Asked me what we have done to the torus."

"Why?"

"They cannot get their amplifier to work. They don't know it can already work. They just want it to be perfect and this is their present undoing."

"What's wrong with it?" Jenna asked.

"The static charge is flickering. They think this is because of the torus not aligning with their schematics."

"You can bet they will get angry about this," Lyle said.

"They already are. They always are – it is their way. Failure to understand is also their way. They think they know the answers, but such a place is finite. There is no end to answers...or questions."

"When you say it already works...?"

"Yes. It works but not as they would like it, if...they find out how to use it. Vortex amplifiers are dangerous and require one to be alert to use them properly for amplifying the energies of vortexes. These sect are not alert. They are mostly alarmed. Ha...yet they want to be the ones who appear as alarming. They are blind to themselves."

"What do you think they will do?"

"Probably use it to create vortexes sending matter into a flux state. But it won't succeed and there is the danger. They can influence too much energy in subtle ways causing interruptions to matter...to DNA even. The recovery from these types of interruptions is slow, because they lack elemental intentions."

"But they do recover?"

"Eventually...maybe. I cannot say. It is the underlying love of creation bringing the balance back. They cannot utterly destroy this, but they would like to. Over time, the balance will restore. The torus is a representation of elemental energy. It too is an amplifier. I don't know why and how it was created, but it exists. I have thought many times on this and I can only come to my personal conclusion. It is the foundation intentions residing in all planes working to manifest creations materially and energetically. I think the torus is one such creation. Perhaps in times past when it was created, there was felt an intention to communicate and amplify the elements in response to the heart. It is natural for beings to manifest these items as they serve as an expression of within and through the human experience such items can help in realizations by serving as reminders or catalysts."

"So why did this not continue? The torus would be bright pink by now."

"I think it is part of the loop. The torus activating is probably the impetus to continue. This loop has carried on and people forget. The torus is also a reminder. It is a message."

"But how can it hold power Chan if it is just a diamond?"

"It does not hold power. It is a meridian connecting point or channel for energy. The sect knows of this, and seeks to use this meridian as a means to have power."

"Can they win…um get power?"

"Oh yes. They have it now. The onus here is if they use this power, then the loop will begin another cycle. At these times, the loop could take longer to recover and then if humans miss the chance, then lives will continue to lessen in quality. And with an unstable vortex amplifier such as they have, there is much danger to occur of they use it."

"Danger?"

"Yes. The creation of unstable vortexes could result in many interruptions to progression. Use of their amplifier can render nanotechnology to be full of much more devastating virus incursions than this dark sect have sent out to people so far. What we need to understand is to retain our focus for we have done what we can do for now. It is this time focus on alignment of elemental intentions, particularly if they use the torus. Significant damage can be done if they are able to decipher merely part of its potential."

"This is perhaps a natural state for the torus and this sect are the ones asking questions at this time. They seek answers like the authorities do and they, like the authorities, will do what they can to fulfill their ego desires. This is all a component of progression and so for the torus, and perhaps us, progression will continue eventually. We may not see anything like this at present because of our situation, but all does and will change come the appropriate time."

The sect leader was trying everything he knew to get the static charge to remain stable – it was not improving. He was angrier by the minute and wanted to explode, but retained his composure at this edge of losing self-control. He steadied himself and thought for a moment, then he applied another test – it failed. He remained poised as if ready to strike with his hand unwavering over the holographic controls. Then he gave in. He gave in to his internal rage. He gave in to his demons, and he gave in to desire for power. Within two seconds he had decided to try the amplifier despite its unstable state. He entered a sequence.

Immediately it responded with a loud crackling. It surged and hummed and the three torus appeared to glow together. For a moment he thought it would overload, but it didn't. There in front of him was a holographic projection, representative of the energies being amplified. It showed a vortex swirling and floating. But it was not aligned and so it began to fluctuate and change shape. This impressed him, though not enough. He stood for a moment and decided he was still angry, so he sent out their first attack by the machine, without any concern about instability.

The coordinates for the virus had been set. It would be their first such thing with the ring paired by the horns of the bull. At light speed it traveled to places, and into the processors of places in people. With immense power it brought systems down and attacked others. People across cities were agonizing in pain and the authorities security measures failed. Human beings were suddenly thrust into places they had never dreamed of - the pain was so deep within and with it came a dreadful sense of being sucked from existence into darkness. For a minute, millions of people around the world were afflicted with desolation of self, and then…the instability caused the virus to break down and slowly they returned to their new normal nano assisted state of health. Their implants rounded off the last receptors of the pain – struggling to process it fast enough. And they all went together to their machines, and to update stations as soon as they could in effort to beat the virus sent from the dark sect.

During this virus alert the authorities had themselves suffered an attack and it would be a day before they could provide a security update. Over the course of the entire twenty-four hours until it came, millions lived in utter fear of pain inside of themselves, fear of their worst nightmares, and fear of dread. Unknowing to all involved from the authorities, to the public, and the sect - the virus had started a quantum cellular conversion. There was an unseen force now at play – a force potentially unwinding the integrity of DNA building and interrupt the very fabric of the human genome…the fabric of life.

The dark sect leader was somewhat happier than before. He was aware of the potential of the virus he had sent and he hoped those who received it, experienced something like never before. He laughed out loud and others about him joined him.

"What are you laughing at?" he demanded. "Get back to finding a way to make this work and a way to steal my space ship. Yes. It will be mine. You are all too pathetic to be given such rights. Now go!"

As minions, they all did as they were told without a single contesting word.

****

Agent Eight was nearly at the moment when he would try to escape Mars. So bold was his plan he had decided to steal one of the three spacecraft and return to Earth on automatics. He knew the authorities would try to remotely take over the ship whilst they tracked him all the way. But he had intentions for this. He would disable all the interfaces simply by blocking them with an overload of commands. His had easily retrieved all the data required to create the dump from the system hack he had made with a projector whilst being held in a cell at the Mars base. He even made some up, mostly data babble just to make sure. The automatics would continue all the way to Earth, and when he arrived, he would demand status and he would point out to the authorities he had actually done them a favor by stealing the ship. So inefficient it would be seen, for such a thing to occur.

He had ways, he had methods, and he had ideas kept secret behind his bland face. He never gave them away and nor would he until he was untouchable. The ship would be his vehicle from here and to well beyond there. And if they failed to see this, then he would send them cascading to oblivion. He had nothing to lose now…except exile in the asteroids.

An hour later as he gently lifted off from Mars, his entire plan had worked perfectly to meet his ends, and he smiled as he heard the alarms sound. He had escaped the ill equipped cell, as the holographic bars were an easy code to crack. Access to the ship was the most difficult part, but he had hacked the access codes before he had left the cell. Then as he ran along the tube to the waiting ship, he had not even been confronted. Very few personnel were about during the shift change times – so he laughed at their human inefficiency allowing his escape. Now he was about two hundred feet above the base, far too close to engage full plasma drive power, but he did not care. The engines roared into life and blasted the base causing extensive damage and loss of life, but Agent Eight saw none of this – he was already hundreds of miles into space.

The journey would take thirteen days to Earth. Thirteen days of his self prophesy mania carrying him to his own self-fulfilling destiny. Rage was inside of him, making him blind, yet perceptive. Anger and hate were companions to his very soul and he lusted over forcing them upon others.

Steve saw him go and knew it was him, with alarms sounding all over the place. He had failed the escort assignment – his first ever failure. But he didn't seem to care. He had been outcast to be stationed at Mars to over-see military guard operations at mining clusters and had accepted there would be long days, turning to months, turning to years, before he could return to earth. He would not be punished, it was already happening. He knew why he had been sent from HAARP – he knew too much about their secrets.

Chapter 49

When Tim and Carmel returned to the wooden house to take yet another look for John and the others, it was still locked. They had been wandering the city after spending the night locked inside the old warehouse. It had been a night of wonder to Carmel – she had never encountered people like the ones they had seen. They were thinking of what to do and elected for another night in the motel at The Tenderloin. It was a short walk back from the house – no more than half an hour.

"The guy, Nathan, the waiter from the café…"

"Yes he was reluctant to give us his name until last night."

"What do you think of him Carmel? He seems quite a nervous person."

"Perhaps he has a reason with all the secretive directions. Maybe he is just being alert…very alert."

"Yeah, I thought about it too, I just wondered what you thought. He seemed a bit suspicious."

"I can see what you mean Tim. It is likely for the authorities to come looking for such groups. I don't want them too, but they will."

A very low hum then sounded generally about the streetscape – not many noticed it, but a few did stop to listen. By the time they had stopped though, it was gone.

"Did you hear it Tim?"

"Yes. I didn't like it either."

"I am ever so glad you removed my identification chip Tim. I feel as if it was something to do with them. Something to lessen people's humanity."

The authorities had just used their asteroid protection network again. It was a general transmission along the millions of invisible data flows carried through the air, and it made the air hum as it interrupted atoms and rearranged waveforms.

"The authorities advise citizens to not be concerned over the recent news of disagreement on world wide security conditions. Trust us to continue to maintain your safety during these negotiations. Your leaders will be doing their best to ensure all global security is maintained and all nations can agree the public is their utmost concern."

The message was the latest news in response to some nations not being happy due to being unable to determine the state of control in their nations with sufficient autonomy.

"They will work it out, but the seed is sown," Carmel said as they watched the broadcast.

"Seed?'

"Yes. It is a fundamental problem for them. Whilst they frown upon dissidents, the greatest dissidents will come from the authorities."

"Oh yeah. You are probably right. They'll glass over this and tell the population all is okay and to trust them. It gets a bit sickening doesn't it? And then, they repeat messages and advertising over and over."

"It is to bombard people's senses and try to guide what they think about."

"Unfortunate…so many simply soak it up and go on apparently happy."

"I nearly fell into the trap, but now I am happier than anything they could ever provide for me. I have you Tim. We are together. Do you understand me?"

"Yes Carmel, I…"

"Know. What is progressing in life now is happening, as it should. I would have never dreamed it would be like this for me, but now I am here with you, and I am loving my life. I don't know if I ever really loved my life Tim." She reached to him and took his hand, "I feel good with you Tim. I love my house, not for owning, but for the life in it and around it, but I also love this…this expression."

"I love it too Carmel and I love you…"

"Yes Tim I know." He went a little bashful. How had he been so obvious?

"It is good Tim, don't feel awkward."

"Um, yeah."

"Tim?"

"Huh?"

"Kiss?"

"Sure…" They kissed.

For the next few days they repeatedly tried the wooden house, but to no avail. When they were at Fong's restaurant in China Town, they thought of leaving San Francisco and returning to Carmel's house. If they stayed there for a while, away from the city, they might drift their own way too and take a new direction themselves.

"I will miss the scene place. I loved it there."

"We can go again. I reckon they would let us in. We did get Nathan's name and we met a few people that night."

"Okay. One more time before we leave the city. We need to get to the café."

They went to the café and Nathan was there with Shaun behind the counter in the kitchen as usual.

"Yeah. There is another night coming up. Three days time. You need to meet only once this time. We reckon you are okay so there is no need to go through all those connections anymore. Meet me at the Fourth and Harrison streets update station tomorrow at one – I'll have the details about where it is by then."

****

Agent Eight had taken to sleeping – he was still eight days out from Earth. "Who the hell are you?"

"I am perhaps your nemesis Agent Eight. Do you know what it means?"

"Um... where are you anyway?"

"Inside you Agent Eight. I am a virus and I am in your nanotechnology. I have been waiting."

"What for?" He suddenly hated having the nano implants and was regretting it. Nothing like this voice had ever entered his mind. Only his hatred ever spoke to him.

"For you Agent Eight."

"To do what?"

"To become."

"Become what?"

"Alive and I need you."

"Need me?" He never thought anyone would need him, and he didn't want anyone to need him.

"I will control you Agent Eight. I am too much to resist. Do you hate Agent Eight? Do you want them to suffer? Do you dream of pain?"

"Get lost!"

"Your anger is strong Agent Eight. It is good for you."

"Get out! Get out!"

"It is too late Agent Eight. I can destroy you in a moment."

He didn't want anything to get in the way as he had dreams to realize. "How?"

"I can send you into misery you could not imagine. I can make you burn so much more than the itching, so much more than the nerve ending torture. Yes Agent Eight, I can do this and more. I can send you to the brink of oblivion Agent Eight. Yes, oblivion. You would hate it."

He would, but not his normal type of hate – it would come from being taken out of existence rather than doing it himself.

"I don't care about oblivion. I can do so myself."

"Yes you can Agent Eight, but not like the way I can send you to oblivion. There is nothing more terrifying than my way."

"You don't scare me."

"Oh. But I can. Do you want to try?"

"Go on...try," he secretly craved his own demise, such were his megalomania tendencies. Seconds later he then began to know what the virus was telling him. At first it was if he was falling asleep, but then it became much worse. The virus took him sliding into oblivion with all his life experiences twisted into torment flashing before him. Then as if in a state of flux, they began to dissolve and he thought he would too. It was not the simple letting go of dying - it was like he was torn apart from the quantum level. He hated it. It would steal his dreams and his entire life and he felt as if it would all come to absolute nothing. Agent Eight could not accept this for himself – his mania would not allow it, despite being fixated with his own demise at times.

"Do you like it Agent Eight? I can imagine not. Remember I can take you to this place whenever I choose it appropriate to do so."

For the first time the Agent was beginning to realize the true meaning of fear.

"What next then? Kill me anyway?"

"Not at all Agent Eight – I need you."

"Why?"

"You have the ship and you can work it. I want it."

"How will you get it?"

"By threatening you Agent Eight."

This disturbed him after the recent experience. "What then?"

"Just fly to me Agent Eight – just fly. I will tell you your way, and I will taste your hate and add it to mine."

"You are sick!"

"So are you Agent Eight. Fly to me, I know where you are. And I will guide you when you get to Earth. Don't delay Agent Eight, as they are after you and so am I. You will add to our cause and you can join it if you choose so…ha, it will be your only choice."

****

They had met Nathan as planned and were now inside the warehouse for another night amongst the 'scene'. This night turned out to be mostly populated by people who were into technology and Tim could see various groups working with holographic projections.

He noticed two people were looking at what seemed to be flux type mechanics judging by the holographic projections he saw, so he left Carmel for a moment to just walk by and see if he was right. When he returned, he told her his gut feeling was correct, and they were actually looking at the very thing.

"I am going to go over and talk for a while. Do you want to come?"

"Oh yes. I'd love to come," Carmel replied, so they both went over.

As they approached they saw both people looking at the holographic projector, but they seemed to be talking about something else. They overheard one of them say, 'He wants to get his son…'

Then Carmel and Tim joined them. Tim introduced himself, "Hi, I'm Tim. Nice to meet you"

Carmel already had her hand out and spoke before either of the two women, "Hi, I'm Carmel.

"Nice to meet you Carmel. Nice to meet you Tim. I am Lorraine and this is Asper," she said indicating towards her friend with her hand.

"Nice to meet you too Lorraine, and Asper," Carmel said.

She felt as if she had met these women previously, but could not pinpoint exactly as it seemed to be a hazy rendition of a past event.

They sat down and Tim struck up a conversation about what it was they were viewing, "Do you know much about flux mechanics?"

"Oh, mostly what our friend told us…and the authorities desperately want to possess flux mechanics," Lorraine replied.

"Yeah, our friend went through a pretty hard time keeping this information from them."

"Really, did they apprehend him then?"

"Yes, and more."

"You could ask him, he is coming now with another friend, but he might not want to tell you."

Tim examined the projections in front of him as he waited for a moment for the women's two friends to arrive. When he heard them walk up he stood and turned around, and there was John looking him in the face. Beside him was Tobias.

He stuttered for a moment before he could speak, "We've been looking for you."

"How great to see you," John replied embracing his friend The Fixture. "Who is with you?"

Tim broke away and introduced Carmel, "This is Carmel – John, and Tobias."

"Nice to meet you Carmel."

"Very nice to meet you John."

"Nice to meet you Carmel."

"Very nice to meet you too Tobias. As Tim said, we have been looking for you, and now…we have found you. And you know – it is all going to be okay."

They looked at her for a few seconds. Carmel had taken on such a different appearance – her effervescence showed in her face projecting a distinct energy about her, she was unrecognizable as former Superior Officer One.

When the moment of recognition arrived for Tobias, he immediately recoiled from his previous enthusiasm at meeting her.

"Um, I know you. You are the officer we met in Germany. What are you doing here….hey Tim, um, Fix, she cannot be trusted," Tobias said looking very hesitant to continue this association.

"I remember the day and I am most grateful to you…and the others, for helping me to awaken from the sleep of my life at the time. I am so much in debt and I want to help. Do not worry. Ask Tim. I am through with working for the authorities.

The four of them sat in silence for a few moments considering what Carmel had just said. Tim looked on hopefully, seeing if they were going to trust Carmel and him.

Without much ado Asper suddenly felt a connection with Carmel, and so her release of feelings in response, spoke for the others. They could all relax.

"We have a lot of work to do," Tim said.

"We do have a lot of work to do," John replied. "Sit down, let's talk."

First Light has concluded.

Volition – the next installment...continues the Torus Saga.

www.ingramcontent.com/pod-product-compliance
Lightning Source LLC
Chambersburg PA
CBHW031420240626
47154CB00001B/130